Praise for Sensing Light

"*Sensing Light* by Mark Jacobson, a doctor who worked with early HIV-infected patients and continues to practice medicine today, is a compelling story of the onset of the AIDS epidemic shown through the eyes of three doctors at a San Francisco public hospital. Although historical fiction, the novel reads like a creative non-fiction exploration of the pathos and uncertainty of those early days when gay men were dying and no one could figure out why. The characters are all too human; their battles both internal and external as they attempt to make sense of the horror around them."

—*GAYLE SHANKS, former president, American Booksellers Association*

"The AIDS epidemic emerges at Ground Zero—San Francisco in the 1980s. This riveting drama poignantly captures the raw emotions at the intersection of patients, health professionals, and a society unprepared for a new epidemic."

—*DIANE HAVLIR, MD, chief of UCSF Division of HIV, Infectious Diseases and Global Medicine at San Francisco General Hospital*

"In his page-turner of a novel, Mark Jacobson drops the reader straight into the action—the early days of the AIDS epidemic in San Francisco, when the then-mysterious disease was killing people in unprecedented and chilling numbers. Only a first-person participant could have created characters so believable and a story so gripping. I loved every word of this unforgettable book."

—*JESSICA O'DWYER, author of* Mamalita: An Adoption Memoir

"Breathing life and emotion into the epidemic's early days, *Sensing Light* is a tribute to the heroism and tragedy of a time when AIDS was a certain death sentence. The characters draw the reader into a world of hope and loss, courage and fear."

—*PAUL VOLBERDING, MD, director of UCSF AIDS Research Institute and former chief of AIDS Program at San Francisco General Hospital (1983–2001)*

Sensing Light

Sensing Light

A NOVEL

MARK A. JACOBSON

Ulysses Press

Published by:
ULYSSES PRESS
P.O. Box 3440
Berkeley, CA 94703
www.ulyssespress.com

ISBN 978-1-61243-570-1
Library of Congress Catalog Number 2015952135

Printed in the United States by United Graphics Inc.

Front cover design: what!design @ whatweb.com
Front cover image: © Alessandro Colle/shutterstock.com

Distributed by Publishers Group West

IN MY OFFICE, AT the back of a dusty file drawer, are stacks of three-by-five-inch index cards. From 1986 to 2000, each time a patient at San Francisco General Hospital was diagnosed with retinitis, a complication of AIDS we rarely see now, I wrote their name on a blank card and used it to keep track of their medication doses, the extent of their eye damage, and their ability to read letters at twenty feet, or at least count fingers or see a hand waving across the room or, if nothing else, sense light from dark.

My drawer has six hundred and twenty cards. Most are very short narratives. Nearly all end in death within two years. The few who survived longer were fortunate enough to have received a new generation of anti HIV drugs that became available in 1996 and allowed their immune systems to recover and stop further eye damage as well as other complications of AIDS. I still see some of these people in clinic today.

This book is dedicated to those who did not survive.

✕ ✕ ✕

Note to the Reader: While I aimed for historical accuracy in portraying the scientific, medical, and political aspects of the AIDS epidemic's first decade, the characters in this novel are purely fictional creations. None are even remotely based on any real person.

The First Case, 1979

I

KEVIN BARTHOLOMEW WAS WRITING medication orders in the residents' room, a den of tattered couches and rickety folding chairs cluttered with the detritus of take-out food delivered from local ethnic restaurants. One of Kevin's fellow senior residents walked in and grabbed a day-pack. He looked at Kevin's scrubs and waist-length white coat, already rumpled and stained with spattered coffee and blood.

"How many hits so far?"

Good question, thought Kevin. He had lost track. He thumbed through his clipboard, searching for a list of patients admitted to his ward team today.

"Six, plus one in the ER waiting for an ICU bed."

"Oh, man! It's only four in the afternoon. You've got sixteen more hours to go."

Kevin gave a fatalistic shrug and continued writing.

"Be a wall."

Kevin kept scribbling.

"No dirtballs you can sweet-talk the ER into dumping back on the street?"

"Nope."

"No one you can transfer to surgery or psychiatry?"

"They're all keepers," Kevin replied with no hint of complaint.

"You're impressive, man."

Kevin stopped writing and squinted at Jay Seward, weighing how much sarcasm there might be in his use of "impressive." Kevin still had trouble deciphering that in compliments from native Californians.

"No, seriously, I mean it," Jay insisted. "Seven admissions by four in the afternoon and I'd be screaming at any ER doc who called me with another hit and throwing charts at any student who asked for help. I'd be in mortal terror my head would never get above water."

"Thanks, Jay, but *not* thinking about that possibility is how I cope."

"Oops, sorry. Well, try to protect your interns. Give all the dirtball admissions to what's his name, that gross slob of a fourth year student you're stuck with."

Kevin frowned. While the macho house staff patter at times soothed his frayed nerves, he wasn't completely comfortable with it, and cruelty was definitely going too far.

What an asshole, he thought, watching Jay leave the room and cross paths in the hallway with a tall, middle-aged, Asian-American attending physician. "Herb Wu" was embroidered on the lapel of the man's pressed, immaculate, knee-length white coat. City Hospital's chief of pulmonary medicine gave Jay a brisk nod. Jay smiled back eagerly, but Herb Wu didn't slow down.

"A kiss-ass, too," Kevin muttered.

He knew Jay wanted to be accepted into a training program for pulmonary specialists, preferably the university one here in San Francisco which included rotations under Herb's supervision at City Hospital. Kevin had also applied for a university fellowship, one in infectious diseases. Though he didn't really care whether he was accepted or not. He was sure one of the local public health clinics would hire him. A clinic job or a fellowship would pay more than his current salary, and both options entailed vastly more sleep than he was getting now.

But it would be cool, he mused, very cool knowing how to use all the microbiology tests at an infectious diseases specialist's disposal, being able to make rare diagnoses like typhoid fever or brucellosis. Even more alluring were the cures when you got the diagnosis right and prescribed the correct antibiotic in time. This reminded him of his latest admission. He jumped up and ran after Herb Wu.

He found Herb in the intensive care unit huddling with house staff discussing a case Kevin had heard about in morning report—an alcoholic in withdrawal who unexpectedly developed heart failure.

"I don't get it," said the junior resident. "His heart rate's rising and his blood pressure's dropping, but he doesn't have a fever or a white count, so I don't think it's sepsis. And he's not agitated. In fact, he's clearing mentally. His crashing can't be due to DT's, can it?"

"His last EKG's OK," added the intern, her hands full of heart monitor tracings and laboratory printouts. "There's less pulmonary edema on this morning's chest film, his cardiac enzymes are normal, and his blood gas is improving. So it can't be a myocardial infarct, or worsening heart failure, or a pulmonary embolism, right?"

"Good thinking, guys," said Herb.

Kevin knew Herb Wu was the child of Chinese immigrants, that English was his second language. Yet Herb had a patrician aura, like the lawyers and corporate executives who lived in Back Bay townhouses and dropped off their Mercedes and BMWs to be serviced at Bartholomew Motors during the summers Kevin had worked in his father's South Boston shop. He supposed Herb's charcoal, razor-cut hair and thick black eyebrows were part of the effect, as well as the way he dressed—Brooks Brothers wool slacks, Oxford shirt, herringbone sports coat. There was also the thin, diagonal scar across his lower lip that suggested mysterious sophistication.

No, Kevin thought, it's his gracious self-assurance. That's what's classy about him

Herb crossed his arms and shook his head.

"We're missing something. Let's see the x-rays again."

Kevin followed the group to a glass box where the intern attached two rectangular sheets of black film and pushed a light switch. The patient's lungs appeared as negative images—black spaces between white rib shadows. The faint patches of white haze in yesterday's x-ray were absent in today's film. Herb peered closely. With the tip of his forefinger, Herb outlined the white heart shadow in each x-ray.

"What do you think?" he asked.

Neither house staff answered.

"The heart's enlarged in both films, yes?"

They nodded in agreement.

"When he was transferred to the ICU, we thought he was in congestive heart failure. You guys gave him a diuretic. He put out a lot of urine. And today we see less fluid in his lungs—just what we wanted to happen. But look carefully at his heart. If anything, it ought to be smaller now. It's not. That's clue number one. If you look at the *shape*, you'll see clue number two. Yesterday, normal like a pear. Today, rounder like an apple."

Kevin understood immediately. Something must be irritating the stiff, fibrous sac surrounding the man's heart. Maybe a virus, or perhaps a toxic effect of one of the medications that had been administered. Whatever the cause, his body's inflammatory response had resulted in fluid accumulating inside the sac, enough fluid to keep his heart from filling completely with blood after each contraction. The condition was called cardiac tamponade and would be fatal if not relieved soon.

"Holy shit!" cried the resident. "He's in tamponade. That explains everything. Wow, thanks Herb."

The two house staff rushed off to gather equipment, thrilled at the prospect of the procedure they were about to do. Kevin felt a pang of envy. He wished this was his patient, that his hands would be the ones to guide in a long needle, suck out the fluid without injuring the beating heart inside, and save this man's life.

Impressive pick-up, he thought, studying the two x-rays. The difference in the two shadows was subtle. Kevin wasn't sure he would have noticed the change in shape if Herb hadn't pointed it out. How could Herb see so much in a chest film?

Kevin suddenly realized Herb had already honed in on the cause before he even compared the films. In the time it took to mount two x-rays on a light box, he had picked up all the clues and walked their strings back, narrowing the possibilities down to the most likely suspect, cardiac tamponade. He was expecting to find a rounder heart.

Now in his third and final year of internal medicine training, Kevin could fully appreciate Herb's skill at diagnosis, particularly his relaxed precision and speed. As an intern, whenever Kevin had been the first to discover the cause of his patient's illness, he would continue contemplating each plausible alternative over and over to convince himself of certainty. He had seen mistaken diagnoses lead to giving the wrong medication with catastrophic results. Even a correct diagnosis could be terrible knowledge if it revealed a grim fate. Eventually, he learned to suppress his fear of lurking dark truths. Now he craved the confidence and accuracy that Herb had.

"Next?" said Herb.

Kevin gave a staccato summary of the case he was admitting to the ICU. Herb stopped smiling as soon as he heard the patient's blood oxygen level.

"Here's his chest film," said Kevin, clipping an x-ray to the light box with a practiced upward twist of the wrist.

Herb sat down and studied the film, tapping his fingers on the desk top. His eyes darted across radiographic landmarks, hunting for signs in the shadows.

"Benign history, right?"

"Other than shooting speed in the remote past. And I believe the remote part. I'll call his clinic doctor to confirm it. Oh, he's had a few STD's. I think he works the bathhouses for income."

"You said *normal* blood count?"

"Except for low lymphocytes. That mean anything?"

"Maybe."

Pointing to the x-ray, so homogenously white that ribs could hardly be distinguished from underlying lung, Herb said, "You can never say never when it comes to TB, but I don't think that's what this is. Sorry, Kevin, no clues here. You can get more sputum for TB testing in the morning, but your patient is in bad shape. We need to go where the money is. He has to be bronched tomorrow."

"God, I was hoping you'd say that. Thanks, Herb."

"We're here to serve."

As Kevin trudged to the ER, he thought about Herb's reaction after hearing the patient was homosexual. There had been no sardonic amusement, no undertone of distaste. That was unusual among the senior medical staff at City Hospital. Not that Kevin would have been offended. Such snide disdain seemed almost respectful when he remembered the overt disgust he had witnessed in South Boston, especially at high school and his father's garage. Of course, none of it had ever been directed at him. Kevin had been too cautious to be discovered until he was sure he could escape.

II

LARRY WINTON STARED AT the emergency room ceiling and tried to concentrate on the drunk lying next to him. Reliably, at five minute intervals, the man would scream, "Just suck my dick, will you!" When no one responded, he would mutter a patronizing "You dumb shitbird" and start snoring again. These outbursts were pleasant compared to the unpredictable howls a black woman on the other side of the hallway was screeching, each ending in a supplication to Jesus.

Hell yes, I'm prejudiced, thought Larry. He smiled, proud that in dire straits his wit remained intact. Larry had stopped believing in Jesus at age sixteen when he ran away to San Francisco. Since then, a decade of professional experience performing fellatio had, for a while, made his life very comfortable.

His brave smirk vanished. Easy to laugh now, he had to admit, now that he could control his fear, which he realized probably had something to do with the twin, dry streams of odorless oxygen flowing from the plastic prongs in his nostrils.

Larry awoke in an alcove, unable to remember falling asleep or being moved. A curtain, more like a negligee, covered the top half of the doorway, blocking only the torsos and heads of people walking by. Larry gathered from bits of passing conversation that the doctors' shift was changing. One group was telling another about the patients they were handing over. They paused outside the curtain.

"In here's a twenty-seven year old male prostitute who's had three months of fever, drenching night sweat, and weight loss. Claims he doesn't shoot drugs."

There were hums of interest.

"Arterial oxygen was fifty before we gave him the nasal prongs. Lungs are a white-out on x-ray. Nothing on the sputum stains, so it's not likely bacterial pneumonia or TB. Medicine's put in the paperwork for an ICU bed. If he gets any worse, he'll have to be tubed."

"So what's the diagnosis?"

"Nobody knows. It's the mystery case of the day."

"Did anyone consider semen aspiration?" someone giggled.

There were a couple of guffaws, and they moved on to the next patient.

Remarks like this were water off a duck's back for Larry, nowhere near as hurtful as the vile things people had said to him as a boy in Fort Worth—including his own devout parents, an often out-of-work teamster and a housewife dependent on her secret stash of vodka. To block those memories, he thought about his prejudice wisecrack and grinned.

The curtain slid open. Kevin entered and immediately noticed Larry was smiling.

"Feel better with the oxygen on?" he asked.

Though the air flowing into Larry's nose was reassuring, any activity elicited hunger for more than he could breathe in. He had no idea what was happening to his body or why it had betrayed him. The uncertainty implicit in Kevin's question, well-meaning as it no doubt was, didn't inspire confidence. No one had explained to him why needles were being stuck in his veins and blood removed in glass vials, what the doctors were listening for with their stethoscopes pressed against his chest, what the x-ray or the phlegm he had coughed into a cup had shown, or what the fluid inching down a plastic tube into his arm was supposed to do.

He needed to believe that someone here had the inclination and ability to help him, and this doctor was the only person Larry had met who remotely seemed to care.

He decided to drop the cool, cowboy façade.

"While I'm lying still, the breathing's OK. But soon as I move, even talk, I'm short of breath again."

"We're going to move you upstairs. I'll be the one responsible for your medical care there."

"Jesus," Larry exploded, "It's a god damn relief to know someone's in charge."

"At your service," said Kevin, giving a little bow.

Grateful for the attention, Larry read the name on the ID badge and inspected Dr. Bartholomew's long, thick, wavy red hair, a shade between auburn and strawberry blond, and his freckles, splayed like a layer of rice grains across his cheeks.

If this guy worked out, Larry thought, and replaced that gut and flabby ass with a six-pack and studly buns, he'd be hot. As his eyes roved over the doctor, Larry saw him stiffen. Is he embarrassed, Larry wondered. Maybe he's in the closet. I'll play along if he can get me out of here alive.

"I think you have pneumonia," Kevin said evenly, "But not the sort of pneumonia we usually see. You're pretty sick, so I'm going to put you in our intensive care unit."

He looked directly at Larry and waited. Surprised to be sounded out for a reaction by someone wearing a white coat, Larry didn't respond until the implications of what Kevin had just said sank in.

"Are you telling me there's an infection in my lungs that could kill me, and you don't know what it is?"

"It might be an infection. Or it could be some other type of disease. I don't know yet."

"Can't you give me something?"

"There's already an antibiotic going into your blood. But to be honest, I can't be sure it's the right medication, and we have a lot to choose from. I've asked a specialist to do a procedure tomorrow. It's called bronchoscopy. He'll pass a little tube down your throat and into your lungs to take a tiny piece of tissue that we can look at under the microscope."

"Ouch!"

"You'll get a sedative. You'll hardly be awake. It'll be over in a few minutes."

"Hey, I'm all for finding out why I can't breathe."

"Then you've come to the right place. I think we can make you better— once we figure out what's causing the problem."

Larry took note of Kevin's New England accent. He suspected frankness would go over better than good-old-boy palaver. He offered his hand, and Kevin shook it.

"Save me, Jesus!" pierced through the emergency room. None of the doctors or nurses seemed to notice, though Kevin did roll his eyes. Shrieking must go with the territory here, Larry supposed, like the Baptist church his parents had sporadically dragged him to.

He recalled the day before he turned sixteen. His father had made him meet with their pastor.

Wouldn't that bastard love to hear *me* screaming "Save me, Jesus," he thought. Well, fuck him.

Larry could still see the scowling, weather-beaten face, the knobby finger poking his chest. He still remembered the man's exact words.

"Sodomy is a mortal sin, son. You'll be condemned to eternal damnation in hell unless you accept Christ and pray for forgiveness."

The next day, Larry bought a one-way bus ticket to San Francisco.

III

ON THE OTHER SIDE of the ER, Kevin checked in with the nurses and reviewed notes and orders. He found his two interns had risen to the occasion and were competently managing the team's other six admissions, which left Kevin free to call the Haight-Ashbury clinic.

"Dr. Howard?" Kevin said, once connected to the physician Larry had told him about. "This is Kevin Bartholomew. I'm a medicine resident at City Hospital."

He liked the cheerful, rich alto voice that replied without condescension, "Call me Gwen."

She recognized Larry Winton's name instantly and lost her good humor on hearing he was being admitted to intensive care.

"Shit! I just saw him two weeks ago. He was complaining of cough and night sweats. I sent him to City Hospital for a sputum induction and x-ray. He never came back. Does he have TB?"

"Chest film doesn't look like it, and the AFB stain I did was negative."

"So what do you think is going on?"

"Don't know yet, but I'm covering him with antibiotics."

"How bad off is he?"

"With nasal prongs, I can barely get his arterial oxygen to seventy."

"Oh, no," she moaned, her voice nearly breaking.

Was she going to cry, Kevin worried. He chewed his lower lip and punched the plunger of his ballpoint pen, waiting for her to calm down. He guessed she wasn't much older than him. Perhaps a dyed-in-the-wool hippy? She did work in Haight-Ashbury.

"I'm coming over to see him. Damn! No, I can't today. I have to pick up my kid in an hour. I'll be there tomorrow morning, OK?"

"Sure. Don't worry. We're on it. He's going to the ICU. The pulmonary attending will bronch him in the morning. It's gonna be pedal to the metal here."

"Oh my God..."

"I'm sorry," he apologized, concerned he may have come across as condescending. "I didn't mean..."

"I know you'll do a full court press," she interrupted. "This is my screw-up. I should have found out what happened when he didn't come back to clinic."

Kevin was astonished. He had never heard anyone senior to him give a mea culpa like this. And there was no way Winton's predicament could be her fault. If he followed up on every patient who didn't return to his continuity clinic, his sleep debt would quickly become incompatible with life.

"Thanks for going the extra mile to call me. You're probably getting slammed with admissions if it's anything like my residency at City Hospital was. I mean internship—I didn't complete residency. Anyway, please tell Larry I'm rooting for him. I'll definitely come to see him tomorrow."

"Absolutely. Oh, I forgot to ask about his medical history."

"Not much there. No prior hospitalizations I know of, certainly no underlying lung disease. He was doing speed when I first met him but cleaned up his act years ago. He mostly saw me for gonorrhea and syphilis—he hustles men for a living. Though now that I think of it, something was going on before the cough and night sweats started. He used to lift weights and wear boutique clothes from North Beach. All that stopped about a year ago. He came to clinic looking disheveled, stressed out, thinner. Maybe it was drugs, but he said he was clean, and he'd never lied to me before."

Kevin sighed, disappointed by the lack of clues. The range of diagnostic possibilities in such a sick patient was way too wide for his comfort zone.

"So, are you a second or third year resident?" Gwen asked.

"Third year. Four more months, and I'm done."

"Then what?"

"I'm not sure. Maybe an ID fellowship. When were you here?"

"1969, just before they built the new hospital."

"Been at the Haight clinic long?"

"Seven years. I only work three days a week."

"That sounds nice."

"It is. Not much money, but I can have a life... Well, at least my daughter can have me in her life."

Kevin imagined a child who would yell "Daddy" and hug him when he came home—a pleasant fantasy.

"How tough is residency these days?" she asked.

"Call is every fourth night, not every third like the days of the giants when you were here."

"Days of the giants?" she laughed. "When I was at City Hospital, the attendings said that same bullshit about how much harder they had it than we did."

"The sleep deprivation is still bad. When I'm on call here, I'm lucky to get half an hour in bed. It's better on the Hill, but they give us a ton more autonomy here."

"Interesting!"

"Is it? Why?"

"I'm thinking about coming back to finish residency."

"All right! Page me when you get here tomorrow. I'll show you around."

"That'd be great. Thanks, Kevin."

IV

"Mr. Winton?"

"Mr. Winton?"

The short, obese young man who had woken him—or was he a teenager, Larry wondered—wore a white jacket two sizes too small. His pockets overflowed with tongue depressors, penlights, and cotton swabs. A mask covered his mouth and nose, drawing attention to the pimples dotting his forehead.

He introduced himself as Dr. Bartholomew's medical student and rolled up his sleeve, revealing columns of tiny words scribbled in ink on his forearm. Reading from the list, he asked Larry about a host of symptoms, ranging from nausea and diarrhea to numbness and tremor. As Larry answered, the student made notes on a sheet of paper full of strange diagrams.

"Mr. Winton, can you tell me today's date, day of the week, and year?"

"Today…."

Larry searched his mind. He wasn't sure. It must be the middle of March.

Frustrated by the interminable questions, he said, "Saint Patty's Day, m'boy."

The student stared at him.

"Never caught a Texas leprechaun?" Larry asked in an Irish brogue. "Ask me where my oil well is."

The student checked his notes against the words on his arm. Dispirited by his failed attempt at humor, Larry closed his eyes. He thought of the mysterious diagrams on the student's clipboard, as inscrutable to him as those in a horoscope he had acquired in 1968.

When Larry got off the bus from Fort Worth, he was met by a middle-aged woman wearing dark eye shadow and a paisley caftan. She dangled a paper template of collapsing circles, radial lines, and arcane symbols. I'll predict your future for a pack of cigarettes, she offered. Just tell me exactly when and where you were born. Larry had liked this idea of a predestination absolving him of any responsibility for his own fate.

By the time Larry arrived in San Francisco, the city's "Summer of Love" was over. There was more "speed"—methamphetamine manufactured by local biker gangs—being sold on Haight Street than LSD. Larry soon sampled all the available drugs. One LSD trip was enough. He wanted to empower his self, not transcend it. Although the pleasure of heroin easily matched that of a good orgasm and lasted longer, he saw what it did to people—the scars and open sores, the degradation addicts were willing to submit to for another high. Speed, on the other hand, wasn't overtly self-destructive. He could listen to music for hours, dance for hours, have sex for hours.

Larry fell in with a tribe of homeless speed freaks, an honorable society compared to heroin addicts. However, surviving in the city with a drug habit required money. Occasionally, he resorted to petty theft, until he learned about the Castro.

Larry discovered he was irresistible to the older, well-off, gay men who had settled in a neighborhood known by its main commercial street, Castro, at the end of World War II. He packaged his lean, six-foot frame into a tight pink tank top and blue jeans worn low to display his flat belly. His cheeks, chiseled by methamphetamine, and a scar on his chin completed the erotic bait. He set the hook with a cowboy persona, half vulnerable, half rugged, brazenly bootlegged from James Dean.

As the gay scene grew exponentially, he graduated from doing tricks on the street to being a kept lover in an elegant furnished apartment. He usually had two or more sugar daddies, discretely scheduled so as not to meet one another. A few were married, had children, and lived in the suburbs. Collectively, their support covered his living expenses, including the upkeep for a pristine, white Thunderbird convertible.

After the medical student left, Larry saw he was being scrutinized by a male nurse. Not examined objectively like a patient would be but sized up on a scale of desirability. The man's layered, shoulder-length hair and thick mustache were familiar. Of course, Larry realized, the nurse was a regular in a

Castro Street fern bar where he had done some higher-end hustling. The man had approached him once and suggested a tryst. When Larry explained what he charged, the man was furious. Must picture himself too hot to have to pay for it, Larry had thought.

He watched the nurse amble to the central ER hub of telephones and chart racks and whisper to a butch-looking clerk he recognized from a downscale, South of Market leather bar. The clerk's mutton chop sideburns were the same. Just his suspenders and chains were missing. Larry recalled being hit on by him with a similar outcome.

Larry had learned early on that such misunderstandings were a professional hazard. One had to cast a wide net in making seductive eye contact. Sometimes a potential client misread the situation. Thrilled that this young stud was attracted to him, the unsuspecting target would strike up a conversation and become hostile on finding out Larry was interested only in commercial transactions.

The two men sneered at him. They seemed to be enjoying his misfortune. Larry was indifferent. His pretense of vulnerability had always been a bigger act than the ruggedness. He still lived the mantra he first heard as a homeless teen in the Haight— "Don't let other people's shit bum you out."

Though there had been one exception to this rule. In 1973, while cruising Haight Street in his T-Bird with the top down, a muscle-bound, blond farm boy from the Salinas Valley hopped into the car and offered to sell him speed. Larry countered with an invitation to lunch. They quickly became lovers and stumbled into an arrangement that permitted intimacy without sacrificing too much pride. Larry helped pay Chris's share of the rent in a lower Haight crash pad. Whenever Larry's apartment was free of clients, Chris stayed over.

After a year, Chris was chafing at his financial dependence. Wanting parity, he escalated from dealing small amounts of speed on the street to bigger buys and distribution. One evening, Chris borrowed the T-Bird to close a deal in Hunter's Point. He didn't return. A week later, a policeman notified Larry that his car, stripped of its tires, doors, and radiator, had been abandoned in an empty parking lot. A body was never found.

Larry quit using drugs and started lifting weights as an outlet for his grief. The change in his physique increased his professional value which led to the most lucrative arrangement of his career, servicing and keeping house for a trio of international airline stewards. Their short layovers in San Francisco allowed Larry the free time to take junior college classes. He even developed an exit strategy for when his marketability declined—obtaining a real estate license.

Then the loss of appetite and fatigue began. Larry went to the Haight Street clinic, but penicillin injections for gonorrhea and syphilis didn't help. He stopped lifting weights at the gym. Soon he was too thin for the airline stewards' taste. They let the apartment lease expire. Larry had to move into a shared flat in the Haight. He worked the streets again—a higher volume at a lower price. Each night, he awoke drenched in sweat. The coughing became constant. He returned to the clinic where Gwen urged him to get a chest x-ray and his sputum tested. He put it off until he couldn't walk a half a block before halting to ease the panting and the pummeling his heart was giving his ribs. Finally giving in, he hailed the cab that brought him to the city's brand new public hospital.

V

HERB LEFT HIS OFFICE at six. Fifteen minutes later, he parked in the driveway of his Tudor home in San Francisco's upscale Forest Hills neighborhood. Inside, his wife was making a salad in the kitchen. He kissed the back of her neck. Cecilia gave him a perfunctory peck, without lingering.

Not my lucky night, he thought. He suppressed the desire aroused by touching her smooth skin, still flawless by his standards.

"Martin needs a poster board for his history project," she said. "Can you get one this evening?"

"Sure. Want some help?"

"Just set the table. I'm almost done. Oh, Allison got an A on her English paper."

"Great!" he said, feigning delight.

He found his ten-year-old daughter sitting next to her younger brother at the top of the stairs.

"Good work, Allison," Herb called out from the landing below. "I told you it was a great essay."

Allison ignored him. She and Martin had their attention focused on a pair of Slinkys perched at the precipice of the landing.

Martin, eight years old and small for his age, counted backwards, "Ten, nine, eight…"

At zero, each tipped their coil forward.

"Go! Go!" they yelled.

Martin's champion made it to the next step and slumped over where it lay quivering. Allison's toppled two steps further.

"Two points for me," she shouted gleefully.

Only when Allison played games with her younger brother, games they had both outgrown, did Herb ever see her animated by joy. Otherwise, she was relentlessly serious. Allison wasn't depressed. They had taken her to a child psychiatrist who confidently dismissed that possibility. She simply had little interest in friends and none in activities that weren't goal-oriented. She approached those that were, such as school, with grave intensity. Cecilia, by dint of more dedicated effort than Herb could apply, had found other topics of conversation—mostly clothes and hair products. Persistently hoping for more emotional currency, Cecilia refused to be disappointed. Herb had already given up. He was certain Allison's austere nature came from his side of the family. He felt all he could manage was to keep it at bay in himself and avoid contaminating his wife and son.

Martin, discouraged by his toy's poor performance, sighed, "Hi, Dad."

Herb bounded up the stairs and tickled him in the ribs.

"No!" his son laughed, scuttling away.

Herb caught him again. Martin collapsed in waves of giggles, punctuated by half-sincere pleas to stop. Herb relented and embraced him in a bear hug.

On his way downstairs, Herb placed a hand on Allison's shoulder. She flinched at his touch. He began praising her essay.

"It was an A-minus." she said with a scowl. "It should have been A-plus."

"You're too hard on yourself. A-minus is fine."

She rolled her eyes and went to her room.

After dinner, as soon as the children deposited their plates in the sink and left the kitchen, Cecilia closed the door behind them. She confronted Herb with a worried frown.

"The MacIntyre execs are unhappy. Their sales have dropped by a third this last quarter."

He stopped loading the dishwasher and sat down. Cecilia was a partner in a downtown advertising firm. MacIntyre was her client, a major source of the revenue she generated for the business.

"There's an emergency meeting tomorrow morning at eight. We need a new marketing strategy, like yesterday. I've got to be there. Six people I supervise, their jobs are on the line."

Although Wednesday was Cecilia's day to drive the kids to school, Winton was his only bronchoscopy case. He could do it at nine instead of eight o'clock.

"Not a problem, honey. I can take the kids to school."

Herb's lack of annoyance was genuine. He felt fortunate, astonishingly lucky, to have Cecilia, a woman so comfortable with herself and others. He believed she was far more than he deserved. But then he had never fully believed he deserved to exist at all.

Herb was born in the spring of 1938. It should have been in Shanghai during the Japanese invasion that laid waste to China. Except his father, a lawyer and diplomat, had been sent to assist the ambassador in Washington DC a few months beforehand. He brought his pregnant wife along and after the war was hired as an immigration specialist by the newly formed United Nations. U.S. citizenship came with the position. Herb grew up in placid, suburban Long Island rather than amid starvation and epidemic cholera.

"It's not just school, Herb. Allison has an orthodontist appointment at nine-thirty. Did you forget she's been complaining her braces hurt?"

"Nine-thirty?" he asked uneasily.

"Yes, nine-thirty."

He squirmed.

"I have a bronch to do, a really sick patient with no diagnosis. I can drop off Martin at school, but I'd have to push back the bronch to eleven if I take Allison to her appointment. Can't your mother take her or one of your sisters?"

"Herb, we're talking about Allison, not Martin. What if she gets into a stubborn snit? She'll refuse to open her mouth if one of us isn't there to talk her down."

"Come on, Cecilia."

"I hate that you have that free pass," she seethed. "Somebody might die if I'm not there. It isn't fair."

He was trapped. The only way out was to concede. Yet Herb wasn't angry. He knew how lonely life could be, how much Cecilia's love sustained him. What he resented was having to choose between his daughter, who gave him no emotional return, and his responsibility for sick patients. He supposed he could do the bronch at eleven. He'd have to page Kevin and the pulmonary fellow first thing in the morning and let them know.

"All right, all right. I'll reschedule the bronch. She'll have to go to the hospital with me after the orthodontist and wait in my office. I'll take her to school when I'm done."

He watched Cecilia relax, her hostility dissipate.

Thank God, he thought, détente at last. Herb was relieved, briefly. With a sinking sensation, he remembered that if the bronchoscopy specimens didn't get to pathology by ten in the morning at the latest, the special stains he planned to request couldn't be completed until the following day, which could delay making a diagnosis for another twenty-four hours. That raised a very disturbing question—whether to tell Kevin to blindly give his patient a steroid infusion. Depending on the type of lung disease, a one day delay in starting steroid treatment might be too long. He had seen someone die from an autoimmune inflammatory condition while waiting for a bronchoscopy result. On the other hand, if an infection was causing the man's deterioration, administering steroids might compromise his immune system enough to kill him.

Herb knew where this was going. He would get no sleep tonight unless he stopped ruminating about the case. He forced himself to think of something else and latched on to Kevin's uncharacteristic behavior that afternoon. Although easily the most thoughtful of all the senior residents and surely the most even-tempered, Kevin had been on edge today. Herb recognized the signs—the lips parted with anticipation, the pressure of speech and gesticulation.

This case had lit a fire in Kevin's belly. To quench it, he would have to find out what was causing Winton's respiratory failure. Herb now had a window of opportunity to sell Kevin on his own career pathway, clinical research. If the bronchoscopy specimens didn't reveal a diagnosis and the patient didn't make it, he would push the pathologists to do an autopsy. Kevin would have to know the cause, with absolute certainty. Then the hypotheses could emerge, and he would be off and running. Herb savored the idea until aware he was still thinking about the specimens that wouldn't get to pathology by ten in the morning.

VI

LARRY AWOKE TO DISCOVER he had been moved again, this time to a bed in a private room. Sweat ran down his forehead, burning his eyes. Despite the oxygen pouring into a plastic shell fitted snugly over his mouth and nose, any physical effort made him gasp for air. He felt a catheter inside his penis and saw electrical wires taped to his chest.

The room's window gave Larry his first view of the outside world since coming to City Hospital. He guessed it was early morning. On the opposite side of the cubicle was a glass wall. Through it, he saw blue-pajama-clad nurses and white-jacketed doctors at work. I'm on display, he thought, like a mannequin in some S&M shop.

He was drifting back to sleep when awoken by a voice softly calling his name. Kevin was sitting next to him on a stool. Larry realized that every doctor, so far, had stood looking down at him. He prepared to receive bad news.

"How's the breathing?" Kevin asked.

"Worse." Larry said and pointed to the oxygen mask. "This contraption is damn uncomfortable."

"Sorry. It's the best we can do right now to get enough oxygen into your lungs. The nasal prongs weren't doing the job."

"And what happens if I don't get enough oxygen into my lungs?"

Kevin sighed.

"Be square with me, doc."

He searched Kevin's face for signs of evasion.

"Your heart and your brain," Kevin embarked cautiously, "need to get enough oxygen for you to make it. We're losing ground."

Larry cut the redneck jive.

"There must be something you can do to fix me!"

"I'm sure there will be, once we have results from the bronchoscopy, once we understand what's causing this. That'll be soon, very soon."

"Yeah, I hope so too, doc. Well, thanks for trying."

Larry extended his hand. Kevin clasped it and gave an encouraging pump.

As he got up to leave, Kevin took a card out of his pocket and examined it. Larry saw his own name printed on the back.

"Is there any family member, any friend you want me to contact?" Kevin asked.

Larry closed his eyes and turned his head away.

VII

AT TEN IN THE morning, Gwen Howard was lucky enough to find a parking spot just four blocks from City Hospital. Walking toward the main entrance, she thought about Kevin Bartholomew, how engaging and appealing he had been on the phone yesterday. Had they been flirting?

Stop it, Gwen ordered herself. He's got to be at least four years younger than me.

Since her divorce, she had dated enough to learn the hard way that men could handle being with a woman who was two, maybe three years older. Any more was inevitably a deal-breaker. Gwen concentrated on the building she was entering.

Though she had already been inside several times to check on sick clinic patients, the place still unnerved her. This modern version of City Hospital with its closed wards and individual rooms was nothing like the brick towers that stood here when she was an intern. The house staff and nurses seemed to work in isolation. It was too white, too bright, too silent for her. Nothing like the old hospital's raucous open wards where she had become adept at sticking intravenous catheters, spinal needles, and bone marrow trephines into desperately ill people. The constant, colorful chatter, even the patients' complaints, had been public reassurance that she was doing her best, all that anyone in her position could be expected to accomplish.

But will my best meet the bar here? Poor Larry Winton was a case in point. Being purely objective, she had to conclude he was in the ICU with respiratory failure because a few weeks earlier, when she saw a tinge of blue in his nail beds and considered calling an ambulance, she had also imagined an emergency room physician complaining about yet another patient unnecessarily sent over by an idiot clinic doc who didn't know what real cyanosis looks like.

"Christ," she said aloud in the empty elevator. "I should have just bit the bullet and called 911. The sub-specialists here would have had plenty of time to figure it out by now."

Gwen hadn't gone into the new ICU on her previous visits. Her self-confidence sunk lower as she looked at the modern equipment. It was all foreign, from intravenous pumps to wall-mounted oxygen valves and chest tube drainage systems. The ventilators had dials to control parameters she had never heard of. It made her re-think applying. How long would it take her to come up to speed? The patients she cared for rarely had anything worse than a bad cold or a sexually transmitted disease. And if she was accepted into the residency, it would mean being here triple the hours she now worked, so much time away from Eva.

Yet Eva did seem to need her less. She was thriving in fourth grade and happy to play in an after-school program until six on the days Gwen worked. And Gwen knew she could find a college girl with a car to cover the nights and weekends on call. It wouldn't be that expensive. Parenting certainly wouldn't get easier once Eva started adolescence. In any case, Gwen's days at the Haight-Ashbury clinic were numbered if she didn't acquire a specialty credential. Health department doctors like her would soon be required to be boarded, and eligibility for a board exam required completing two additional years of hospital training after internship. The clincher was Proctor, the private school Eva attended. Its tuition was eroding her savings, and her ex-husband Daniel refused to help. He believed private schools were politically incorrect.

A middle-aged nurse, a good ten years older than Gwen, asked, "Can I help you?"

"I'm Dr. Howard from Health Center 3."

The nurse gave her a disinterested, faintly disapproving look.

Is it my appearance, Gwen wondered. Hair too long, dress too short for thirty-five? She was proud of her trim, tennis-toned body. A pretty face, too, she'd always been told.

"A patient of mine is here. Larry Winton."

The nurse pointed to a red-haired man in a white jacket seated on a stool. He was watching a heart monitor.

"Winton is his."

Gwen studied Kevin. What gorgeous green eyes, she thought. He could be cute if he lost twenty pounds. She halted further fantasy. He indeed was too young for her. But this reminded her of another plus in doing of a residency—so many opportunities to meet men.

As Gwen approached Kevin, she saw he was exhausted.

"Hi, I'm Gwen Howard. We talked about Larry Winton yesterday?"

Kevin immediately brightened. He stood up and offered his hand.

"It's great you came by. He hasn't had any visitors."

"That doesn't surprise me. He's kind of a loner."

Kevin looked at his wristwatch.

"He's going to be bronched soon. You want to see him now?"

"Sure," she said, her pluck fading again.

Kevin led her to Larry's room. She slipped past him, rolled a stool to the head of the bed, and sat down.

Larry had a vacant expression. With each inhalation, the hollows of his neck retracted and he lifted his shoulders. To the uninitiated, he might be meditating or practicing yoga. The sad irony, Gwen knew, was that no one, not even the world's greatest marathon runner, could sustain this level of breathing work for more than a day or two.

"Hi, doc," he said, his words echoing inside the oxygen mask. "What're you doing here?"

"He called me," she said with a nod toward Kevin.

"What do you think? Is it TB?"

"Maybe," she said, trying to sound hopeful.

Larry looked skeptically at her, then at Kevin.

"I don't know what it is," Gwen confessed. "I am so, so sorry this happened."

"Not your fault, doc. I fucked up. Blew off your advice. Shoulda got my ass here sooner. Don't worry. They're doing all they can."

"I know they are," she fervently agreed.

Larry's smile was fractured by the curved, translucent shell covering his mouth. Gwen bit her lips and turned away. In the doorway, she saw two people in white gowns and masks. They hovered there like wraiths. Behind them stood a middle-aged Asian-American man wearing a sport jacket and tie. He was frowning.

Herb apologized for being late. Kevin handed him the most recent arterial blood gas results. Herb glanced at the numbers, checked the oxygen flow valve by Larry's bed, and gave a barely perceptible shake of his head.

"Time to go," said Kevin.

Larry recoiled.

"They do this every day here," Gwen murmured. "You'll be OK."

While Larry was being moved to a gurney, Kevin introduced Gwen to Herb.

"What do you think?" she asked, struggling to tamp down her anxiety.

"Not TB," Herb answered. "Though I've been wrong about that before. Hypersensitivity pneumonitis, cocci, sarcoid? It could be anything. Let's hope the bronch washings tell us something, at least a clue as to whether steroids might help."

Gwen liked the self-deprecation, but he sounded pessimistic. Laying crepe was what they called it when she was an intern.

VIII

THE PULMONARY FELLOW AND medical assistant transferred Larry to a recliner chair and proceeded to ignore him as they sorted through boxes of bottles and syringes. Herb, now gowned and masked too, entered the bronchoscopy suite. Larry grabbed the armrests and pushed himself back into the chair. His lips were trembling.

Like a caged rabbit, Herb thought. A tide of empathy rose. He fought it off and diverted his gaze. Maintaining cool objectivity was essential, he believed, for performing this procedure with minimal risk to the patient's safety as well as to his own mental health.

"There's nothing to be scared about, Mr. Winton."

Herb balked. He couldn't pretend the consequences of his being late were potentially disastrous. He had to be completely present, whatever the cost to his equilibrium.

He placed his hands on Larry's shoulders and looked into his eyes.

"You'll get through this just fine," he vowed. "I promise."

Saying those words stirred up memories he couldn't suppress.

In seventh grade, during a field trip to Manhattan, Herb's class traipsed across Madison Square Park to see the statues of famous Americans. Herb lingered too long in front of the Civil War admiral who had famously yelled, "Damn the torpedoes, full speed ahead." On realizing his classmates were gone, he jogged in widening circles around the park until finally giving up. He trudged in search of a subway station and soon faced a massive stretch of identical, fifteen-story red-brick apartment buildings. Just beyond was the East River. He turned around and saw six rough-looking teenagers blocking his path.

"Whatchya doin' here, chink?" shouted the gang's apparent leader. "This ain't Chinatown."

"I'm lost," Herb confessed. "How do I get to the Long Island Rail Road?"

"What! Peter Cooper Village ain't good enough for you, chink? You wanta go to the suburbs?"

Herb retreated. He didn't notice one of the boys creep behind him and crouch down. Falling backwards, Herb's head slammed on the sidewalk. The leader lifted him by the collar and slugged him, splitting his lower lip.

"Get outta here you little shit," he yelled as they ran away.

Too stunned to sit up, Herb lay patting his scalp and lip gashes in a feeble attempt to stanch the bleeding. Eventually, there were sirens. Herb was taken by ambulance to a hospital, propped up in a wheelchair, and rolled to an exam room where a pale, freckled, middle-aged man clad in green scrubs knelt down and looked into Herb's eyes.

"I'm going make you numb, lad," he said in an Irish accent, "Clean your cuts and sew them shut. Are you brave enough to lie still for that?"

Herb submitted willingly. No white adult had ever made such direct eye contact with him, not even a schoolteacher. That alone sufficed to convince him the man must be well-intentioned.

"You'll get through it just fine," the doctor promised.

Herb's faith wavered when an anesthetic injected into the wounds burned hard enough to make him shed tears, but the warm, rinsing liquids that followed restored his trust, as did the doctor's chipper apology, "Sorry, lad," each time Herb felt a dull yank from sutures piercing and pulling his skin together. He had been given a pain pill that kicked in as the last thread was tied. The throbbing ceased, and true numbness came—a neutral buzz, constant, predictable, bearable.

Herb was asleep when his mother arrived. She bundled him into a taxi and brought him home. He spent the rest of the night buffeting between dreadful dreams and conscious pain. At some point during this fugue state, his father appeared, demanding information. Herb's mouth was too swollen to make intelligible words.

His father returned at six in the morning. He made Herb get dressed and eat cereal. Though moving his lips was excruciating, Herb didn't complain. He didn't have to be told this was his own fault for not paying attention. His father drove them to a police station in lower Manhattan. They went from office to office through mustard-colored hallways reeking of stale tobacco smoke. Fluttering fluorescent lights made Herb dizzy. He found a bathroom and vomited.

His father insisted a criminal report be filed. Flash bulbs lacerated Herb's headache as photographs were taken for evidence. The presiding officer was good-natured. Too good-natured. As his father filled out forms, the man grinned. Other policemen were smirking or outright laughing. Herb was incredulous his father couldn't see he was the butt of their joke. Then he realized his father actually had noticed and was refusing to acknowledge the fact. Herb began to despise him.

Regaining self-control, Herb said, "You need to be relaxed for this. I'm going to give you a medication that'll help. I'll be surprised if you remember the experience afterwards. Ready?"

Larry nodded meekly. He watched Herb attach a syringe to his intravenous tubing and the fellow adjust dials on an ominous black box connected to a two foot length of cable.

"You'll be getting sleepy soon."

Alarmed by a burning sensation in his arm, Larry tensed. Pleasure suddenly bloomed in the back of his head. The fatigue, fear, and relentless labor of breathing dissipated.

Herb was speaking rapidly. Larry was unable to comprehend. Was it a foreign language? Latin? As the ceiling lights dimmed, Herb's face was bathed by the glow emanating from the bronchoscope dials.

Now everything made sense to Larry. He remembered a priest, a regular on Haight Street, who wore a black Nehru jacket over his clerical collar. The man chatted with street people about hustling and drugs, but he didn't proselytize. Instead, he helped them find housing, food, or a place to detox. He had never approached Larry until seeing him short of breath. When asked if he needed assistance, Larry declined. The priest gave him a card with the address of a local parish church. Once a half-block walk became the limit of his endurance, Larry reconsidered his options. He hoped Catholics had a different perspective on sin than Baptists.

The Sunday before he was admitted to City Hospital, Larry took a bus from Haight Street to Saint Ignatius. The street priest was at the pulpit, wrapped in a white robe, giving a sermon about purgatory. The term was vaguely familiar to Larry. He supposed it had something to do with suffering for your sins. The priest explained that individuals whose lives never strayed from virtue went straight to heaven while those who had never hesitated in being selfish went straight to hell. Purgatory was a waiting room for people who had made any effort to atone for their misdeeds.

"Mr. Winton," said Herb. "You're going to feel a tube go down your throat. Take in a long, slow breath."

Larry did his best to cooperate. He understood what was happening. This doctor was Saint Peter. He had come to see Larry and decide whether to send him to heaven or hell. Fair enough, thought Larry, and he relaxed.

IX

AFTER DROPPING OFF ALLISON at school, Herb returned to his office. He found a note from Kevin taped to the door, asking him to attend noon conference. The case to be discussed would be Larry Winton. Herb knew Kevin's team had just admitted fourteen patients to the wards in addition to Winton in the ICU, which meant Kevin would have already been awake for twenty-eight consecutive hours when the conference began. He wondered why Flagler, the elderly head of infectious diseases, said the residents were getting soft.

Herb sat at his desk dictating reports and letters for the rest of the morning. His office, part of an interior suite, had white walls and floors. Hospital wards fanned out in all directions, allowing Herb to see patients, teach, and conduct research with maximal efficiency. He didn't mind working in a windowless hive. There was more than enough drama here to distract him. Seven years into this job, Herb was absolutely certain it would never become boring.

In the conference room, a chief resident sat on either side of Flagler who motioned Herb to join them at the "pontificators' table." Kevin stood at a blackboard that spanned the entire east wall. Chalk in hand, he made notes while his medical student summarized the case. Kevin wrote acronyms, distilling the salient features of Larry Winton's history, physical exam findings, and laboratory results into an even briefer synopsis. He asked Herb to comment on the chest x-ray. Herb pointed out the obvious. Both lung fields were solid white throughout.

Kevin continued to make notes as the discussion proceeded. Larry Winton's *clinical* diagnosis was severe pneumonia. The *differential* diagnosis Kevin scribbled on the board, a list of all plausible causes of his pneumonia in the order of their probability, numbered twenty by the end of the hour when people began leaving. Yet the process was hardly finished. It had been easy enough to achieve consensus in eliminating common causes. It was the obscure autoimmune, allergic, and infectious diseases that generated controversy. Kevin gained energy with each comment he wrote for or against a rare illness. He drew arrows connecting candidate diagnoses to tests which could confirm or exclude the condition and medications that could treat it. Since some tests could help nail down or rule out more than one diagnosis and some drugs could treat more than one disease, his arrows branched and crossed forming a web.

Herb left after two hours and worked in his office until four-thirty. On his way out of the hospital, he walked by the conference room. Kevin was still there, holding a stub of chalk, erasing and re-writing in the few empty interstices remaining on the blackboard. Herb was about to insist Kevin go home and sleep when his pager sounded. A moment later so did Kevin's. Both displayed the ICU phone number, followed by 9-1-1. They looked at each other, said "Winton" simultaneously, and ran to the unit.

X

Larry awoke from a nightmare. He had been kidnapped by his high school football team, hog-tied, and taken to the Trinity River. The boys were screaming "Die, homo, die!" as the quarterback dunked his head. Larry fought fiercely, thrashing to get his mouth above water for the half-second it took to get another small breath.

He opened his eyes to see he was in the glass cubicle, not Texas. But his frantic struggle to get more oxygen hadn't ended. He grasped the bed rails and rocked backward to maximize inhalation then forward to expel every bit of air. Kevin was sitting next to him, extracting blood from the arterial catheter in his wrist. Dark purple liquid pulsed into the syringe, a familiar sight to Larry from his days of shooting speed, though something about it was wrong. Whenever a shooter's point hit a vein, blood of this same purple hue would seep slowly into the syringe. It wouldn't pulse like this. And if he hit an artery by mistake, the backflow would pulse like this, but the color was always bright red.

Kevin looked dejectedly at the syringe. He signaled to the pulmonary fellow waiting at the nurse's station. She carried a toolbox into Larry's room and removed trays filled with hollow plastic tubes and chrome instruments. Larry was terrified again. Were they going to cut a hole in his neck?

Kevin was talking about a machine that pumped oxygen into the lungs. Larry couldn't concentrate on what he was saying. Kevin moved on to another issue.

"Mr. Winton, is there a family member I can contact?"

"Don't...bother," he answered between breaths.

A technician wheeled in a mechanical ventilator.

"As soon as the tube is in place," said Kevin, no longer able to hide his anxiety, "we'll turn the machine on. Then your lungs will get enough oxygen. OK?"

Larry was listening now.

"You'll have an uncontrollable urge to cough the tube out. We have to put you to sleep so the machine can do the work of breathing for you. It can't help you if you're fighting it. You understand?"

"Doc...will I ...wake up? Or is this…just...easy way out?"

"No! Not at all! We're buying time. We still don't have all the bronchoscopy results. Once we know what's causing your pneumonia, we can start treating it with the right drug."

"OK…I'll be…good soldier."

As the fellow sprayed numbing medicine into Larry's throat, Herb entered.

Praise God, Larry thought, Saint Peter's back in charge.

Now the fellow was holding a short length of clear plastic piping, half an inch in diameter and covered with lubricating jelly, in front of Larry's face. She instructed him to swallow as she thrust the tube into his left nostril. He retched. She forced the tube farther until it jammed into the back of his throat. He retched again.

Larry saw Herb wince.

"One more swallow," she coaxed.

He tried to comply.

"Now inhale."

Larry obeyed and felt the tube slide down his throat. He coughed violently.

"We're in!" she yelled triumphantly.

"Inflate the cuff," Herb calmly decreed.

Kevin attached an empty syringe to a side port on the tube. He pushed the plunger down, expanding a balloon-like sheath at the tube's other end, which sealed off Larry's windpipe. Kevin secured the tube to his nose and cheeks with strips of fabric tape. Herb pressed the ventilator power switch on.

A rush of air inflated Larry's lungs. His terror was submerged in a wave of self-disgust. His body, once an object of desire, had been diminished to flesh of medical interest only. It repelled him. He wanted to be rid of it.

Kevin stroked his hand. Larry remembered being touched this way long before he had ever been penetrated or sucked for someone else's gratification. A protective touch.

His mother had done that when he was a little boy and had measles. In a darkened bedroom on a steamy summer afternoon, Larry had been fitful. He couldn't sleep, couldn't find a comfortable position to rest. Sensing his frustration, his mother gently swept away the wet strands of hair stuck to his forehead.

As the intravenous anesthetic arrived in his brain, Larry began to cry. His craving to be sheltered vanished.

XI

WAITING FOR HER DAUGHTER outside of Proctor, Gwen saw Eva's new teacher open the school's front door. When he had been introduced to parents during the tense meeting after Eva's old teacher abruptly quit, she had appreciated his engagement and composure. His strong jaw, impish smile, and lithe figure didn't escape her attention either.

He must be a dancer or a runner, she thought. Probably younger than me, but not by much. He might not be gay either.

Eva's teacher recognized her immediately. She imagined touching his chocolate skin, his closely sheared, woolly hair. Aware he had glanced at her bare left ring finger and was looking at her with more interest and enthusiasm than a fourth grader's mother should expect, she blushed.

"Eva's mom, right?" he said eagerly.

"Yeah," she whispered.

Hoping he wouldn't think she was imitating some sultry film star, her blush deepened. For God's sake, she thought, he'll only be her teacher until June.

"Mr. Parsons, right?"

"Just to the students. I'm Rick."

"OK. Hi, Rick."

"Hi..?"

"Gwen."

"Gwen," he said, clearly taking pleasure in pronouncing her name. "So… Eva's doing well here."

"I can tell. She likes school. She likes you, too."

"The academic part is easy for her," he said, lowering his voice professorially. "That helps a lot."

Seeing a giddy sparkle in his eyes at odds with such an earnest assessment, she was emboldened to move beyond talking about Eva.

"So…is this job fun for you?"

"It is. Doesn't pay well, but it is fun. Plus, I get to do something useful. At least I'm not making bombs."

And there was the grin she was anticipating. Gwen crossed her arms, looked down, and giggled.

"You like what you do?" he asked with an intensity that could hardly be misconstrued as making idle conversation.

"I do. I'm proud of it, too."

She met his eyes again and thought how wonderful it would be to have this in common—enjoying your work and feeling it made a positive social contribution—how much it would help in building sustainable intimacy. She remembered once sharing that bond with Daniel. It was the main reason she agreed to marry him. What a mistake that had been. But this man didn't take himself so seriously.

As Rick started to ask what she did, Eva stomped between them. She scowled and dug a shoulder into Gwen, knocking her off balance. Gwen regained her footing and gave Eva an exasperated frown.

Though tempted to say, "Use your words, Eva, instead of hitting," she realized forbearance would make a better impression than treating her daughter like a four year old.

"How was your day, darling?" said Gwen, her sarcasm unconcealed.

"Fine," Eva growled.

Smiling at Rick, Gwen said, "I think this girl is tired."

"Yeah," he agreed wistfully.

"See you."

Eva took her hand as they walked toward her car.

"Bye," he sang out to them.

I can wait until June, thought Gwen. Hope you can.

After cleaning the dinner dishes, Gwen plopped on their overstuffed couch, purchased at a flea market. Eva crawled onto her lap and braided Gwen's hair, blond when Eva was a baby, now sandy brown. At eight o'clock, Eva jumped up to turn on the television set. While her focus was on the screen, Gwen watched her laugh at the situation comedy. Eva had Daniel's loose black curls and aquiline nose and was as quick-witted as her father. Unlike Daniel, she could appreciate the humor of others.

Eva leaned forward in anticipation of her favorite moment, when the loveable bigot would call his son-in-law "Meathead." Gwen marveled at how much happier Eva seemed than she had been at this age. What would Eva's favorite memory be in twenty years? Watching television at night with her single, working mom? She hoped Eva would have better than that, but laughing at Archie Bunker together would be good enough.

Gwen's best memory from fourth grade was reading alone in her bedroom. That was the year her family disintegrated and she started working hard at school so she could eventually escape to college.

At the first chords of the show's closing theme, Gwen said, "Time for bed."

Eva did her Frankenstein imitation, arms stretched out, legs stiff, rocking from side to side. As Gwen guided Eva to the bathroom, she thought of how "time for bed" might sound if said seductively to Rick.

"God, I'm pathetic," she muttered.

Eva went to sleep, and Gwen lay awake listening to her favorite jazz cassette. She loved the piano's quirky melodic line, its unexpected shifts in tempo and key, the naked emotion of the music. She wished she had someone to snuggle next to, someone comfortable with life's capriciousness. This made her think of Daniel, a man with no tolerance for uncertainty. Her fantasy was replaced by resentment.

"What had I been thinking, marrying him?"

They met the summer of 1964 in Hinds County, Mississippi. Gwen, about to be a senior at Stanford, and Daniel, a law school student, were volunteers in a voter registration campaign. Sixty-seven black churches, businesses, and homes were bombed or burned that summer. Three volunteers were murdered by Klansmen. The danger bred fear, but it also fueled their idealism. Gwen was intoxicated by the political discussions and by Daniel, a master at debating the issues. She consented to marry him after graduation.

Their marriage fared well while the rigors of medical school and internship distracted her from Daniel's pettiness, the judgmental comments aimed at her. She didn't fully understand her mistake until Eva turned one, and she was ready to find a job. Gwen wanted to hire a nanny. Daniel, now a public defender, was adamantly opposed. He wanted Eva in day-care, like working-class children. Their kitchen became a courtroom where she was pilloried for her reactionary tendencies and bourgeois conventions. Civility disappeared once Gwen, concerned that Daniel rarely held Eva, started criticizing his failure to bond with their daughter. His attacks on her selfishness and privilege escalated. The day he categorically refused to try couples therapy, she faced reality and began looking for an attorney. Daniel fought it like a death row case. It took them three years to settle the divorce terms. Meanwhile, both her parents had died. She used her inheritance to buy a two-bedroom bungalow in the Oakland hills.

Angry with herself for replaying the same old complaints and rationalizations, Gwen turned off the cassette. She thought about being a medicine resident. She wasn't ambivalent. She had to change her life. That decided, she fell asleep.

Just as the sky lightened, Gwen awoke from a dream. She had been in her childhood bed, almost asleep, when startled by loud noise. Her parents' voices were raised in argument, unheard of in this household. Over and over, they shouted, "Larry! Larry!"

The dream had been eerily precise. Every detail—the feel of her pillow and blanket, the plaid pajamas she was wearing, the pine odor of the cleaning solution her mother used to mop the floors—was identical to the real event, except for the name they had shouted.

Gwen's older brother, Jack, had been sixteen at the time. His temper was igniting at the least frustration. The morning after her parents' argument woke her, Jack slammed a window shut, shattering the pane. He was still upstairs when she left the house. At recess, a girl with an older sister at Pasadena High told her Jack had been suspended from school for fighting.

Jack's name continued to be shouted behind her parents' bedroom door. A week later, her father moved out of the house.

Jack went back to school, briefly. He was arrested for car theft and sent to juvenile hall. Her mother wept fiercely, but Gwen didn't offer comfort.

She was infuriated by her mother's incompetence and terrified of the consequences. Jack was a criminal, her father had abandoned them, and her remaining parent was falling apart.

After three months in detention, Jack came home. Her mother wouldn't discuss Jack with her, yet she demanded Gwen's presence whenever she spoke to him, leaving Gwen to wonder if she needed her daughter's moral support or simply a witness in order to confront him. The same day Gwen received a letter from her father announcing he was divorcing her mother and moving to New York City, Jack informed them he had flunked out of high school.

Her mother finally took a stand. She refused to give Jack spending money. He got a job as a dishwasher in a drive-in restaurant. Jack had odd hours and often didn't return at night. Then he stopped coming home at all.

When Jack eventually did reappear, his lips were dry and cracked. His hands trembled, and he smelled of vomit. The few words he said were untethered to each other. Her mother sat speechless, dabbing her eyes.

"What are your plans?" Gwen asked him meekly, prepared to receive a volley of verbal abuse.

Head down, Jack didn't answer. He gave her a furtive, hangdog glance.

"Please, Jack. We need to know."

"I'm going to enlist," he said, staring at his plate.

"Enlist?"

"In the army."

"Why?"

"So I won't have to steal to pay for brandy. Sooner or later, probably sooner, I'll get caught and go to prison. No juvenile hall next time."

"How will joining the army help?"

"I can't drink, except when they give me a pass. Then I can use my paycheck to cover bar bills."

"That's silly. You don't have to join the army to stop drinking."

"Easy for you to say," he snarled. "You don't have to live with being like this."

The next morning, they drove Jack to a recruitment center where he boarded a bus for boot-camp in the Mohave Desert. Gwen saw him once more. He came to her high school graduation dressed in a spotless, starched khaki uniform. They corresponded by letter afterwards. She was certain he would have come to her college graduation too, if it hadn't been for a sniper's bullet in Vietnam.

XII

KEVIN WAS BACK IN the ICU at dawn. He found every oxygen reading from Larry Winton's arterial blood line had been less than fifty since midnight. Larry's cheeks were the dusky grey-blue of dying violets. It was miraculous he hadn't died yet from a cardiac arrest. Kevin adjusted and re-adjusted ventilator settings, without seeing any improvement.

After rounding with his interns and student on the team's other patients, Kevin returned to the ICU to write a progress note. Slumped on a stool, he transcribed data onto a clean sheet of lined paper—breathing and heart rates, sodium and potassium levels, blood carbon dioxide and oxygen pressures. As soon as he finished listing the facts, he was defeated. All he could write in the "Assessment" section of the note was "Idiopathic pneumonia. Grim prognosis." Neither Kevin nor any of the attending physicians involved in the case could explain the cause of Larry Winton's impending demise.

Twenty-seven years old and a benign medical history, Kevin thought. OK, he used to shoot drugs, but that was years ago. He was gay, but why would that matter? *What did I miss?* Previously healthy twenty-seven-year-olds admitted to the hospital do not die unless the house staff royally blow it. *Shit!*

He wrote "Plan" and left the rest of the page blank. His only plan was to wait for Herb to bring news from pathology and deliver an opinion on whether this patient's life might be salvageable.

He looked up as Gwen was entering Larry's room. He saw her flinch on discovering Larry paralyzed and comatose, an endotracheal tube in his nose, a gastric suction tube in his mouth. Still, Kevin was glad to see her. He wanted to commiserate.

"What did the bronch show?" she asked when he appeared at the bedside.

"Not much. More confirmation it's not bacterial pneumonia or TB. There are still some special stains pending."

"God, I completely blew it. He was in my exam room two weeks ago. Our social worker would have given him a taxi voucher to come here the same day if I'd just asked."

"Hey, we're all in the dark. Herb and Flagler don't even have a good guess as to what the diagnosis is. If nobody can figure out why he's dying, a delayed diagnosis doesn't change the inevitable."

"Thanks, Kevin, but if a bronch had been done two weeks ago and it was negative, you'd have had time to get a surgeon to do an open lung biopsy before he was this far gone."

"Maybe," he conceded, chastened by having underestimated her clinical acumen, "though elective OR procedures like that get pushed back for days by all the trauma cases coming here. Actually, I'm afraid we're going to find something I should have thought about when he first walked in the ER door. That'll be on me."

Gwen nodded sympathetically then frowned.

"Then the two weeks before that are on me."

"I don't think so. The bar is totally different for a clinic doc. You'd need ESP to pick out the one in ten thousand patients with a cough and weight loss who's going to turn out to be a zebra *and* crash like this."

"Maybe."

She looked at the ICU entrance and said, "Uh-oh."

Kevin turned around to see Herb marching toward them. He jumped up to intercept Herb at the nurse's station.

"What's his arterial oxygen?" Herb demanded.

Herb had never spoken to him so curtly. It unnerved Kevin. He responded immediately, forthrightly, as he had when a schoolboy, caught red-handed committing a venial sin by one of the nuns.

"It's been in the forties since midnight," Kevin confessed, half-expecting Herb would order him to say thirty Hail Mary's.

Instead, Herb's shoulders sagged. Head bent down, he whispered an expletive. When Herb lifted his gaze, Kevin saw no anger, only resignation.

Gwen joined them. Herb mechanically acknowledged her presence.

"The silver stain is positive for Pneumocystis," said Herb.

"That's what the path showed?" said Kevin in disbelief. "Isn't Pneumocystis a parasite?"

"That's right."

"I thought it just occurred in immunocompromised people?"

"Exactly."

Gwen, who knew even less about Pneumocystis than Kevin, asked if the infection could be treated.

"We can give him trimethoprim-sulfamethoxazole. Though at this point, it's not likely to make a difference."

Holding up the blood gas printout as evidence, Herb added, "He's had so much lung destruction, the odds of his ever getting off the ventilator are nil. And with these numbers, he's had enough hypoxic brain damage that if he does survive, it'll be in a vegetative state."

Kevin and Gwen reddened simultaneously.

Gwen stared at Kevin. How could he possibly think it was his fault now, she asked herself.

"Guys," Herb said gently, "treating Pneumocystis pneumonia is just winning a battle. You still lose the war if the underlying immune deficiency can't be reversed."

Neither Kevin nor Gwen was mollified.

Herb looked away and said, "You're right. There's no good excuse for losing a patient to a treatable infection, especially when it's one you've seen before."

Gwen's remorse was supplanted by amazement. This senior specialist had just taken on the entire responsibility for Larry Winton's imminent death, while two other candidates stood by, ready and willing to accept the blame.

"You're sure it's Pneumocystis?" asked Kevin, his eyes deflected downward.

"Think about it. The x-ray appearance, the time course of his illness, the negative micro studies, no history of an autoimmune condition to account for his lung disease. At NIH, I saw kids with leukemia who developed Pneumocystis pneumonia on chemotherapy. Clinical course and findings *exactly* like this case. Which is why I asked the lab to do a silver stain on the bronch washing. They thought I was nuts, but the slide had textbook cysts. Lots of them. Of course, that raises the question of why the hell this young man's immune system wasn't working. He wasn't getting chemotherapy. He wasn't getting steroids. He didn't have a history of serious infections like someone with a congenital immune deficiency would have. It doesn't make sense."

Perplexed, Gwen nodded in agreement. Kevin went off to retrieve the chart and began writing a medication order for trimethoprim-sulfamethox-azole. As he asked Herb about the dose, she returned to Larry's room. She watched the monitor tracking his heart's electrical activity. A white dot moved across the screen, forming a series of identical waves. Suddenly, the pattern disintegrated into chaotic spikes.

"Code Blue!" she screamed.

Kevin rushed in, followed by Herb and two nurses. The white dot now made a flat line as it crossed the screen. Reflexively, Kevin stacked the heels of his palms over Larry's sternum. Arms outstretched, he rocked up and down until he saw Herb shaking his head mournfully.

Kevin stopped rocking. He looked at the wall clock. He was supposed to say the time of death out loud. He couldn't make himself do it.

XIII

THE IMPORTED LIGHT BEER Kevin opened on returning to his studio apartment was the only sign of any sophistication or health consciousness acquired since he had moved to San Francisco. He felt lonelier than usual tonight and thought of his mother. He hadn't talked to her in weeks. His wristwatch showed seven o'clock, not too late to call Boston.

Francine Bartholomew had prematurely turned gray while Kevin was in high school. When he and his older sister, Katherine, were children, their slim, reserved mother was the obvious source of their red hair and green eyes. The daughter of a policeman, a bully who expected to be served by women, she had all ambition, beyond that of making a good marriage, snuffed out at an early age. Intelligent enough to have gone on to college, she quit school at sixteen to work as a cashier. At twenty, she moved from the modest bedroom she shared with two sisters into smaller boarding house quarters with her new husband. He had set one condition to his marriage offer—a taboo on her working outside the home.

His mother didn't answer on the first ring, which struck Kevin as strange. Then he realized it wasn't Sunday, the usual evening he called her.

"Hello," his father gruffly answered.

Paralyzed by the sound of this voice he hadn't heard in three years, Kevin was mute. There was a loud clack as the receiver on the other end of the line slammed down. Angry, and at the same time curious, he dialed the number again.

"Who is it?" yelled his father.

"Hi, Dad."

There was a pause before his father spoke again, now from a distance. Kevin imagined the old man holding the receiver at arm's length to prevent contamination.

"It's your son, Francine."

After another pause, he heard his mother's voice.

"Kev, are you all right?"

"I'm good, Mom. Sorry I haven't called in so long. It's been super busy at work."

"You're sure nothing's wrong?"

"Everything's fine. Don't worry, they haven't cut my salary."

Kevin knew this would calm her. By her standards, he was already making a decent living—though she had no idea what it cost to live in San Francisco—and he would be doing much, much better in the near future. If he reassured her on that point, maybe she could control her other fears. Maybe they could even have a pleasant chat.

"Dad OK?"

"The same. The doctor doesn't seem concerned."

Their conversation followed a well-trod path. They kept to the ruts like pack mules, both pretending his father hadn't just refused to talk to him.

Kevin's parents still lived in the tiny three-bedroom brick row house where he and Katherine had grown up, nestled in an all-white, all working-class, virtually all Irish-Catholic, South Boston neighborhood. A safe, comfortable world until he turned fourteen and discovered how different he was from everyone else.

"Kevin, could you come home next month for Douglas's confirmation?"

His mother had deviated from the script. He deflected her question by asking the date. But instead of scrambling for an excuse, he remembered that Douglas was the youngest of Katherine's four children. His confirmation would be the last family event at Saint Brigid's until someone married or died, more likely the latter. Kevin understood how important this must be to his mother. She didn't ask much of him. He really should go.

He promised to check his schedule and steered them back to a familiar trail by mentioning the weather. As Francine chanted her litany of Boston's winter horrors—treacherous black ice, merciless cold winds, unreliable coal furnaces—he thought of how a trip east would also mean having to deal with his sister and brother-in-law. That could be as bad as seeing his father.

Kevin's childhood with Katherine, a willowy attractive girl precociously adept at making friends, was a peaceful coexistence despite her ignoring him in elementary school and treating him with icy superiority in high school. His animosity came later, while he was an undergraduate at U Mass still living at home. By then, he had a circle of gay friends, kept secret from his family. One Saturday night, he was strolling across Harvard Square with a couple holding hands. They ran into Katherine and her fiancé, Ben, a Vietnam veteran. It took Katherine a brief inspection for the nickel to drop. Kevin watched the corners of her mouth turn down in disgust and her lips form the words, "This explains everything."

To Ben, having a faggot as a future brother-in-law was a joke, at first. Then Kevin graduated from U Mass and was drafted. At his induction physical, Kevin was graphically credible in describing his sexual preferences. He fabricated a weak story for his family. A bad knee, the same implausible excuse he had employed to avoid gym class, made him ineligible. Ben saw through the charade. Having risked his life in Vietnam, he was furious. Kevin's father and mother didn't press the point, but Katherine did. Kevin lashed back. His anti-war sentiments came roaring out of the closet. He berated Katherine in front of them, challenging her assumptions about who the real aggressors were in Southeast Asia, knowing she wouldn't play her trump card. Outing him would devastate their parents, and she would have to bear the consequences. He could leave South Boston. She couldn't.

After two years of working construction, Kevin started medical school. A scholarship and loan allowed him to move from the brick row house to an apartment shared with other students. Yet he was still uneasy about being openly gay. There was always the possibility he might run into his parents or someone they knew. The simplest solution was to go away for residency training.

Ironically, just before he moved to California, his father overheard him telling a friend on the telephone how he could finally be out of the closet in San Francisco. Since then, his father had refused to speak to him. That was doubly ironic now. Kevin had found being a single, gay man here more lonely than liberating.

His mother signaled she was ready to end with her standard remark about how expensive long distance calls were. Departing from the script a second time, she pleaded with him again to return for his nephew's confirmation.

She's never asked me twice in the same call to come to Boston, he thought. Is there something she's not telling me? Could she or Dad have a terminal illness? Despite his aversion to seeing them, Kevin hadn't abandoned all hope of salvaging these relationships.

"I love you, Mom," he said in a rush. "I'll try to get to Douglas's confirmation."

He hung up the phone and headed out to a bar in the Castro. Kevin was exhausted. He didn't expect to meet anyone who would be interested in more than a quick fling, which no longer appealed to him. It only exacerbated his loneliness. But he did think another drink or two and the opportunity to talk about anything other than medicine, however superficial and awkward, would distract him enough to fall asleep when he came home.

XIV

THREE MONTHS LATER, KEVIN ran into Gwen outside the City Hospital auditorium.

"Hey," he said, pleasantly surprised, "What are you doing here?"

Before she could reply, he deduced the answer.

"You *are* serious about coming back if you're here for an update on septic shock. That's not outpatient medicine."

"I've been interviewed," Gwen said, unable to contain her excitement. "There aren't openings for this July, but there will be next year. They all but offered me a position."

"Great! I'll still be here. Flagler's taking me on as a fellow."

"Fantastic!"

Once they were seated inside, Kevin said, "I was going to call you. Larry Winton's autopsy report is done."

"What did it show?" Gwen whispered as the lecturer stepped to the podium.

"It's complicated. Don't worry, we didn't miss anything reversible. I'll explain later."

After grand rounds, Kevin hailed Herb and told both of them about the autopsy findings. In addition to the lung destruction caused by Pneumocystis pneumonia, every one of Larry Winton's lymph nodes from his neck to his pelvis was shrunken and scarred.

"That fits with the low lymphocyte count in his blood," said Herb. "And having no immune system left would be why he got Pneumocystis. But what wiped out his immune system?"

"There's no smoking gun," Kevin lamented. "All the slides were negative, except for some cytomegalovirus inclusions in the liver and gut. The pathologist said that was more likely a result of immune suppression than the cause. He's seen the same thing in transplant patients."

"Sorry, Kevin. I'm afraid the Winton case is going to remain a mystery. It happens."

"I tried to reach his family," said Gwen. "I called the phone number we had and went to the last address he used. No luck. If I'd been able to contact a relative, I could have found out about his family history. Most immune deficiency syndromes are inherited, aren't they?"

"Good thought, Gwen," Herb said.

"I'd like to write up the case for publication," Kevin volunteered. "I'll put it together if you'll edit the draft."

"Kevin, I would love to help you publish something, but a single case of unexplained immune deficiency won't appeal to any broadly read journal. If there was an identifiable cause, like a toxin that hasn't been reported before, you could easily get it accepted. Or if you had a series of patients like this one tied together by a common thread, even if it was only geographic location. You could sell that to reviewers. But one case with a mysterious cause won't be perceived as advancing knowledge."

"Yeah," Kevin reluctantly agreed.

"You'll be here another two years. I'm sure Pneumocystis will be the first thing we think of if someone with progressive pulmonary disease and no obvious diagnosis is admitted. And if we do find more patients with Pneumocystis, you could investigate family histories and environmental exposures and get one of the immunologists on the Hill to figure out what's behind it."

Gwen gave Kevin's shoulder a fist-bump.

"I'll help if you lead the charge," she said.

"That's right," said Kevin, his mood upbeat again, "Gwen will be here. She's going to finish her medicine residency."

Herb met Gwen's eyes. Though he was well aware of how attractive she was, he limited his regard to other virtues he esteemed in house staff. She wouldn't have come to the ICU twice while Winton was dying if she didn't feel responsible for her patient, didn't care deeply about what was happening to him.

"Your clinic experience will be a big plus here," Herb said. "We have attendings greener than you."

Flushing, Gwen asked, "Kevin told you about me?"

"No, Flagler. I ran into him right after he interviewed you. He was impressed. But don't expect him to acknowledge it to you."

"How flattering. I'm glad he thinks my experience will be an asset. I wish I did."

"Oh my! And self-deprecating, too? We'll see how long that lasts here."

"You're in if you've got Flagler's vote," Kevin crowed. "This is a great time to be in medicine, Gwen. Huge changes are coming. Molecular techniques like DNA cloning are going to revolutionize diagnostics. Biotech companies will be making totally new kinds of treatment possible."

"Brave new world," she mused.

"And we'll be right at the cutting edge! It's going to be cool, very cool."

An Epidemic, 1981

I

AFTER KEVIN'S FELLOWSHIP ENDED, he was hired as an attending physician at City Hospital. His nights and weekends were generally free of responsibilities, and he wasn't lonely anymore.

One hour past sunrise on the last Sunday of November, he stood exposed to a wet Pacific wind, shivering at the high point of an East Bay trail. Donning the fleece jacket and wool cap he had taken off during the steep hike up didn't make him warmer. Neither did cuddling with his lover, Marco, who was four inches shorter and had the sinewy physique of a long-distance runner. Kevin jammed his hands under his armpits and jogged in place.

He looked west across the bay beyond Mount Tamalpais to the Farallon Islands then east to where the Contra Costa hills, tinged with green after a week of early November rain, rolled toward the Sacramento River delta and faded into haze.

"On clearer days, you can see snow on Sierra peaks from here," said Marco.

With his black hair in curly ringlets, sparse silky beard, strong chin, and deep set eyes, Marco could be the object of a Latin Adonis or Che Guevara fantasy. Both appealed to Kevin's prurient interest. He slipped a hand into the gap between Marco's jeans and the hollow of his back and lightly brushed his olive skin.

"That too cold?" he asked solicitously.

"I'll warm you up," said Marco and leaned his head against Kevin's shoulder.

"This view is incredible!" Kevin exclaimed. "What a great idea to come here."

"Hah! You weren't so happy when I woke you up at four thirty. See, you should listen to me more often."

"You're right about that," Kevin concurred with a carefree laugh.

Squinting at the horizon, he asked, "How far do you think Mount Tam is from here?"

"Twenty miles, *más o menos*"

"Twenty miles *como la cuerva vuela*?"

"*Sí*," said Marco, amused by Kevin's literal translation of "as the crow flies."

"If we had a telescope, the kind amateur astronomers use, do you think we could see people standing on Tam peak?"

"I haven't a clue, *mi amor*. But you know what? You have a lot of curiosity for someone who claims not to be a real scientist."

Kevin gave him an enigmatic glance, seductive enough to entice Marco into kissing him. As Marco's tongue darted inside Kevin's mouth, a shrill, insistent beeping sounded. Startled, Marco drew back. He saw Kevin's neck pulsing and his pupils dilate.

"Adrenergic response to your pager, or was I arousing you?"

"Both, unfortunately."

Marco parked in front of the massive, Art Deco building on the Berkeley campus where he was completing a post-doctoral fellowship in cell biology. They had stopped at a pay phone on the way there. Kevin had called the hospital and was told about a patient brought by ambulance to the emergency room, somebody of consequence from the mayor's office. The medical resident on call said the patient had fever and altered mental status. She also suspected he had Gay-Related Immune Deficiency.

Marco offered his car keys. Kevin gave him a contrite smile.

"*Querido*, it's OK. I can run my gels now instead of tomorrow. I'll have the data one day sooner for those obsessive-compulsive *Science* editors holding my paper hostage."

After two years of coddling and massaging embryonic mouse cells, Marco needed results from just one more experiment to parry a final reviewer's objection to publishing his paper in a prestigious journal.

"Really? You're not disappointed?"

"Kevin, I think you're confusing me with someone else's long-suffering, submissive wife. I'm happy to go to work. I'll page you when the blots are developed. You can pick me up at the BART station, and we'll go out to celebrate."

"No, no. I'll drive back as soon as I'm done. Then you won't have to wait. I don't mind hanging out here until you're finished."

"So now you're going to do penance?"

Kevin looked away, and Marco sighed. They had been through this script before. Feeling guilty, Kevin would shut down. Marco, annoyed that he wasn't responding, would criticize him for not breaking free of his psychic chains. Catholic bondage Marco called it. If particularly irritated, Marco would raise Kevin's refusal to tell his family about his live-in lover as a prime example, and Kevin would retreat further.

Marco had looked up the common noun "catholic" in an English dictionary and informed him the meaning was "of liberal scope, inclusive of all humanity." Kevin believed class difference was the underlying issue. He had mentioned that possibility once, and Marco gave him the silent treatment for a week.

It's all right for Marco to rail about the prejudice, homophobia, and narrow mindedness of South Boston, Kevin had brooded, but not for me to point out how the privilege of growing up in a luxurious Mexican villa and attending an elite Jesuit boarding school in Europe has given him the freedom to become whomever he wants to be.

Time to lighten up, thought Kevin.

He smirked and said, "What kind of penance did you have in mind?"

Marco's stern disapproval dissolved.

"Touché," he chuckled. "Penance later. Now that I'm here, I'm going to run the gels. But first…"

Marco sat on a bench and opened his arms. Kevin sat on his lap, and Marco massaged Kevin's neck.

"That's an impressive talent you have," Marco murmured, "Making things funny when they get too heavy. I've never been with someone who could do that."

Paralyzed by the compliment, Kevin didn't reply.

"Don't give up on teaching me, *querido*."

"You sure?"

Marco dangled his car keys and said, "Go my son. Your sins have been forgiven."

Kevin kissed him on the cheek and took the keys.

"*Qué injusticia*," Marco grumbled as he watched Kevin drive away. To keep from dwelling on the benighted souls who had raised and still haunted his lover, Marco recalled the night they met.

A crowd of fifteen thousand had filled Castro Street for the 1980 annual Halloween bacchanalia. Half were in costume while the rest gawked at them. Alcohol was the drug of choice here, and lines of riot police filled the neighborhood to prevent a repeat of the previous year's melee when gangs of fag-bashers from nearby blue collar suburbs had attacked gay men. Marco had come with Robert, a fellow grad student. Both were dressed as lab rats in white coats. Lengths of rope served for tails and pieces of broom straw taped to their cheeks for whiskers. As they crossed Castro Street, a skinny teenager sliced off Robert's tail with a switchblade. He ran away whooping, swinging the trophy over his head. Robert cursed the boy who returned to confront him and jabbed the knife at his testicles. He missed low by an inch, slicing through the femoral artery. Robert collapsed in a pool of blood which expanded at an alarming rate.

A hefty, six foot pirate appeared, bedecked in a white flounce shirt and a blue bandana that couldn't contain his thick red hair. A policeman recognized the pirate, called him "Doc," and cordoned off space for him to work. Kevin pulled down Robert's pants, carefully inserted his bare thumb and forefinger into Robert's wound, and pinched the artery. The bleeding stopped.

Marco was amazed by Kevin's equanimity as he was helping EMTs lift Robert into an ambulance while keeping a firm hold on the artery and reassuring Marco that his friend would be fine. Kevin talked the driver into letting Marco ride with them. In the ambulance, Marco got Kevin's phone number. The following evening, Marco brought over an expensive Medoc which they had just begun to explore when other appetites took precedence.

Driving west on the Bay Bridge, Kevin tried to soothe himself. He envisioned the panorama they had seen at the top of the trail. That failed to calm him. The brief telephone call had put him in red alert mode. Kevin had become the local expert on immune deficiencies at City Hospital. Everyone would expect him to provide definitive guidance on what tests to perform and what medications to administer to this patient.

Kevin tried harder to imagine the scene before his pager beeped. He wondered how he and Marco might have looked to a passing stranger. Did their physical differences make them an odd couple? Would a passer-by be repelled by seeing them kiss? Furious for having that last thought, Kevin pounded the dashboard. How could he allow a scintilla of the old self-hatred back into his consciousness? Why couldn't he shed it? He was living in San Francisco now. Being gay was totally acceptable here. What was his problem?

II

DANA PEARLSTEIN, A PETITE junior resident, pushed a somnolent man on a gurney toward the only unoccupied bed in City Hospital's intensive care unit. Dana had two months of experience leading a medicine team and was twenty-six hours into her on-call shift. Her impeccable make-up remained intact, but her confidence, appropriately tenuous at this point in her training, was waning, especially with her last admission. She'd heard rumors the patient had a lot of clout in local politics, and he was gravely ill.

Once Dana saw Kevin enter the ICU, her hunched-up shoulders relaxed. Kevin looked at the toothpaste-advertisement smile she gave him, the thin man asleep on the gurney, the familiar intravenous solutions, portable cardiac monitor, and oxygen tank, then back to Dana's smile. He calmed down.

As Dana was handing admission orders to an ICU clerk, Kevin grabbed her stethoscope and took over wheeling the patient to his room. He signaled Dana that he would return in a moment. Kevin noticed a scaly rash on the man's forehead, a severe type of dandruff common in Gay-Related Immune Deficiency, and the hollow shape of his temples, a sign of muscle wasting. The man didn't react to Kevin's calling out his name.

"Mr. Miller," Kevin said shaking him gently, "Are you OK?"

"I don't know," the patient mumbled.

Further questioning revealed he was disoriented to place and time. Kevin listened to his heart and lungs, felt his abdomen, flexed his neck, and used a tongue blade and penlight to look inside his mouth. In addition to the patient's confusion, there was another abnormality. A white layer, like thinly spread cottage cheese, covered the roof of his mouth.

Kevin sat down at the ICU conference table with Dana and her medical student, and she launched into her case presentation—an account of Mr. Miller's symptoms and history, her physical exam findings, the laboratory and x-ray results, and finally her formulation of a differential diagnosis and plan of action.

"Mr. Miller is a forty-two year old white male with no prior hospitalizations or chronic diseases. He works as an assistant to the mayor of San Francisco and lives alone in the Marina."

Dana arched her eyes in feigned surprise. City Hospital patients rarely came from this upscale neighborhood.

According to a friend who discovered Mr. Miller yesterday on the kitchen floor of his apartment, he had been well until a week ago when he began complaining of fatigue and headache. Then he stopped coming to the office or answering his phone. Per the friend, Miller was gay. He didn't use drugs or frequent bathhouses.

Dana's physical exam findings were identical to Kevin's. The blood test results were unremarkable except for anemia and an extremely low lymphocyte count. Dana's intern had done a spinal tap which showed no white blood cells to suggest meningitis or red blood cells to suggest a brain hemorrhage.

Kevin was pleased by Dana's presentation—fluent, precise, thorough yet succinct enough to communicate in less than five minutes all the elements he required in deciding what to do next. She had clearly mastered one important skill for leading an inpatient medicine team. She could sift through massive amounts of information, discard the dross, and communicate the essential data in the minimum time necessary without sounding manic.

"I think the white stuff in his mouth is thrush," Dana concluded. "That and his low lymphocyte count fit with GRID."

"What's thrush? What's GRID?" asked the student, a frumpy young woman who wore thick-lens glasses.

"Thrush is like athlete's foot but in the mouth," said Dana. "It's a superficial fungal infection caused by Candida. And GRID is Gay-Related Immune Deficiency."

Turning to Kevin, she added, "Here's the expert."

"That's OK," he said deferentially. "Let's hear you explain it."

Dana eagerly accepted the challenge. She talked about the clusters of gay men in New York, Los Angeles, and San Francisco recently diagnosed with a rare form of skin cancer, Kaposi's sarcoma, or Pneumocystis pneumonia.

All had been previously healthy. Since Pneumocystis only caused disease in people with profoundly impaired immune systems, the syndrome had been named Gay-Related Immune Deficiency. A preliminary investigation by the Centers for Disease Control identified two common denominators among GRID patients—past gonorrhea and syphilis infections and a lifetime history of hundreds of sexual partners.

Dana looked to Kevin. He nodded with approval.

"Kevin has seen, what, ten Pneumocystis cases here?"

He nodded, less enthusiastically.

"And in his clinic he's seeing lots of gay men who have enlarged lymph nodes and thrush. A couple of them have gone on to develop Kaposi's or Pneumocystis."

"Have you biopsied their lymph nodes?" asked the student.

Noting the name on her ID badge, he answered, "Good question, Gail. We did, at first. But the results have been negative—no underlying infection or malignancy."

Dana chimed in, "Kevin just gave grand rounds. Didn't you say the number of new patients coming to City Hospital with the pre-GRID lymph node syndrome has doubled in the last four months?"

He nodded somberly.

Gail frowned as she considered the implications of that fact.

Returning to the case at hand, Kevin said, "The low lymphocyte count is a good pick-up, Dana. And that's definitely thrush in his mouth. So he's got pre-GRID, if not GRID itself. But why's he confused and barely arousable? What's wrong with his brain?"

"He could be septic. He has a temperature of a hundred and two. Blood cultures are cooking. I already started him on broad-spectrum antibiotics."

"That's good. No downside to covering him for sepsis. But why would he have bacteria in his blood?"

"I don't know. His spinal fluid showed no cells, so it's not meningitis. The chest x-ray and brain scan are clear."

"You sure it's not meningitis? What about cryptococcal meningitis? That's a GRID-related infection, and the patients can't mount an inflammatory response when the fungus invades their brain. So, typically, we *don't* see cells in the spinal fluid."

Dana flushed and left to find a telephone. While she dialed the laboratory, Kevin explained the test she was requesting to Gail.

"India ink stain. Very low-tech assay. A fourth grader could do it. The lab will put a drop of Miller's spinal fluid on a slide, then add a drop of India ink. Cryptococcus has a capsule that can't absorb the ink. If the bug is there, they'll see white dots on a black background. Which reminds me, Dana, when you tapped Miller, what was his opening pressure?"

"Sorry," said Dana, now mortified, "We were in a rush to get samples to the lab. I forgot to measure the pressure."

"*I* was watching the pressure." Gail interjected. "When the intern got the needle in, spinal fluid rose up the manometer so fast it would have spilled over the top if he hadn't opened the valve to fill specimen tubes in time."

"Good observation skills, Gail." Kevin said. "That's exactly what we need to know. So Miller *does* have elevated intracranial pressure. If the India ink is positive, he'll need repeated spinal taps, every twelve hours, to lower the pressure on his brain. Done a tap before, Gail?"

"No," she replied timidly.

"This is your chance. If you just saw a lumbar puncture, then you're ready to do one."

Gail beamed.

The phone rang. Kevin picked it up and listened for a moment.

"It's Cryptococcus," he announced.

Dana hurried out, Gail in tow, to write orders for an antifungal medication and gather equipment for another spinal tap.

III

KEVIN RETURNED TO MILLER'S room and was surprised to find Gwen at the bedside making notes on a clipboard.

"Hey, how come you're here?"

"I just started a pulmonary elective. It's the fellow's day off, so I'm pre-rounding before the attending comes in. Herb paged me and said I should see Miller. But he doesn't have any respiratory issues. I don't get why we're consulting. What's up?"

Kevin couldn't enlighten her, and it troubled him that Herb had already heard about the case. He was certain Dana wouldn't have asked for a pulmonary consult, which meant someone higher up in the hospital chain of command must have contacted Herb. He deflected her question.

"What do you think is going on with him?"

"He has GRID, that's for sure. I'm guessing some kind of opportunistic infection, too."

"You're right. It's cryptococcal meningitis. How do you know for sure he has GRID?"

Gwen bent Miller's left ear forward, revealing a small purplish nodule.

"And there's more," she added, rolling the patient on his side and pointing at a tiny, similar lesion on Miller's back, hidden in a skin fold.

"Wow! Good pick-up."

"You're a good teacher."

"Maybe, but you seem to be better at putting knowledge into practice than me."

"That's not true. Doing a thorough skin exam is a spinal cord reflex for me from all those years in the Haight Street clinic hunting for signs of secondary syphilis."

"Yeah, right," he said dryly. "I'm sure no higher cortical function is involved."

Unable to dodge the compliment, she grinned.

Trifecta, he thought, happy with himself for provoking her amusement, pride, and affection, all with one remark.

When Gwen began her residency, Kevin was still in his fellowship, toiling in Flagler's laboratory to make sense out of how the mouse immune system responded to bacterial infection. During her first rotation at City Hospital, he was glad to show her the ropes on the medical wards. It was an excuse to escape from what was becoming tedium. Once he appreciated how at ease she was with herself and others, he sought opportunities to be with her, hoping it might rub off on him. She took the next step, suggesting they double-date. Their respective boyfriends, Marco and Rick, found each other kindred spirits and poked gentle fun at the two more reserved doctors. The evening was a wild success.

"How are things at home?" asked Gwen.

"OK. Better, actually. You?"

"Good enough."

"Good enough?"

"Maybe they could be better. I shouldn't complain. So what happened with you two? You'd been fighting a lot."

"I don't know…"

She waited.

"OK," he confessed. "We decided to get some relationship advice from friends, an older gay couple who've been together for years. Now we're working at not letting conflicts stew. They call it 'immediate decompression of tension.'"

"Kevin, that sounds like New Age psychobabble. I can't picture you and Marco constantly talking about your feelings."

"Hardly. Come on, you know what I mean. Don't you?"

"Not really. Have you guys figured out how to avoid getting annoyed with each other?"

"No, we're just taking it less seriously when it happens. It usually means one of us either needs more freedom or wants more reassurance he's loved. And if the other can accept that without being threatened by it, the tension defuses."

Gwen stared at him, her mouth open.

"That's an astonishing insight for…"

"For what?"

"Umm…"

Kevin grinned slyly.

"You were going to say a man, weren't you? An astonishing insight for a man. Oh my God, Gwen! I am so disappointed. You are the last person I would have suspected of such blatant sexism. I guess it just goes to show how ingrained the prejudice men have to deal with is. In fact, you're a textbook demonstration of why we're so oppressed. It's terrible that mothers still pass on such garbage to their daughters. Even someone as enlightened as you can't shed the bigotry."

"Stop," Gwen giggled. "I was going to say 'a person of your age.'"

Kevin shook his head no.

"After I said 'a man,'" Gwen admitted, "I was going to say 'and a person of your age, but...'"

"Gotcha," Kevin exulted, pecking victoriously at her with his index fingers.

"Stop," she laughed. "You're very lucky. Do you know that?"

"What do you mean?"

"I don't have that kind of openness with Rick. I tell him what I'm feeling, but he's the 'still-waters-run-deep' type. And I'm never sure how deep they are or where they're running."

"Rick? He seems pretty extroverted to me."

"Now you're being dense, Kevin. I'm talking about what he says to me when he's pissed off."

"What does he say?"

"Nothing."

"And you know he's pissed because…?"

"That's the point. Sometimes I don't know whether he's angry or not, and he won't admit to it. I know he's no saint. You should hear what he says about the demanding parents at his school. They can push his buttons."

"I can't believe you're all that difficult to live with."

"I'm not perfect."

"Maybe he doesn't expect perfect. Maybe you're good enough. Maybe he doesn't have anything to complain about."

"Kevin, that's too good to be true."

"Is it?"

"Oh, my goodness. You're more romantic than I thought."

Kevin suddenly noticed Herb at the nurses' station and waved at him.

"Thanks for coming by," said Kevin.

He stifled the impulse to ask why Herb was consulting on the case.

"Sorry to step on your toes, but this is a command performance," said Herb. "The mayor's office called Ray at home an hour ago, and he paged me."

"The mayor called the chief of medicine at home?"

"Mr. Miller's 'an important member of her team.' I gather it's not so much his job in public housing as his role as a political advisor. She is *very* concerned he gets the best possible care here."

Kevin frowned.

"You, my friend, have nothing to worry about. I heard you already made the diagnosis by telepathy."

Gwen clapped. Kevin forced a weak smile.

"Look, Kevin, this is a great opportunity for us. The mayor will find out first hand what the reality of this epidemic is. She'll get how serious a problem it's going to be for San Francisco. She'll understand our commitment to caring for these people and what we need to be able to do it adequately. Department of Public Health money is our lifeline, and the DPH director reports directly to her."

"Yeah," said Kevin, now almost as uneasy about Herb's involvement as the mayor's.

After Larry Winton died, Herb had urged Kevin to get specialized training in infectious diseases. He didn't push Kevin to become a pulmonary specialist yet clearly wanted him to stay at City Hospital. As more cases of GRID were diagnosed during Kevin's fellowship, Herb encouraged him to develop ideas for GRID-related research and offered advice. But Flagler wanted Kevin at the bench, working with microbes and mice. That effort culminated in Kevin submitting a funding proposal to the National Institutes of Health which was summarily NERF'd—not even recommended for further consideration.

Flagler had no intention of keeping Kevin in his division, but two weeks before the fellowship was to end, the chief of medicine at City Hospital drummed up salary support for a physician to manage the care of the hospital's increasing volume of GRID and pre-GRID patients. Kevin took the position, which came with a university faculty appointment in the department of medicine. Herb renewed his encouragement, suggesting Kevin investigate what was causing GRID and what factors predicted how long patients survived. Kevin wondered if Herb had somehow influenced the chief's decision to hire him, though he couldn't grasp why Herb thought he would be successful in clinical research after his failure in the lab.

Kevin led Herb into Miller's room where they found him unresponsive to shouting, shaking, or Herb's grinding his knuckles on the patient's sternum.

"That's it." Herb said. "We need to intubate and hyperventilate him. The house staff can do another tap after we're done."

Kevin concurred, and Gwen collected the equipment to pass a plastic tube down Miller's windpipe. As Herb was setting ventilator dials, a man with a thick mane of gray hair appeared. He wore an Armani suit and a blue power tie.

"I'm Tom Redding from the mayor's office. She's on a trade mission in Mexico. Otherwise, she'd be here. How's Michael?"

Kevin froze, so Herb took over.

"I'm Herb Wu, in charge of the ICU today. This is Dr. Bartholomew, our expert in immune deficiency diseases."

"Michael has the gay cancer? Is he going to die?"

Mastering his timidity, Kevin said, "Mr. Miller has a fungus infection in his brain. He's in a coma. I don't want to be rude, but we have to put him on a breathing machine and drain out spinal fluid right away."

Redding, horrified, stepped back.

"I didn't mean to interrupt. I'm just. ..devastated."

"No need for apology. Please understand we're doing everything we can to control the infection and prevent permanent brain damage."

Eyes welling with tears, Redding stuttered, "How can...How can this be happening to *him*? He's brilliant, unselfish. He doesn't deserve this."

Over the next two hours, Mr. Miller was stabilized. Dana helped Gail pass a needle into his spinal canal and remove enough fluid to normalize his pressure for the moment. But Miller remained comatose. By one o'clock, there was nothing else they could do except hope the antifungal drug would work. Kevin and Herb left the ICU together.

"Wednesday afternoon at four-thirty?" said Herb at the hospital entrance.

"I'll be there. The protocol's almost finished. I'll bring the latest version."

"Outstanding!"

Looking at the ground, Kevin formulated a delicate question.

"Herb?" he asked, glancing up.

Herb was already halfway across the street. As Kevin watched Herb walk to the parking lot, he thought of their discussion last summer, just after he'd been hired as City Hospital's immune deficiency specialist. Herb was pressing him to write a protocol outline, and Kevin had probed Herb's motivation.

"So, why are you so interested in Pneumocystis?"

"It's a mysterious pathogen. No one can grow it *in vitro*. There are no good animal models for understanding how it causes pneumonia. Treatment outcomes are unpredictable."

Kevin gazed at him for an impertinently long time.

Herb sighed and conceded, "Guess I'm drawn to diseases that are fatal to young people. Like leukemia when I was at NIH. Moth to the flame maybe..."

The next day, Kevin agreed to take on the project.

IV

Herb came home to find Martin donning his cleats and shin guards. At three o'clock, they met the other Jaguars at Dolores Park. Although team sports had never captured Herb's imagination, soccer had captured Martin's. Herb embraced the opportunity to share his son's passion. The previous summer, he had even spent eight consecutive weekends in a coaching course so the Jaguars could move up to Class III competition.

Once the boys were done with stretching exercises and dribbling drills, Herb split them into squads for scrimmaging. He was pleased to see the defense, where Martin always played, forcing the offense to the sidelines where angling a shot through the goal was difficult. Martin, as sweeper, was the last defender protecting the goalie. Any mistake he made gave the opposition a fifty-fifty chance to score.

Herb watched the offense methodically pass the ball from one side of the field to the other, even backwards, as they attempted to spread the defense apart. A large enough space opened near the goal for the team's best striker to sprint downfield in time to receive a well-placed pass. He was about to take a shot when Martin arrived and booted the ball away.

As the coach, Herb couldn't demonstrate favoritism.

He calmly called out, "Good move, Martin."

Martin showed no acknowledgement.

Excellent, Herb thought, he doesn't need to revel in his victories.

Next, Herb had the boys do a passing drill, which required no supervision on his part. He sat on a bench and let himself enjoy watching Martin gracefully swivel and feint.

The boys scrimmaged again. This time, the striker made an excellent foot fake. Martin took the bait. His opponent tapped the ball in the other direction, ran past Martin, and was inside the goalie's box before Martin recovered.

Herb had to clench his jaw to keep from laughing.

"Nice touch, Jeremy," he shouted neutrally and nodded for them to play on.

In the final half hour of practice, Herb had the Jaguars work on their greatest weakness, defending against corner kicks. It was just a matter of communication, he believed. In the chaos that ensued as the ball sailed from the corner of the field into a crowd of boys jockeying for position directly in front of the goal, leadership was essential. Someone had to see that every offensive player was covered. This had to be the sweeper's responsibility.

But kick after kick, the defenders invariably clustered around the best strikers, leaving others free to score when the ball came their way. Martin repeatedly lost the boy he should have been guarding and doubled up against a player who was already covered. He paid no attention to what the other defenders were doing.

After the offense scored on three successive corner kicks, Herb raised his hands in frustration.

"What are you *doing*, Martin?" he yelled.

The boys looked back and forth between father and son. Martin stood with his arms crossed, waiting for play to resume. He stubbornly ignored his father's question.

Herb recognized his error, but it was too late to retract.

"Scrimmage," he called wearily and rolled the ball into the middle of the field.

All Herb wanted to be was a better, or at least a kinder, father than his own had been. When Martin was born, he had been confident of his ability to do that. Now he wasn't so sure.

By five, the boys could no longer see the ball in the growing darkness. Herb ended practice with three short whistles and dolefully picked up the orange cones he had set down to mark boundaries on the park lawn.

It was an unseasonably warm evening, and Cecilia asked Herb to go for a walk with her after dinner. Still regretting his lapse on the soccer field, he told Cecilia about it. She was sympathetic but had no advice.

"It's inevitable, honey," she said. "Sooner or later, he needs to separate from you."

"At ten? Isn't that a little early?"

"It's uglier when it happens in the teens. Think about my sisters' kids."

Herb had to assume she was right. Cecilia and Robbie Cohen, his best friend since college, were the only people with whom he had ever substantively discussed parenting. He trusted their judgment more than his own. My God, he thought, what if I had to do this alone? What could be harder than that?

V

GWEN LEFT THE HOSPITAL at noon and met Rick and Eva at a nearby BART station. They had lunch at a taqueria Eva chose from the dozens of Mexican restaurants in the neighborhood before driving to Ocean Beach. Now, beneath a hazy, late afternoon sky that seemed finger-painted blue, the three padded barefoot on the sand. An angry surf hurled bright wet sparks at them. Gwen and Rick, holding hands, trailed behind Eva.

The previous weekend, Gwen had cut her hair short. It had darkened to dusty brown in the last year. She expected it might turn gray by the time she turned forty. Since the prospect of coloring her hair was unappealing, she hoped a shorter length would make the transition less noticeable. Her face, creamy white all summer and fall, finally had a tan after three consecutive weekends in the sun.

These free weekends, once morning rounds ended, were the best part of being on a consult elective. Not that she was complaining. Residency wasn't nearly as difficult as she had anticipated. Despite the long hours and sleep deprivation, it felt more like a booster shot than boot camp. Two weeks into her first ward rotation, managing medical problems she almost never saw in the Haight had become routine. Within months, her clinical judgment, acquired over years of outpatient practice, and her life experience of child-rearing and divorce had made her a sage among the other junior residents.

She watched pink seep into the western sky. Advancing shreds of stratus clouds absorbed the pigment. Turning seaward, she bumped into Rick. Eight inches taller than her and still thin with a faint ripple of muscle, he grabbed her to keep them both from tripping. Their eyes met. Rick brushed his lips against hers. He looked southward. They resumed walking.

How lovely, she thought. He can be present and not say anything. How unlike Daniel who always became ominously opaque whenever he did stop talking. Cut it out, she ordered herself. I'm over that marriage.

Eva, now as tall as Gwen, had been tiptoeing on an invisible, curving tightrope just beyond the tide's reach. Skinny and angular, she high-stepped into the shallows, a black-wigged flamingo. Bored with that game, she ran to Rick and tagged him.

"You're it," she cried.

"Good thing I didn't jog this morning," he said to Gwen.

While Eva and Rick chased each other in and out of the tide, Gwen brooded over the nasty argument she had with her daughter the night before. Eva wanted her own telephone and her own private number. She had picked out the model—a Princess handset, the same one that came on the market when Gwen was her age. Eva had a precise color in mind to express her true persona—coral green. The idea of a pre-teen having her own phone made Gwen uncomfortable. She wouldn't know how late Eva stayed up at night gossiping. The privilege might spoil her. Gwen certainly didn't have her own phone as a teenager. Too late, after escalation, Gwen remembered the mantra her best friend, Nan, had told her to recite in such situations.

"She's twelve, impulsive, passionate, unsure of herself—a toxic combination— but completely normal, age-appropriate behavior. She's twelve, impulsive….."

The tension had soon evaporated, like a passing thunderstorm. Still, Gwen worried this might be the harbinger of bigger trouble to come.

Eva came up to her, panting.

"You know, Mom," she said, "It would be a lot more fun if you joined us. If that's not too much for you."

Gwen gritted her teeth and smiled congenially. Tag was not too much for her. She could still play three sets of tennis with a speed, skill, and ferocity few twelve year olds could match—surely not Eva who had neither the drive nor the athleticism requisite for competitive sports. Eva must be parroting some insufferable character from a television show. Her patronizing attitude made Gwen reconsider their lunch at the greasy spoon. She hadn't tried to talk Eva into going elsewhere. She hadn't even grumbled about it. Afterwards, Eva showed no gratitude. Gwen was luxuriating in the languid stroll, basking in unobstructed views of ocean and sky. She didn't feel like running around.

"You know, Eva," Gwen said, "I'd be more inclined to play if you asked me in a nicer way."

Eva's eyes narrowed to slits.

When Rick arrived, Eva said, "Mom doesn't want to play with us. She has too many important things to think about."

"I didn't say that!" Gwen protested.

Eva was standing between Gwen and Rick. She turned to Gwen with a malicious grin then to Rick with doe-eyed innocence.

Rick kicked the sand and looked at his watch.

"Let's turn around," he said. "I think Billy and Laura will be at the fire pit by the time we get there, *with their golden retrievers.*"

Eva had forgotten what Rick's friends were bringing to the bonfire picnic. She raced off, screaming, "Dogs!"

"Maybe I should get her a dog," said Gwen. "Would that help?"

"I'm not going to be feeding a dog and picking up its poop every day. Are you?"

"She's old enough to take care of a pet."

"I think you've got those developmental milestones confused."

"OK, but if I gave her dog, then maybe she'd get it. I'm her mother, I love her unconditionally. We don't need to be at war. And she'd grow into the responsibility."

"That's right, and while you're harping, 'Did you walk the dog? Did you feed the dog?' she'll be resenting all those helpful reminders."

Gwen giggled.

Rick was relieved to see she wasn't serious about the idea.

"Thanks," she said and touched his cheek.

They held hands again and followed Eva.

As Rick watched the waves break, his mind wandered to surfing, his main avocation prior to running marathons, which led him to think about his younger sister. Years ago, he had bought her an airplane ticket to California as a college graduation gift and taught her how to surf.

Now she's a partner in a Chicago law firm, he thought with a mix of irony and self-pity, while I'm four years older and still teaching middle school. Hold on, what's with the "while" and "still" in that sentence? Like what I do isn't as important as what she does?

Rick was proud of his little sister's success in a world dominated by white men, though it had ceased to surprise him. He saw what was happening in his own classroom. The boys were so much more vulnerable and inept than the girls. Gwen had told him she'd been an aberration on graduating from medical school in 1969, but now fifty percent of new doctors were women. He had no doubt that in another generation a majority of the educated elite would be women.

Five minutes after the sun's last ruby drop disappeared over the horizon, they were at a campfire being warmed by driftwood flames. A pair of golden retrievers looked expectantly at Eva. They leapt joyfully when she picked up a stick. Eva ran off with the dogs, and the adults flew into conversation about local ethnic restaurants and California nouvelle cuisine. Gwen wasn't shy. She spoke more than Rick did.

He was proud of her charm and confidence. A bonus, he had told a friend, in a beautiful woman who already blows me away by loving passionately without being needy. If she wants, I'll marry her. Yet Gwen had never brought up the subject. He guessed she had even less trust in the institution than he did. Rick had been in long-term relationships before. He had considered marriage once, ambivalently. But if Gwen were to push, he would commit in a second.

A bottle of brandy was circulating. Gwen took a sip and gave it to Rick. A drop remained on her lower lip. Rick leaned over to lick it off.

VI

Marco had begun running polyacrylamide gels as soon as Kevin left. He turned on an electrical current to separate the proteins in his experimental brews and prepared the equipment and reagents for his next steps. Two hours later, he switched off the current, peeled the slippery panels from their glass plates, bound them to nitrocellulose paper, and immersed the gels in electrophoresis trays. After another two hours, he bathed the blotted sheets in a series of monoclonal antibody solutions and washes. Six hours after starting, he was ready to add substrate for the final stain. Marco traversed the great laboratory, passing floor-to-ceiling windows, to a row of ventilated hoods. His only spectators were the redwood trees just outside, swaying in the breeze.

He envisaged blue bands about to emerge. Up to now he had been too subsumed with each step of the experiment—measuring reagents, manipulating gels, carefully timing each incubation and wash—to imagine how the blots would look. As he poured in substrate, the imminence of having evidence he could photograph and send to the journal editor thrilled him. He concentrated on the undulating sheets of paper, on *where* he wanted to see blue bands appear.

As he lifted each tray onto a rocker, he willed the bands to be in the locations he had predicted, visible proof of his hypothesis. Marco was on a roll. All the nitrocellulose sheets, so fragile they would crack like an egg shell if mishandled slightly, had peeled off the gels without a single tear. The photos would be impressive.

He saw the positive control columns first.

Perfecto, he thought, as a thick smudge flowered where his control protein ought to be. The negative control strip was pure white. Perfect again. Columns of blue bands appeared. *Exactamente*.

He was satisfied until he noticed the bands increased in size from left to right, not from right to left as he had expected.

"What? No! This can't be. Unbelievable! Did I reverse the enzyme concentrations? *Chíngame, que pendejo soy*!"

Kevin arrived to find him crouched over a lab bench, head in hands.

"Uh-oh. What happened?"

"I don't know. It's all wrong, and I can't figure out why. I remember exactly what I did yesterday when I loaded the gels. The tubes are still in the correct order. How I could have made a mistake?"

"What's the problem?"

"The replicates with more enzyme shows *less* protein on the blot, not more."

Kevin gave him a sympathetic pat.

"What did I do wrong?" Marco implored.

"You're asking me?"

"Even a contaminant can't explain these results. Maybe, if the enzyme I used acted on another molecule in the cell…which could have blocked the reaction…No, that's ridiculous."

Kevin had no idea what enzyme or blocking molecule Marco was talking about but felt he had to say something.

"Why's it ridiculous?"

Marco gave him a dismissive frown. Then his eyes opened wide.

"*Sangre de Cristo*!" he shouted. "Of course, the new pathway the Cambridge people just found, it must be here, too. That's the only possible explanation. You're a genius, Kevin!"

Baffled and delighted, Kevin asked, "Can you tell me what we just discovered?"

In a cozy French restaurant on Russian Hill, Marco was elaborating, for the second time that evening, on what a breakthrough this was. His research focused on stem cells obtained from the earliest stage of a developing mouse embryo. A stem cell could proliferate indefinitely, and its progeny could mature into all the different kinds of cells that constitute an adult mouse—gut, brain, bone, skin, muscle, and more. In theory, a living, reproducing mouse could be grown from a single stem cell *after* Marco and his colleagues had altered its DNA. If feasible, such a technique could advance at warp speed the understanding of how genetics and disease interact.

Marco's unexpected results suggested a new way for scientists to stimulate stem cell growth. He knew precisely what molecules to look for now in order to explain his findings. Before the entrees were served, he had envisioned a set of experiments to confirm his new hypothesis as well as assure his paper's acceptance by the journal. Although Kevin was excited and amused, the terminology of cutting-edge cellular biology was hard to follow. Keeping up his end of the conversation was becoming tedious. He was glad to see Marco turn his attention from science to food.

Marco made quick work of his scallops. As a waitress emptied the rest of a Napa Valley chardonnay into his glass, he reached under her arm to pick at Kevin's cassoulet. Kevin thought ruefully about Marco's daily six mile run—the obvious reason he could eat voraciously and not gain weight. Kevin carefully watched his own diet, rarely had more than one drink, consistently took in fewer calories than Marco, yet still was twenty pounds overweight. Marco had been urging him for months to run with him, promising that he'd slow down to an easy jog. But Kevin hated exercise as much as he hated professional sports. Both were associated with his father's auto repair shop— the heavy engine blocks and transmissions he had lugged around, the radio station always tuned to a game, the frozen bolts and scraped knuckles, the omnipresent black grease.

"I'm…what's the term? I know, thunderstruck," said Marco. "That's an English word? It sounds German. I'm thunderstruck you can get food this good in America. And it's not even expensive."

"This isn't cheap," Kevin remonstrated.

"Don't worry, sweetheart. My treat. It's the least we can do for ourselves after our vacation day was so *abruptly interrupted*. See what I mean. That sounds German too."

"I'm sorry, baby."

"Don't be sorry. You were a hero today. Didn't Herb say how much it will help the cause?"

Marco pumped his fist and leaned back to study Kevin. He held up his wineglass.

"I'm so proud of you."

Kevin laughed self-consciously.

He caressed Marco's thigh under the table and asked, "Is this what…what being in love is?"

"Oh yes," Marco answered, his eyes sparkling, "I think so. *De veras*, I do."

VII

ON WEDNESDAYS, KEVIN HAD a morning clinic and came to work early to look in on his hospitalized patients beforehand. Today would be Mr. Miller's fourth day in the ICU, and Kevin wasn't hopeful about his recovery. He decided to see Miller last, after checking on two ward patients who had Pneumocystis pneumonia.

One was nearing the end of treatment, able to stomach medication by mouth and being weaned from nasal oxygen. He could likely go home tomorrow. A thirty-five year old investment banker with a private doctor in Pacific Heights, he had never been to City Hospital before collapsing in his office downtown and being brought to the ER by ambulance.

The banker was staring at the wall, expressionless, when Kevin peeked into the room.

"How's it going?" said Kevin as he entered.

"How much time do I have?" asked the man in a monotone. "A few months? A year?"

Kevin sat down on the edge of the bed. He had learned by trial and error it was better to listen first, get a handle on a patient's understanding of his disease and what he feared, then discuss prognosis. But this man's replies to open-ended questions had been "I don't know" up to now. He had shown no curiosity about his condition. Kevin presumed he was reacting to his diagnosis with disbelief and numbness—it can't be happening to me. Clearly, he had moved to the next stage, depression. No, Kevin reconsidered, anger and bargaining are supposed to occur before depression.

The banker was mute, waiting for him to speak. Kevin couldn't deflect the question and maintain credibility. He had to take a stab at it.

"Maybe longer, if you're monitored closely, if we get on top of infections like this one sooner."

"That's pathetic! You don't even know what's causing the disease, do you? All you can do is try to treat the complications of having a crippled immune system, right? And mine has already been destroyed, hasn't it? It's not going to get better, so it's just a matter of time. And not much time. And most of it spent feeling shitty, right?"

Kevin was at a loss. The banker had moved the wrong way, from depression to anger, in a blink. These stages of grief weren't as orderly as one would think from reading the literature on death and dying. And patients like this were the most difficult, the ones with penetrating, merciless intellects that turned on themselves and their physicians. The best he could do now was to apologize.

"I'm sorry…I can promise we'll do whatever we can to help you. There is research going on. We might have answers soon."

Still refusing to look at him, the banker screamed, "*I am fucked. Fucked!*"

He lay down, covered his head with a pillow, and asked Kevin to leave.

Across the hall was a patient Kevin knew well, Danny, a fifty-two-year-old denizen of the South of Market bondage-and-discipline scene. Underneath the metal spikes and chains was a puckish, sweet-tempered man reconciled to the inevitable. Danny had been admitted the previous night with his third episode of Pneumocystis, a severe one. What little was left of his lungs was full of frothy fluid that blocked oxygen from diffusing into his blood. The pulmonologist on call had told Kevin it was futile to put him on a ventilator. Kevin hadn't argued. Danny would die in a few days no matter what they did.

He stood in the doorway watching Danny's labored breathing. Though he saw morphine dripping into Danny's vein and knew his patient wasn't conscious, Kevin couldn't help but imagine being frantic with air hunger, the desperate compulsion to expel smothering liquid inside his lungs, the clawing need to inhale more air, the inability to gratify either urge. He left the ward trying to erase the intrusive picture in his mind of an abandoned car being crushed by a metal compactor.

In the ICU, Kevin found Dana looking at a printout of Miller's blood test results. He glanced at the numbers, which indicated no further deterioration, and began lecturing her on how important it was they stay aggressive in lowering the pressure squeezing the patient's brain. He stopped when her medical student, Gail, walked past carrying a long spinal needle.

Dana changed the subject.

"So what do you think?" she asked. "Is the culprit behind GRID a toxin, a virus, or an autoimmune disease?"

Dana had worked in an immunology laboratory between college and medical school and planned to do an oncology fellowship. Her interest in GRID had been piqued when Kevin informed her that scientists at UCLA had discovered a subset of lymphocytes called helper T cells were greatly diminished in the blood of GRID patients. This deficit was almost certainly the proximate reason for their vulnerability to opportunistic infections like Pneumocystis pneumonia or cryptococcal meningitis—infections caused by microbes unable to invade people with intact immune systems.

"I don't know," Kevin answered. "Those are the major suspects. Most epidemiologists think some kind of virus is knocking off helper T cells. But the jury's out."

"You're too cautious. Don't you like to speculate?"

"Not really, but you can."

"Hey, I just thought of something. This is a chance to figure out which T cell functions are critical in preventing opportunistic infections. Cancer and transplant patients get Pneumocystis, but their immune systems are too blitzed by chemotherapy for anyone to get useful data. If an immunologist compared lymphocytes from your pre-GRID patients and those with full-blown GRID, maybe she could tease out exactly *how* T cells prevent opportunistic infections."

"Sounds like you're describing your future fellowship research."

"Maybe so. Thanks for the idea!"

"It's *your* idea."

"I wouldn't have thought of it if I wasn't taking care of *your* patient."

The irony of this conversation wasn't lost on Kevin. He'd chosen his specialty over oncology largely because infections often had definitive cures and cancer didn't. Yet, here he was attempting to treat the "gay cancer" with no effective medications other than short term fixes for the opportunistic infections that complicated the syndrome. He was constantly dealing with death and dying. Now he'd inspired the career of a future oncologist.

VIII

HERB WAS IN GOLDEN Gate Park at dawn on Wednesday, jogging under a cotton ceiling of fog. He loved this type of sky, the range of hues—off-white, pearl, cinder, gunmetal, silver, slate—and the bracing clarity, nothing bleached by direct sunlight or hidden by glare. The fog also made it cool enough to run comfortably in a polypropylene shirt that wicked away the sweat. After two miles, he had passed through the stiffness, burning in his sternum, and cramping in his side. It was effortless now. He was being carried by the rhythm of running, the cadence of his pace and breathing in four-four time. Soon there would be an exhilarating taste in the back of his throat, like glacial water with a pinch of gunpowder. He could sustain this pace for an hour, a slower one for two or three, before lactic acid accumulating in his muscles finally undid him in a surge of nausea and exhaustion.

Herb began running seriously as a fifth grader, motivated by his father's enthusiasm for the upcoming 1948 Summer Olympics, the first to be held since the 1936 games in Berlin. Like all United Nations staff, his father viewed renewal of the Olympics as a perfect metaphor for the fledgling organization—an amicable competition that all countries could participate in equally and peacefully.

Herb was the fastest boy in his elementary school and fantasized about track-and-field record holders. His favorite athlete was Jesse Owens, the black American who had won four gold medals in 1936. Looking in a full-length mirror, Herb focused on his long, muscular legs instead of his eyelids, which made him the butt of classmates' jokes. What if he trained to be the fastest boy in his town, Herb wondered, or the whole of Long Island? Who would dare tease him then?

He wheedled his mother into driving around the neighborhood while he studied the odometer and a street map until settling on the best course. He started jogging every other day, adding a kilometer to his distance each week. As soon as he could run ten kilometers without stopping to catch his breath, he ratcheted the effort up, and his times came down. He read about training regimens at the library. He searched local newspapers for reports of high school track meets and went to several, making notes on the runners' form and clocking their speeds.

Once the Olympics began, Herb rode a bus each afternoon to UN headquarters where he watched newsreels of the day's highlights with his father. They had good-natured arguments over which countries would win. Herb had more conversation with him in those two weeks than the entire rest of his childhood.

Herb was fascinated by Emil Zatopek, the Czech who broke the world record for ten kilometers, running it in under thirty minutes—a superhuman feat to a boy who couldn't cover the distance in less than an hour. The agony on Zatopek's face in finish-line phsotos convinced Herb that anyone capable of enduring great pain could be a winner in life. He vowed to emulate his hero's example.

The following summer, he trained for a one-mile race in a countywide competition. The day before the event, his father called from the UN. There was an international crisis. He couldn't leave.

His mother drove him to the Nassau county fairgrounds. Surrounded by dense forest in full leaf, they milled awkwardly among the young athletes and proud parents—all white. Herb's race was the last. Their wait was interminable. He kept expecting to hear a disparaging comment, but every glance in their direction was politely tolerant. Herb's mile was over in six minutes. He came in second and was satisfied. This was no village contest, he explained to his mother. It represented half the population of Long Island.

Afterwards, they went to an exhibition hall. Each boy who had won or placed in a dash, jump, or throw was escorted to the stage by his father and received a medal. The mile awards were given at the end of the ceremony. Herb's mother leapt up when his name was called. He glared at her, shaking his head no, and walked to the stage alone.

Herb was in the ICU by nine, seated at a small conference table, ready for the interns to present their new admissions. He raised his baton, a ballpoint pen wrapped in black electrical tape to conceal the pharmaceutical company logo. The first act opened—a tale of an elderly emphysematous man brought to the ER in respiratory distress. Herb listened carefully, taking notes as the drama unfolded. He enjoyed the house staff, their alternating banter and solemnity. It still surprised him when they appreciated the constructive feedback he could provide.

Next, he had consultation rounds with his new fellow, Harry Simpson, and Gwen. Harry had earned a PhD in physiology during medical school and planned a laboratory-based career in academic medicine. Herb had heard from pulmonologists at the other university-affiliated hospitals that Harry was bright, knowledgeable, and reasonably competent as a clinician. Once Harry started his rotation at City Hospital, Herb learned something else about his new fellow. Harry was terrified by GRID.

Ward residents and attending physicians complained that Harry tried to talk them out of requesting consults on GRID patients. Those Harry couldn't brush off, he assigned Gwen to evaluate. He called in sick both times GRID cases were scheduled for bronchoscopy.

"Bronchoscopy entails minimal exposure to blood," Herb pointed out to him. "Plus, you're wearing a protective gown, a mask, gloves, and goggles."

Herb showed his fellow epidemiologic papers as evidence there was no risk from such contact. Though Harry claimed to concur, his behavior didn't change. More disappointed than outraged, Herb was counting the days until Harry's month at City Hospital would be over.

Herb, Harry, and Gwen began at the bedside of a young man just admitted with severe abdominal pain. Exploratory surgery was being considered. Because he had two prior episodes of Pneumocystis pneumonia, the surgical team wanted advice from a pulmonary consultant before operating. Harry's pallid complexion whitened a shade as they entered the room.

While Herb was listening to the patient's lungs, a group of scrub-clad residents and students came in, led by their attending surgeon, Jared Hart. The descendant of three generations of Montana ranchers, Hart was a remarkable character even by City Hospital standards. Five feet, two inches tall, with a huge handlebar mustache, he had a basso voice, swore liberally, kept the pocket of his long, white coat full of Havana cigars, and occasionally addressed female students and interns by their chest circumference and breast cup size rather than their name. Herb stepped aside, yielding access to the surgeon.

Hart pressed the back of his ungloved hand against the delirious young man's wet forehead.

Holding up one finger and flicking off a drop of sweat, he announced, "Fever!"

He dug his heel of his palm into the patient's abdomen. The man flinched. Hart abruptly pulled his hand back. The patient howled in agony from the ripping sensation this maneuver induced.

Holding up two fingers, Hart said, "Right lower quadrant *rebound* tenderness!"

He snatched the chart from an intern and thumbed through the pages with a flourish to the laboratory results section.

"Leukocytosis!" he shouted and held up three fingers. "His white count is 18,000. That's three out of three criteria for appendicitis. We'll operate today."

All of Hart's coterie, as well as Harry and Gwen, stood wide-eyed and silent. Herb had seen this performance before and wasn't impressed.

"Any objections, Dr. Wu?"

"He won't survive without surgery, Jared. Please proceed. Just keep the ventilator pressures on the low side so the blebs I saw on his chest film don't rupture."

"But, Dr. Hart," objected a resident. "Is it safe for us to operate? We heard a lecture by Dr. Bartholomew, and he said these patients' immune deficiency might be transmitted by contact with their blood."

Hart eyed him coldly and said, "We're surgeons, Dr. Bryan. We take those risks. We might experience fear, but we aren't influenced by it. A resident I trained with contracted hepatitis B from an accidental scalpel wound. He died of cirrhosis. In Vietnam, two of my colleagues were blown to smithereens in an operating theater ten yards away from mine."

With a sneer, Hart delivered the coup de grâce.

"It's an occupational hazard, Dr. Bryan. If it makes you uncomfortable, find another job."

Hart marched out of the room. His team docilely followed.

Herb had never heard this soliloquy and rather liked it, though he suspected its veracity. Given his height, had Hart really been inducted into the military? Herb turned to share the question but checked himself on seeing Harry's crimson cheeks and ears. Better to save it for later, he decided, when he and Gwen would be alone.

In the afternoon, Harry went to a seminar, and Gwen helped Herb with bronchoscopies. Their first patient was a scrawny, wrinkled man who had smoked a pack of cigarettes a day for fifty years. A week ago, his doctor ordered a routine chest x-ray that revealed a spot the size of quarter in his right lung.

The man's pupils dilated when Gwen rolled a gurney into his room. The fear he exuded didn't abate until she gave him an intravenous sedative in the bronchoscopy suite. Now he was in a dopey, half-sleep state.

While Herb advanced the bronchoscope, Gwen looked through a second eyepiece. She could see images from the tip of the fiberoptic cable as it snaked past the vocal cords and headed south along the trachea, past glistening pink mucosa stained with nicotine. Herb made a sharp turn into the right mainstem bronchus and came to a sudden halt in front of a fungating mass that blocked any further passage. Gwen cringed. It was the coin lesion on the x-ray, magnified to the size of a boulder.

She held the bronchoscope as he manipulated a sheathed wire running alongside the cable and connected at the tip to a tiny forceps. Before the procedure, Herb had showed her how squeezing the trigger at his end of the wire closed the sharp metal teeth at the other end. Through the lens, she watched the instrument bite off a piece of tumor.

"Ugh," she cried and immediately regretted her outburst.

She whispered an apology.

"Don't worry," said Herb. "He's too deep to remember any of this."

"Poor guy."

"It is what it is."

To Gwen, his comment didn't sound callous. She heard simultaneous sympathy, philosophical detachment, and sadness. An ideal attitude, she thought. After working with Herb for three weeks, she was in awe of how centered he was, always balanced between objectivity and empathy. Gwen wished she could do that. She had contemplated asking him to teach her how, though it was inconceivable making such a request wouldn't embarrass both of them. He was handsome, too. She momentarily wondered why she hadn't married someone like him instead of Daniel. Instantly, she knew the answer. It would be intimidating to live with anyone so perfect.

The forceps bit off two more pieces of the tumor, and Herb retracted it into the sheath. Gwen set the bronchoscope down, donned latex gloves, and opened a vial of formalin. Herb withdrew the wire. When the forceps appeared, Gwen grabbed the stainless steel pincers and placed it in the formalin. Herb released the trigger. They watched, neither commenting, as shreds of malignant tissue floated to the bottom of the vial.

Gwen rolled the patient back to the wards. She finished gathering information on two new consults, then met up with Herb in his office where she presented the new cases. Herb took note of how efficient, thorough, and concise she was. It made listening to her presentations a pleasure, and it spoke volumes to him about her character. He had observed that those who went into medicine solely for prestige or money tended to invest little energy in being accurate or to the point.

He also enjoyed her sense of humor. Gwen was the kind of resident he wanted his division to recruit into its fellowship program. However, she clearly wasn't excited enough by procedures to become a pulmonologist. Perhaps an infectious diseases fellowship, he mused. Not that it mattered because Kevin would have to expand his GRID clinic soon, within a year at most, and his affection for Gwen was transparent. He was certain Kevin would find a position for her.

The two new consults were a routine exacerbation of emphysema and a rare autoimmune lung disease. After discussing the cases, Gwen had a question about the man they had biopsied earlier.

"What do you think his prognosis is?"

"Based on the big mediastinal lymph nodes we saw on his chest film, it has to be bleak."

"It could still be small cell, couldn't it? Then chemo would be an option, even with metastases, right?"

"True, which is why we had to get tissue. But a small, asymptomatic tumor like this; odds are less than one in five a small cell lung cancer would present that way."

"Based on the literature or your own experience?"

"Both."

He opened a drawer of photocopied articles and handed her one.

"Here's a large series. I've seen the same thing here. We get a case or two a month. Nearly all the small, asymptomatic tumors are squamous cell carcinomas. And as you well know, once they've metastasized, school's out."

Gwen considered the implications of regularly giving this news to people for whom chemotherapy couldn't help, having to tell each one he had at most a year or two to live.

"Herb, does telling these patients their diagnosis depress you?"

She's definitely not going into pulmonology, he thought. She might not join Kevin either.

"It makes me sad for them, but not depressed."

Been there done that, he thought.

"The sadness doesn't stay with you, doesn't bleed into the rest of your life?"

"Not anymore."

"That's a neat trick," sighed Gwen. "I need to learn how to do it."

"You're a quick study. Stick around. It won't take you long."

IX

Marco was already setting up gels in the laboratory before Kevin left for work. He took a break at noon, set down a stack of data printouts in his nook of a carrel, and had lunch—a thermos of strong coffee and a peanut butter and jelly sandwich. While eating, he gazed at the shelf of bound notebooks he had filled during his three years here. His heels bounced on the floor. He was so close to confirming a radical, new hypothesis, it was hard to stay calm.

Since moving to Berkeley, Marco had only chipped away at creating new knowledge. Once his current experiments were finished and the revised manuscript accepted for publication, his apprenticeship with Professor Goldstein would officially end. He would be promoted to full membership in the team attempting to create clones of genetically identical mice from stem cells. Everyone in the lab believed comparing clones of mice that had a single altered gene to clones of unaltered mice was going to become the gold standard for proving what any particular gene did, at least in mice. And because mouse and human genes were so similar, their experiments would create new paradigms for understanding human diseases.

His eyes strayed to a photo of Kevin with a turquoise lake and snow-capped mountains in the background. Kevin had a rare, contented smile. Marco's neck muscles relaxed. He had taken the picture last summer in the high Sierras. They had backpacked for a week through alpine meadows dotted with marigold, paintbrush, and penstemon. Each morning they scrambled up boulder fields to find the loneliest outposts of life where only one or two flowers could survive. Marco took photos and kept a meticulous log. At their camp, Kevin gathered wood, made fires, and cooked. The modest effort required to survive in such an austere, exquisite place made him glow with satisfaction.

Marco's attention wandered to the data printouts. He reached for a pencil but moved past it, picked up the telephone, and dialed Kevin's pager.

After his morning clinic, Kevin boarded a shuttle to the Hill, the university complex of hospitals, health science schools, and research institutes towering over Golden Gate Park. As he entered a classroom, his pager vibrated and displayed the phone number of Marco's lab. The instructor was explaining the difference between a t-test and a Chi-square test. Kevin wanted to hear this and made a mental note to call Marco later.

He had begun auditing this introductory biostatistics course once he accepted the handwriting on the wall. To have job security, he had to obtain grants. As a physician who didn't perform expensive procedures like bronchoscopy, he had no other income-generating options. A grasp of the methods used in biostatistical analysis was one of the skills he needed to submit competitive proposals.

Yet Kevin was still ambivalent about research. Not only had he failed in Flagler's lab, he had also been burned when he tried to publish a report of the first three Pneumocystis patients they had seen at City Hospital. Herb and he had hypothesized a combination of drug use and multiple bouts of syphilis and gonorrhea infection, features common to all their cases, might have irreversibly damaged the immune system. While typing his final draft, a phone call came from Atlanta. The CDC had investigated five Pneumocystis cases in Los Angeles, all in gay men with a history of many sexually transmitted infections. Their results would be published before Kevin could get his manuscript submitted. The CDC asked him to collaborate. They offered to include the details of his cases in their national dataset, for *their* statisticians to analyze. Eventually, his name would be on some papers, but not as first author.

He couldn't have refused even if he wanted. Though he had been slapped in the face by fate, his mood soon improved. He was actually glad to not be alone in dealing with this disease. Nevertheless, the academic clock was ticking. He desperately needed funding, and a first-author publication would have been a foot in the door, giving him scientific credibility to grant review committees. He was back at square one.

Kevin's pager buzzed again while he stood outside in the drizzle waiting for a shuttle bus. He saw Marco's number, but there was no phone nearby. He couldn't respond until he got to City Hospital.

Over the ocean, a dark curtain of rain was moving inland. Being exposed to inclement weather on the Hill, to forces beyond his control, evoked memories of his ward assignments in the university hospital across the street. He had hated those months, the arrogance of the attending physicians, the lack of resident autonomy, the ambience of social Darwinism. The approaching shuttle reminded him of the deliverance he had felt at moving on to rotations at the Veterans Administration and public hospitals where the mean-spirited competition that house staff exhibited on the Hill softened into collegiality. How strange life's zigzags are, Kevin thought, as he compared those memories to his new appreciation of the Hill's scientific resources.

He was still ahead of the storm sweeping across the city when he got off the shuttle. He walked toward his office in one of the original red-brick buildings constructed after the 1906 earthquake. Its bronze gargoyles, weathered green, were set against a blackening sky. He remembered he should check on his inpatients before meeting Herb at four-thirty. Kevin turned back and passed through motion-triggered, sliding-glass doors into the modern hospital. He had forgotten Marco's page.

X

KEVIN WENT TO SEE Miller last. Flipping through the chart revealed nothing had changed since the morning. He consoled himself with the fact that at least the antifungal infusions hadn't harmed Miller's kidneys yet.

"Give me an order sheet from the chart."

Dana stood before him, a hand outstretched, her lips pressed tight.

"Why the foul mood?"

"Well, Gail tapped him again this morning, and his pressure was still high. So neurology told us to keep hyperventilating him. Which means we have to continue sedating and paralyzing him so he won't buck the ventilator. Which means we can't assess whether his neurologic status is getting better or worse. Which means I have to say I don't know to all the people who are asking about his prognosis."

"Who's asking?"

"The chief of medicine, the health department director, the hospital administrator, a nosy reporter I refused to talk to."

"Wonderful," Kevin groaned. "Any more city pols come by?"

"No," said Dana, grinning mischievously. "What, you don't like being a celebrity? The famous immune deficiency doctor?"

Kevin grimaced.

"Just kidding."

Dana's pager beeped. She looked irritated on seeing the number displayed and went to the nurse's station to make a phone call. She returned ashen.

"My father's in an ER back east with crushing chest pain and EKG changes. I need to get out of here."

Ten minutes later, Gwen, the back-up resident for the month, came into the ICU. She had been paged by the chief resident who told her the bad news—she would have to drop her pulmonary elective and cover for Dana whose team also happened to be on call today. They had four new admissions so far, and two were unstable. Dana gave Gwen her set of index cards, to-do lists for each of her team's patients.

As she walked out the door, Kevin gave a condolence frown to Gwen.

"It's OK," she said with a shrug.

Dana's interns and student arrived, and Gwen spread Dana's cards on the conference table. She sent one intern to the ER to take care of a sixty-five year old Salvadoran woman who had a dangerously rapid heart rhythm.

"Massage her carotid artery," she instructed him. "If that doesn't work dunk her face in a bucket of ice water. If she's still in atrial fibrillation, push digoxin until her pulse slows down."

She assigned the other intern to manage the admission with a bleeding stomach ulcer.

"Make sure he's got two large bore IV's running wide open," Gwen advised. "If his blood pressure drops, grab the IV bag and squeeze it, *hard*. Draw a hematocrit every hour and spin it yourself. Dana ordered four units of packed cells half an hour ago. Ride herd on the blood bank if there aren't at least two units already there when you get to the ICU."

She gave the other two admissions to the medical student and phoned Proctor, leaving a message for Rick that she wouldn't be home until tomorrow night.

"Wow," said Kevin, "Superwoman takes charge."

Gwen wondered if she heard a gentle edge of mockery. She could never quite pin that down with Kevin, one of the many entertaining aspects of being his friend. It took her a moment to be sure it was there, an undercurrent in his admiration. Despite an effort to keep from smiling, the corners of her mouth rose.

"I can help with Miller," Kevin offered.

"That'd be nice. Thanks."

Kevin searched her face and asked, "You sure you're OK?"

"I'm fine. It's no big deal. Rick is used to this."

"It must be hard on Eva."

"You've got to be kidding. If I disappeared completely from her life, she'd be ecstatic."

Kevin wrinkled his brow.

"Believe me, she is not longing for any more attention than she's getting from me. And she'd be happier with less."

"You really think she doesn't mind all the time you're away?"

"Did you want to spend time with either of your parents when you were twelve?"

Kevin tried to recall being twelve.

"Wrong question. You were a boy. Have to add two years. Did you want your parents interfering in your life when you were fourteen?"

"God, no."

"See what I mean."

That would be a major downside of having children, thought Kevin. They grow up and become difficult. He and Marco had talked of adopting. They were mutually relieved to discover the other had fantasized about the possibility and was nowhere close to considering it seriously yet.

"You think conflict with your child is inevitable?"

"Unfortunately, I'm afraid most of us do have to reject our parents in order to believe we're individuals in charge of our own fate. Though maybe if I were more psychologically minded, more astute at parenting, I could avoid some of the nastier battles."

"It sounds hard," said Kevin.

"Not any harder than what we do here, once you know the ropes."

"How so?"

"Understanding what motivates someone's bad behavior, figuring out how not to take it personally. Sound familiar?"

"Yeah…but she's your daughter. How could you not take it personally?"

"You're a smart cookie, Kevin. That is precisely the problem. Most of the time I do take it personally."

Holding the bell of his stethoscope to his mouth, Kevin imitated a newsreel reporter from the 1930s.

"Can you believe it folks? She can do all this and still be the mother of a teenage girl. Only her daughter's kryptonite can stop this woman."

Gwen laughed as Kevin headed off to find Miller's chart.

She had never had a male friend like Kevin, adoring her in an utterly asexual way. I've always had pals at work I could be comfortable with, she thought, but no man, other than a lover, has ever shown me this much appreciation. Wrong, she corrected herself, except for my father.

The summer after Gwen's brother joined the army, her father came out from New York. Her mother, now a dentist's receptionist, had saved enough money for a week vacation at a desert spa. Children were not allowed. Gwen had no choice but to accompany her father on a fishing trip.

Driving east through the empty desert, she was sullen while he remained doggedly cheerful. He let her pick radio stations and control the volume. She was surprised to find he didn't mind listening to loud rock and roll. Turning north, they drove along the eastern slope of the Sierras, stopping at rustic, lakeside lodges to fish and stay the night. She hadn't seen air this clear before. The sky's rich blue color and the steep rock walls above tree line entranced her. Each day they cast lures from a rowboat beneath snow-capped peaks. Her father complimented her repeatedly on her skill at casting.

Gwen's first two catches were too small to keep. Tossing the quivering, iridescent creatures back to freedom thrilled her. On the second day, she caught a trout big enough to eat. As her father was about to impale its jaw on a stringer, Gwen yelled, "Don't!" She held out her hands, demanding the fish. He chuckled at her audacity and let her drop it in the water.

Every evening, he had a single beer, which made Gwen wary, though its only discernible effect was to make him more agreeable. By the end of the trip, it was difficult for her to be angry with him. Still, on principle, she refused to kiss him good-bye. He was disappointed but not put off. He asked her if she'd like to see New York. Unable to hide her excitement, Gwen said yes.

The following summer, she rode east in an air-conditioned bus, studying her transcontinental highway map and calculating distances when not engrossed in the new landscapes. On a moonless night, the coach crossed the eastern Colorado plains. Gwen saw a carpet of stars falling to the horizon—a sixty mile radius away in all directions, the driver told her. The only terrestrial light was from a lone, distant farm house.

She imagined a family with a girl her age living there. She worried the isolation might make them lonely. No, she decided, they were contented, humble people, grateful to live at the center of such a peaceful world. But the girl would need to leave home soon to seek her fortune in a great metropolis.

. Her father's apartment was on the thirty-eighth floor of a building in midtown Manhattan. He let Gwen have his bedroom and slept on the couch. He bought her a subway pass and urged her to see the city while he was at work. She spent the first two weeks exploring neighborhoods from the Battery to Washington Heights and the rest of the trip inside museums.

At the Metropolitan Museum of Art, Gwen was drawn to the ancient marble sculptures. Her favorites were Jupiter astride an eagle and a nude Aphrodite. Perfect human forms carved over two thousand years ago, they defied life's impermanence. She was equally intrigued by the Cloisters, a castle filled with medieval art perched on a bluff above the Hudson River. She went there for the ambience, not the tapestries or sculptures, and pretended to be a princess in fifteenth century France, safe behind the parapets while wars raged below.

On her last evening in New York, her father took her out to a fancy Italian restaurant. He drank two cocktails before dinner and turned gloomy.

"I'm going to miss you," he said.

Gwen flushed. She fended off her own conflicting emotions and tried to understand what he meant. His sentiment sounded genuine, but she wondered if he had some other agenda. Was he hoping she would take care of him when he became old and feeble?

"Are you lonely?" she asked.

That question flustered him.

"Sometimes," he acknowledged.

"Why don't you get married again?"

"I don't think so. One alimony is enough."

"Huh?"

"Honey," he explained sadly, "All the women I've met here are just like your mother. They want a man to take care of them. That's ultimately a no-win proposition. They end up resenting their dependence. It's a vicious circle."

Gwen was offended. He had no right to insult her mother. Nevertheless, she recognized the truth in what he said.

"You're strong, Gwen, and smart enough to make your own way in the world. You'll go to college, won't you? I'll give you all the help I can. I promise."

"College," she said softly, exhilarated by his confidence in her potential.

"You could do it, Gwen. Finish college and get a good job before you settle down with someone. It's best to have an exit strategy."

On the ride back to California, she was on the lookout for lone farmhouses, especially at sunset. She didn't find one that had moved her, though in Utah a crow perched atop a dying fir caught her attention. Its glassy black eyes tracked her bus for miles. Gwen felt its steely tenacity stirring inside her.

XI

WHILE WAITING FOR KEVIN, Herb continued to craft text for their grant proposal. In such endeavors, he always used a number two wooden pencil capped with an oversized pink eraser and wrote on a yellow legal pad. He was holding the pencil by its point, bouncing the eraser up and down on his desk. A faint smile appeared as he thought about how obviously fundable the idea was, how the grant was writing itself. He hadn't shown any of this text to Kevin yet. He wanted Kevin to design the study with a minimum of assistance and feel ownership of the effort. He'd sneak in these paragraphs, articulating the rationale and larger significance of their proposal, later.

Herb's name would have to be listed as the principal investigator. His track record of publications was essential to getting them funded. Afterwards, he planned to recede into the background while Kevin ran the project and subsequently authored a paper describing the results. Herb was pleased by the personal closure his scheme entailed. He had become a wily mentor like the ones at the National Institutes of Health who had seduced him into a career of clinical research.

Herb had entered this pathway unintentionally. In 1968, after being deferred from military conscription for four years of medical school, three years of residency, and a year of pulmonary fellowship, he had run out of dodges. The army urgently needed doctors for its escalating war in Southeast Asia. Herb was newly married, and Cecilia wanted to get pregnant. He saw a flyer posted for a position at NIH, which was hiring young MDs to help conduct experimental treatment trials. Several perks came with the job—training in clinical research methods and another draft deferment. He applied immediately.

When Herb arrived in Washington DC, protests roiled the nation's capital. College students wearing army fatigues manned barricades and cursed at police and National Guard troops. The kids were impassioned and cocky. They had just forced a sitting president to renounce his bid for re-election.

Cecilia was self-assured too—about her ability to handle the MBA program at Georgetown, pregnancy, and motherhood. Allison was born a few months after they arrived, an easy baby who slept through the night at six weeks and wasn't prone to crying spells. They could take her with them anywhere—restaurants, parties, movies. Herb carried Allison on his back in public places and received smiles from passers-by instead of furtive, xenophobic glances.

It was also in Washington that he started jogging again. Out Embassy Row, through Rock Creek Park, up Connecticut Avenue past the Zoo, or to the Lincoln Memorial, through the middle of the Mall, and on to Congress. The exercise calmed him, reinforced his own nascent self-confidence.

Kevin came into Herb's office holding a stapled, ten page document at arm's length, as though unsure of its odor.

"It can't be that bad," Herb laughed.

"We'll see," Kevin replied.

While Herb read the draft and made notes in the margins, Kevin thought of the question he hadn't asked yesterday.

Ten minutes later, Herb declared, "This is great! Besides a few typo corrections, all we need is to complete the analytic plan and justify the sample size. Then it'll be ready to plug into our grant application."

"Do you really think it has a chance of being funded?"

"More than a chance. I'll be very, very surprised if it's rejected."

Kevin wasn't convinced.

"There's always luck involved," Herb admitted. "We don't know who will be on the study section panel or what their biases are. But even if it's not funded on the first round, I'm sure a resubmission can address any criticisms raised."

"You've been lucky, haven't you?"

"Absolutely. My whole career was an accident. The only reason I went to NIH was to get out of the draft."

"I don't want to go to NIH."

"You don't have to go to NIH. There's plenty of opportunity right here."

"But I'm not lucky."

"Look, I know you had a bad experience with Flagler, but this is clinical research, not a laboratory experiment where every possible variable is under your control. It's about how patients react to a disease and respond to its treatment. Lots of uncertainty, many plausible interpretations of the data. You're the kind of person who's capable of dealing with the messiness and sorting it out."

"So how did things work out so well for you?"

"Simply being in the right place at the right time, like you are now. When I showed up at NIH, the oncologists were investigating new chemotherapy regimens for children with leukemia, more toxic drug combinations than had ever been given before. The patients got so immune suppressed they were sitting ducks for opportunistic pneumonias like Pneumocystis. Serendipitously, the year I started, a company invented a flexible bronchoscope and wanted someone at NIH to try it out. There I was with the right training, the right patients, the right tool, and all these NIH microbiology and pathology labs happy to collaborate with me. A wide open road to success, and I took advantage of it. It wasn't hard to publish a dozen articles during the two years I was there, which made me marketable enough to be offered this job."

"Sounds too good to be true."

"Perhaps, but let's talk about how your stars are aligned. There are lots of GRID patients here, the disease isn't going away any time soon, and no one understands it. That is a huge opportunity for someone with your skills and training. Not only will this grant be funded, you'll be able to use the results to leverage bigger grants afterwards, which, by the way, should be more than enough to make the university change your academic appointment from temporary to permanent. *If* that's what you really want."

Kevin disliked being probed. Impulsively, he turned the tables.

"Herb, why did you choose me? Why not one of your pulmonary fellows?"

Taken aback, Herb said, "What? Am I pushing you? Isn't this what you want? To figure out why people are dying from GRID and how to stop it?"

"Of course I do. But why choose me? Because I'm gay?"

Kevin tensed, expecting Herb to be defensive, if not hostile. Instead, Herb sighed, plopped his elbows on the desk, and rested his chin on intertwined fingers.

"I see," Herb said, peering over his reading glasses. "Kevin, there are two reasons. One, it's obvious you're deeply disturbed by this disease. I can tell because I've been watching you since you were an intern. On the surface, you're a lot like me—a relatively calm person in this madhouse of high-strung prima donnas. Anyway, that first case—I'd never seen you so upset. You may not realize it yet, but you *need* to figure GRID out. It's going to haunt you until you do. And without that sort of passion, it's hard to accomplish much as a clinical researcher. The second reason is you have the smarts and drive to pull it off. There isn't anyone else here who has that combination of talent and motivation, which is why it has to be you."

Kevin's cheeks burned. He tried to maintain a skeptical expression.

"I'm not selfless," Herb added. "Getting grants funded is good for my career too."

Herb offered his hand. Kevin tentatively clasped it.

XII

Making good on his promise, Kevin met Marco after work at a men's clothing store on Union Square. Two weeks earlier, scientists from a local biotech company interested in GRID had taken Kevin to dinner at an expensive restaurant. The next day, he swore to Marco's delight that he would never again go to such a place wearing frayed Rockports. Exploiting this window of opportunity, Marco hinted he might also have use for more than one tie.

Kevin was inspecting loafers when Marco arrived with opinions about color.

"A brown could match your eyes and hair," said Marco, "if it's the *right* brown."

Marco went through the store's entire inventory before settling on three pairs. While Kevin tried them on, Marco's eyes raced back and forth between the shoes and Kevin's face. He decided the first pair had too boxy a shape and the second made Kevin's skin look pasty. Kevin had been hoping he would pick the third pair, which had a matte finish. Shiny leather shoes seemed too pretentious to him.

Marco leaned against a mirror and gave Kevin a thumbs-up sign. Then he frowned.

"This is the tragedy of optics. You can only see your gorgeous green eyes in a mirror, which makes them twice as far away from you as they are from me."

Kevin blew him a kiss.

Next they shopped for ties. Kevin followed as Marco led him through the racks and selected six candidates. Holding each one loosely knotted below Kevin's chin, he described the plusses and minuses of the color, pattern, and brightness, what it did to enhance Kevin's natural beauty. The last tie, yellow silk with diagonal, emerald stripes, particularly appealed to Kevin.

"You like it?"

"*Bello*," said Marco, flaring his nostrils ever so slightly.

Kevin had never been inside a high-end men's clothing store before and was reluctant to leave. Now he wished he could afford a whole new wardrobe.

They grabbed a slice of pizza, and Marco went home, while Kevin drove to a meeting at the public health department. Marco was reading journals in bed when he returned.

"What was that about?" asked Marco.

"Bathhouses."

"Bathhouses? They think saunas will cure GRID?"

"Very funny. The health department thinks bathhouses are breeding the epidemic. They're planning an educational campaign to warn people to use condoms and not share drugs inside those places."

Marco was drowsy and didn't want to hear a lecture. He asked about Kevin's meeting with Herb.

"I gave him a draft of the protocol today," said Kevin.

Marco sat upright.

"And?"

"He liked it…a lot, actually."

"*Fantástico*! This is the opportunity to get the academic credentials you need, *querido*."

Opportunity to screw up, thought Kevin.

Kevin didn't want to talk about the grant. He asked if they were on for lunch tomorrow after Marco's symposium at the Hill. Kevin also had meetings there in the morning. They agreed on the cafeteria at noon. Marco mumbled something about gene splicing and fell asleep.

Kevin lay next to Marco, watching him at rest. He thought of Marco's self-assurance in generating and testing his own scientific ideas. Where did it come from? Was it from growing up with more money and parental love than he had received? Marco's father, an oil company executive, was a conservative, politically and socially. He may have been disappointed on finding out Marco was gay, but he was demonstratively fond of his son and civil to his son's lover. Was getting unconditional affection the key to having confidence?

Kevin had only experimented with mice, never with human subjects, sick people, dying people. It was easy to imagine the mistakes he might make—recruiting inappropriate patients, not following the protocol correctly, errors in his analysis of the data. And if he did it all flawlessly, in the end there still might be nothing of importance to show for the effort.

When Kevin first told Marco about Herb's suggestion they apply for NIH funding, Marco urged him to collaborate. Kevin was hesitant. He had already failed once at grant writing. A nasty argument ensued after Marco, whose view of academic reality was not sanguine, pointed out the facts of life.

"You won't last as a pure clinician," Marco had said. "The university can always replace you with younger, cheaper doctors who are right out of training. How many faculty at City Hospital have you seen promoted on the basis of their clinical work alone? But if you're bringing in grant money, you become necessary. The university needs those overhead dollars."

Kevin knew all this and didn't want to hear it from his lover. Since then, Marco had been circumspect whenever they discussed Kevin's career.

As he tried to fall asleep, Kevin soothed himself with a saving grace. At least he had a firmer grasp on how microbes killed humans than he ever had on how antibiotics killed microbes.

XIII

Early the next morning, Kevin backed his 1969 Rambler sedan into the street, shifted into second gear, and let the engine brake his descent to Castro Street. The car had 120,000 miles on the odometer and numerous dents when Kevin bought it five years ago. Its smooth ride and excellent visibility were nice features, but Kevin had chosen the Rambler because of its reliable straight six, large engine compartment, and seven hundred dollar price tag. After stripping the air conditioner, unnecessary in San Francisco's climate, he had enough room to change the fan belt, clean the head, or replace the starter without having to jack the vehicle up and work underneath it on his back. He could make repairs without getting filthy or lacerating his hands. Space was the ultimate luxury for a mechanic.

Although the Rambler's squared-off frame and clunky, horizontal grille offended Marco's aesthetic sensibility, he had become reconciled to the car. It helped that Kevin didn't object to their exclusively using Marco's Alfa Romeo convertible when traveling together. Kevin wouldn't open the hood of the fragile Alfa unless there was an emergency. Marco frequently had to take it in to the local dealer for repairs. The 1969 Rambler had a track record of outstanding durability—its crowning merit from Kevin's perspective.

As a teenager, Kevin had no effeminate traits. However, his lack of pugnacity or enthusiasm for sports did make him suspect. His disinterest in girls' bodies might have sealed the verdict if not for the mechanic camouflage. Kevin knew his regular presence in the garage and competence with tools saved him from persecution. Yet he hated the charade and was repelled by car culture, which made the Rambler's uncoolness to automobile aficionados another virtue.

The sky had cleared. As Kevin rolled downhill, he saw the Marin headlands in the distance, a richer green after yesterday's rain. He had some time before his appointments on the Hill and detoured into Buena Vista Park. Mothers were pushing strollers in the parking lot. No men were cruising for sex at this hour. Relieved there wouldn't be any awkward encounters, Kevin trotted up a short footpath. At the crest, he saw the twin, cream spires of St. Ignatius Church rise from the valley below. Evergreen ridges in the Presidio formed a backdrop. Just beyond loomed the orange-vermillion towers of the Golden Gate Bridge.

The ocean view through the glass walls on the twelfth floor of the Hill's new medical science complex was also spectacular. Given his second chance in a week to see the Farallon Islands, Kevin didn't mind waiting in the hallway.

Raymond Johnson, an overweight, bald man in his fifties, was twenty minutes late. The immunologist sported a silver goatee and square-rimmed, tortoise shell glasses. Johnson apologized, but he neither smiled nor shook Kevin's hand. He hastily ushered his visitor through a high-ceilinged laboratory into his office.

Kevin knew Johnson's academic niche was investigating rare, inherited immune deficiency syndromes and that one of the instruments he caught a glimpse of could count helper T lymphocytes in blood. Kevin's acquaintances at UCLA had used a similar device in their study about to be published in the *New England Journal of Medicine*. Johnson had the only laboratory on the Hill capable of measuring these unique cells.

The meeting had been Kevin's idea. He called Johnson and proposed they talk about some common interests. Kevin hoped once Johnson heard details of the UCLA report and understood Kevin had a cohort of GRID patients willing to donate a little blood, the immunologist would be thrilled to collaborate. Johnson was well-funded. He could cover the salary of a research assistant for Kevin if he wanted.

Johnson sat in a black leather armchair and directed Kevin to a small plastic seat across from his desk. He leaned back and opened his hands. Kevin took the cue to explain GRID, tossing in the UCLA group's results along with the fact that their paper had been accepted by a prestigious journal. He described his patients at City Hospital then waited for immunologist's eager response.

"I'm surprised the *Journal* accepted the manuscript. As a reviewer, I was unimpressed—such a small sample size. Apparently, the other reviewers were more indulgent. It is an interesting observation, although not very illuminating. The money question is what's driving the loss of T helper cells. Are they destroyed, or is there a failure of production? And what's the underlying cause—a toxin, virus, occult malignancy, or some new pathogen no one has ever seen before?"

"I … I'm not sure," said Kevin, flummoxed. "I don't have a hypothesis yet."

Johnson smiled tightly.

"That would be a good place to start, wouldn't it?" he said.

As Johnson rose to escort Kevin out, he added, "My plate is full right now. Let's discuss this in six months or a year when you have a clearer idea of what you're looking for."

Kevin's next appointment was in the basement of the medical center's oldest building. This meeting had not been initiated by Kevin. A PhD in the oncology division, Rajiv Singh, had called him requesting blood specimens from GRID patients. Kevin queried oncologists at City Hospital but only learned Singh was studying a rare virus that caused leukemia in cats.

Kevin entered a tiny laboratory and found a short, wiry man sitting erect on a stool, writing numbers in a bound notebook. On seeing Kevin, he jumped up, pumped Kevin's hand, and began explaining what the various pieces of equipment measured. The instrument Singh was most proud of could detect reverse transcriptase—a signature enzyme uniquely present in a class of organisms called retroviruses.

"Do you think GRID might be caused by a retrovirus?" Kevin asked.

"It's a reasonable hypothesis. Maybe a retrovirus infects helper T lymphocytes and destroys them. You know what? I could look for reverse transcriptase in the lymphocytes of your patients."

"I can get you blood samples," said Kevin, "But there's going to be a problem. GRID patients have very few T cells."

"Then I'll need a lot of blood," said Singh with a wide grin.

Although Kevin doubted the plausibility of Singh's hypothesis, he had no other opportunities on the horizon for partnering with a basic scientist. He volunteered to submit an institutional review board application, which would permit him to collect blood from his patients and allow Singh to assay the specimens.

"That's exactly what I was hoping to hear you say," said Singh, patting Kevin on the back.

XIV

Kevin was still dejected when he met Marco in the university hospital cafeteria and told him about his meetings with Johnson and Singh.

"So you're batting five hundred, yes?" said Marco.

"I guess so. But it's more like my team acquired a walk-on and lost a top draft choice."

"Oh, I thought you didn't know anything about baseball?"

"Unfortunately, I do. I just don't like talking about it—except when I'm angry."

Marco laughed and stroked Kevin's cheek.

"We'll change the subject. You want to hear about my symposium?"

"Absolutely!"

"I know how science gets you aroused," Marco whispered conspiratorially. "Are you sure you want to discuss it in public?"

Kevin finally smiled.

Marco's symposium was a gathering of two groups with converging interests, his own laboratory at Berkeley, run by the cell biologist Isaac Goldstein, and the Wilmer laboratory on the Hill, which specialized in gene splicing—excising natural genes from a cell and inserting modified ones. In collaboration, the two groups might be the first to create a gene-knockout mouse by removing a normal gene from a mouse stem cell, replacing it with a gene that couldn't function, and growing the altered stem cell into a mature adult mouse in which every cell had the faulty gene.

"Wilmer's lab is in the same boat we are. They're getting scooped by people at Oxford just like we were last month by the Cambridge group that published their paper in *Cell* on the same day Goldstein submitted our paper to *Nature*."

"So the Brits are your common enemy?"

"*Exactamente*! Which is why Goldstein and Wilmer are ready to trust each other enough to join forces."

"So, how did it go?"

"*Querido*, you would have loved it. When I get there, all the Wilmer people are sitting on one side of the room and our people are on the other. Nobody is talking. Complete silence."

"Sounds unpleasant."

"Right. So I sit down right in the middle of the Wilmer group who give me these uncomfortable social smiles. Then the data presentation begins. All the post-docs are edgy, trying to figure out what information is OK to give. They don't want to reveal too much. It was like, how you say, a strip show. Then Goldstein takes the big leap. He puts some very hot, unpublished data on the overhead projector. The Wilmer people's eyes get big. They lick their lips. I'm surprised nobody makes a wolf whistle. Then the anti-Brit jokes begin. After that, everybody is good buddies, sharing all their data."

Kevin laughed.

"The best thing was that nobody picked at details, like whether enough replicate experiments had been done or the controls were adequate. People asked about what the data meant, which showed they really respected each other's work. In no time, we came up with a consensus research plan."

"And you promised you'd be faithful to me."

"Aha! I knew that story would cheer you up."

Well aware of what this collaboration implied for Marco, Kevin exclaimed, "What a fabulous opportunity for you!"

Marco beamed, and Kevin tipped his own coffee cup against Marco's in a celebratory toast.

XV

ALL THE CITY HOSPITAL medicine house staff and faculty had been invited to a party on Saturday night at the home of their newly recruited chief, Ray Hernandez. While riding in the passenger seat as the Alpha Romeo swerved on a narrow, winding road in the East Bay hills, Kevin told Marco the little he knew about Ray. The new chief had grown up in Fresno, the child of Mexican immigrants and, like Kevin, was the first person in his family to go to college.

"So what do you think of him so far?" asked Marco.

"I've only met him once. Mostly, he praised the work I'm doing."

"That's good."

"I don't know. Herb says he's very ambitious, and not just for himself. He's gung ho on academic success for everybody in the department. I wonder if he's softening us up for painful changes."

"Has Gwen met him?"

"Yeah. She likes him. He runs morning report with the residents. She says he doesn't teach by intimidation. That's an anomaly for a chief of medicine."

"Then don't be pessimistic. If I were you, I'd enjoy it while you can. Maybe he's taken one of those new management courses in team building and wants to inspire loyalty instead of fear."

"Right," said Kevin dismissively.

They found the address in a wooded dell. Long shadows and waning sunlight filtered by fir needles fell upon a rambling house with a redwood-shingled roof and cedar-plank walls. At the stairway leading down to the chief's front door, they ran into Rick and Gwen.

Kevin and Marco took turns pecking cheeks with Gwen. Kevin shook hands with Rick, but Rick and Marco gave each other daffy grins. Rick wet his lips and aimed them at Marco's cheek. He missed, planting a kiss on Marco's ear. Both erupted in laughter.

"Uh-oh," said Gwen. "They haven't even started drinking yet."

Peering down the rickety wooden stairway at the chief's house, Rick said, "This is your new boss's house? It looks like something from *The Hobbit*."

"Or Hansel and Gretel," said Gwen, gripping his arm.

"What's a hobbit?" Marco asked.

As Kevin was about to answer, the front door creaked open. All four stepped back.

Herb peeked out and waved at them.

"Come on in," he called merrily. "Ray won't bite."

Kevin and Gwen glanced at each other. Neither had ever seen Herb in such an expansive mood. Taking the initiative, Kevin led the way down the stairs.

Herb showed them into a living room crowded with shelves of books on Native American art and handicrafts. Bright Huichol yarn paintings from northwest Mexico hung on the walls. Cecilia Wu, Ray, and Ray's wife were chatting by the fireplace. The new chief, a portly man with a salt and pepper goatee, was delighted to see them, especially Gwen.

"I hope more house staff are coming," said Ray.

"Don't worry," said Gwen. "They'll all be here. No one I've worked with at City Hospital would miss a free meal."

The doorbell rang, and Ray let in six interns. Marco walked around the room examining the yarn paintings.

"Who's the collector?" he asked.

"Ray," said the chief's wife.

Marco began another question but Herb interrupted, insisting, "Let me get you some wine. You have to catch up with us."

He led the two couples to the kitchen. An array of bottles and long stemmed glasses covered several marble counters.

"I brought this one," said Herb as he opened a magnum and poured five generous servings. "It's from Oregon, the new frontier for boutique Pinot Noirs."

Their conversation moved from wine to geopolitics—the rise of Solidarity in Poland and the Ayatollah in Iran. After a few minutes, Marco wandered back to the living room where he found an encyclopedic collection of world music to explore. A new group of boisterous interns came into the kitchen for wine. Rick drifted away with them.

Herb could knock off a half-liter of wine and hardly feel it. He had already passed that benchmark and noticed Kevin and Gwen were matching him ounce for ounce. Curious about a Zinfandel on the counter from a winery he didn't know, Herb opened the bottle. He filled Kevin's and Gwen's glasses, then his own. They stared at him in surprise.

"It's a party," Herb said with an authority that quickly disintegrated into silly laughter.

"All right!" shouted Kevin, raising his glass.

"This'll be a first," he said in a stage whisper to Gwen. "I don't know anyone who can say they've seen Herb Wu drunk."

Kevin and Herb took long sips then eyed Gwen's full glass. Smiling serenely, she downed a larger amount, then held it up for their inspection. Herb and Kevin took even larger swallows. Herb immediately topped off all three.

Kevin shook his head in wonder.

"You have to be able to drink seriously to make it in academic medicine," Herb pronounced.

"It's a requirement?" asked Gwen.

"It is."

"Perhaps I should reconsider my career plans. I was going to look for a clinic job after residency."

"You should reconsider that," said Herb, no longer facetious. "GRID is going to be the next big thing. Not just because of the epidemic we're dealing with here. Understanding what causes this immune deficiency could revolutionize transplant medicine. Think about it. You could get in on the ground floor."

Kevin nodded in agreement.

"It's a great career opportunity," Herb added mischievously, "for someone with your clinical skills."

Kevin wagged his finger at Herb and said accusingly, "Herb, you are such a slut. First you hit on me. Now you're hitting on Gwen?"

Gwen's laughter was loud and shrill. Herb's face reddened, but he was tickled by Kevin's absurdity.

"Very clever."

"Wait," Gwen interjected. "What'll happen to poor Kevin? You've seduced and abandoned him."

Herb rose to the occasion with faux lugubrious sympathy.

"I feel bad for him. He's hooked now. He'll never be able to stop working. I guess by default he'll end up becoming an academic superstar."

Gwen whooped and clapped. It was Kevin's turn to be embarrassed. He bore it good naturedly until realizing what game they were playing.

"Herb, what you said about Gwen's skills is right on. What do you see in her future?"

Herb put his thumb under his chin and studied Gwen.

"I think Gwen could be more than a master clinician," he said with no mockery. "This disease is eventually going to affect a lot of people. How the country deals with it will be controversial at best. Gwen has the even temper and maturity to communicate to the public about it very effectively."

Gwen's face was crimson, which caused Herb and Kevin to laugh. They slapped each other's backs.

Kevin suddenly wondered where Marco was. He went to the living room and found Marco talking excitedly with Ray in Spanish. Gwen and Herb had followed Kevin, and the three could see Rick through French doors outside on the deck, huddled in a circle of house staff passing a joint. Rick caught Marco's eye and motioned him to join them. Marco glanced around the room. He noticed two young women taking off their coats in the foyer.

Pointing to them, he asked Ray, "Interns or residents?"

Ray went to greet them, and Marco slipped out onto the deck.

"Different strokes," Herb chuckled.

Gwen laughed, but Kevin was no longer paying attention. After four glasses of wine, his mood was swinging down the register to sad reflection.

"Herb," Kevin said. "Remember last summer when you told me about working with doomed young people. I don't get how it doesn't depress you. Unless it actually does and you're incredibly good at hiding it."

"Doomed young people?" Herb echoed blankly.

Once he grasped Kevin wasn't referring to the pot-smoking interns on the deck but was back to GRID again, he said, "It makes me feel…privileged. Don't you, both of you, feel that way?"

Kevin and Gwen hesitated.

"You should. The bad things you see happen to these patients aren't your fault. You have every right to feel good about helping them. There aren't many jobs in the world that are this ethically unambiguous. That's reason enough to be grateful. Hell, this would be God's work, if any of us believed in God."

Kevin and Gwen stared at Herb, their mouths open.

"Sorry for the sermon," said Herb, briskly shaking his head to clear away the fog inside. "I guess it was an anti-sermon."

Before Kevin or Gwen could respond, Herb shepherded them back to the kitchen for refills. He began praising Oregon wines again. But Kevin, intrigued by what Herb had just said, pursued it.

"Herb, why do you assume we don't believe in God?"

"Ha! That's my little secret. I have a sixth sense for it. I'm right aren't I?"

"Yeah," Kevin answered then looked at Gwen.

"How did you know?" she asked.

"It's not magic. I've done my own local survey."

"You survey people about whether they believe in God?" said Kevin, flabbergasted.

"I ask my patients, colleagues too. I'm more curious about that than how they experience physical attraction or jealousy or other transparent emotions. Anyway, I lack the courage to question people I don't know intimately about things you two are probably very comfortable talking about with strangers. I kind of missed out on the '60s."

"Why do you do it?"

"Because I'm fascinated by faith and the lack of it. And most people don't seem to feel that asking about their religious beliefs is intrusive."

"So what have you discovered?"

"Among doctors in the Bay Area, the ones I know, the vast majority don't believe in God. So maybe I was guessing about you and Gwen. The odds were in my favor."

"Herb," Gwen objected,. "from what I've seen, you lead with knowing, not guessing."

"Aha! That's why it's a fascinating question. The state of another's faith isn't knowable. There's no blood test, no radiographic image to confirm its presence or absence. There's just subjective report."

"I beg to differ," said Kevin, his speech now slurred. "Saints are the gold standard for having faith, aren't they? The Catholic Church has objective criteria for sainthood. To be a saint, you can't just say you believe. There has to be evidence, like a miracle others have witnessed."

'Fair enough," Herb agreed, "But only a tiny fraction of people who profess faith in God are saints. Sainthood is a very, very rare condition. You can't generalize from that."

"Good one, Herb," Kevin laughed. "Did you go to a Jesuit college?"

"Wait a second, Herb." Gwen interrupted. "You didn't answer Kevin's question. How did you know neither of us believes in God?"

"I didn't know. I guessed. There's no tell, like in poker. But what's odd is I'm virtually always right. I certainly have a better batting average for that than for making the right diagnosis in the ICU."

"That would be batting a thousand," Kevin protested.

"OK, I'll show you. I'll putting my nickel down that you both believed in God as children and were done with faith by the time you graduated from high school."

Kevin and Gwen's mouths dropped open again.

"Herb," said Gwen. "That's an eerie talent."

Herb had a self-satisfied smile.

"Did you believe in God as kid?" asked Kevin.

"Nope. I come from a long line of atheists. Superstitious ones, but atheists at the core."

"I'm missing something," said Gwen.

"Let me refill your glass," offered Herb.

"No. I've had enough to drink. I meant this conversation is getting too deep for me. I stopped thinking about big ideas when I quit the Socialist Worker's Party in the early seventies. I'm just a simple Valley Girl from Pasadena."

"Oh, right," snorted Kevin.

"You were in the sectarian left?" Herb asked, amused.

"For a few years," Gwen replied airily. "I was horizontally recruited."

Kevin snorted again.

"By my future husband," she said with indignation.

Gwen looked suspiciously at Herb.

"Were you…?"

"No, no," Herb cut her off. "Attempts were made, but they failed."

Kevin snorted again.

"Vertical attempts, Kevin. Dogma has never appealed to me."

"You're over my head now," confessed Kevin as he held out his glass for more wine.

Herb started talking about northern California Zinfandels.

When the three returned to the living room, Rick and Marco were entering through the French doors, followed by Ray.

"You've got to hear this," Ray said to them.

He knelt in front of a shelf of record albums. His eyes, usually at raptor-like attention, were unfocused. On finding the album he wanted, Ray delicately removed a vinyl disc. He showed it to Marco and Rick who both nodded in beatific approval. Kevin snuck behind Marco, peered over his shoulder, and scurried back to Gwen and Herb.

"Ravi Shankar," he tittered.

Ray ceremoniously set the record on a turntable and gently set the needle down. Rick and Marco appeared to be meditating on the spinning disc.

Gwen covered her mouth to muffle her laughter.

The three men stood in a small circle, swaying to the sitar's melody and the tabla's rhythm.

Kevin began guffawing through his clenched teeth.

"I'm leaving," he said. "Ray deserves more respect than this."

"Me too," said Gwen.

But they couldn't move, paralyzed by the sight of their lovers in a stoned séance with their boss.

"Time for coffee," said Herb.

He steered them toward the kitchen.

XVI

Herb finished ICU sign-out rounds early on Monday, picked up Martin at school, ran soccer practice at Dolores Park, then circled back to the hospital. When he arrived at his office, there was an urgent message posted on the door from a name he didn't recognize, an Elliot Reed from the local blood bank. It was almost six o'clock. He dialed the number anyway.

A gravelly voice answered, "Elliot Reed."

"This is Herb Wu from City Hospital returning your call."

"Thanks for getting back to me so quickly. I need to locate the doctor of a patient named Anna Polchevek. Would that be you?"

Herb's heart sank. Sister Anna was a nun in her mid-sixties, a heavy smoker with chronic bronchitis whom Herb had been seeing in lung clinic for the last ten years. She had a ruddy complexion, wore an Isadora Duncan scarf over her habit, and made airy gestures while speaking. She mixed quaint phrases such as "Dear me" or "My goodness" with four letter words for various bodily functions. At her appointments, Sister Anna always inquired about his family.

"Yes," Herb replied, his mouth dry as he recalled an episode of pneumonia she had a year ago. She was severely anemic at the time, and he had ordered a blood transfusion for her.

"Someone from the CDC is tracking GRID cases. He asked me to check if any of the names and birth dates on their list of cases match any of our blood donors."

Reed paused.

What's he waiting for, Herb fumed. Am I supposed to connect the dots so he won't have to say anything else?

"There was one match," Reed said evenly. "Two units of packed red cells from that donor were given to your patient Polchevek last January, apparently before the donor got sick."

Herb expected to hear more. Then he understood Reed was only remaining on the line to verify Herb had received the information.

"So what am I supposed to tell her?"

"You'll have to talk to the CDC and find out what they recommend."

"Shit!" hissed Herb.

"Sorry, I don't know anything about GRID. Obviously, this can't be good, but I can't advise you on what to tell her. Try the CDC."

"Thanks," Herb said icily and hung up the phone.

He paced inside his office until he was calm enough to call the convent. When Sister Anna came to the phone, he apologized for bothering her and asked if she would come to clinic tomorrow. His excuse was to explain the results of her recent x-rays. She agreed and had no questions.

XVII

Kevin spent all Monday in clinic. At dusk, he went across the street to see inpatients where he ran into Gwen. She had been on call since Sunday morning.

"Last progress note," she said, closing a chart. "I'm out of here."

"Get any sleep?"

"I did! A whole, uninterrupted hour."

She didn't seem in a rush, so he brought up her post-residency plans, urging her again to apply for a general internal medicine attending position at City Hospital. Gwen said she had submitted the application and had also scheduled interviews at several public health clinics around the Bay Area.

"Stay here," he pleaded. "The residents take care of the scut, and you'll get to teach them. You might get woken by a phone call in the middle of night once a month, if that. It'll be more fun than working in a public health clinic and way less time away from your family than this is."

"Any job will be easier than this, Kevin. You know I'd love to be hired here. But they're not making any promises. I need other options."

He put a hand to his forehead and gnashed his teeth in an operatic imitation of despair. Gwen's laughter stopped when her pager sounded.

"Damn!" she cried on seeing the number. "The ICU. Five more minutes, and I would have been signed out."

"I'll be there in a bit," he said as she hurried off. "If it's about Miller, I can take care of it."

"You're sweet," she called back to him.

Miller's sedation had been temporarily lightened that afternoon to look for signs of recovery. He became agitated and yanked out his intravenous line. A nurse attempted to re-insert a new one but had no success. Per hospital policy, a medicine resident had to take the next try. If that failed, a surgeon could be called in to dissect down to a vein.

Gwen found Miller motionless except for the periodic rise and fall of his chest each time the ventilator pumped air into his lungs. She scrubbed his forearm with iodine and alcohol, tied a rubber tourniquet above his elbow, opened an intravenous catheter kit, and donned a pair of sterile gloves. Using the tip of her gloved finger, Gwen stroked Miller's skin, hunting for an engorged vein. Finding a promising bulge, she drove in a needle encased inside a white Teflon tube. Blood appeared. Satisfied she was in the right place, Gwen slid the white catheter off the needle into his vein. She was reaching backward to drop the needle in a sharps container when she felt wetness on her ankle. Turning her head, she saw blood dripping from the catheter onto her leg. Reaching back to pick up a piece of tubing, Gwen impaled the fleshy part of her left palm on the needle she was still gripping with her right hand.

Gwen stared at the needle for a numb moment before pulling it out. Eva crossed her mind. She's only twelve years old, Gwen thought. Then all thinking was submerged by a flood of nausea and disbelief.

As Kevin entered the ICU, he saw Gwen leave Miller's room. Her eyes were oddly glazed. She was wandering, not walking purposefully. This was beyond any post-call torpor. She passed him with no sign of recognition. Kevin followed her out the rear door into a resident sleeping room. She collapsed on a bed.

"What's wrong?"

"Unbelievably stupid!" she sobbed. "I stuck myself."

"When?...Miller?"

She nodded yes and began shaking. Kevin sat next to her.

"Let me see."

Gwen opened her palm. A bead of blood covered the puncture wound.

"It went in deep."

She finally looked at him. The apprehension she saw in his face registered.

"Unbelievably fucking stupid!" she screamed.

Kevin disappeared and returned seconds later with a basin of iodine solution. He plunged Gwen's hand into the basin and held it down. The force of his hand on hers, pressing it to the bottom of the sterilizing bath, soothed her.

"Thank you," she said, sniffling.

"Gwen, I know you've heard about IV drug users in New York with the syndrome. But think about it. A lot of immune deficiency patients have been hospitalized in the last two years, and not just here. Lots of hospital staff have had accidental needle sticks. Nobody has gotten sick."

"Kevin, what about that nurse in Los Angeles who…"

He cut her short.

"Urban legend. The CDC has been searching hard and hasn't been able to document a single case in a health care worker who didn't have other risk factors—that's code for being gay or injecting drugs. You don't cruise bars in the Castro, do you? Been shooting heroin or speed with your buddies in the Haight lately?"

Gwen tried to smile.

"I'd be scared too, but think about facts. If whatever causes this disease can be transmitted by an accidental needle-stick, it hasn't happened yet. Which means the risk has got to be very, very low."

She looked at the basin and said, "Kevin, the only thing reassuring me is the smell of iodine."

They lapsed into silence, hands immersed together for the next five minutes. Then she stood up.

"Think that's long enough?"

"Probably. Go home, Gwen. I'll take care of Miller."

"No, I don't want anyone else to know about this. If someone sees you putting in his IV, they'll ask questions."

"I'm not going to tell anyone. Come on, Gwen. You've been here for thirty-six hours. If I tell people you don't feel well and I'm mopping up for you, they won't start wondering if you stuck yourself. They might think you're getting soft or maybe that I'm not really gay and have the hots for you."

She didn't smile.

"I need to go back to work and stop thinking about this."

"Gwen, you need to go home. Get some sleep."

She gave him a look of utter incredulity.

"You've got to be kidding."

"OK. If you can't sleep, at least get some rest."

"Right," she said, washing off the iodine.

"Talk to Rick. He'll be there for you."

She didn't respond. Head bowed, Kevin followed her back into the ICU.

XVIII

THE MOMENT KEVIN OPENED his front door, Marco shouted from the bedroom, "Your mother called."

"Did you talk to her?"

"Briefly."

Marco's evasive reply fueled Kevin's rising panic.

He ran to the bedroom and demanded, "What did she say?"

"She wants you to call her back, tonight. It's an emergency."

"Details?"

"Come on, Kevin. I didn't ask. She doesn't even know who I am."

Kevin blanched. His mother had never done anything like this since he had moved to California. Either his father, Katherine, or one of Katherine's children, must have died or be seriously ill.

His mother didn't answer until the sixth ring.

"Mom! What happened?"

"Kevin, your father went to the doctor today… He has lung cancer."

"Jesus, Mom… I'm sorry."

"They say it can't be cured."

"Is there anything I can do?"

His mother started weeping.

"I wish there was. He says he won't talk to you. I don't know if you should come home or not."

Kevin wanted to be supportive but couldn't control his rising anger. He remembered a stifling August afternoon in the garage, sitting on a brake fluid drum, cleaning used lug nuts and wheel studs with a wire brush while two mechanics carried on a lively conversation.

Kevin had tried not to listen as they mimicked Red Sox radio announcers and described the delectability or ugliness of every woman who walked past the open garage door. They expertly analyzed visible body parts and speculated on what was hidden underneath halter tops or shorts. To Kevin, it was cruel and demeaning. His father was standing right beside them, repairing a transmission. It was impossible that he could be naïve enough not to understand what they were saying. Yet he didn't tell them to stop.

No, Kevin thought, my father doesn't judge other people, just me.

"Will you ask him something?"

"All right."

"Ask him how much more he needs to punish me? Tell him that people don't get life sentences unless they commit murder. I don't think being gay qualifies. Tell him it's time to commute my sentence."

After a long pause, she said, "Say that again, Kevin, so I can write it down."

His catharsis didn't last long. Ten minutes after hanging up, Kevin was distraught. He had no information and doubted it was possible to get any more from his mother. He would have to call Katherine, a most unpleasant prospect. As he dialed her phone number, he tried to be positive. When he last saw her, two years ago, it hadn't been as bad as he anticipated. Though she barely concealed her cold sarcasm, at one point she did ask about his work with genuine interest. Neither of his parents had ever done that. And at the end of her son's confirmation service, she confided in him—another quantum leap. She planned to stop being a stay-at-home mom. Douglas was old enough for her to get a job without feeling guilty. She had enrolled in a training program to become a licensed vocational nurse.

"It's Kevin. I heard about Dad…"

"Well, isn't it nice of you to call."

There was no mistaking her indictment. A wave of resentment passed through him. He made no effort to suppress it. Instead, he took a deep breath and imagined the hair color, freckles, and jaunty tip of the nose they had in common. He thought of what they shared only with each other—growing up beholden to these two people, now so diminished.

"I know I'm not the perfect son who turns the other cheek. But what can I do if he won't talk to me?"

He prepared to be lambasted again.

She surprised him by saying, "OK, that's fair."

"So what should I do, come to Boston and force myself on him?"

Kevin was even more surprised to hear himself make that suggestion.

"Yes!" she said, her voice breaking as she gave in to grief.

He had heard her cry before, behind the closed door of her bedroom, but not since she was a girl and never in his presence.

"He's going to die, isn't he?" she wailed.

"I don't know. I mean yes, but I don't know when. Some people with incurable lung cancer die in a month or two, some live for three or four years. The prognosis depends on the biopsy and x-ray results, and he doesn't want me to know anything. For sure, he won't give his doctors permission to talk to me, and it's a long shot I'll be able to get Mom to ask them the right questions."

"Is there anything I can do?"

"Let me think."

He grabbed on to one redeeming fact. As stubborn a bastard as the old man was, he had provided each of them with a tiny space, eight by ten feet, that was inviolate, exclusively theirs. At age thirty-three, after years of taking care of people who had been given far, far less in their childhood than he, Kevin appreciated that gift.

"Would he let you go with him to his next doctor's appointment?"

"I guess."

"With real information, I could give you an idea of what to expect. How much time he's likely got left. How much radiation or chemotherapy might extend it and what the typical side effects would be if he's offered one of those treatments. Once you know that, you can help him figure out what he wants to do."

"Fat chance he'll want my advice."

Before he could respond, she blurted, "Come home, Kevin. Would you? Please."

Kevin was trapped. Now he had to go. At least he had friends to stay with in Boston. Sleeping under the same roof with his father or Ben would be out of the question.

"OK. You get more information, and I'll see when I can get time off."

Kevin hung up the phone and poured two inches of tequila into a glass tumbler. He downed it while undressing in the kitchen. He went to the bedroom, grabbed the journal Marco was reading, and tossed it on the floor.

After sex, Kevin gave Marco a terse account of his family drama and refused to discuss it further. That door closed, Marco asked how Miller was doing.

"The same. I don't think he's going to walk out of the hospital."

Marco waited for details, but Kevin didn't elaborate.

"So, did you find out anything more about his past? Was he into bathhouses and poppers like the others?"

"I don't know. The friend who brought him to the ER wasn't sure."

Marco nodded solemnly. He knew that nearly all of Kevin's patients, prior to getting sick, had regularly inhaled amyl nitrate sold on the street in glass ampules that could be broken or popped to release the vapor. He also knew the explanation for GRID Kevin secretly favored had to do with the drug's effect of enhancing orgasm by dilating blood vessels in the penis and anus, thus allowing access for vast numbers of sexually transmitted microbes to invade the body and destroy the immune system.

Although Kevin had never gone to a bathhouse, Marco had before they met. Not to the extent of Kevin's patients, a dozen anonymous partners at most. But Marco couldn't tolerate poppers. The one time he sampled the stimulant, he became too nauseated to have sex.

As Kevin looked into Marco's eyes, the tequila resurged in his head with the promise of sleep.

He resisted it long enough to kiss Marco on the lips and say, "Don't worry, baby. We're safe."

XIX

Gwen got home at eleven. Rick and Eva were already asleep. She sat at the kitchen table, arms wrapped around her chest, trembling.

I need a plan, she thought. No, two plans. One for dealing with the fear. Another for what I'm going to say to Eva and Rick. She started on the latter, thinking of words that wouldn't suck the three of them into a self-perpetuating cycle of anxiety. An hour later, she had made no progress.

Eva's backpack lay on the table. Gwen noticed a folded piece of paper spilling out the top. She opened it. The first line was in someone else's handwriting, the second in Eva's.

"Why him?"

"Because there isn't any other boy I like."

"You're wasting your time."

"Why?"

"Because of the way he looks at Carla. Sorry, he doesn't look at you that way."

Gwen was afraid to put the note back. Refolding it would be handling a razor blade by the cutting edge. She was ashamed and instantly realized shame was a convenient way to erase the glimpse she just had of Eva's vulnerability. Gwen stared at the stove, ignoring the note on the table, denying it would pop into her mind whenever she was unguarded, a reminder she might not be there when Eva finally did need her mother's comfort.

Gwen climbed into bed and rustled the sheets. Rick didn't wake up. What could she tell him anyway, besides the essential facts. She had been stuck, deep in the hand, with a bloody needle from an immune deficiency patient. Of course, he would understand the implications. She might die as a result. They would have to take precautions for his protection. More than ever, she was glad they weren't married. She couldn't tolerate the thought of being a burden, seeing him bear the responsibility for taking care of her.

Gwen ruminated over what to say, if anything, then lost the will to continue, approached sleep, became alert again, looked at the clock, felt dread twisting her intestines, and weighed her options once more. By two in the morning, she knew this wasn't going to work. She had to deal directly, definitively, with her own fear before considering what to tell Eva and Rick.

She could think of only one solution. She shut her eyes tightly and forced herself to imagine Eva distraught, using drugs, casual sex, anything to fill the emptiness after her mother's death. A great moan passed through her, loud enough to stir Rick. She cast out this vision of a desolate Eva. She was absolutely certain she had the resolve never to let it back in.

Suddenly, she could think rationally. Gwen understood that in the worst case scenario she would survive until Eva graduated from high school, which was enough. It was futile and dangerous to think of the future beyond Eva turning eighteen. And there was no sense in telling Eva about the needle-stick. That could only do her damage.

Rick was sitting up, looking at her with concern.

"What's going on?" he asked.

"I stuck myself…"

She had begun calmly but now lost control.

"With a bloody needle," she sobbed, "from a GRID patient."

This is the last time I cry, she swore silently.

Rick breathed in and in. His diaphragm was in spasm. He couldn't exhale. He couldn't even speak. He touched her tentatively, afraid she might become hysterical.

Gwen knew he hadn't a clue about what she needed him to say or do. This had to make him feel inadequate, if not somehow at fault. She took his hand and squeezed.

"Jesus!" he expelled.

He reached for her and said. "I'm here for you, baby."

Gwen curled into him and whispered, "Please say that again."

XX

KEVIN AWOKE IN THE middle of the night and couldn't go back to sleep. He sat at his desk calculating and typing, trying not to think about Gwen or Boston. Four hours later, he had a headache. His protocol, he decided, was at the point where "better is the enemy of good." He had learned this shibboleth from the mechanics in his father's garage and still believed in its wisdom.

Marco, who had arisen at six to run at a nearby high school track, returned soaked in sweat.

"Nice run?" Kevin asked, rubbing his scalp to ease the pain.

"*Así, así*. I didn't push myself today."

"No? What was your time?"

"Thirty-five minutes, *más o menos*."

"Christ, Marco! That's under a six-minute-mile pace. You don't call that pushing yourself?"

"Sweetheart, I'd be happy to jog ten-minute miles with you. Just two miles, three times a week, would be so, so good for your body."

"Marco, you knew when you met me I'd never be buff."

"I love your body. You know I don't want muscles. I want health. You've got a family history of coronary disease, and you're already in your thirties."

"I have a headache, too. Let's change the subject...Oh, my God! I forgot to tell you about Gwen."

After Kevin finished recounting the details of her accident, Marco asked, "Is there anything we can we do?"

"I wish, but it's not the sort of thing you can bring over a casserole for."

"What?"

"It's an American custom. Sorry, that was a stupid thing say. The truth is I don't know what to do. Wait until she's ready to talk about it, I guess."

"You think they might want to know how we deal with the uncertainty?"

"That's not a good idea. We can ignore it. She can't. She's got a kid."

Marco turned sarcastic.

"I could tell her about your *macho* attitude. *Que será, será*, eh?"

"Marco, come on. If anyone's anxious here, it's me."

"Ignoring the sword over our heads was my idea?"

"Jesus, Marco! I worry enough already. I don't need to add that to the list. Anyway, there's nothing we can do now, besides staying monogamous, and that still works for me."

Marco leaned against Kevin and massaged his neck.

"Don't get upset, sweetheart. We're on the same page."

At noon, Kevin was leaving clinic when his pager beeped and displayed the ICU phone number. He had heard "Code Blue" announced on the intercom earlier and hoped it wasn't Miller.

Kevin reached the ICU breathless from running up four flights of stairs. He found Gwen standing over Miller, her arms extended, her palms on his sternum. She rocked downward at one second intervals, counting the compressions aloud. As soon as she saw Kevin, she let her medical student have a turn.

"Miller arrested twenty minutes ago. I was just waiting for you or Herb to OK pronouncing him dead."

He glanced at the flat line on the monitor and agreed they should give up. With no heart activity after this long, there was zero chance of survival. Gwen signaled her student to stop. She stated the time of death for the nurse keeping the resuscitation log.

As they walked back to the unit's central work station, Gwen looked straight ahead.

"You OK?" he said.

"I'm fine, Kevin." she said with enough force to make it clear he shouldn't ask again.

He watched her write a final order in Miller's chart and depart. As the door was closing behind her, Tom Redding appeared. Kevin saw him talk to the first nurse he encountered. His posture sagged with the news of Miller's death.

Kevin offered his condolences and escorted him to the bedside.

"I'm so sorry." Kevin said. "We did everything we could…"

"I have no doubt of that. What you people are doing here is tremendous. But I have some questions. I've been looking into GRID. What the CDC is reporting makes it sound like an epidemic. If the number of patients is doubling every couple of months, isn't that an epidemic?"

"We think so."

"And the federal government, what are they doing? I've heard there's no research going on, other than the CDC tracking cases."

"Not yet."

"That's not right. It wasn't how the feds responded to the Legionnaires' outbreak. We'll be talking to some congressmen, pressuring them to lean on NIH. And by the way, the mayor is going to beef up funding for your clinic."

Kevin met Herb in the cafeteria. On sitting down, he handed Herb his revised protocol, fifteen pages long. While Herb read, Kevin concentrated on his sandwich.

When Herb turned the last page, he said, "This is perfect, Kevin."

He thumbed through his leather-bound pocket calendar.

"We have plenty of time before the submission deadline. I'll just add a little more background, tidy up the rationale, reference a few of my own papers, put in preliminary data from the patients we've scoped so far, stick in some boiler-plate text and window dressing…Oh, the budget. What do you think, how about thirty percent of your salary for three years?"

"Is it OK to ask for that much?"

"If we ask for less, the reviewers might not believe you're committed to doing the work."

"Herb, that would be fantastic! I could quit doing general medicine clinic and just see immunodeficiency patients. That would give me enough time to do this study and get other ones started."

"Good. That's what NIH salary support is supposed to do. Thirty percent it is."

Herb scribbled numbers in the margins of the document then looked up curiously.

"Other ones? Do you have any specific ideas in mind?"

"Actually, there is one I've been meaning to run by you. It's for an interventional trial."

"Really?"

Herb chuckled to himself, thinking the hook had indeed been set.

"Tell me about it."

Kevin pitched a proposal for treating GRID patients with interferon, a molecule naturally made by human white blood cells in response to viral infections such as influenza. Herb knew that a biotech company had devised a method for synthesizing interferon and was developing it as an experimental treatment for cancer. He liked Kevin's idea. It made sense to explore whether the agent could reverse the progressive loss of lymphocytes in GRID.

"It's a plausible hypothesis. It ought to be tested. But you'll need a different mentor than me. An oncologist experienced in treating cancer with interferon, like Sprinson at the VA, would be a good choice."

"I'll call him."

"And you'll need a lab-based collaborator, an immunologist who can measure helper T cells in blood samples."

"Yeah," Kevin muttered, frowning. "That might be a problem."

XXI

Laurie Hampton, the newest nurse on the ICU staff, noticed Herb enter the unit. She looked at her watch. Ten minutes, she thought, before he starts rounding with the residents.

Laurie had met Herb in the ER a year ago when a heroin overdose arrived in cardiac arrest. The resuscitation wasn't going well, and the ICU team had come to assist. Laurie suggested they try a different medication. She had mentioned it earlier to the ER attending who hadn't bothered to respond. Herb not only agreed, he punctuated his approval with a thumbs-up sign, rare praise coming from a doctor, which was why eleven months later, desperate to leave the ER, she arranged to be transferred to the ICU.

More than a tad overweight, Rubenesque according to her lover Tanya, Laurie was from southern Illinois. She had worked in a Carbondale hospital and lived alone for twenty years before admitting to herself that she wanted to be with a woman. Not possible, she felt, in small-town Illinois, so she moved to San Francisco. Now in her forties and in love for the first time, she had never been happier. Until a recent flail in the ER with an intoxicated, combative patient.

An intern had drawn blood and was holding the uncapped syringe when the man swung at him. The intern jerked back reflexively. The uncapped needle jammed into Laurie's thigh, an inch deep. There were rumors the patient had the new gay-related disease, that it might be transmitted by infected blood. She had been sent to Employee Health, given vaccines for tetanus and hepatitis, and advised to return if she became sick.

She had to talk to someone soon, she realized. The fear was paralyzing her. She couldn't keep working in this state. Transferring to the ICU had helped, for a while. Then the nightmares recurred. Fanged maggots invaded her blood stream. They were breeding inside her spleen and preparing attacks on other vital organs. She awoke gasping, her chest pounding.

Herb was alone at the sink, washing his hands. Guessing this would be her best chance, Laurie approached him.

"Can I speak with you—privately?"

"Sure."

Taking note of her dilated pupils and the droplets of sweat at her temples, Herb led her to an empty room.

"What's up, Laurie?"

She stammered. Her tongue felt too thick. Averting her eyes, she described the needle-stick incident.

"And all Employee Health told you was to come back if you get sick?" Herb asked, attempting to suppress his outrage. "They gave you no information about the patient, didn't offer you any counseling?"

"They said I should have my blood checked for hepatitis in a month. That's all. I'd really appreciate your advice."

Herb heard no complaint, only apprehension and the desire to preserve her dignity. She clearly didn't want to be a victim.

"Let me see what I can find out. I'll talk to our GRID expert, Kevin Bartholomew, and get back to you tomorrow. OK?"

"That would be great, Herb."

He wanted to give her a sympathetic touch. But concerned she might think it inappropriate, he didn't act on the impulse. She left to start an intravenous medication.

Herb pretended to skim through a chart. With Laurie's presence no longer threatening to arouse untamable feelings, he reconsidered that decision. Inappropriate? What a pathetic excuse.

Herb first conceded there was a problem during his residency. He tried psychotherapy but found the mandatory self-revelation humiliating. After seeing how senior physicians at NIH maintained a balanced distance in dealing with young leukemic patients and their distraught families, an era of rationalization began. Despite his incapacity for expressing strong emotions, Herb felt them deeply and was well attuned to how others showed them. He determined by trial and error the minimum amount of emotional juice needed to appear credibly caring to people facing devastating loss. He gave only the minimum, just enough so he wouldn't be drained and depressed for days afterwards. Damage control, he told himself. When in a charitable mood, he was reassured that he hadn't completely succumbed to the impediment. At moments like this, however, he couldn't avoid the truth. He was bottled up inside and making no substantive effort to change.

Once rounds were over, Herb drove to the airport. He reached the gate of an inbound flight from New York City as his mother was walking out the jet way. He hadn't seen Chen for a year and was delighted to discover her lush white hair and vigorous gait hadn't changed. In a few days she would turn seventy, he marveled.

"You didn't need to come, Herb. I could have taken the shuttle. Don't you have to be at work?"

"I've got time to drive you to the house. You can surprise the kids when they get home from school."

Chen was elated, but only briefly.

"Oh," she said mournfully, "The happiness those darlings give me makes me sad your father never got to know them."

He had heard this plaint before and was confident his father, if he were still alive, would pay little, if any, attention to his grandchildren. He didn't doubt his mother's unconditional love for Allison and Martin. He felt guilty about how long it had been since Chen last saw them and had to remind himself this was her issue with Cecilia's family that kept her from visiting more often.

"Any plans for while I'm here?"

He understood her real question.

"Cecilia's parents are out of town, so it'll just be Will and Andrea coming for dinner on Saturday night."

Chen was pleased. She liked these old friends of Herb and Cecilia. Though he was quite sure she had chosen to like them before she ever met them, based solely on his telling her they both had parents who belonged to the elite, educated class in China prior to immigrating. Socializing with Cecilia's family, on the other hand, had always made her uncomfortable. His wife's great-great-grandparents had been peasants in China, lucky enough to escape to California when workers were imported to build the transcontinental railroad.

As Herb drove from the airport parking lot to the freeway, he brooded over an incident that happened during his mother's first trip to San Francisco. Cecilia and he had brought her along to a red egg and ginger banquet in honor of a cousin's newborn baby. The sheer number of Chang relatives and their raucous chatter made Chen ill at ease. She spoke little until the conversation shifted to the People's Republic of China. Chen said it was tragic how Mao was destroying the world's oldest civilization. Another cousin, a radical college student, retorted that Mao's rule had ended the world's longest history of state-sanctioned slavery. This interchange quieted all cross-table talk. The young man took the attention as a cue to pull out Mao's *Little Red Book* and quote aloud from the Chairman's sayings. The older Changs quickly tired of his rant and ordered him to shut up. As soon as they moved on to other topics, Chen asked Herb if they could leave. Now he wondered if her discomfort with the Changs was less about class and political differences than about seeing a close-knit, argumentative family in action.

Herb was back in clinic by four to meet Sister Anna. He hid his clenched fists under the desk as he calmly told her about the source of the donated blood she had received. Her equanimity was unshaken by his explanation of GRID, which delicately alluded to its primary mode of transmission and acknowledged the disease might be transmitted by blood as well.

When he was done, she asked, "How likely is this to do me in before the lungs go?"

Herb opened his hands helplessly.

"You're more worried than me," Sister Anna scolded. "Are you afraid the bishop will sue you for poisoning a daughter of the church who's still in her prime?"

He couldn't smile.

"I'm afraid of losing you," he confessed.

"That's most flattering."

Mired in despair, he couldn't stop frowning.

"Herb, I know what's coming. The modus operandi doesn't matter to me."

He knew that Sister Anna had worked for years as a pastoral counselor, that she probably had more experience talking with people about dying than he did. She might also be right about the ineluctable obliteration of her airways trumping any complications of GRID. None of this helped him.

"I feel responsible. Hell, I *am* responsible. I made the decision to give you that transfusion."

"And it would be a terrible thing for you to bear if I was a young person, not already stricken by an incurable disease. But really, Herb, what difference does this make? I certainly don't blame you."

Her eyes sparkled as she added, "If you feel so guilty, perhaps you should talk to someone, a professional, about it."

Herb managed a weak smile.

XXII

Kevin walked to the clinic waiting room doorway and called the first name on his afternoon schedule, a new patient, Tommy Paulson. A short, slender man with thinning brown hair stood up. Kevin introduced himself and ushered the man into an exam room.

Once they were seated, he affably asked, "What brings you here?"

Speaking to the floor, Mr. Paulson said, "I read about you in the *Advocate*. You're the gay cancer specialist, right?"

"I am," said Kevin, deferentially subduing his usual upbeat approach. "Why don't you tell me about yourself, where you're from, what you do, whether you've ever been hospitalized or take any regular medications. Then we'll get into the concerns that brought you here."

Tommy Paulson was shy. He gave an abbreviated account of growing up in rural Pennsylvania and obtaining an engineering degree in college. He was thirty, lived alone, and worked for a construction firm. He had never been in a long-term relationship. There had been no health problems, other than an episode of gonorrhea, until a flu-like illness began six months ago. The fatigue had persisted. Then he started having diarrhea. He had already been to one doctor who ordered blood and stool tests which failed to reveal a cause for his symptoms. Two weeks ago, he noticed a white substance coating the roof of his mouth and made the appointment to see Kevin.

A physical exam confirmed Tommy had thrush. The lab results he showed Kevin included a lymphocyte count well below the lower limit of normal. There was going to be bad news to give, but this was not the time. Kevin needed to go through the motions of ordering and interpreting more tests. He needed more contact to establish credibility and rapport before Tommy would believe his prognosis and trust Kevin to help make the rest of his life as bearable as possible.

Though pressed by his new patient to make a diagnosis on the spot, Kevin stood his ground.

"There are viral and parasitic infections, some autoimmune diseases too, that can cause a prolonged illness like this. Let's find out for sure what we're dealing with, OK?"

Tommy was mollified, which Kevin used as an opportunity to ask what drew him to engineering. Tommy described the blueprints he created, the pride that came from seeing his drawings transformed into office buildings and industrial plants.

Kevin imagined a ten-year-old Tommy spending rainy days assembling an Erector Set. He envisioned a boy so adept with his fingers he wouldn't be frustrated by working hex nuts onto bolts in a tight space. Kevin had done it as a child. He hadn't minded the repetitious fabrication—constructing girders, tying and cross-bracing them into a bridge, even adding a second or third tier. Anticipating the completion was half the fun.

Kevin gave Tommy a return appointment slip and was about to say goodbye when he sensed his patient wasn't finished.

"Any other questions?"

Tommy declined. He started to leave but paused at the doorway.

"I don't get it. I mean, yeah, I tried the bathhouse scene a few times. It wasn't for me. I'd only had sex with a couple of people before that, and there's been nobody since. And I never, ever used poppers. I just don't get it. There are all these men who've been at the glory holes forever. They're fine. Why me?"

Kevin had no answer.

XXIII

ON SATURDAY, ONE OF the chief residents rounded with Gwen's interns so she could have a day off. Rick was already out running when she awoke. Eva wouldn't be up for hours. Gwen got of bed and made coffee. She sat at the kitchen table, mulling over the strategy she had settled on. The more she considered it, the sounder it seemed. She was going to be living for her daughter and lover now. Their inner peace mattered more than hers. She could be oblivious to the uncertainty of her own fate as long as she was sure they were all right. It was a relief to have clarity at last. Gwen was ready to put her plan into action.

She went to a neighborhood pharmacy. Avoiding all eye contact, she purchased a packet of condoms. When she came home, Rick was at the kitchen table, grading history quizzes. She sat next to him, resting her head on his shoulder. He gave her a long inquiring look and returned to work. She sat still, trying to be mindless, unable to sustain it. She stroked his calf. He stretched languidly. Her hand drifted to his back. He kept marking papers. She kissed him on the neck.

Rick let go of his red pen. They rose as a unit, moved to the bedroom, undressed, and lay down wrapped around each other. She wanted sex but was too scared to take pleasure in it. Rick felt the tension in her thighs, the absence of her familiar abandon. He stopped moving. Gwen nestled under his arm. She began to cry softly.

"It's going to be OK," he said. "We'll get through this. We will."

Looking up, she saw his wet eyes and believed him.

XXIV

KEVIN AND MARCO ALSO slept in on Saturday morning. They awoke to bright sunlight and after breakfast drove north to a trailhead in Point Reyes. The fog here hadn't burned off yet. Fortunately, the path they chose stayed close to the floor of a winding, forested canyon, protecting them from cold sea breezes. By the time the trail climbed to an exposed, grassy plateau, they were warm from their brisk pace and invigorated by the sudden drop in temperature.

Two hours after leaving the car, they arrived at a bluff overlooking the ocean. The hike had flown by for Kevin. Not a muscle or joint was protesting. He was energized. Maybe Marco is right about exercise, he thought.

Marco ran the last hundred yards to the cliff's edge. He searched the water below and waved excitedly. His thick eyebrows were bouncing in delight. Kevin caught up with him and faced an expanse of gray, wind-battered sea. Marco pointed to a band of clear water where dark shapes, diamonds and crosses, floated beneath the surface.

"Bat rays and leopard sharks," Marco exulted.

Staring in awe, Kevin said, "Holy Mother …"

"Holy what?"

Kevin laughed and spread his arms wide.

"This is what the church wants," he proclaimed.

Marco looked puzzled.

"For us to be dazzled and spellbound before God's great creation."

"*Querido*, I think their first priority is having us be passive and guilty so we're easy to manipulate."

"That's only because they decided to raise fortunes and build cathedrals instead of celebrating mass in places like this that would have cost nothing."

"*Dios mio*. He's a visionary now. Move over Joan of Arc, make room for Saint Kevin of Distressed Automobiles."

On their way home, they stopped at the road's high point to view a rolling carpet of round hills, lush early this year from a series of October storms. The late afternoon sun was behind them as they silently watched swells of grass slowly change hue from deep emerald to a soft pine shade.

This was how Kevin had always imagined serenity would feel.

"What are you thinking?" he asked Marco.

"That winter is my favorite season here. These green hills, they go on forever, full of possibility."

Kevin kissed him on the lips.

A Plague, 1984

I

KEVIN WAS DRIVING TO City Hospital, headed in the opposite direction from the downtown hotel where he was supposed to be lecturing in two hours at the department's annual conference on new developments in internal medicine. Ray Hernandez had told him four hundred physicians were registered to attend. He had never spoken to so large an audience of doctors and had been worrying about it all week, until paged last night by an intern. His clinic patient, Tommy Paulson, had been admitted. Now Kevin's anxiety was about him.

This was Tommy's third hospitalization for dehydration in a month. The cause was a gut parasite resistant to all available drugs. Maximum doses of constipating medications couldn't prevent him from having ten to twenty watery stools a day. After his last admission, Kevin arranged for a home care company to give him continuous intravenous fluid infusions in his apartment. Despite such aggressive treatment, Tommy was severely dehydrated again. Kevin had to prepare him for the end.

As soon as Kevin entered the room, Tommy saw the resignation on his face. Before he could say hello, Tommy began wailing.

He sat on the bed and held Tommy's hand.

"I am so, so sorry…"

Kevin considered praising Tommy for how courageously he had struggled, what an inspiration he had been to everyone in the AIDS program, but these expressions of heartfelt empathy and battle metaphors were becoming trite. In any case, he had learned that his initial take on Tommy's capacity for insight was an underestimation. No cliché would ring true for him. Kevin needed a new approach to end-of-life conversations—a more creative, more authentic one.

To keep doing this work, Kevin was realizing, he had to be sure he was providing comfort, which at a minimum meant giving his dying patients the respect of a spontaneous reaction.

An idea came. Kevin lay down on the bed.

"Hey, Tommy. Tommy," he sang softly like a lullaby.

This seemed to calm Tommy.

"Let's try something," Kevin suggested. "It's a thought experiment."

"A what?"

"You'll see. Tell me about your favorite childhood memory, one that makes you feel really, really good."

Tommy concentrated.

"OK. Playing tag on the bank of the Susquehanna River."

"Why's it your favorite?"

"The warm sunlight. Cool, thick grass you could almost bounce on. After tag, I jumped in the water. I was completely free then. Now I can't even get out of bed on my own."

"Perfect! Now, can you to imagine that place in the year 1900?"

"I guess so. It probably wasn't much different than when I was kid."

"Can you imagine *yourself* there in 1900?"

"Me? At the Susquehanna?"

"Yes, in 1900, not 1950, a lifetime before you were born, even before your parents were born."

"I'll try…"

"Tell me what you're doing."

Tommy's limbs relaxed as he thought.

"Floating on the river, being carried downstream by the current."

"Are you afraid?"

"No, the water's buoying me up."

Kevin patted his knee.

"That's where you're going, my friend. You're going to be part of that river again."

"Huh… Hey, that's a nice trick, Doc. It's less scary thinking about it your way. Guess I've already been dead, haven't I."

"Exactly! Can you be OK with that?"

"It's gotta be better than this."

Kevin kissed Tommy on the forehead and said goodbye.

II

KEVIN'S BELLY STARTED TO cramp as he watched Ray Hernandez stride toward the podium. Scanning the hotel ballroom, he couldn't see an empty seat. There had to be at least five hundred people here. He became aware of another unpleasant sensation. Sweat was running down his flanks.

Kevin had spoken to audiences of two hundred doctors. Ray had told him speaking to two thousand wouldn't be any more intimidating. From the podium, he explained, you can make out at most two hundred faces. The rest are a blur in the background. Kevin was not reassured.

"It's my great honor to welcome you," said Ray, beaming with charm.

Kevin focused on his boss's amplified voice, confident and mellifluous. He hoped he could mimic it. Although he had been wary when the new chief of medicine took over at City Hospital, unsure of what it would mean for his fledgling career, it was hard not to like Ray. Especially once it was apparent that Ray wanted to see him succeed as much as Herb did. This kind of regard from an older man had been outside his experience before coming to San Francisco. Even Kevin's own father had shown little interest in what he might make of himself.

"Our opening lecture will be given by one of the world's experts on a new disease that has captured the medical community's attention, Acquired Immune Deficiency Syndrome—AIDS for short. Many of you know the syndrome by its former name, GRID, which was changed when it became obvious the disease is not exclusively 'gay-related.'"

Kevin's heart was racing. He tried thinking of someplace tranquil. Ray's home came to mind.

"Our speaker, Kevin Bartholomew, leads the AIDS program at City Hospital, a new division of our department of medicine which I established because the number of patients with this condition is growing so rapidly in

San Francisco. But take note. AIDS won't be limited to a few 'liberal' US cities. It will become an important disease globally—as you'll hear when Kevin shows you data emerging from other parts of the world."

In a last ditch attempt to control his anxiety, Kevin visualized Ray's collection of yarn paintings, the tremulous combinations of bright colors, plush zigzag, and round shapes—the sun, a man aiming a bow and arrow, peyote cactus. But it was time to walk to the podium now.

It'll be over soon, he thought grimly.

"We're also proud of Kevin's creative productivity. This year alone, he's published papers in the *Annals*, the *Journal of Infectious Diseases*, and…"

Ray savored the moment, keeping the best for last, a feather in his cap for having supported Kevin from the beginning.

"The *New England Journal of Medicine*," he boomed.

Stuttering, Kevin thanked Ray. He stared at a Post-It sticking to his palm. Scribbled on it was the first sentence of his talk. The words made sense, but he didn't know what to say next. He pressed a button that advanced a slide carousel at the back of the room. A sketch appeared on the screen depicting the structure of a novel retrovirus named HTLV-III. Laboratories in Paris, San Francisco, and NIH had just simultaneously discovered it in lymph nodes removed from patients with AIDS. Those with the syndrome of milder signs and symptoms that often preceded AIDS—AIDS-related complex, or ARC—also had HTLV-III in their lymph nodes.

Speaking to the screen, the words flowed. Kevin guided the audience through a series of figures that demonstrated how the retrovirus reproduced itself. Logically, effortlessly now, he described HTLV-III tricking human helper T lymphocytes into swallowing it and, once inside, hijacking the cells into making new viral particles.

His listeners were intrigued and a bit frightened by this devious pathogen that targeted the cell most responsible for coordinating human immune defenses against invading microbes. Kevin could have been telling a ghost story at a campfire as he explained the current hypothesis for the source of the epidemic. There was a reservoir of HTLV-III in a remote central African forest from which the retrovirus had crossed from chimpanzees to humans, who then transported and transmitted it around the world.

The room hushed when he said patients with AIDS were the tip of the iceberg. A larger population of people with ARC and a far, far larger population of asymptomatic HTLV-III- infected individuals might all eventually progress to AIDS. Worse, this was a global epidemic. The number of new AIDS cases in the Americas, Europe, and Australia was doubling every six months. His bleakest slide estimated that a quarter of a million people in the United States alone were already carrying the virus.

He ended with three "good news" slides. First, the risk of viral transmission to health care workers exposed to AIDS patients' blood appeared to be very, very low. Only one proven case had been documented, a nurse in England who had no risk factors other than an accidental needle-stick. Second, a diagnostic antibody test was being developed. As soon as it was proved to identify retrovirus carriers accurately, any infected blood donors could be screened out, eliminating transmission of the retrovirus by transfusions. The antibody test could also be used as a public health tool to prevent further sexual transmission. Third, and most important, understanding the structure of HTLV-III had given bench scientists targets for designing drugs to treat the infection and halt the immune system damage it caused.

Kevin finished by thanking Ray for the invitation to speak. He glanced at the red digital timer below the podium. It read twenty-nine minutes. He pressed the reset button, gratified his lecture was done before the timer reached thirty and a light would begin to flash. He heard a crackling din like surf. He looked up from the timer to see everyone in the hall clapping.

III

KEVIN STAYED FOR THE rest of the conference. During the breaks, he received many compliments on his talk. Returning to an empty apartment didn't sour his mood. He opened a beer and put his feet up on the kitchen table. His only regret was Marco's absence. Earlier that week, Marco's mother had been in a car crash. It still wasn't clear she would survive. When Kevin came home, there was a telegram from Mexico City on the doorstep. Marco said her prognosis was better but not good enough for him to be flying back any time soon.

Pacing through the two-bedroom apartment, Kevin wished he could share his elation. Gwen would be the perfect person—someone he was sure wouldn't be threatened by his success. But it was Friday night. She would be with her family. She had a life outside work.

In the living room, he studied a framed print, enlarged from a photo Marco had taken of Pico de Orizaba, the highest mountain in Mexico. Marco had climbed to the summit on his eighteenth birthday. Suddenly exhausted, Kevin sprawled on the couch.

I should be humble, he thought, not jubilant. Herb and Ray made this possible. I happened to be in the right place at the right time, and they gave me the chance to do something worthwhile—incredibly worthwhile.

Looking at the photograph, he wondered if Marco really would share his joy. Kevin was already traveling a lot to attend scientific meetings and confer with pharmaceutical companies interested in drug development. Now he'd probably be invited to give talks in other cities, maybe other countries. He'd be getting more requests for interviews from reporters. The demands on his time would increase. Exponentially increase, he realized. How would he handle that? Would he become arrogant? He had seen it occur in others on the academic medicine fast track. And even if he was a paragon of humility, would Marco be threatened by his rising star? Marco had seemed distant recently. What if their relationship couldn't survive such a major change in status?

Kevin got up and rummaged through the bathroom cabinet for Marco's bottle of Halcion, prescribed months ago while he was churning out his first NIH grant application and suffered from insomnia. Kevin washed a tablet down with another beer.

IV

HERB WAS ALSO AT a conference, in Washington DC. His day began with a jog through Rock Creek Park. The trail he followed was overgrown. Bottomland weeds going to seed and tree branches thick with deciduous leaves pressed in on him. Though he had started out at sunrise, it was already unseasonably warm and humid for September.

"What a jungle," he complained, swatting bugs away from his face.

Herb was not enjoying this run. The heat was debilitating. Odd, he thought, it didn't bother me fifteen years ago. Do I sweat less now? He did not want to entertain the fact that he had just been jogging nine-minute miles, not the seven-minute miles he once ran here. Half an hour later, Herb was back in his hotel room, showering. Afterwards, shaving in front of a mirror, he saw new gray hairs and was more discouraged.

The meeting had been organized by the American Association of Blood Banks in response to pressure from the CDC, several congressmen, and a patient advocacy group. They were all urging the AABB to implement a national policy of screening volunteer blood donors for antibodies to hepatitis B virus. A blood test that could accurately identify and exclude potential donors infected with HTLV-III was being developed but was not yet available. However, studies showed that most individuals infected with HTLV-III had previously been infected with hepatitis B and had antibodies to the latter virus that could be detected in serum. Screening donors for hepatitis B antibodies and excluding those who tested positive could go a long ways toward preventing HTLV-III transmission by transfusion.

Herb had been invited at the CDC's request. As an AIDS expert, the director of an ICU where hundreds of transfusions were administered annually, and co-author of an article on transfusion-related AIDS, he was a bargain for the CDC—a triple-threat consultant for the price of one federally discounted coach airline ticket.

Though he was wearing a wool sports coat, Herb shivered in the hotel conference room. The flickering fluorescent lights, loud humming of air conditioners, and lack of windows were disorienting. To clear his mind, he speculated about the other attendees. It wasn't difficult to deduce who was from the AABB. The CDC folks wore rumpled clothes, had glasses instead of contact lenses, and carried worn leather satchels stuffed with documents. The reporters looked skeptical. The advocacy people were fuming. That left a scattering of pasty, clean-shaven, white men in suits, sweating despite the cold air.

The conference opened with a frontal attack by the CDC—an announcement that their field investigations had verified eighty AIDS cases caused by contaminated transfusions. They projected a graph of solid black bars representing new transfusion-associated AIDS cases, which had quadrupled in the last two years. On the right hand side were gray bars representing estimates for future years that towered over the black bars.

In addition to the unlucky cancer patients, individuals undergoing surgery, and trauma victims who had received infected blood, there was a group which had been much harder hit—hemophiliacs dependent upon frequent transfusions of concentrated clotting factors. Without these Factor VIII transfusions, the slightest injury caused painful, crippling bleeding inside their joints. Factor VIII could only be obtained by pooling donated plasma, thus multiplying these patients' risk of becoming infected with the AIDS virus. The CDC said fifty hemophiliacs now met criteria for an AIDS diagnosis. They showed another ominous graph summarizing results from hemophiliacs who had no symptoms or signs of the syndrome. Ninety percent of them had tested positive for HTLV-III.

Three men in the back row stood up and waved canes.

"Murderers! Murderers!" they yelled. "You know you can make Factor VIII safe!"

As uniformed security guards shoved the hobbling demonstrators out of the room, photo bulbs flashed. Echoing chants of "Make Eight Safe! Make Eight Safe!" receded down the hallway.

The next presentation was by a petite pediatrician from New York who had taken care of four infants with transfusion-associated AIDS. While she spoke, photos of the babies were projected on the screen. Some were jaundiced. Some had ulcerated lips. All were profoundly gaunt. Herb was getting queasy. It was a familiar visceral reaction. He had experienced it as a boy on discovering a photograph of starving babies in his parents' bedroom. He feared he might vomit. Yet thinking about that photo actually calmed his stomach. He dwelled on the memory, wondering if this was one of those "Aha" moments his therapist had hoped he would have.

The year Herb was in fifth grade, his mother worked evenings in a Manhattan department store. His father was interceding in a Balkan crisis that fall, so Herb came home to an empty house after school. He made his own dinner and amused himself until bedtime by listening to the *Cisco Kid* and *Captain Midnight* on the radio, reading biographies of famous Americans, or thumbing through his collection of Superman comic books. When bored with these activities, he would daydream.

He saw parallels between his own life and Superman's childhood. Herb had a special power of sorts, running fast. If he didn't come from another planet, his father and mother might as well have. Were the parents he lived with, like Clark Kent's, people who had adopted him? Depending on his mood, Herb imagined his true father and mother were royalty, sports stars, or famous scientists like the Curies. In his fantasies, he fit into the larger world seamlessly. He would meet his real parents and cease to look Chinese.

As he embellished stories of his fantasy father and mother, Herb became more and more certain that the pseudo-parents he lived with were hiding crucial information from him. One evening, he sneaked into their bedroom to search for evidence of his secret past. He wasn't breaking any explicit rules, but Herb knew he was behaving badly. He felt guilty yet compelled to go through each of their shelves and drawers systematically. There were no surprises—other than musty smelling undergarments he wished he hadn't found—until he uncovered a flat wooden box lying beneath his mother's sweaters. Inside were envelopes containing flimsy sheets of translucent paper, letters written in Chinese characters. Below these were photographs of Chinese men in suits and ties and women in high-collared dresses posing in front of a modest white, clapboard house.

The photograph at the bottom was of Chinese adults in white uniforms standing at attention between two rows of cribs. In each crib lay a skeletally thin infant. The baby closest to the photographer was looking straight at the camera. His eyes were set so deep in their sockets Herb couldn't tell whether he was Chinese or not. Along the bottom, someone had written in English cursive "Nanking, 1938."

Nauseated, Herb put the photographs back into the box. He couldn't read Chinese, so the letters were useless. There was no solution to the mystery of his origins here, but there was the incriminating fact that he had been born in 1938, which raised the possibility *he* might have been one of those starving babies. Had his parents lied to him about being born in New York? And if he had been a baby in that photo, why had he been spared?

Herb was in the living room devising an interrogation plan when his mother came home.

"How was work, mother?" he asked politely.

"Fine. It's too late for you to be up. Go to bed."

"Is your store near the hospital where I was born?"

"No. Mt. Sinai is at 100th Street. I work in mid-town. Now go to bed."

"Does the hospital have my birth certificate? If I went there, could I see it?"

"I suppose so. Why do you want to know?"

"Why wasn't I born in China, like you and father?"

"You know why. We came here before you were born."

"Why you did you leave before I was born?"

"Because of your father's job. President Lin sent him in the United States."

"Why did he send father then? Why didn't he wait until after I was born?"

"Why are you asking me all these questions at eleven o'clock at night? Go to bed!"

Having failed with his mother, Herb had no option other than getting information from his father. The challenge was finding an opportunity to be alone with him. If his mother were present, she would surely cut Herb off by saying, "Your father works so hard. Let him relax."

In December, his father returned from Eastern Europe. Herb had his chance when his mother was assigned additional weekend shifts at the department store and his father decided, in an impulse of American do-it-yourself gumption, to stay home and paint the kitchen. Herb volunteered to help. He enjoyed taping the baseboards and window moldings, seeing the walls transformed to immaculate off-white surfaces, and the companionship of his father. He almost forgot his plan for a stealthy inquest. Then they stripped the baseboard tape. There were a few streaks of paint underneath. His father blamed Herb.

As they were cleaning up, Herb asked about China. Buoyed by his practical accomplishment, his father was in a talkative mood. He rambled on about Qing Dynasty culture, the revolutions preceding World War II, and his own ancestry. Of course, none of this provided any useful clues. Herb still felt estranged but lacked the proof he was someone else's child.

Herb rose as he heard his name spoken from the podium and his credentials cited. At the microphone, he reached inside his jacket pocket. He touched his prepared notes and left them there.

"Thank you for the kind introduction," he extemporized. "I want to speak primarily as a physician who administers blood and plasma to acutely bleeding patients. We don't have time to get consent for such transfusions. Our patients and their families have to trust our judgment, and we have to trust that of our local blood bankers. In San Francisco, that trust is well-placed. Our blood banks are screening out virtually all donated blood that could transmit the AIDS virus. They reject any units that test positive for hepatitis B antibody.

"The epidemiologic data presented today make it clear that the risk of acquiring transfusion-associated AIDS is no longer limited to a half dozen geographic locales. The entire country is at risk. Yes, hepatitis antibody screening will increase the cost of blood products, but the public accepts that health care is expensive. They won't accept getting a fatal disease from a transfusion when there is a proven means to prevent it."

Herb was dizzy. He opted to quit while ahead. He thanked the audience and walked unsteadily to his seat.

During lunch, the AABB leadership met in private session and voted against the proposal. The AABB director read a brief statement afterwards acknowledging there was anecdotal evidence of the AIDS virus being transmitted by contaminated blood products. However, their consensus was that such events were extremely rare. Implementing a policy of testing all donated blood for hepatitis B antibodies would be prohibitively expensive, on the order of one hundred million dollars per year.

Irate, Herb turned to the San Francisco blood bank director sitting next to him, one of the minority already screening donated blood.

"One hundred million dollars? That's far-fetched. With economy of scale, wouldn't performing four million hepatitis assays a year drive the price way down? These people are bankers. Don't they understand how capitalism works?"

"Look, Herb," the local director replied, "An HTLV-III antibody test will be approved by the FDA and on the shelves in six months. Then blood banks will get insurance companies or the government to foot the bill, and everyone will adopt screening. That's what this is really about."

Herb had been able to avoid thinking of Sister Anna during the meeting. Now he stopped trying. In clinic, he didn't need to review her chart to know she was losing weight at an alarming rate. Kevin had told him her T cells were dropping precipitously. Even with normal lungs she wouldn't survive a year.

It had been Sister Anna who urged him to give therapy another go. After eighteen months of weekly sessions with an angular, bald psychologist in his sixties, Herb had just "graduated." The experience had attuned him to appreciate the half-full portion of his glass and taught him how to loosen the leashes on his less-threatening emotions, like the righteous indignation he had now.

Herb imagined the AABB leaders running for cover when the story of Sister Anna's death hit the news. He could see the headline, "Nun Dies of AIDS, Blood Bank Policies Faulted." But why wait, he asked himself. I bet she'd love to rattle these peoples' cages. He thought of the impact she could have on the public. Maybe I should persuade her to talk to a reporter.

V

WITH KEVIN AWAY LECTURING and one of their nurse-practitioners out sick, Gwen had a busy Friday morning clinic. Though she wasn't falling behind, each time she looked at her schedule Gwen felt anxious. It was the name at the bottom, the one she had added on late yesterday, that was disturbing her.

At his last appointment, Ed Greames was in the terminal phase of AIDS. Millions of slow-growing mycobacteria were reproducing in his lymph nodes, liver, spleen, and gut, metabolizing their way through his body. His symptoms initially improved on antibiotics, but the mycobacteria were becoming resistant to these drugs, gathering their minions for a final assault.

This week, Greames called complaining of right leg weakness. Gwen sent him to the ER where a brain scan revealed a mass, almost certainly a lymphoma—inoperable, incurable. Before the scan, the best he could anticipate was six months of worsening fevers, diarrhea, and weight loss. In a sense, his death would be caused by starvation. The neurologist who had seen Greames yesterday told Gwen that scenario would be superseded by progressive loss of motor function and speech in weeks with seizures likely along the way. Radiation therapy might prolong the inevitable by a month or two, but the patient would have to undergo a brain biopsy to confirm the diagnosis for any radiation oncologist to treat him. Beyond that, all she could offer was home hospice care from visiting nurses who were savvy in the use of morphine, steroids, creams, and tranquilizers to ease suffering at the end of life.

Ed Greames could still walk into the exam room. A tall, thin, graceful man with graying, jet black hair, he wobbled in on a cane. A proud man, a successful architect prior to his illness, Greames was angry.

"The neurologist explained it all to me," Greames said, interrupting her greeting. "I'm not interested in radiation. I want it to end, as soon as possible."

"OK... Can I get a little more information first?"

Greames answered her questions and let her examine him. Gwen's laying on of hands diffused some of his bitterness.

Five minutes later, he repeated his request. He was lucid, realistic, and hopeless.

It was a snap decision for Gwen. She knew what the risks were, where she would be crossing the line, but she couldn't refuse to help him. She wrote two prescriptions and gave them to him.

"The morphine is for pain, the phenobarbital to prevent seizures. Be careful with these medications. They're dangerous. For example, if you were to take an overdose, say the entire contents of both bottles all at once, you'd fall asleep, stop breathing in a few hours, and die."

Greames's face softened.

"That is most instructive, Dr. Howard. You're very kind."

He gazed at the slips of paper.

"I'll use these carefully," he promised.

"I know you will."

"Though actually, I might need a few weeks to take care of things before I leave."

"Of course," said Gwen with relief. "Let me know if there's anything I can do. There are hospice nurses who do house calls. I can arrange for home attendant help, too."

"I don't think so," said Greames, his voice flat and distant now. "My young friend can take of everything. Thanks anyway."

VI

After clinic, Gwen found a message in her mailbox. Charlie Sawyer from the CDC called. She had met Charlie the previous spring at a meeting in Atlanta and learned he was seeking collaborators to field test an assay he was developing to diagnose HTLV-III infection. As the assistant director of the AIDS program at City Hospital, Gwen had access to hundreds of AIDS and ARC patients getting routine blood draws who would be willing to donate an extra tube for research. She eagerly agreed to help.

Gwen had another agenda in joining the project. Since her needle-stick, whenever she had a cold or was tired, the fear she might be infected had to be dealt with or suppressed, usually the latter. Checking her lymphocyte count, which she did on each equinox and solstice for good luck, and seeing a robustly normal number made it easier for her to believe she had dodged the bullet, but it wasn't definitive proof. In June, after listening to Charlie's caveats about the assay's accuracy problems, Gwen sent him a sample of her serum. Ten days of tension, punctuated by panic attacks, ensued before she received the result—HTLV-III antibodies *not* detected.

Charlie had warned her that the test was still a work in progress. Her result could be a false negative. He promised to check her serum again once the improved accuracy of his next generation assay was verified. She had told Rick the news with restrained optimism. Charlie had also talked her into enlisting health care workers at City Hospital as study subjects. Their samples would be run the moment his new version was validated.

Gwen dialed the number in Atlanta. Charlie answered and excitedly told her his next generation assay was ready for prime time. He was packing test kits to ship to her as they spoke. The City Hospital staff's specimens she had stored in a basement freezer could finally be thawed.

"Charlie," she asked awkwardly, "can I send you my serum now? I mean it would be weird to run it in our lab."

"That's not necessary."

"I don't understand. You said…"

"Gwen," he interrupted, "I saved an aliquot of the serum you sent me in June. I already ran it with the new assay so you wouldn't have to wait for the results like last time. I can guess how that must feel. Anyway, you're not infected."

Gwen was mute as she absorbed the news.

"This version of the assay has a less than five percent probability of false negatives, Gwen. And because you were antibody negative before, even though it was using a less accurate test, the probability is actually way, way lower because of the multiplicative… I don't think you want a statistics lecture right now. Suffice it to say you are *not* going to get AIDS."

Gwen had the presence of mind to thank him, which she kept repeating until he begged off.

"I'll get back to you in a month. We want to follow those City Hospital results very, very closely."

VII

WHEN GWEN CAME HOME, she opened the front door and stood in the hallway listening. Eva was supposed to go directly from school to a friend's house for a sleepover. The only sound was a distant thrum of running water. She crept through the house. The noise came from the bathroom. It had to be Rick in the shower. She imagined sliding her fingers over his wet back. Euphoric, her inner thighs tingling, she sat at the kitchen table waiting for the water to stop.

Rick was out of the shower with a towel around his waist when Gwen entered naked. She pulled away his towel, and rubbed her hips against him.

"I'm negative," she said.

"Negative?"

"My antibody result. This time for sure. No more testing required to confirm it."

Rick lips parted. Then he froze. Gwen grasped his shoulders and wrapped her legs around him. He began a question. She preempted it with the answer.

"No more condoms."

Rick had been quickly convinced, as much by Gwen's passion as her logic. Now he lay beside her deliciously spent. They hadn't come simultaneously in years.

"Remind you of the early days of our love?" she asked dreamily.

"Oh, yes," he laughed.

She stuck her tongue in his mouth and stroked his flaccid penis.

"Afraid I need recovery time."

"No problem, we've got all night."

With a contented hum, she tucked her head under his arm.

She suddenly considered another complication of having sex without protection. Her initial reaction was not to worry. I'm forty years old. My period just ended two days ago. I won't forget to use a diaphragm next time. Then she realized they had never had The Talk.

Of course not, she thought. We hadn't been a couple long enough for it to come up when the needle-stick happened. But now we've been together five years. And Rick is thirty-eight. He's never said anything about wanting children of his own. But under the circumstances, why would he have? Ugh, we have to go there. There won't be a better time than right now.

"Hey, honey…you know what we've never talked about?"

"Um…there are lots things we haven't talked about... What's on your mind?"

"I guess I'd like to know… how you feel about having children."

"We have a child. I still think of her as a child. So I'm guessing you mean… having a baby?"

"Yeah."

"Is that something you want?"

"I was sort of trying to find out what you want."

"I guess I asked you first. Do you want to have a baby?"

This was not how she had hoped the conversation would go, but they were in too deep now. She was going to have to show her hand first.

"I'm…open to the possibility."

"That doesn't sound like you want to have a baby."

"Rick, what do you want?"

"I like our life the way it is. Eva treats me like I'm her father even if she doesn't call me Dad. Hell, she hardly ever sees Daniel. I feel like she's *my* daughter, too. And I get all the interaction with kids I can handle at school."

"Really? You'd be OK if we didn't…?"

"Absolutely."

Gwen returned to her snuggling spot, and Rick's mind idly wandered. He wondered whether she would keep working so hard. After her residency was over, he had assumed she continued working sixty hour weeks to distract herself from worrying about being infected. Now, he realized that assumption was about to be tested. And what if she didn't ease up? What would that say about their relationship? He didn't want to follow this thread. Instead, he thought of a cartoon he had saved from the *New Yorker*. He hadn't shown it to her yet. Four men in business suits were seated at a bar. Each had an open briefcase spilling out documents onto the counter. The bartender was shutting one. "No more work for you tonight, buddy!" was the caption. Should he give it to her? What if she didn't think it was funny?

VIII

Gwen and Rick drove to San Francisco on Saturday morning. They parked by Golden Gate Park and strolled into a meadow where Gwen spotted three middle-aged men and a young woman sitting on a blanket. She had a meeting with these activists. He planned to take a leisurely run to the ocean.

"Is that Hippy Hill?" Rick asked, pointing toward a nearby slope.

"Maybe, I don't know."

In fact, she did remember smoking pot there during medical school. But Gwen wasn't in the mood to wax nostalgic.

"I don't have a good feeling about this," she confided.

"Really? They seem like just what you need now. Community people putting pressure on the government to develop drugs for AIDS."

"I hope you're right."

The man with a beard and shaved scalp Gwen knew well. Holden was one of her clinic patients. He had arranged the meeting. She recognized the others from television interviews after the candlelight march in July when thousands had filled the Civic Center demanding federal action on AIDS. Holden had told her about the woman, Rebecca Wolman. Very thin with closely cropped her, she had a master's degree in public policy from Berkeley. The leaders of the San Francisco AIDS Action Committee, the largest AIDS activist group west of the Mississippi, had hired her to be their executive director. When Gwen had heard her speak, Rebecca was on fire with a formidable, controlled rage as she described what AIDS was doing to gay men and other marginalized people and what had to be done to stop the epidemic.

"Dr. Howard," said Rebecca graciously, "We know how busy you are. We really appreciate your taking the time to meet with us."

Slick too, thought Gwen. It was easy to foresee how this ambitious young woman's public persona would blossom as the epidemic spread. She was going to be quoted by the press, a lot.

Rick excused himself and jogged off.

Gwen was curious about SFAAC, and the activists asked about how the AIDS clinic was funded and what research was being conducted at City Hospital and elsewhere in the university. They spent an hour in collegial discussion. Gwen was impressed by how knowledgeable they were.

Getting down to the real reason they had requested the meeting, Rebecca said SFAAC was intending to take action in a way they believed would increase pressure on the government to put more money into AIDS patient care and research.

"It'll be a symbolic protest with the dramatic power to grab the media's attention and generate public outrage. We'll make the average American viscerally aware of the wave of death this disease has caused."

Gwen wasn't sure what "viscerally aware" meant, but it made her uneasy. She also realized Rebecca had done her homework. Gwen's history of civil rights activism must be the reason SFAAC wanted to meet with her instead of Kevin.

SFAAC's strategy, Rebecca explained, was to have fifty activists, incognito in business attire, mingling among the convergence of shoppers and office workers in downtown San Francisco's Union Square on the Friday after Thanksgiving. At precisely four thirty, each activist would open a shopping bag, remove a plastic squirt bottle containing fresh cow's blood, spray passers-by, and scream "AIDS means death! You're next!" Each bag would hold six bottles of blood. Rebecca estimated they should be able to "contaminate" one thousand "victims"—one-sixth the cumulative number of AIDS cases recently reported by the CDC. Because the Saturday after Thanksgiving was typically a slow news day, they expected to get national television and front-page newspaper coverage.

Gwen was appalled. She was certain such a "direct action" would do far more harm than good in swaying public opinion. As she formulated a diplomatic way to say this, Rick jogged up to them.

Rebecca, interpreting Gwen's silence as tacit approval, said, "All of us in SFAAC think the action will be much more powerful if you and Kevin are involved. We'd like you to be arrested with us and make a statement to the press afterwards."

Rick coughed to mask his gasp. He walked away, head bent down so they wouldn't see it shake in disbelief.

"Rebecca," said Gwen, maintaining her composure, "Kevin and I would lose all our credibility if we publicly supported this action, let alone if we participated and were arrested."

"What? You'd be heroes to people with AIDS!"

"I'm talking about our credibility with the City Public Health Department and NIH. They're the source of all our funding, and they're already skeptical about Kevin and me. They wonder if we're just using the money they're giving us to create our own little fiefdom. They're seeing more and more people dying while the problem and the costs keep getting bigger."

"We're wondering the same thing," Rebecca lashed back. "We see Drs. Bartholomew's and Howard's names in the newspaper. We hear about the grants you're getting. It's obvious AIDS is benefiting your careers. Here's your chance to prove which side you're on."

Gwen was close to losing her temper. For a second, she saw Eva standing before her instead of Rebecca—an edifying vision. She was not going to allow herself to be provoked. Gwen walled off her emotions and thought through what to say next.

Lifting her hands, she said, "Let's cool down. I appreciate that you folks have a very important role in raising public awareness and empathy for people with AIDS. I respect your courage and imagination. I just don't agree with your tactics. I'm afraid your demonstration will play poorly in the press, and I'm concerned the media will spin this in a way that could make the general public more repelled by people with AIDS than sympathetic to their plight.

"Please understand, Kevin and my jobs are to do the best we can *medically* for our patients. That requires a lot of money. The only funding we have is from government agencies. Believe me, we've talked to a number of nonprofit foundations. They aren't interested in helping."

Rebecca sneered.

"Please, Rebecca, Holden, all of you. Think about what we're doing at City Hospital. There's no other place with a clinic like ours, dedicated solely to this disease, or an inpatient unit like the one we just opened. Of course, the country needs a huge, federally-sponsored research effort to develop a cure for AIDS. It's your job to build that kind of political commitment. If Kevin and I advocate stridently for more government dollars, we'll look self-serving."

Rebecca gave the men a cynical half-smile then turned to her.

"They have you exactly where they want you, quietly providing custodial care for a bunch of dying outcasts. The Reagan administration won't do anything of substance to stop this epidemic or to find a cure, unless we raise the stakes and force them."

Dumbfounded, Gwen stared at Rebecca who said to the men, "Shall we?"

As the group departed, Holden gave Gwen a sad, short wave goodbye.

Rick was at her side again and slipped his arm around her waist.

"I thought all those sixties hippies that were into political theater had retired by now," he said.

She didn't laugh.

IX

BACK IN THE EAST Bay by noon, Gwen dropped Rick off at home then drove further up into the hills. She parked in front of a large ranch house and steeled herself to deal with Eva's unpredictable moods. Waiting in the front hallway, she looked around the spacious living room through bay view windows to a deck and hot tub. Uh-oh, she thought.

Eva, now taller than her mother, came downstairs and eyed Gwen darkly. She politely thanked her friend's mother for hosting the sleepover. Inside the car, she started in as Gwen was backing out of the driveway.

"Why can't we live in a bigger house? You're a doctor. Most doctors are rich. Why can't you get a job that pays more money?"

"Sorry, Eva, I'm not qualified for any of those mega-buck jobs."

Gwen had learned to pick battles with her daughter carefully. Passing on this one was a no-brainer. She was grateful Eva had survived her first year of high school unscathed and willing to cut her some more slack.

Though the meeting in Golden Gate Park had reined in Gwen's euphoria, the rest of her weekend was luxuriously uneventful. She prepared slides for a medical school lecture, caught up on overdue clinic progress reports and performance evaluations, and went for a long walk with Rick.

On Sunday evening, while making dinner, she called out for Eva to set the table. She got no response and went to her daughter's bedroom. The door was closed. She could hear Eva talking on the phone.

She was about to knock but stopped short when Eva said desperately, "Are you sure she doesn't like me?"

Gwen gave her another pass.

At dinner, Eva was morose. Her face had no muscle tone. Rick's attempt to cheer her up made Gwen laugh. Eva gave them an accusatory glance and stomped off to her room.

After dinner, the phone rang. Gwen snuck up to Eva's door and heard happy chatter. She returned in an hour and heard giggling.

"Kiddo," she said loudly, "Is your homework done?"

A moment later, Eva bounded out. She grabbed her backpack and sat at the kitchen table, completing work sheets for her Spanish class. At ten o'clock, Gwen checked again and found Eva in front of a mirror, holding two tubes from her collection of lip glosses.

"Tough decisionsville?" she inquired.

Eva's eyes darted between the mirror and each shade of gloss. She didn't answer.

Bemused, Gwen climbed into bed where Rick was engrossed in the Sunday newspaper. When I was her age, she thought, friends weren't *that* important, were they? No, not for me, not until I met Nan in college.

She had a vague, unsettling sense of guilt, as though something shameful from her past was approaching consciousness. She grabbed the Sunday magazine section and set to work on the crossword puzzle.

The alarm went off at six-thirty the next morning. Gwen promptly arose and crossed the hall to mobilize Eva, who needed to be at the school bus stop in forty-five minutes. Eva muttered a protest that wasn't overtly hostile. A good sign, thought Gwen.

Coffee, juice, and a bowl of cereal later, Gwen was waiting at the breakfast table, her annoyance growing. She was about to yell an ultimatum when Eva appeared in the kitchen doorway, somnolent but dressed with a coral green backpack slung over her shoulder.

Gwen dropped her off as the school bus door was closing and headed onto the freeway toward the Bay Bridge. She mused over how different high school was for Eva than it had been for her. Just the racial and cultural diversity her daughter had to negotiate seemed daunting. She had heard from other parents that neither black nor Asian kids would socialize with whites. There were exclusive cliques too, like the girls who made the soccer team. At age fifteen, Gwen and her classmates were a monochromatic rock-and-roll nation, united against their parents' authority. It had been a simple generational conflict.

Remembering high school perturbed her. She turned her mind to the content for a talk she had been invited to give in Chicago.

X

KEVIN WAS IN HIS office before seven on Monday morning studying a spreadsheet. He had already mined from this data, gathered from everyone with AIDS or ARC seen at City Hospital since the epidemic began, material for half a dozen publications. Now it dawned on him that the substance for two more papers was here. The first time he looked up at the wall clock, it was eight-fifteen. He cursed. The weekly clinic meeting started at eight. On his way out the door, Kevin realized he didn't have to go. Gwen had volunteered to take over as clinic medical director. Elated, he returned to his data.

In 1981, Kevin could easily handle being the sole primary care doctor for all AIDS and ARC patients coming to City Hospital. By mid-1982, there were too many for him to manage alone, even with the help of a nurse-practitioner. He talked Ray Hernandez into hiring Gwen to share the load. Once she was on board supervising the treatment of hospitalized AIDS patients, Kevin only had to juggle keeping his research afloat and running the clinic. He soon deferred to Gwen's judgment there as well. Kevin discovered she could tell unerringly which patient complaining of a headache just needed reassurance and pain medication and which one had to be admitted for an emergent brain scan, or which one with a fever would be fine to rest at home and drink lots of fluids and which would die if not immediately given industrial strength antibiotics and sent to the ICU.

Now that a laboratory on the Hill was willing to measure T cells in blood samples, Kevin's top priority was his Phase 1 trial of suramin. Of all the drugs Rajiv Singh had pulled off the shelf to screen, ancient suramin, used in Africa since the 1920s to treat sleeping sickness, most potently disabled the retrovirus in a test tube. Although the medication had serious side effects, there were no better candidates. Conducting this trial while simultaneously moving his other studies forward absorbed virtually all of Kevin's attention.

He didn't look up from the spreadsheet again for another hour. Then a rustling noise startled him. He saw a small envelope slide underneath his door. Inside, he found a familiar pressed flower, a purple wild iris glued to a beige vellum card. He had seen it before mounted under glass. It was part of a wildflower collection in Gwen's office. Written in firm cursive were the words "Negative. Definitively."

He ran to her office.

"By Charlie's *new* assay?" Kevin asked, trying to keep from shouting.

Gwen smiled beatifically.

He slumped onto a chair.

"That's...fantastic," he said, his voice catching.

"Oh my God, Kevin. I don't want you to cry."

"I'm not going to cry. I'm just...so happy...for you, for all of us."

She sat on his lap and hugged him. Kevin ran his fingers through her hair, much finer than his own or Marco's. Suddenly afraid he might be overstepping the boundaries of their friendship, he stopped. Gwen sighed contentedly. More Catholic guilt, he could imagine Marco saying.

"What color's your hair?" he asked.

"Golden brown—if you pretend the gray streaks aren't there. That's the closest match I've found. Think I should dye my hair?"

"No. It looks terrific. It's better than terrific. It's you."

"What a lovely thing to say, Kevin." She kissed him on the cheek.

"So Rick knows, doesn't he?"

"No, I'm going to torture him for a few more weeks. Of course he knows. I found out on Friday. We celebrated this weekend."

A sly grin crept over Kevin's face.

Blushing and laughing, she said, "Let's go out to dinner soon. We need to catch up."

"Absolutely. We need to celebrate, too...with our clothes on."

Gwen crumpled a piece of paper and threw it at him.

XI

GWEN'S LAST PATIENT OF the afternoon was a heroin addict, a woman with no lymphocytes, no visible body fat, and barely any muscle mass. Skin hung loosely from her skeleton. She was accompanied by a stout, six-foot-six counselor wearing a tie-dyed tee-shirt and flannel pajama bottoms. His long grey hair and bushy beard were each held together at the end by a rubber band.

Gwen had helped Janet get through a lengthy hospitalization for an opportunistic brain infection, consulting with the house staff and dropping by to encourage her daily. This was Janet's first visit to the AIDS clinic. She had been feisty and foul-mouthed on the ward. Today she was subdued, her responses monosyllabic. After examining her, Gwen went over her medication list, reinforcing how many of each pill she should be taking and at what time. When asked if she had any questions, Janet shook her head no.

She's numb, Gwen thought. She finally gets that she's going to die soon.

"Janet, let's have the lab draw your blood and the front desk make you a follow-up appointment. Then check back here with me before you leave, OK."

Gwen hoped she might open up after a break.

As Janet left, the counselor whispered, "Guess she's not ready to talk about it yet."

"You know her well, Greg?"

"No. I just met her today, half an hour before we came in here."

"She's still using. Those are fresh needle tracks on her forearms."

"That's no surprise. She's in denial about her feelings. Heroin's a good way to keep them at bay. But I'll be in the waiting room at her next appointment, lying in wait for her."

He chuckled at the bad pun.

"Thank you for doing this," said Gwen, trying not to stare at the man's remarkably pale blue eyes.

"I should be thanking you for giving me this opportunity."

Gwen had seen many people with end-stage disease uplifted by Greg's support. She knew little about his organization, Shanti, other than the name was a Sanskrit word meaning "tranquility." The group had been counseling terminal cancer patients for years and recently began extending its services to those with AIDS.

Gwen looked outside her door to be sure there were no more patients to be seen. She glanced at her watch. She could go home now. Instead, she opted to sit down.

"So tell me," she asked, "how do you manage doing this day in and day out without becoming despondent?"

"It's not that hard. You just have to stay focused on embodying the Shanti core principles. Empowerment. Genuineness. Empathy. Service."

"I have to admit I'm suspicious of big ideas solving problems. Though you seem to avoid being sucked into despair. That's a challenge for me. How do you do it?"

"The principles really work if I apply them consistently. There's the rub—consistency. When I listen carefully to a dying person and respond honestly with an open heart, whatever sadness I feel passes through me. And afterwards…."

Greg placed his hand on his chest, drew it away toward the window, and said, "It's gone."

"Sometimes," Gwen said, wavering over how much to reveal, "A lot of the time, actually, the sadness stays with me."

"Have you thought about what's sustaining it? I mean in doing this work, sometimes sadness comes from empathizing with what our client feels. And sometimes it comes from guilt we have because our client is dying and we're not, which is about our feelings not theirs. In Shanti, we try to be mindful our mission is to *empower* the dying, which can take guilt out of the picture. There's still empathic sadness, which can hurt a lot, but that doesn't usually last long once your interaction is over."

Greg halted for a moment.

"Maybe we have an unfair advantage. See, we believe our clients can resolve their own death issues with a little help. They don't need us to be directive. But what you're doing here is based on all the special knowledge you have. Your patients can't make choices about their medical care without your advice. I guess you have to be directive."

Treading lightly, Greg added, "That must be a burden."

Gwen gave a downcast nod.

Then she brightened and said, "You're using your empathy."

Greg laughed.

"Thanks for being here for these folks," she said. "They need your help so much."

"No, no. It's nothing anyone needs to thank me for. It's not *all* selfless. I get a lot in return once my clients move beyond their denial and understand life is not about who dies with the most toys."

Gwen was alone in her exam room, ruminating over their conversation, when she remembered Janet. She ran to the waiting room. Janet was gone. Angry at the front desk staff for letting Janet leave, furious the clinic had no on-site psychiatric services, Gwen got into the elevator and repeatedly punched the down button. Outside, she jogged around the building twice. Janet had vanished.

Back in the elevator, she found a more suitable target to punish. Gwen hadn't allowed herself to think of Frieda last night or this morning. Defenseless now, the memories broke through. She began to cry.

Gwen met Frieda Lowenstein in her freshman high school home room. The frizzy-haired girl instantly assumed intimacy with her. Frieda was the most audacious girl Gwen had ever encountered. Her excitability was contagious, her Jewishness exotic. Frieda was also big on self-improvement. She told Gwen that on the basis of her looks alone she could be much more popular, if it was of any importance to her. Gwen readily agreed it wasn't. She had never been so flattered.

They had sleepovers on weekends at Frieda's house where there was a color television set, an extensive collection of teen magazines and top-forty vinyl recordings, and a refrigerator stocked with chopped chicken liver and cream cheese to slather on bagels for a snack.

They discussed the merits of various brassieres and sanitary pads and lamented the injustice that boys didn't have to put up with any of this. They shared what little knowledge they had about sex. Photos of Vic Damone, James Dean, and Rock Hudson adorning Frieda's bedroom wall made Gwen dimly aware of yearnings for mysterious sensations and release. However, she mistrusted boys, as did Frieda, who only had sisters. In any case, romance was still a hypothetical issue. No boys had demonstrated interest in either of them, so far.

Frieda stopped growing in ninth grade but didn't stop gaining weight. On entering tenth grade, her breasts were large enough to be a source of embarrassment. She knew she bore a passing resemblance to the young Elizabeth Taylor in *National Velvet* and tried to draw attention to her face instead with lipstick and make-up. Meanwhile, Gwen had grown three inches over the summer. Her breasts and hips were modestly proportioned. Her nose had turned cute. She let her straight blond hair grow long and tied it in a ponytail.

Pheromones permeated their classrooms now. The boys were markedly taller and had deeper voices. Gwen was approached by previously taciturn Rusty, who sported a new flat-top and had an attractive bulge in his neck. She didn't brush him off. He confided that there was a cabal of the most popular kids in school. You could join only as a couple. The reward was being invited to make-out parties. Gwen was curious. She accepted the offer to be his girlfriend.

When Frieda showed no interest in hearing about this unfolding drama, Gwen assumed her friend was distracted, nervous over who would ask her. Rusty seemed no great prize to Gwen. She didn't consider Frieda might be jealous.

The next Saturday night, Gwen was in a crowded basement jitterbugging to Bill Haley and the Comets. She noted Frieda's absence but gave it no more thought once the slow dancing started. In the morning, she awoke feeling guilty. She called her friend's house. Mrs. Lowenstein promised Frieda would call her back soon. The phone didn't ring that day.

At school, Frieda ignored her. Despite understanding now how tough it would be for her not to be jealous if the tables had been turned, Gwen believed it wasn't her fault Frieda lacked the self-control to stay out of her refrigerator or that none of the boys wanted a fat girlfriend.

The parties continued. Though Gwen made a few girlfriends, she wasn't comfortable enough to trust any of them with her secrets, not like she had been with Frieda. She missed Frieda and plotted ways for them to make up. Gwen intended to be generous, to take full responsibility for their estrangement.

After Thanksgiving, Frieda wasn't at school. No one, not even their home room teacher, knew why. Gwen called for days until finally Mrs. Lowenstein answered the phone and told her Frieda was in LA Children's Hospital, seriously ill. She urged her to visit.

Gwen had never been inside a hospital. Just the word frightened her. She dutifully took a bus to the twelve-story pavilion on Sunset Boulevard. Frieda was on the top floor in a private room that smelled of bleach. Her skin was as white and fragile as tissue paper. Blue blotches covered her arms. Her body had shrunk. Plastic tubes descended from glass bottles hanging high above her bed and converged beneath a square of gauze taped to her neck. Frieda looked terrified.

"What happened?" asked Gwen, tears streaming down her cheeks.

"There's something wrong with my blood," sobbed Frieda. "Nobody will explain it to me, and they won't let me go home."

Gwen sat on the bed. She touched her friend sympathetically. Frieda pushed her away.

"I can't stand it anymore," Frieda screamed. "I'd kill myself if I knew how."

Gwen blanched. Both girls were too distraught to notice Frieda's father come into the room. He immediately insisted Gwen leave.

"I'm sorry, I'm so sorry," Gwen cried as a nurse escorted her to the elevator.

Two weeks later, her mother showed her an obituary in the Los Angeles Times. Gwen read one phrase and rushed to the toilet to throw up.

"Frieda Lowenstein, age 15, died of leukemia… "

At the funeral, Gwen had to use her mother as a crutch to walk into the sanctuary. She was relieved no one seemed affronted by her presence. They were all weeping or overwhelmed by grief, except for the rabbi who led the service. His calm incantations were soothing. She followed little of his eulogy, but he did say one thing that stuck in her mind.

"The death of a child is our ultimate test of faith."

Gwen had always half-heartedly hoped God would take care of her. Frieda's death now made faith a cruel joke. At best, her death was senseless. And if Frieda didn't deserve to be spared, why would Gwen?

XII

BECAUSE RAY HERNANDEZ WAS about to leave for a sabbatical in Argentina, his annual holiday party was early this year, on a Sunday in late September. The day started out hot and windless. By four in the afternoon, the temperature had reached one hundred degrees. Like most houses in sight of the bay, Ray's didn't have air conditioning, so the party moved outdoors.

Kevin, Gwen, and Herb, all barefoot and wearing shorts, sat on collapsible beach chairs. It was pleasant to drink chilled white wine under the shade of fir trees while Ray's children, armed with spray bottles, showered mist on them.

"This is the first time in a month I've been able to sit down and relax for a couple of hours," complained Gwen. "It took me forever to catch up with the backlog I had after the Paris meeting."

"Me too," said Kevin.

"Me three," Herb chuckled.

Gwen and Kevin looked dourly at him.

"It wasn't my idea to have an international AIDS conference in Paris."

"That's what I thought," growled Kevin. "The mentors around here only take credit for the productivity they spawn, not the misery."

"It's not Herb's fault," Gwen said, her words beginning to slur. "You remember what he said to you, right here, a few years ago?"

"In there," she corrected herself, pointing at Ray's house. "He said you'd never be able to stop working. It was already out of control."

"I've been exonerated," Herb sang with gleeful satisfaction. "She's right. I warned you. You could have bailed out then."

"I'm not blaming you, Herb. I'm just stating a fact. Between work-related travel, work at home, and work at work, I have no social life."

"Same here. It's what happens in a crisis."

"There's the empathy I was looking for."

Gwen giggled.

"OK, then how about this?" Herb suggested, "It would be God's work…"

"If any of us believed in God," said Kevin and Gwen together.

"I must be repeating myself. When did I say that? Not today. But it was at one of Ray's parties, wasn't it? Yes, years ago. And you guys remember?"

"Of course we remember," said Gwen.

"It's our ethos," Kevin chimed in. "That's the best thing about working at City Hospital. We've got this rational, humanistic, shared belief system. We don't need religion. What a fucking relief."

"I'm impressed, Kevin," said Herb sincerely. "That's a perfect way to put it."

"A fucking relief?"

"No, our ethos—a rational, humanistic, shared belief system. Somebody should write it down. I want to quote you."

Gwen turned glum and said, "Living up to those beliefs is a bear and a half. We have to be saints."

"Saints?" asked Kevin.

"You know, rise to every occasion with thoughtful compassion. No matter what shit people throw at us."

"The bar isn't that high," said Herb. "We just have to be honest, benevolent, and fair. That's no more than exhibiting plain human decency. It's hardly sainthood."

"Thanks, Herb," Kevin said, slapping himself on one cheek then the other. "I needed to hear that."

Herb giggled, which tickled Gwen. Her hilarity became a coughing spasm, which seemed the height of silliness to Kevin. He shook with laughter.

Ray happened to be passing by and stared at the threesome.

"Jesus H. Christ," he roared. "These are the people who are going to save us from the worst plague in modern history? God help us."

"Don't look at me, or at Gwen," said Herb, pointing at Kevin. "He's the one trained in infectious diseases. It's his bread and butter. The pathogen is known. There are targets for drug development."

"True," Ray agreed. "Get on it, Bartholomew. I expect results. Pronto."

Kevin saluted.

"Yes sir!" he shouted.

Ray nodded agreeably and wobbled on.

"That reminds me," said Herb, "I had a little tête-à-tête with Ray yesterday. He totally agrees with what I've been saying. You are so in the right place at the right time."

"You can't be serious," protested Kevin. "Don't take this the wrong way, Herb, but you don't have friends who are dying of AIDS. I do."

"Sorry. You're right. We have to stop talking about work."

"I have an idea," proposed Gwen. "I remember something Herb showed us at one of Ray's parties. He can tell whether a person believes in God or not. But he didn't explain how he does it. I want to know. Tell us, Herb. Please?"

"Yeah! That's a very cool skill. How do you do it?" Kevin appealed.

"It's not ESP," Herb replied. "Maybe it's pattern recognition. I've been asking patients whether they believe in God since I was a fellow at NIH. I have a lot of data to draw from."

"OK, then what's the pattern of an atheist?" asked Gwen.

"I don't know. I've never tried to articulate the patterns. Maybe there aren't any. Maybe it's intuition"

"Why don't you deconstruct what you're doing?" said Kevin. "Then you could write about it."

"No!" Herb harrumphed. "Why would anyone other than me be interested? I don't have a hypothesis. I don't even care *why* people have faith or not. I'm just curious *whether* they do or don't. And, by the way, I haven't noticed any association between belief and patient survival, or the severity of suffering. Not that there's any plausible reason why either would correlate with faith."

While Kevin and Gwen pondered his response, Herb snuck off to rummage through Ray's ice chest for a Sauvignon Blanc—one tart enough to keep them all alert. He returned, uttering the wine's variety, appellation, and year like a practiced sommelier. As Herb refilled their glasses, he changed the subject.

"Kevin, I want to apologize about my poor choice of words earlier. I didn't mean just being in the right place at the right time for academic success. You have a rare opportunity. The world values entrepreneurship so much more than altruism. Few people ever get the chance in their work lives to do something this undeniably beneficial for others. You should embrace it. Both of you should."

"Ah, the wisdom that comes from criticism and self-criticism," said Gwen.

"This isn't about politics," countered Herb.

"What!" she objected. "What could be any more political than AIDS? You should hear what SFAAC plans to do."

"Spare me. I was in DC and saw the hemophiliacs raising Cain, bless their hearts. But I thought we were talking about the personal, not the political. Gwen, you're the one who brought up sainthood. Is that a political requirement for doing this work?"

"Oh," she said, woozily. "I guess you're right."

"We have got to stop talking about AIDS," Kevin demanded, "and anything else work-related."

"Fair enough," Gwen agreed. "And politics, too. Shall we talk about wine? No we did that already. Movies? Restaurants?"

There was an awkward pause until Kevin said with a crafty smile, "Let's go back to religion. Herb weaseled out of explaining how he knew neither of us believes in God but we did as children. How did you do that?"

"No fair. You wouldn't ask Houdini how he did a magic trick, would you?"

"Don't lead us on and leave us hanging!" howled Kevin.

"Herb's got a secret," Gwen sang, "Good for you, Herb. We should all have a secret or two. The world needs more magic."

"Thanks a lot," said Kevin petulantly. "I want to know how he does it."

"Poor Kevin. Some things will have to remain mysteries, won't they."

He pouted for a moment then launched into a high-pitched giggle that made Herb and Gwen laugh just as Ray walked by again.

Ray gazed indulgently at them. He squatted, putting one hand on Kevin's knee and the other on Gwen's to keep his balance.

"You three are a paradigm shift."

Kevin and Gwen were nonplussed. Herb nodded knowingly.

"This university's rise from obscurity was built on social Darwinism," explained Ray. "My predecessors pitted faculty like you against each other.

That strategy worked for a while, but we've entered a new era. From now on, the winners will be those best at collaborating. Obviously, it's quite a challenge for people who don't enjoy each other's company to collaborate. We don't seem to have that problem here, do we?"

"It's the least of our problems," said Kevin, "But this is a party, so we won't bother you with our more substantive ones."

"I appreciate that," said Ray as he stood up. "I'm sure I'll get to hear all about it before I'm off to Buenos Aires."

Herb turned to Gwen and said, "I'm confused. Both these guys tell me they're from working-class families. Yet they talk to each other with the graciousness of old-money fraternity brothers."

"That's what's great about America," Ray proclaimed. "Everyone gets to re-invent themselves."

"To collaboration!" Gwen shouted, lifting her glass. "If I learned anything from the sixties, it's that when people value their uniqueness more than what they have in common, there's always conflict, even if they agree on principles. But when their commonality takes precedence, there's collaboration. Either way, stuff gets done and the world changes, but it's a hell of a lot healthier when there's no conflict."

They all stared at Gwen, moved by her rhetoric.

"Well said," acknowledged Ray, lifting his glass. "To our future stateswoman."

As Ray ambled away, Gwen asked, "So, speaking of re-inventing yourself, what's your long range plan, Kevin?"

Herb hunched forward to hear better.

"I don't think long range." said Kevin, a touch defensively. "Trying to keep our ship afloat is all I can do."

"We're just curious," said Herb, "You're younger. You have more potential for re-invention than either of us."

"It's OK if you don't want to talk about it," said Gwen.

"Right," agreed Herb.

"Though if you want a safe place to explore the possibilities," she added, "We're here to listen."

Herb opened his arms and said, "You can run anything by us. It'll stay completely confidential."

Kevin resisted the impulse to make light of their banter. He'd heard the undercurrent of sincerity. He wondered if he should try something out for size.

"All right," he said, "I wish there was a clinical trials group with sites across the country. I have friends who are AIDS docs in New York, Seattle, Los Angeles, Chicago. They're savvy and have good ideas we could test collectively."

"You want to run the group?" asked Herb.

"I'd be willing to, but I'd be fine with just being part of it."

"You could run it," said Gwen. "You totally could do it."

"Sooner or later," Herb piped in, "NIH will have to fund a system like that. Two, actually. One for treatment and one for prevention. Take your pick."

Herb slouched back in his chair, pretending disinterest, while Gwen crouched forward in anticipation.

"OK," said Kevin. "What I'm thinking…what I really want to do…"

She leaned farther forward.

"What I want most of all…"

Gwen was half on her feet.

"Is to keep it a mystery."

She blew a raspberry at Kevin and plopped down on the front end of her beach chair, which tipped forward, depositing her butt-first on the grass. Herb guffawed, rolling side to side until he leaned too far and upended his chair. He landed on his belly.

The rest of the party had stopped talking and were staring at them.

Ray muttered, "I better tone down a notch this cheerleading for collaboration."

XIII

KEVIN CAME HOME FROM work on Monday to find a letter from Marco full of love and longing to be together. Later that evening, Marco called from Mexico City with bad news. His mother had a major setback, a blood clot in the lungs. He talked of how she had been the most important pserson in his life, how this might be his last chance to give back a little of what she had given him. Marco's reaction to Kevin's account of his debut in the big-league lecture arena was a terse "that's nice."

On Wednesday, Kevin was paged by the hospital operator for an outside emergency call. Katherine was on the line. She told him their father had just passed away.

At seven the next morning, four o'clock West Coast time, Kevin was riding in a taxi through downtown Boston. He wore sunglasses to fend off the bright sunlight and felt well rested, having conked out for the entire plane ride. Taking one Halcion on a red-eye is reasonable, he thought. He disregarded the fact that the bottle containing a dozen pills when Marco left for Mexico was now empty.

The taxi dropped him off on a block of identical brick row houses. He wasn't sure which one he had grown up in. A door opened, and there stood his mother. Francine had more gray hair and wrinkles than when he last visited three years ago but looked less haggard than he was expecting. She wore a house dress Kevin hadn't seen before, made of blue, permanent-press fabric with buttons down the front from the collar to the hemline. The kind Sears or JC Penney periodically puts on sale, he thought, the uniform of a domestic servant. The dress was new. He suspected a good deal of delibera-tion had gone into its purchase.

His mother ran down the flight of stairs and hugged him. She hadn't done that since the day he departed for residency training, and it had been a forced gesture then. This hug wasn't restrained. The cache of resentment he was hoarding, a secret he kept even from himself, vanished.

"How are you?" he asked.

"I'm fine. Everything has been taken care of."

He sensed she wasn't devastated by his father's death. Yet somehow she had changed. Following her into the kitchen, he watched her gait. It was relaxed, not an act of careful consideration. Kevin was fascinated by the metamorphosis.

"There must be something I can do," he said.

"Your being here is enough."

Nothing she had said was steeped in abnegation, her default mode of being in the world. As Francine sat down at the Formica table she had manned for forty years, she didn't search for crumbs to wipe off. Kevin put it together. She was relieved.

"Tell me about your life in San Francisco," she asked.

That bombshell disabled Kevin's habitual censoring of what he said to her.

"Do you really want to know?"

"Of course I do."

"Mom, you haven't asked anything about my personal life since I left Boston eight years ago."

"I'm sorry, dear."

Now, Francine's posture drooped mournfully.

"Mom, you don't have to apologize. I never blamed you."

She studied him and waited.

"Honest. Things are OK between you and me."

"Well…That's good then."

Kevin eagerly nodded in agreement.

Francine cradled his hands in hers. He watched her face as a rare and wonderful transformation occurred. She smiled.

The life in San Francisco he told her of only involved his work, which did entail having to explain AIDS. Once he saw her reaction, her fear for his safety, he began asking who would be at the funeral and about the priest who would officiate. After that topic was exhausted, he asked what she planned to do with her time. He knew the garage had been sold and the house paid off. There had been enough money left over to buy an annuity. Adding social security, it was highly improbable she would spend half her monthly income before the next checks arrived.

"You should travel," he suggested.

She squirmed and pursed her lips.

"You can afford to take Katherine with you. Then you wouldn't have to go alone."

Francine looked askance at him. Kevin momentarily considered inviting them to San Francisco. With his father dead, it wouldn't cause a nuclear family holocaust. But no, he wasn't ready for that yet.

The animation slowly drained from their conversation. The silences increased. Kevin kept at the questions. Her answers were short but not rude. Did she want him to stop prying? Was she not saying so out of politeness? Possibly, though she obviously appreciated his interest in her. On the other hand, she had said his presence was enough to content her. Perhaps they didn't have to talk.

The funeral was at Saint Brigid's. A larger mass of bricks than a row house, thought Kevin. That's all it is, with some stained glass, incense, and Latin inside to embellish the homilies. Listening to the rotund, middle-aged priest recite the opening rite, he was skeptical of the man's sincerity. This prayer can't mean more to him than a random string of words. Kevin reproached himself. Who am I to judge?

He contemplated the building to keep from thinking of the body in the casket, the dead man who could still elicit a flood of anger, grief, and guilt. He estimated the age of the bricks. Fifty years old at most, he calculated. His father had been an altar boy when this incarnation of the church was built. Strange, he thought. When I was an altar boy, Saint Brigid's seemed ancient. Maybe it's me that's ancient. I was an altar boy a quarter of a century ago.

Kevin tried to remember what had possessed him to apply. Of course, it had been his mother's cajoling and his bowing to her will. Then a pressed and folded surplice appeared on his bedspread. He had never worn a uniform other than on Halloween. He put on the bleached white garment, admiring the lace bands above the hem and around the wrists. He looked in a mirror and saw someone with a purpose in life.

The biggest challenge, memorizing Latin prayers, was a piece of cake after his mother taught him what the words meant. The responsibilities of mass quickly became rote, and Kevin would stop thinking during the service. This mindless state was so pleasant he actually looked forward to mass, believing he was in a state of exaltation there. He loved the equanimity of the altar. There was no struggle for power, no battle for survival between mortal humanity and the eternal divine.

His new avocation had other benefits. At school, the nuns were more willing to give him the benefit of the doubt. So was his father at home.

Because I was an altar boy? What a fucking hypocrite he was.

Kevin tried concentrating on other people to avoid wallowing in his feelings about the old man. He watched Katherine. The one downside of being an altar boy had been his sister's disapproval. Katherine strove to be the most popular seventh grader at Saint Brigid's. Altar boys were the antithesis of cool, and he had put her status at risk. Worse, their parents' credence in his new angelic persona threatened a hostile realignment of family political forces against her. That must have been the last straw, he thought, because she had devised a plot to torture him.

His mother went to the grocery store once a week and bought four boxes of cereal, no more. There were no mitigating circumstances that would change this rule. Suddenly, half-full cereal boxes were disappearing. When Kevin appealed, he was told he could have oatmeal with a single, level teaspoon of sugar until she went shopping again.

The choice between spiritual sustenance and Sugar Pops had been a tough one. Reminding himself that Christ had suffered on the cross for him, he filled the chalice with wafers, turned missal pages, and recited prayers. Kevin didn't expect Katherine to repent. He reasoned correctly that she would soon be distracted by other dramas and would ignore him once again.

He continued to steal glances at Katherine. She was the only person at the funeral who seemed truly sad. He imagined what her life was like now.

He knew she worked thirty hours a week at a rehabilitation center for brain-damaged patients. None of her four children, three boys and a girl, were terribly difficult. Francine had told him that Ben was good with the two older boys, using humor rather than abuse to keep them in line. In fact, Ben, not Katherine, made sure they finished their homework. Who would have thought? Katherine had just her daughter and the youngest boy, Douglas, to stay on top of, and they were both courteous, docile children. It was doable, he supposed, though she couldn't possibly have any time for herself.

After the burial, they went to Katherine's row house. While Ben and the kids dived into a platter of pastries, Kevin had coffee with his sister and mother in the living room. Katherine talked about the rehab center. She rhapsodized over her charges' achievements, ranging from bladder control to comprehensible speech. This was a revelation. He didn't remember her ever being compassionate toward those less fortunate than her.

Ben drove Francine home, and the children went to a nearby playground, leaving Kevin and Katherine alone.

"Your kids seem good," said Kevin.

"I count my blessings. There's not a bully among them, and they're all doing fine at school."

She blushed.

"Actually, the teachers say Emily and Douglas are gifted. Like you, I guess."

The compliment burrowed inside him. He couldn't detect a shred of sarcasm in what she had said.

"Why, thank you, Katherine. I believe that's the nicest thing you've ever said about me."

He had spoken playfully, his words leached of acidity. They eyed each other, looking for the hidden venom. Both burst into laughter.

In the thaw that followed, Kevin told her about Marco. Instead of being repelled, she was pleased to discover he wasn't alone in the world. Though unlike his mother, Katherine could articulate her concerns.

"Aren't you worried about AIDS?" she asked.

"Not really. We've been monogamous for years."

She nodded pensively, clearly wanting to believe him but unconvinced.

"It must be hard for you, taking care of so many dying young men you can…"

"Identify with?"

"Yes. A lot of our patients don't get better either. When they're old, it doesn't get to me. But when they're my age or younger, it's tough. Last year, we had a woman, a mom with four kids like me, who had been in a car wreck. She couldn't speak or feed herself. And she understood what was going on, that she wasn't making progress in rehab. Sometimes I'd come home and couldn't eat. I'd feel guilty for being able to talk to my children."

Kevin was stunned. How could this woman be his big sister?

"I don't know," he sputtered. "Maybe I've grown a harder shell than you."

Katherine raised her eyebrows. With a thin, doubtful smile, she shook her head no.

They heard the front door open. Douglas, a chunky, freckled twelve-year-old, walked in. He stood in front of Katherine, demanding her attention.

"Mom, I've been outside long enough. Can I read in my room?"

Like a prelate, she lifted her hand, granting him dispensation.

Kevin was intrigued that a son of Katherine and Ben would prefer reading in his room to playing outdoors. He asked Douglas what book he wanted to get back to.

"*A Tale of Two Cities*," Douglas confessed reluctantly.

"What do you think of it?"

"It's OK. I have to read it for school."

"I read it when I was your age, *twice*. 'It was the best of times, it was the worst of times.' Right?"

"Uh-huh."

"And the last sentence of the book can still give me chills. When Sidney Carton is taken to the… Oops. I won't spoil it for you."

"That's OK. I know how it ends."

"So you're reading it again, too!"

With a shy grin, Douglas retreated to his bedroom.

XIV

ON SATURDAY MORNING, HERB went for an early morning jog. When he returned, Martin was in the kitchen eating cereal.

"I've got a surprise," Herb said.

"Yeah," Martin said indifferently.

"Come upstairs when you're done."

Herb settled into the spare bedroom, which housed his new home computer. He turned on the Macintosh, opened a package that had come in yesterday's mail, removed a floppy disc, and inserted it.

"What's that?" Martin asked from the doorway.

"Tetris."

Clusters of squares in various shapes drifted down from the top of the screen. Using the cursor keys, Herb rotated the falling tetronimoes and moved them sideways.

"It's a game," Herb explained as he let Martin have the chair. "If you can arrange these things to form an unbroken line, you get points. Try it."

Martin caught on quickly, manipulating the falling tetronimoes one, then two, then three seconds before they reached the bottom. He gave shouts of triumph each time he completed a line.

Herb enjoyed seeing his son at play. Since starting high school, Martin had become guarded and inaccessible, like his older sister. Herb hoped he had finally found something fun they do together, a pathway to wider-ranging and more personal conversations. Impulsively, he tested the possibility.

"How are you getting along with kids at school?"

Distracted, Martin misplaced three consecutive tetronimoes.

"Fine," he said and stood up. "Thanks, Dad."

After Martin left the den, Herb watched the screen. Blocks were piling on top of each other. What was he doing wrong? He feared history was repeating itself. His father hadn't put a fraction of the effort he had put into connecting with his son. Was alienation an inherited Wu defect, irreparable?

Herb and Cecilia had a date that afternoon. They drove downtown to a matinee at the new concert hall, which had perfect acoustics, she told him. Still disturbed by the Tetris fiasco, he grumbled about Martin while she sat next to him knitting.

"He's not confiding in me either." she said. "I'm not worried about it. It's normal for a thirteen-year-old boy to be uncomfortable sharing anything private with his parents. His hormones and body are changing. You shouldn't take it personally."

Herb knew it was unrealistic to assume a boy Martin's age would admire his father. But a little affection was a fair expectation, wasn't it?

"Thanks," he replied curtly.

Cecilia stopped knitting.

"What's with that tone?"

"What tone?"

"You know what tone."

"You're assuming innuendo that isn't there."

"Right," she said dryly and returned to her knitting.

Inside the concert hall, he asked her, "Who's performing?"

"The Berlin Philharmonic."

"That's supposed to be the world's best orchestra, isn't it?"

"I think so."

Herb was suddenly aware the word "Berlin" had caused him no distress whatsoever. Now he recalled Cecilia telling him weeks ago it would be the Berlin Philharmonic. He hadn't reacted then either. It had been twenty-five years since he had heard the word "Berlin" without flinching.

They had dinner at a nouvelle cuisine restaurant Herb had heard was terrific. He had two glasses of a very smooth cabernet and let go of his annoyance with Cecilia's earlier lack of sympathy. He thought of her calmness during two pregnancies, her resilience when they were robbed the week after moving into their first home, her unpredictable earthiness. He touched the curve of her ear and let his fingers trail down her neck.

"This is nice."

"It is," she murmured and held his hand.

"Another glass of wine?"

"Herb, are you trying to get into my pants?"

He looked away innocently.

"It's working," she said and speared her fork into the bouillabaisse.

XV

HERB AWOKE WITH A headache. He kept his eyes shut. The brightness was irritating. Did I have too much to drink last night, he wondered. Herb remembered the restaurant though not the wine they ordered, which was odd. He couldn't remember what time he went to bed either. Guess I did have too much to drink. Oh well, it's Sunday. He went back to sleep.

He woke again determined to brave the light. Squinting, he saw a white tile ceiling with bare fluorescent bulbs. He turned left and bumped his nose against the chrome side railing of a gurney. A medicine resident he recognized walked by. Her name eluded him. Dressed in scrubs, she was staring at him. Her eyebrows were furrowed. Oh no…this isn't a dream, is it.

Herb turned the other way and saw Cecilia, Martin, and Allison. He sat up, discovered he was clothed only in a hospital gown, open in the back, and immediately lay down.

"What's going on?" he cried out.

No one answered. Martin and Allison looked at each other and rolled their eyes.

"What's happening?" he implored them.

"It's your turn to tell him," said Allison to Cecilia. "I did it last time and Martin the time before."

"Please, Cecilia! What am I doing here?"

Cecilia wearily explained that after dinner, on their way to the car, a Muni bus had nearly hit them. Herb pushed her out of the way then jumped, but not soon enough. As the bus swerved, it delivered a glancing blow that knocked him off balance. He landed on his head and was transiently unconscious. Once he came to, Herb was confused, unable to remember anything that had occurred after dinner. Six hours later in the City Hospital ER, he was asking his family every five minutes where he was and how he got here.

After each explanation, he was again surprised to hear the news. Cecilia told him a CT scan of his brain had been done. The ER physician said it was normal.

"Then I can go home."

His children and wife lunged toward him, yelling "No!" in unison.

Herb touched a cherry-size swelling on the side of his skull that throbbed painfully. He acquiesced.

Since all the ER rooms were filled with more gravely injured patients, Herb spent the night in the hallway. He didn't complain. He pretended to sleep so he wouldn't see the passing house staff's morbid curiosity. Yes, it can happen to us too, he wanted to scream.

In the morning, Jared Hart, sans his retinue of surgical residents and students, came by and carefully examined him.

"No motor deficits," Hart concluded. "Are you thinking clearly now?"

"More or less," Herb hedged. To admit otherwise would be beyond mortification. But how he could not be truthful? His mind, not just his reputation, was on the line.

"I still have amnesia for about six hours of last night. Otherwise, my memory seems intact."

Hart rubbed his chin skeptically.

"I'm not quite playing with a full deck. Maybe it's stress from the trauma?"

"That'd be par for the course. But if you're not back to normal in a few days, you need to be seen by a neurologist. OK?"

"Sure," said Herb, noncommittally.

"I'm serious about that, Herb. I'm not trying to cover my ass. I'm trying to cover yours."

Cecilia picked him up at the ER entrance. On the ride home, he insisted he was fine.

"I think there's still time for me to round on the ICU patients."

She stopped the car and stared at him.

"You've got to be kidding."

He began to argue. Seeing her jaw clamped tight, he hesitated.

"Herb, what did the ER doctors say about going back to work?"

"We didn't talk about it."

Cecilia and Herb had played chess when they were dating. They had been well-matched. She expected this response. She knew she had him in check and prepared her final move.

"If you had asked them if it was OK for you to go in to work today, what do you honestly think they would have said? 'Sure, no problem' or 'Gee, that doesn't sound like good idea?'"

"Never mind."

A compassionate victor, she said, "Isn't it possible, honey, that your judgment is a bit off right now? Let's take it one step at a time, OK?"

Cecilia set a hand on his knee and started the car. He looked out the passenger window and worried.

Once home, he called the ICU and was told another pulmonologist had already come in to round with the residents. Herb wanted an update because he indisputably would be at the hospital tomorrow. In addition, he wanted to test his ability to remember details about old patients and search his fund of knowledge for relevant facts when told about the new ones. After hanging up, he couldn't point to any glaring cognitive deficits. He was also aware he hadn't second-guessed a single decision made by the back-up attending.

Herb tried to nap that afternoon but couldn't stop fretting over his mental acuity. He kept multiplying and dividing numbers and recalling names of interns who had rotated through the ICU.

He got up and found Allison studying for a history test. He quizzed her, repeating each question after four minutes to check his own short term memory until she demanded he leave her alone.

Just before dinner, Martin shouted from upstairs, "The bathroom sink's stopped up."

Herb found Martin inspecting his face in the mirror, clearly unhappy with what he saw. His adolescent growth spurt was underway and had started with his nose. Herb had heard Cecilia assure him the rest of his face would catch up soon. It appeared he was losing faith in her infallibility, too.

"What are you going to do, Dad?"

It was more an accusation than an inquiry. Herb looked at the sink full of soapy water. His mind went blank. To buy time, he asked Martin what he thought.

"Gee, Dad," Martin exploded. "Can't you even fix a clogged sink?"

Afraid the answer was no, he stalled.

"I'm curious about how your mind works, how you'd approach the problem."

Martin turned away. Herb knew he had compounded his error. Martin most definitely did *not* want his father to have a clue as to how his mind worked. Herb had to answer the question or suffer a quantum drop in his son's esteem. He noticed a toilet plunger.

"Let's try this," he said, picking it up.

Martin had thought of using the plunger but hadn't suggested it, fearful it would be a gross sanitary violation. Among other things, his father's unassailably superior grasp of this mysterious and embarrassing subject galled him.

Cecilia came in the bathroom, took one look, and said, "I'll phone a plumber in the morning."

Of course, Herb chided himself. Why didn't I think of that?

Martin glanced at Herb. His eyebrows were furrowed. It was an expression Herb had seen recently. He couldn't place where or when.

XVI

Herb was at work Monday morning, supervising his fellow as she performed bronchoscopies. He hovered behind her, looking through the second eyepiece, ready to step in if needed. Mostly, he re-oriented her while she steered the instrument tip inside the patient's lung, reminding her to suction whenever fluid accumulated and clouded their view. At the same time, he was explaining disease mechanisms to the resident and medical student assigned to the pulmonary consult service that month and letting them peek at airway abnormalities.

The first two procedures went smoothly. Herb wasn't encouraged. He knew that before the accident he could have been doing both clinical and teaching tasks and simultaneously planning the outline of a manuscript.

A problem occurred during the third bronchoscopy. The fellow, attempting to direct the tip into a small airway, got stuck. She tried unsuccessfully to retract it, which made the patient cough violently. Herb couldn't think of any advice to give her. Meanwhile, she told the resident to administer more sedation and kept maneuvering the lever. One minute later—a very long minute for Herb—she freed up the tip, redirected it to another part of the lung, and adroitly completed the procedure.

"Thanks for letting me work it out, Herb," she said afterwards. "That was a real confidence builder."

"Well, part of training is learning how to get out of trouble, isn't it?"

As his team was exiting the suite, he overheard the resident whisper to the student, "See what I mean? That's why he's a legendary teacher."

Ashamed by being complimented when he wasn't even capable of doing his job competently, Herb thought, I don't need a neurologist's help. He knew what he had—a cognitive dysfunction in problem solving, relatively mild in severity but incapacitating for this occupation. And he knew what a neurologist could do about it—absolutely nothing. It would get better, or it wouldn't.

Herb had no difficulty seeing the irony here. He had applied his skills and insight to his own problem and identified the correct solution. He would have to go on sick leave. He decided to allow himself one more day before concluding he was too impaired to work.

His pager beeped and displayed the lung clinic phone number. He had forgotten Sister Anna was coming at eleven for her airflow to be measured.

Sister Anna was in a jovial mood.

"God is giving me a last laugh, Herb," she said. "I told the bishop I have AIDS. He was utterly befuddled. So I said, 'the gay plague.' Oh, Lord, was the expression on his face a treat! I could see the wheels turning. He must have been imagining me humping a bisexual man. Then I told him about the transfusion. My, my, did the color in his cheeks rise. Guilt, no doubt, for having those sinful thoughts of me *in flagrante delicto*."

Herb smiled, though in his current distress he was reacting to Sister Anna's ability to speak in whole sentences without catching her breath rather than sharing her amusement.

"How's the breathing?"

"A tad better with the new inhalers. The cough and fatigue are the same, annoying but manageable. I suppose this is as good as it's going to be from here on out."

He heard no trace of self-pity. She spoke of her misfortune as if it was another's, someone she didn't even know. The clarity with which she saw her future froze him. He couldn't formulate a reply.

"I know I don't have much time, Herb. It's all right. I'm at peace with it."

"I believe you. You seem so serene. It's impressive."

"There's no deep secret involved," she said, coughing. "No religious mystery. I'm not anticipating an ecstatic afterlife. I've had a good run. That makes me content. But I can't claim to have achieved any higher spiritual state."

Herb wanted to ask her more but checked himself. She was his patient. He wasn't hers.

She gazed soberly at him.

"What's bothering you, Herb?"

Her question unfettered him. He told her the story of his accident and subsequent troubles.

"It must be very frightening," said Sister Anna, her tone contemplative.

"It is. Everything I do here is at stake."

"You seem normal."

"You're being deceived by appearances."

She started to speak and stopped. He had a presentiment she was holding back something of great importance.

"What are you thinking?" he asked.

"Have you thought through the worse case scenario?"

"Not…in any detail."

"Your intellect isn't the only way to be in the world, Herb. There's love. You've got that too, don't you, with your family and friends?"

He looked away.

"I see. Perhaps not as much as you could have if you applied yourself to it, like you do to making the right medical decisions."

Herb felt naked, more than naked, as though a supernatural surgeon had painlessly opened his chest and exposed the vulnerable truth inside.

"Thank you, Sister," he said in a rush. "I value your advice. I truly do. I'm sure it's the best I'll get."

After Sister Anna left, Herb was relieved he had forgotten to bring up her talking to the press. The blood banks would change their policies soon whether her story made the news or not. She didn't need the satisfaction of embarrassing them. Neither did he.

XVII

Herb went from clinic to the monthly department meeting, Ray's last before his sabbatical began. Since Ray wanted him to counsel the young assistant chief of medicine who would be in charge during his absence, he had to attend. Though able to follow the discussion, Herb made no comments about the department's ongoing financial woes, despite several prodding glances from Ray. As he was leaving, Kevin stopped him.

"Are you OK?"

"I'm fine."

"Really?"

"It was a little concussion."

"Then…do you have time for coffee? I need your advice about the suramin trial."

"To be honest, Kevin, my mental powers are not quite back to a hundred percent yet. You sure you want advice from me?"

"Herb, if you're functioning at twenty percent, that's better than me with all eight cylinders firing."

They sat in a corner of the empty cafeteria. To postpone having to deal with another intellectual challenge, Herb asked about Kevin's weekend. His probing, warm curiosity surprised Kevin. Herb gave an apologetic shrug. He hadn't meant to pry.

"It was pretty intense," said Kevin.

"What happened?"

"I was in Boston, at my father's funeral."

"Oh, I'm sorry. Was his death unexpected?"

"Hardly. He lived for three years after being diagnosed with inoperable lung cancer. It must have been a joy for my mother to have it drag out that long."

"You sound angry," said Herb, leaning forward, elbows on the table, chin resting on his interlaced fingers.

"I know. I shouldn't be."

"No?"

"He wasn't a kind man. In fact, he was a stubborn bastard. But I never took the initiative to work things out. I assumed he'd eventually accept who I was and want my forgiveness. That never happened."

Herb's forehead wrinkled as he concentrated.

"What do you think, Herb? If I didn't try to repair things between us, do I have the right to be angry at him now?"

"Why not? He was the parent. In the big picture, didn't he have a bigger share of responsibility for the relationship than you?"

Kevin thought for a moment and said, "Maybe you're right."

Hoping he was on a roll, Herb said, "And if you're like me, you're probably mad at yourself, too."

"Huh…you think?"

"Definitely. And I know what I'm talking about."

"How so?"

"I didn't have much of a relationship with my father. That's an overstatement. He never showed me affection. Then he died when I was twenty-one. Nothing was resolved—I mean for me it wasn't. I'm sure he never saw any problem between us."

"You still sound angry."

"Just sarcastic. I got over it. Other people came into my life. His significance receded."

"Gee, that's inspiring."

"Sorry if I sound flippant, but it's true. If nothing else, age does give one perspective on stuff like this. I was angry well into my thirties. Now I think I should have been grateful. Growing up as the only Asian kid in an all-white suburb of New York City had to be far better than living through World War II in China."

"Was your dad just indifferent or abusive?"

"I'd say he took indifference to a level that approached cruelty. Here's an example. He traveled a lot for work, but he did happen to be in town the weekend I graduated from high school. And, by the way, my class had voted me most likely to succeed. He didn't bother to come to the ceremony. It wasn't important to him. I was just another piece of furniture at home, nothing more."

"And you're not still angry?"

"Oh, I guess there's a spark or two left. But mostly when I think of him, I'm sad. He was such an unhappy person."

"That's a lofty view. Wish I had it."

"You will. And when you do, you'll accept that you weren't responsible for what happened. Neither was your father. Shit happens. And when there's no love, it's not rational to feel loss or guilt."

"I don't think that attitude is going to work for me. I have a few good memories to feed the guilt."

Kevin could hear his father's voice, shouting and laughing, "Kev, this is gonna be a huge problem!" At the end of the first summer Kevin spent in the garage, his father had tested the twelve-year-old boy's mastery of the socket wrench. Kevin scooted under a car and unscrewed oil pan bolts while his father called out five second intervals. He slid back out, oil pan in hand, in eighty seconds. "That's faster than Jones," his father had said sotto voce with a wink. "I can't fire him. He's got three kids at home. He needs the job more than you do."

Kevin's nostrils flared. His eyelids turned red.

Herb had been running on pure emotion. Now he was at a loss for the right thing to say. He had to start thinking again.

"Then you're lucky, Kevin. I don't have a single fond recollection."

"But you've got so much confidence. Isn't that supposed to come from good fathering?"

"Who knows."

"Maybe we should be in a self-help group."

They both laughed, but Herb couldn't sustain the humor. The desolation of his childhood felt too close. Wanting to hold onto his connection with Kevin, he confided the difficulties he had been having since the accident.

"It's terrifying," he said at the end of his account. "This is how I've made my way in the world. I can't let myself imagine what it would be like if I don't recover."

Kevin grabbed Herb's wrists and squeezed. Herb didn't withdraw.

Looking him straight in the eyes, Kevin said, "You're going to recover completely. You've got to believe that, Herb. I do. I'm absolutely sure of it."

XVIII

FROM THE CAFETERIA, KEVIN drove across town to the Department of Public Health. Entering the building required passing through a gauntlet of protesters who carried placards reading "Out of the Baths, Into the Ovens." They shrieked curses at him.

His mouth was dry as he opened the conference room door. Sixty people were inside, all standing though there were more than enough empty chairs to accommodate everyone. Members of two gay Democratic clubs, enraged by each other's presence, appeared ready to throw punches at the least provocation. One was pressuring health department officials to shut down the bath houses. The other waved the American flag and Bill of Rights, charging that closure would violate their constitutionally guaranteed freedom. While Gwen usually handled AIDS policy issues for their program, a gay man had to represent them here.

Both sides heckled him, shouting, "Where do you stand on this, Bartholomew?"

Kevin trotted to the front of the room to take refuge with the rest of the speakers.

An attorney for the bath house owners, a man in his early thirties wearing a three piece suit and designer eyeglasses, followed him.

"What's your position, Bartholomew?" he screamed.

Kevin refused to respond.

The lawyer pulled at Kevin's sleeve and screamed at a higher pitch, "Doctor, I'm talking to you!"

Kevin yanked his arm away.

"You'll hear what I have to say, publicly," he replied coldly. "I'm on the schedule."

Kevin found it baffling that any educated gay men believed bath-house closure was a threat to individual rights. Every sane person he knew thought knowingly transmitting the retrovirus was de facto homicide. How could permitting unsafe sex to go on in public bath houses be different from abetting murder, he would argue. The data were incontrovertible. For a gay man living in San Francisco, the more bath-house sexual encounters he had had, the greater his risk of being infected with the AIDS virus. Kevin had no ambivalence about taking sides in this dispute.

After his turn at the microphone, Kevin knew he had come across as uninspired. He had cited statistics and made analogies. The bath houses were as causally linked to AIDS as mosquito swamps were to yellow fever. It was that simple. But neither his delivery nor his rhetoric had been compelling.

The other side didn't mention the one argument for keeping bath houses open that might make sense—the damage had already been done, the majority of bath-house patrons were probably already infected. Gwen and Kevin had been briefed by the health department about a recent survey. One out of twelve men interviewed in local bath houses reported persistent swollen lymph nodes, an almost certain sign of HTLV-III infection in the ARC stage of disease, which meant an even larger proportion must be infected and asymptomatic, invisible below the iceberg's water line, continuing to transmit the infection. The health department had also hired private detectives to document what practices occurred in bath houses. They reported most sexual activity included anal intercourse, almost always sans condom. Soon, the only people whom closure could protect would be the next generation of young gay men.

When Kevin left the meeting, the slick attorney followed him into the hall.

"You're disgusting, Bartholomew," he taunted.

"Excuse me?" said Kevin, his hands involuntarily forming fists.

"You think you're some selfless, compassionate healer, don't you? That's a convenient delusion. You're really a self-loathing homosexual. You want to take away the freedom of others to rationalize your own guilt. I bet you're a Catholic, aren't you?"

Kevin smirked. His fists relaxed. The dart had missed its mark. Catholic guilt was at the bottom of his problem list now.

"And you're a lawyer, right?" he said with contempt. "Isn't that supposed to be someone who can defend his position by arguing on the basis of rules, facts, and logic? And the best you can do is a scummy slur. How pathetic. Where did you go to law school? One of those places that advertises inside a matchbook cover?"

"Fuck yourself, Bartholomew."

The lawyer showed Kevin his extended middle finger.

"Go back to law school," Kevin said as he walked away, "You missed the part about murder. It's not protected by the Bill of Rights."

XIX

Gwen left clinic early that afternoon wearing capris and a tee-shirt. She drove to Noe Valley where her best friend, Nan, had just claimed a tennis court. Their bond, forged twenty years ago while sharing seats on the bench of the Stanford women's varsity team, had endured despite the divergent directions their lives had taken. Nan married a lawyer right after college—they did have that in common. She became a suburban matron and didn't work outside the home again. Her daily life was unaffected by the turmoil of the 1960s that so influenced Gwen. Nan's three children were all older than Eva, and Gwen often thought of Nan as an older sister—except on the tennis court where her speed, powerful swing, and natural blond hair made Gwen feel like Nan's doddering old aunt.

They lost touch during Gwen's years in medical school but reconnected when Eva was born. Nan would come to San Francisco and provide advice and support. A few years later, Nan's youngest child was diagnosed with a kidney tumor. Gwen would drive to Menlo Park, their roles reversed.

After volleying for ten minutes, they began a set. Gwen's first serve nicked the net.

"Let," hollered Nan, shifting her center of gravity from one foot to the other.

Where does that energy come from, wondered Gwen.

She lost in short order by a double fault, two long returns, and another double fault. The second game started with Nan's serve getting by her. It was one she would have been able to return a year ago. In college, she had been well-matched against Nan on the court. Not anymore.

Gwen set her hands on her hips and shouted, "You may have to play the outer lines for this to be competition."

"It used to be about winning, Gwen. Now it's about exercise."

"Uh-huh," wheezed Gwen as she rushed the baseline and returned a serve over Nan's head as she was creeping up to the net. Nan raced back. She had to lob her return, allowing Gwen to send a forehand smash which Nan could only watch. They both laughed.

There was another bond they shared. Sophomores on the Stanford tennis team traditionally strengthened their forearms and got their art requirement out of the way at the same time by taking a studio course in carving marble. Their team mates were soon bored with the repetitive hammering, but Gwen and Nan were entranced by shaping stone blocks into human forms. They still made dates to visit local museums whenever sculpture exhibits were in town.

As they walked off the court, Nan said, "We're on for the De Young next weekend, right?"

"Absolutely! I'm not missing a chance to see some of the Pergamon collection."

"Hey, how's Eva?"

"The same. At least she's not pregnant or doing drugs. I guess I should be grateful."

"That's for damn sure."

"Actually, if I can think objectively and ignore how she treats me, it does seem that for fourteen, she's doing all right."

Nan slung an arm around Gwen's shoulders.

"There you go," she said. "That's a winning attitude."

XX

FROM TENNIS, GWEN WALKED to a neighborhood Italian restaurant. Inside, Kevin was seated with an open bottle of Chianti on the table. He filled two glasses as soon as he saw her.

"Sorry about your father," said Gwen.

"I'm not. Let's talk about something else."

He had anticipated Gwen bringing this subject up and decided he didn't have the stamina to sort through his conflicted emotions again today.

"OK, we won't go there. What's happening with Marco's mother?"

"I just got a telegram. She's finally out of the woods. He's coming home the day after tomorrow."

"Yay!"

"After four operations and a pulmonary embolism, she left the hospital with her mind and mobility intact. Can't ask for more than that, can you."

"I guess what he's gone through makes what we do seem easy."

Kevin showed her a little smile which quickly faded. He was still tense from the tantrum session at the health department. He told her about the debacle.

"Did the director make a decision?"

"He thinks there isn't enough community consensus to force closure."

"Shit!"

She had already given Kevin the short version of her meeting with the AIDS Action Committee. Now she went into the gory details.

Kevin was sinking into pessimism. He realized they had to stop talking about work. He asked how Rick and Eva were doing.

"Oh, he's the good guy. I'm the witch."

Uh-oh, thought Kevin, this might be a mistake too.

"He truly is the good guy. He doesn't lose his temper like I do. Plus, he's not the father who abandoned her. She can blame me for that."

Kevin winced.

"Don't worry. I'm not going to cry."

"Aren't you being a little hard on yourself? Think about how much experience Rick has with kids. And he's not her father. She can't push his buttons like she can yours."

"I know. Rick has the clinical distance to see her as a patient with a treatable condition."

Kevin laughed.

"So when did you say Marco is coming back?"

"Wednesday evening," he answered blithely.

Hearing his blatantly counterfeit tone, Kevin shuddered. He couldn't pretend not to notice it. Something was wrong between him and Marco. He didn't understand it, had no desire to think or talk about it, but knew he needed to, that he should use this opportunity to get Gwen's help.

She looked at him with concern.

"I'm worried…" he said.

He couldn't articulate the fear any further. It was too amorphous.

Gwen turned pale.

"I'm worried," he faltered, grasping for safe words to hang onto, "about what…this academic status thing might do to us."

"Oh," she said, the color returning to her face. "You think he'll be envious?"

Kevin was relieved. She had given a name to the distress, one he could handle.

"Maybe. It's not something we've ever talked about. But I see where you're going. I do need to make sure things stay real between us."

"Right! Marco isn't that competitive, is he? You two can work it out. Just don't say anything he could remotely interpret as lording it over him."

"Me?" he exclaimed in mock offense, "Lord *my* status over Marco? Don't tempt me."

Aware his back muscles were painfully taut, Kevin stretched his neck. Was that a panic attack, he wondered. Will that be the price of fame?

Dishes of steaming osso buco and risotto, redolent with garlic, were brought to the table. Eating was an excuse for dropping the matter.

As their plates were being taken away, Kevin asked, "Was Eva a Girl Scout?"

"Girl Scout? Do you think if I had made her join Girl Scouts, she'd be better behaved now?"

"No, no. I'm just curious. How about you? Were you a Girl Scout?"

"Yeah…"

Gwen recalled a muggy spring afternoon, the smell of chalk and starched clothes mixed with acrid sweat. She had been standing in a line of uniformed girls, waiting to march into the school assembly hall. She was adjusting the front of her Girl Scout dress. It didn't seem right. She had forgotten how many buttons were supposed to show below the belt. She'd been told, repeatedly, how important it was that everyone look exactly the same when they filed onto the stage. Was her scarf completely under her collar? Her sash at the right angle? She could only see the back of the girl ahead of her. There was no way to check. Her anxiety turned into suspicion. Why was it so important that everyone look alike? What if she wanted to be different?

"When?"

"In elementary school. It was part of Pasadena 1950s conformity. All the girls joined. The uniform was chic when we were ten. By the time we were twelve, it was passé, and anyone seen wearing it was ridiculed. So I quit. Sorry, Kevin. Girl Scouts wasn't particularly meaningful for me. Was Boy Scouts for you?"

"I've been trying to figure that out."

"Why?"

"It's about understanding where my values came from. All I got at home was 'don't waste money,' 'do your chores,' 'don't lie.' And the Church was mostly about not having evil thoughts or committing sins. But Boy Scouts actually had positive ideals. Some were even altruistic. I bought into it. There were these twelve values we had to recite out loud at troop meetings. I'm blanking on the first ones. The last four were 'thrifty, brave, clean, and reverent.' Brave is good. I'd like to have more courage."

"Interesting. Girl Scouts had same thing. I remember 'respectful' and 'considerate' were on their list. I couldn't buy into it. I saw how well those values were working for my mother. She was *so* respectful and *so* considerate, and it made her so miserable."

Kevin folded his hands below his chin.

"Now we are getting someplace," he said in a parody of a Viennese accent. "The unhappy childhood that drives great accomplishment in adult life."

"Indeed. It was grist for my mill."

"You've been in therapy?"

"Kevin, I've been divorced. It's *de rigueur*. Have you?"

"Once…"

Gwen leaned forward conspiratorially.

"So, tell me about it."

"You really want to hear this?"

"Of course I do!"

"OK…I guess things came to a head when I moved to San Francisco expecting to fall in love and leave my neuroses back in Boston. None of that happened. Residency was exhausting. Whenever I did escape from the hospital, I'd see all these men who were openly out and looked genuinely gay—I'm using the nineteenth century definition of the word. Big surprise, I sank into depression. I tried therapy because I was desperate."

"Did it help?"

"Not at first. The therapist thought my problems stemmed from low self-esteem. He made me describe my strengths. That was round one—lukewarm results. Round two was examining values, what we were just talking about, and choosing which ones I wanted to direct my life. That's when I began to believe the person I want to be—fair, empathetic, competent, not needing to control others—was in reach."

"And it worked?"

"I wasn't cured overnight, but it was a turning point."

"Impressive! Therapy wasn't nearly so high-minded or transformative for me. Mostly it was about the anger—at my parents, at Daniel, at myself—that was poisoning my life. I needed to exorcise it or at least be able control it."

"But you're so *not* an angry person."

"Aha!" she said, assuming the Viennese accent. "This is the result of years of hard work on the couch."

They were laughing as the waiter arrived with the check.

"That's what we like to see," he said. "Happy customers."

XXI

Gwen had a hangover the next morning. The headache lingered into her mid-afternoon meeting in a hospital conference room. Thirty nurses, medical assistants, and laboratory technicians sat around the perimeter. They looked tired after finishing their eight hour shift and uneasy about the subject to be discussed. Gwen introduced herself and explained the specifics of what had been advertised in flyers posted throughout the City Hospital corridors. They could sign up here to get a blood test that would determine if they had been infected with the AIDS virus. In addition, they could opt to have the test repeated every six months.

"It's *voluntary* screening," Gwen said. "I want you to be clear about three things. First, all results will be kept strictly confidential. Second, screening is being implemented for our protection, to learn how to make our jobs safer. Third—this hopefully is just hypothetical—if someone were to be infected from a needle stick or scalpel wound, the antibody results could be used to document it was due to the occupational exposure rather than…some other behavior."

Lilly, a Filipina nursing supervisor, exactly Gwen's age, raised her hand.

"Yes?" said Gwen, recalling a framed photograph of three children she had seen on Lilly's desk.

"How long before we know the result?"

"We only have enough lab tech support to run the assay once a week, and we have to schedule a counseling session to give you the result. So right now it's taking about two weeks from the time your blood is drawn until you can get the result."

"That's a long wait," objected a middle-aged black ICU nurse.

"I couldn't agree more, but regulations require a counselor to be present when you get the result, whether it's negative or positive. Most employees at City Hospital want to participate, and there aren't enough counselors to schedule it any sooner. Once we've completed this round of screening, we can spread out the follow-up testing. Then the waiting time will get shorter."

A young, blond woman with a Swedish accent said, "I have a friend who was tested in a research study. He says it's very frightening, waiting to find out."

"Honey," said an older gay man, "The folks I know who've been through it say the waiting is ice-cold terror."

There was a collective, introspective lull. Gwen looked around the room to see if anyone had an question. She saw doubt and vacillation, though no one appeared ready to articulate it. She invited comments and was met with silence.

A few people walked out. The rest got in line to sign a consent form and choose a date for their blood draw. As the last staff somberly exited, a public health nurse hurried in. The woman was assisting Gwen in this project and held one of the manila folders they were using to keep each participant's records.

"Can we talk?" she whispered urgently to Gwen.

"Sure, what's up?"

She didn't speak until the room was empty and she had shut the door.

"One of the stored samples is positive. It's a woman. Her only risk factor is a needle-stick three years ago."

Gwen felt her chest pound. The pace of her breathing involuntarily sped up. She couldn't remember the drill for dealing with an infected health care worker. After her own close call, she had never really believed it could happen to anyone else here. What was she supposed to do now?

"Who is it?" Gwen asked.

"You sure you want to know? Her post-test counseling visit is next week. We can't tell her before then, can we?"

"No!"

Gwen considered the implications. If she knew who it was, that could help her prepare to handle the woman's reaction. But what if it was someone she worked with in clinic? What if they interacted before the disclosure meeting?

How could she not be tense and artificial? And afterwards, wouldn't that be seen as a betrayal?

"When's the appointment?"

"Monday, three o'clock. Can you be there?"

"Of course I'll be there."

Gwen deliberated, eyes fixed on the manila folder. She held out her hand.

As soon as Gwen was alone in her office, she opened the folder. It slipped from her moist, shaking fingers onto the floor. She wiped her palms on her skirt, clenched and unclenched her fists, and tried again.

It was a name she didn't recognize—one small mercy—Laurie Hampton, an ICU nurse. Another was her age, forty-seven. Future pregnancies wouldn't be an issue. Gwen read the account of a needle-stick exposure. The source patient had later been diagnosed with Pneumocystis pneumonia. The file was small, just the incident report, a behavioral questionnaire that had every box checked 'No,' a signed consent form, a phone number and address in Daly City, and a woman named Tanya listed as an emergency contact.

Gwen noticed a page stapled behind the report. It was a photocopy of a letter dated a month after the incident. Herb Wu had written to City Hospital's head administrator demanding the hospital refer Ms. Hampton to a psychotherapist and pay all costs.

She closed the folder and chewed on her ballpoint pen. Suddenly, the pen snapped. She watched in horror as a drop of black ink fell from her lip onto the file's cover, obliterating Laurie Hampton's identification number.

XXII

Kevin's hangover, milder than Gwen's, was gone by end of his morning clinic. He had a pleasant break in the early afternoon. A ward team presented their most interesting cases to him, and he did a little teaching. When he returned to clinic, he passed the waiting room where three of his suramin trial subjects sat fidgeting. Their study folders were in his exam room. He found a note on top from his research assistant alerting him to new lab test results inside. Kevin picked up one labeled HW.

On his way to get the patient, he opened the folder. His assistant had highlighted three abnormal results with a fluorescent yellow marker—creatinine 3.5, blood urea nitrogen 40, urine protein 4+. Dazed by the bright halos encircling numbers that indicated imminent kidney failure, Kevin leaned against a wall. To fend off mounting dread, he concentrated on what he had learned about suramin toxicity. Individuals who had received the drug for sleeping sickness often suffered kidney injury as a side effect. It began with innocuous amounts of serum proteins leaking into urine. If suramin continued to be administered, it could lead to irreversible kidney failure.

"That's why we check a weekly urinalysis," he complained aloud. "Kidney toxicity isn't supposed to happen this fast."

This patient's urine had shown a trace amount of protein last week, though not enough to meet the protocol criteria for stopping treatment.

Kevin went to the waiting room.

"Hubert?" he called softly.

Mr. Wilson had requested Kevin use his first name. It wasn't Kevin's style, but he adapted to what his patients wanted. A slender, blond, twenty-eight year old man stood up. Hubert was a graphic artist for a downtown advertising firm and quite a success at the job from the rumors Kevin's assistant had heard. Other than a birthmark on his neck, Hubert had remarkably smooth, unblemished skin.

In the exam room, Kevin asked how he was feeling.

"Not great," he replied, quickly adding, "But no worse than when I started the trial."

"More fatigue?"

"Not really."

"All right if I examine you?"

"Sure."

Kevin shone a light in Hubert's mouth, palpated his neck and under his arms for lymph nodes, listened to his heart and lungs, and pressed a hand on his belly. Everything looked, sounded, felt normal.

Despite three years of working with people who had a fatal disease, Kevin still hated giving bad news. He calmly told Hubert about the lab results while suppressing a deluge of guilt. Hubert must have been receiving real suramin, he said, not placebo, because there was no other plausible reason for the kidney damage. It was severe enough that the medication had to be discontinued at once.

"No!" Hubert protested. "I don't want to stop. This is my last chance."

Kevin had been at international meetings, cultivating connections with NIH scientists and pharmaceutical companies, learning all he could about drugs developed for other chronic viral infections. He knew Hubert was right. There was little on the horizon more promising than suramin. Given that Hubert's helper T cell count was less than two hundred, it was hard for Kevin to spin this as anything other than the final door closing.

"Hubert, more suramin infusions would permanently destroy your kidneys. You'd need dialysis forever."

"So the choice is between living with kidney failure or dying from AIDS? That's a no brainer."

"Sorry, I'm not being clear. There is no choice. According to the protocol rules, if toxicity this serious occurs, the drug has to be stopped. Permanently."

Hubert sat still, his lips pressed tightly together.

"If I gave you another dose of suramin, I'd be violating the most fundamental rule of human research—do no harm. And if the FDA or the university found out, they wouldn't let me, wouldn't let anyone at City Hospital conduct another treatment trial for AIDS."

Hubert's head drooped.

"Let your kidneys recover. Then you could be eligible for the next study that comes along."

Hubert gave a short snort of disgust. Kevin wheedled him into making an appointment in two weeks to check how his kidneys were doing off the drug. Hubert's mechanical consent intimated he might never be back. He left without acknowledging Kevin's good bye. From the exam room doorway, Kevin watched him shuffle toward the elevator.

"Fuck," Kevin swore. "I can't do this anymore."

He stared at Hubert's folder, blinking, his vision blurred.

"I don't have time for this bullshit," he hissed, wiping his eyes with a sleeve.

He grabbed the next folder and marched out to get the patient.

XXIII

IT MUST BE A dream. How could she not have felt the earthquake? Still, the ER staff were saying it had been the big one. She heard sirens approaching the emergency room.

"Ambulance alert!" screamed a ward clerk. "Six hundred AIDS patients on their way, all critically injured. ETA five minutes."

In moments, they would be awash in infected blood. Men in white plastic jumpsuits walked through the hallways fumigating doctors and nurses in preparation for the onslaught. Covered with oily disinfectant, damp hair stuck to her neck, she waited. The sirens kept howling but didn't come closer.

Waking in the dark, Gwen realized the telephone was ringing. Her digital clock showed five a.m.

She picked up the receiver and mumbled, "Hello."

"Dr. Howard, it's the answering service. I have a Terrell Hunt on the line. He says your patient, Ed Greames, is dying. I told him he should call an ambulance, but he insists Mr. Greames told him not to."

Gwen remembered the two prescriptions she had written and sat upright, wide awake.

"Connect me please."

Gwen had met Ed Greames' boy lover once in clinic. She thought his name was Timmy, perhaps because he looked like the child actor who shared top billing with Lassie in her favorite girlhood television show. Allegedly nineteen years old, Terrell acted the part of a devoted son or nephew.

She heard the operator say, "Dr. Howard is on the line."

A pleading voice, punctuated by static from the tenuous phone connection, said, "I don't…to do. How…know when he's dead?"

"Slow down, Terrell. Tell me what happened."

"Ed took the death cocktail."

"Is he breathing?"

"Sort of…stops and starts."

"Terrell, find the pill bottles and see if they're empty."

"What difference…" he shouted. "Are the police…arrest me? Do I need to get out of here?"

"Don't go anywhere, Terrell! Give me your address. I'll be there in half an hour."

Her mind raced as she sped across the Bay Bridge. This was the first time she had intentionally given a patient the means to end his life. She hadn't thought through how it might play out. What if Greames didn't swallow all the pills or couldn't keep them down, and then Terrell called an ambulance? Would Terrell, or Ed, if he woke up, tell the ER doc that Gwen had written the fatal prescriptions? Would that trigger a criminal investigation? Or if Ed did die at home, would people from the coroner's office come and find empty morphine and phenobarbital bottles that had her name printed on them as the prescribing physician? Would they call the police? How could she honor Ed Greames' wishes without losing her medical license and facing manslaughter charges?

A band of orange light rose above the East Bay hills as she descended into Eureka Valley. It was spreading across the sky when she found the address, a second floor Victorian flat off Castro Street. She rang the bell. The door promptly buzzed open.

Gwen climbed a dark stairway and entered a high-ceiling living room decorated with splendid millwork. Ed Greames lay on a couch. He didn't respond to her shouting his name or rubbing his collarbone. He was breathing, intermittently, and had faint heart sounds. She couldn't feel a pulse.

From behind her, Terrell asked, "Is he dead yet?"

"No," she answered, thinking minutes, an hour at most.

Then she reconsidered. What if his phenobarbital levels had already peaked? God, what is the half-life of that drug? It's long, isn't it?

She turned to the boy and said, "Timmy, I mean Terrell, what did he take? Which medications?"

"I don't know"

"Think hard. It's important."

"He told me he was going to take the death cocktail, but I didn't see him do it."

"*When* did he take it?"

"Probably when he went to sleep, maybe two in the morning."

Gwen demanded he show her all of Ed's pill bottles. Terrell led her into the kitchen where medication containers littered the breakfast table. She inspected each bottle, several times. None were labeled morphine or phenobarbital.

"Are you sure this is everything?"

"I don't know," he answered defensively. "I just fed him and cleaned him. I didn't deal with his pills."

Gwen couldn't remember the precise words of their conversation, but she had seen Ed write down the names of the drugs and the number of pills. She studied the boy. Nineteen might be pushing it a year or two. Gwen chose to believe him. Ed must have taken the pills four hours ago. In his terminal state, he would absorb the medication slowly. That meant his blood morphine levels should be peaking now, possibly the phenobarbital as well.

Terrell twitched. His eyebrows knitted. Gwen saw a frightened kid, only a few years older than Eva. She was appalled by the questions she had just asked him, the tone she had used. This had to stop being about what she was risking and start being about what he had already lost.

"Terrell, you did the right thing. No one is going to accuse you of a crime. OK?"

He looked doubtfully at her.

"We have to wait until he goes. It won't be long. Are you OK with that?"

"Like I have some other choice? If I leave now, you can tell the police I killed him."

"As soon as he dies, I'll call the coroner. They'll send people to take the body away. I'll do the talking. There won't be any police."

Terrell crouched on a stool with the posture of a dog about to be struck.

"Look, they'll see evidence that someone else has been living here. They just need to see you here, so it won't look like we're hiding anything. OK?"

He reluctantly acceded then slipped away to the bedroom.

Gwen sat next to Ed Greames. She watched him breathe in crescendo-decrescendo cycles, each ending in a protracted period of no movement. Then his airflow would fitfully recover and his respirations mount again in depth and frequency.

It had been over a year since Gwen's last death vigil. She'd done it many times during her training and again in the first months after City Hospital opened a special AIDS ward. Gwen believed being present at a death was a great privilege. As an intern, she had hoped witnessing the transition from warm, pulsatile life into cold, motionless death might give her insight into the mystery of her own being, of all life. She would hold patients' wrists, feel their pulse stop, their skin temperature drop, their bodies transform from a volitional creatures into inanimate objects. There was a disconnect, like the reversal between figure and ground in an optical illusion, but there was never an epiphany. The only revelation was how unfathomable the mystery remained.

Ed's gasping was more forlorn than desperate. He was tired out, ready to quit. Gwen concentrated on the rise and fall of his chest, which calmed her. After another half an hour, Ed paused at the end of a cycle. Five minutes later, he still hadn't taken a breath. Gwen placed her stethoscope over his heart. There was no sound. His skin was distinctly cooler. She covered him with a blanket.

Gwen dialed information and asked the operator to connect her to the coroner. While listening to the rings, she again worried the coroner's staff would search the apartment. What if they found the two pill bottles she had missed—the ones with her name on the label? Would Terrell say something indiscreet?

On the twelfth ring, there was a click.

"Coroner's office," a gruff voice said.

"This is Dr. Gwen Howard from City Hospital. I'm on a home visit. I have a death to report."

XXIV

Herb awoke on Wednesday feeling more like his old self. Morning ICU rounds went well. A case of bacterial pneumonia in an elderly woman, complicated by septic shock, kidney failure, and allergies to the antibiotics usually administered, didn't flummox him in the least. As he was writing progress notes, Herb hummed a melody, a tune he first heard in a blues club while living in Washington DC. Recalling the title, *I Got My Mojo Working*, he laughed out loud.

"It's nice to see you in a good mood."

He looked up to see Laurie Hampton. She had her arms folded and an amused smile.

"It's nice to be pain free," he said touching the pea-size lump on his head. "I guess you know about my little accident last weekend?"

"Do you think there's anyone in this unit who doesn't know about it?"

He shrugged amiably.

"Sorry to rain on your parade, Herb, but Boyce's parents want to talk to an attending."

He knew the case well, a twenty-four year old with severe Pneumocystis pneumonia. The patient's family and friends were absolutely certain he wasn't gay or bisexual and that he had never injected drugs.

"They still don't believe he has AIDS," she said. "They've heard about the new antibody test and asked the resident to order it. He told them it's not available yet. Now they're demanding to see the 'doctor in charge.'"

Laurie pointed her finger at Herb.

"The resident's right. The assay hasn't been approved by the FDA. It can only be used in a research protocol."

"They need to hear it from you, Herb."

She pointed at the door of the family room.

"Will do."

When Herb left the room, Laurie was hovering outside the door.

"How did it go?" she asked.

"They're having a hard time coping, and I validated that's a normal, appropriate response. They're willing to face facts and not make unreasonable demands."

Instantly ashamed of what he had just said, Herb berated himself. Who am I to tell her about coping? She's known for three years her fate is a coin toss that might land tails-down at any moment. How could I have been so stupid?

Laurie didn't react to his remark.

Maybe she's in Gwen's study, he hoped. Maybe she found out she's not infected.

He glanced at Laurie, who was gazing pensively at the young man lying unconscious and paralyzed while a ventilator kept him alive. She turned to Herb with unguarded eyes, seeming as fragile as when she had told him about the needle-stick in 1981. They hadn't spoken of it since. He felt his neck pulse bounding. He thrust his hands into his pockets so she wouldn't see them trembling.

"Herb, do you have a few minutes to talk?"

He waited a second too long before answering, "Sure."

By then, Laurie had reset the corners of her mouth into a managerial smile.

"Actually, I need to start an IV," she said. "I'll catch you later."

XXV

HERB WENT TO HIS office after rounds. He was on the phone when Kevin tapped on his half-open door. Herb waved him in, motioning him to sit down. While Herb finished his call, Kevin inspected the leaded-glass lamp on his desk and the photographs of the Chrysler and Empire State buildings hanging on his walls.

Before this week, Kevin had assumed Herb's fondness for geometric patterns simply resonated with his cerebral, tranquil, interior reality. Now he wondered if Art Deco was a metaphor for the serenity Herb still aspired to have. That thought further discouraged Kevin. If inner peace was a mirage for Herb, what chance did he have of ever finding contentment.

Kevin kept glancing back at the Chrysler Building's terraced crown as he told Herb about Hubert's kidney damage.

"There's nothing worse than harming someone you're trying to help," Herb commiserated. "I saw that happen in spades with patients on experimental chemotherapy at NIH. Many of them died as a direct result of the drugs' bone marrow toxicity. It was hard to watch, Kevin, but it was better than giving up. Those people were under a death sentence, and the investigational regimens were their final appeal. Sound familiar? Most did survive a little longer, and that time was huge for them and their families. I got to see a lot of unadulterated love there. It was inspiring."

"Yeah," sighed Kevin, his eyes moist. "Thanks for the pep talk."

"I should thank you. I'm realizing I could have that experience again if I got more involved with your patients. Please don't take this the wrong way. I have no desire to poach on your territory. But there are other AIDS opportunistic infections nobody here is working on—like Mycobacterium avium, for example."

Kevin stared at Herb, raised his palm, and said, "That's an offer I can't refuse."

Their hands slapped.

"Let's go for it, Kevin. We should be testing all kinds of treatment strategies here. There's cytomegalovirus and Cryptococcus, too."

"All right! If we can be this fired up when we're teaching our residents and fellows about AIDS, they'll happily recruit patients for us."

"Brother, you've seen the light. The only missing piece is talking a pharmacologist into joining us. Oh, and getting some of the local private practice docs to refer their AIDS patients here."

"Yeah," said Kevin, his enthusiasm fading as the image of Hubert Wilson shambling toward the elevator came back to haunt him.

"Damn, Herb, what can I do for this poor guy? It's not like I can tell him a grateful nation appreciates his sacrifice. He might have to end his life on dialysis."

"Hmm. What's the mechanism of suramin nephrotoxicity?"

"Renal tubular injury from what I've read."

"I heard a nephrologist on the Hill give grand round rounds last year on renal tubular toxins. His name is...um...Hightower. He's investigating prostaglandin infusions to prevent kidney failure after toxin exposure. Call him. Maybe there's something you can do to reverse your patient's kidney damage or at least keep it from getting worse."

"What a great idea! I should have thought of that. Say, Herb, what exactly is your problem-solving deficit?"

Herb gave him a faint smile.

As Kevin was departing, Herb's pager sounded. He dialed the number displayed. Gwen answered on the first ring. She asked him to come to her office.

"It's about Laurie Hampton," she said.

XXVI

GWEN JUMPED UP FROM her chair when Herb arrived and closed the door behind him. She made him sit down and showed him a slip of paper. Herb looked at Laurie's antibody result. He put his head in his hands.

"We're telling her Monday afternoon."

"I can be there."

"No! Christ, I've already violated confidentiality by letting you know."

Furious with herself for this lapse, for her weakness in needing to confide in someone, nearly in tears over it now, Gwen apologized which led to further explanations until the whole Ed Greames story flooded out.

"I've never done anything like that before," she said, only half believing she had really been in Greames' apartment a few hours ago, that it wasn't part of her earthquake dream.

"I understand," he said. "I've done something like that, worse actually. I didn't just write a script. I administered the medication myself."

"You?" she said, unable to imagine him even considering such an act. "I don't believe it."

"Yes, me, while I was at NIH."

"Oh, my God!"

"I was covering the Clinical Center. A ten-year-old boy with leukemia who'd failed two previous rounds of chemo was admitted. The oncologist suggested a course of deep salvage therapy to the parents. I think they were ready to accept it was over, but after hearing his pitch, they couldn't write off the possibility of a miracle. So they agreed. I happened to know that every leukemic at the Center who'd failed prior regimens had died within two weeks of getting this one. But I wasn't an oncologist and had to keep my mouth shut. Predictably, the boy's platelets fell through the floor. Soon he was choking from nosebleeds despite transfusions. The oncologist came by, told the parents how sorry he was, wrote a do not resuscitate order, and left. The mother became hysterical, the father catatonic, and the kid couldn't stop retching blood. That's when I decided to play God, the merciful God we all wanted to trust in as children."

"How did you do it without the staff seeing?"

"A lot of morphine was pushed on the unit. I put an empty vial in my pocket and looked for used syringes and open ampules by a bedside. I'd go in to examine the patient, which meant closing the drapes. It only took a couple of hours to squirrel away a hundred milligrams. Then I pushed it into the boy's IV. Seconds later, he stopped breathing. I waited until he flat-lined before calling a nurse."

Gwen rolled her chair next to Herb and stared at him.

"Weren't you terrified someone would report you?"

"For a week I was scared shitless. We had a baby. My wife wasn't working. If I had lost my license…"

"Oh no," she moaned.

"But after that week went by and nobody said anything or looked suspiciously at me, being caught seemed more and more implausible. My rationality got back in control."

She shook her head slowly.

"Gwen, you and I aren't the only ones who've ever done this. And here's the important part. For months afterwards, I kept waiting for justice to be meted out. Yet my inexcusable hubris went unpunished. No panic attacks, no insomnia, no self-recriminations. In fact, the more I went over it, the more convinced I was that I'd done the most decent thing possible, and the more certain I was that I'd chosen the only option I could live with. I was no hero, but I was no monster either. I did what had to be done to end a family's unbearable suffering. Fortunately for me, I've never had to do it again."

Herb's tale gave Gwen enough solace for exhaustion to take over. She slumped against his shoulder. Immediately, she felt him stiffen. Herb inched away from her. She stood up and started apologizing.

"No, Gwen. This is my problem. Hell, if we can't even be here for each other in situations like this…"

He couldn't complete the sentence.

"That would be pathetic, wouldn't it," said Gwen.

"Exactly."

She made a fist to show her steadfastness.

He clasped it and gave her an encouraging squeeze.

"You'll do fine on Monday," he said.

On his way home from the hospital, Herb thought of Sister Anna. He wanted to ask her about the confessional booth. What went on inside there suddenly intrigued him.

XXVII

AFTER CLINIC, KEVIN DROVE to the airport to pick up Marco. The moment he got out of the Rambler, his anxiety grew with a vengeance. He tried to think objectively. Of course Marco was going to be jealous, but they could work through it, couldn't they? If not, there was couples therapy. Reasoning didn't help. Thinking of Marco only intensified his fear.

Inside the terminal, he distracted himself by adding up all the frequent flier miles he had accumulated in the last year. He had been to meetings in Atlanta, Paris, Washington DC, New York, and Chicago. There were other young physicians from academic medical centers around the country at these conferences, people like Kevin who were dedicating their careers to AIDS research. They had made a tradition of going out to dinner, getting inebriated, and revealing their personal histories and dreams. They called themselves "AIDS doctors" with a mixture of self-deprecation and pride. Kevin reveled in their fraternity. The scientific sessions were exhilarating, too. It had dawned on him that he had something worthwhile to contribute. He was reminded of a talk he had just been invited to give at an Australian symposium in January, the middle of the summer there, and a European meeting scheduled for March.

As Kevin was calculating how much time he would have to write papers on these long flights, the door to the jet way opened. Passengers began trickling out.

Marco emerged, head down. The tip of his tongue kept reappearing to wet his lips. He looked up, and Kevin saw his pupils were dilated. The mobile eyebrows he always used in greeting people didn't move.

After the strangeness of their perfunctory kiss, the barriers Kevin had been carefully constructing crumbled. He could no longer ignore the conspicuous evidence. Marco's flu last summer had never quite resolved. He had stopped running months ago.

No, thought Kevin frantically. He didn't say he was sick on the phone or in his letters. He must be over it by now.

But Marco didn't look well. He was pale and had lost weight. Kevin recalled waking in the middle of the night while Marco was changing his tee shirt. The bed sheet had been damp. Kevin had gone back to sleep, believing it was a nightmare—a recurrent nightmare because it had happened more than once.

Kevin was reeling. He couldn't remain suspended in disbelief any longer. There were no rational explanations left.

Tugging at his arm, Marco led him to a vacant gate. Refusing to speak, Marco watched the passing crowd, waiting until no one was nearby before he turned to face Kevin. Marco opened his mouth wide and shrieked as he pointed to the white plaques inside.

A Holocaust, 1986

I

BOTH HAD SLEPT RESTLESSLY, Kevin barely at all. Marco's morning started with a headache followed by nausea and dizziness. At last, he was sleeping again. Kevin stood alone in the kitchen, brewing a cup of coffee, drained of all feeling except a dull, throbbing stomach ache. His mind was empty except for a single nagging question. Why doesn't he want to end it?

Marco was always plagued by one symptom or another, often in such agony Kevin could hardly bear to be with him. Sleep came only when he was too tired to react. His weight was down to a hundred and ten pounds. Half his lush hair was gone. His formerly taut abdomen was distended. The muscles that once rippled through his legs and buttocks had evaporated, leaving dismal convexities. New lines and folds appeared daily in his face.

Marco said he was unafraid of death, and Kevin believed him. They had talked about what to do if life became intolerable. At Marco's request, Kevin had obtained sufficient morphine and phenobarbital. The bottles were in plain view, on top of their bedroom dresser. Obviously, Marco wasn't ready yet, but if their situations had been reversed, Kevin was sure he would be by now.

When sorrow surged, Kevin made no effort to halt it. He would lock himself in a bathroom. After a paroxysm of crying, he was able to cope again.

He occasionally imagined a future after Marco's death. One fantasy he conjured up involved a remote Irish monastery where he knelt praying in a brown-hooded robe. A useful fantasy because when indulged in, Kevin became so incensed by his absurd, maudlin self-pity that he could turn his attention to the outside world, which at this particular moment meant his meeting on Monday with the AIDS Action Committee. They were calling him a Nazi for not storming Burroughs Wellcome corporate headquarters with a sub-machine gun to demand AZT for the masses.

Anger was a good antidote for desolation, like an itch that distracts one from pain. However, Kevin had thought this through. The rational approach was a better strategy for this meeting. His plans for the hour or two he might have free until Marco woke up included writing a hand-out to give to the committee members.

Sitting at his new home computer, Kevin typed confidently. He knew the data. He had been a local investigator in the multicenter trial that proved AZT's efficacy.

> The Facts
> **AZT treatment did prolong AIDS patients' survival in this trial.** 16 people randomly assigned to receive placebo died compared to 1 assigned to receive AZT.
> **Consider the context.** It was a very short study. People were on their randomly assigned treatment for just four months. There have been no other trials to date.
> **Consider the toxicity.** 21% of those getting active drug had severe anemia requiring multiple blood transfusions compared to 4% of those who received placebo.
> What's Not Known
> Is it safe to take AZT for any longer than four months?
> Will survival after a longer course of AZT be any better than taking nothing?
> What if the trial had been continued for a full year? Might there have been more deaths on AZT than on placebo?
> What Needs To Be Done
> An observational study of AZT treatment with longer fol-low-up, exactly the protocol that Burroughs Wellcome and the FDA are collaborating to implement. No one will get placebo. Everyone will get AZT. Everyone will be monitored rigorously and uniformly.

The phone rang. Kevin didn't pick it up. He waited as the answering machine played its message. He heard a familiar voice, a friend from Marco's lab. She asked how he was doing. She also wanted to know if he was taking AZT yet. A well-meaning inquiry, one might suppose, if her tone hadn't been that of a police detective. This irked Kevin. He knew watching Marco's body deteriorate gave his friends a heightened awareness of how tenuous their own lives were. But some had the magical belief that a search and destroy mission to get every bit of medical information about Marco's condition could abolish their own anxiety. They justified their intrusion by thinking they were being sympathetic, never considering how their questions might make Marco and Kevin feel.

There was something else troubling Kevin. How could he explain to this woman why Marco wasn't taking AZT when he was the local gatekeeper, controlling access to the drug? In the randomized trial, Marco hadn't met the entry criteria, which had been designed in a careful balancing act to include those most likely to benefit, people with advanced immune suppression who still had the physical reserve to tolerate AZT's toxicity, and exclude patients such as Marco who had already been wasted by multiple complications of AIDS. For the same reasons, Marco would be excluded from the compassionate-use AZT distribution planned by the FDA and Burroughs Wellcome. Kevin had seen the anemia and the muscle toxicity AZT caused. He knew the drug would be at best a double-edged sword for Marco. He had also talked to Rajiv Singh, whose assessment was more pessimistic.

"I hear NIH can culture the retrovirus from the blood of patients taking AZT," Rajiv had said. "So, obviously it's no cure. Short-term benefit—that's plausible. But the virus will mutate and become resistant. Then these patients will be left with only the drug's toxic side effects."

Kevin wanted to call the woman back and tell her he was pulling strings to get hold of the drug for Marco, who was willing to suffer for his friends so they could rest assured that everything possible was being done.

Kevin was making another cup of coffee when the phone rang again. He intended to let this one go to the answering machine too, but Marco picked up the bedroom extension.

"*Hola*," said Marco with artificial cheeriness.

Don't pretend, thought Kevin, his temper re-ignited. Let them hear your misery. Drag your words out. Show them your despair. Tough shit if they can't take it. This is about you, not them.

"*Katarina, mi corazón!*" Marco crooned.

It was Kevin's sister. He calmed down and listened for a while. He knew Marco loved chatting with Katherine. He wanted to hear the genuine animation in Marco's half of the conversation.

Kevin was still surprised by the remarkable change his relationship with his sister had undergone since their father's death. Not only had their animosities been buried. When he told her that Marco was sick, she insisted on coming to visit them in San Francisco. He was amazed to see the rapport that developed instantly between Katherine and Marco. His sister was as astonished to see him feeding, cleaning, and caring for Marco.

Kevin went back to his computer. He stopped paying attention until Marco said sadly, "Poor Douglas... I know...Yes, teenage boys can be very cruel."

Kevin sighed. He couldn't concentrate on work now.

Moments later Marco shouted for him to pick up the phone.

They began with small talk. Kevin automatically asked about Ben and the kids. He immediately regretted it. Her claim that they were fine rang so false he winced. He knew this, of all things, was where he should be helping her, yet he avoided mentioning Douglas's name whenever they talked. I can't go there, he kept saying to Marco. It'll just make her worry more.

Marco, in a wheelchair, rolled into the study. His were eyes blazing.

"Tell her," he whispered. "You can't help her with Douglas if you're not honest about yourself."

Marco wheeled around, and left the room.

Kevin put his hand to his forehead. He'd run out of excuses that made sense.

"Katherine," he said gently, "Remember when you asked me about the blood test?"

There was no noise on the line.

"Katherine? Hello?"

"I'm here," she said in a small, fearful voice he had only heard once before.

As a child, Katherine was afraid of nothing, except the dark. When he was six and she eight, a thunderstorm caused a power failure early one evening while their parents were out on an errand. Kevin thought it an adventure to find his way through the pitch-black house. He made a game of getting from the living room to his bedroom without tripping or bumping into anything. He was too focused on the quest to heed Katherine's plaintive calls. Finally, she sobbed, 'Kevin, are you OK?' It was miraculous. She had always been bigger and stronger, and she flaunted it. This was the first chink in her armor he had ever seen. It was the opportunity of a lifetime to torture her. But he had heard her vulnerability and her concern for his safety. He was shocked to discover he felt protective. Naturally, the sentiment soon disappeared. After dinner that night, she slapped him for taking more than his share of dessert.

"I got tested, Katherine. I'm positive."

The line was silent.

"But my T cells are OK. Fifteen percent of infected people, they never drop into the danger zone."

There was a soft exhalation of air.

"And if my T cells eventually do go down, I can take AZT. Though there'll probably be better drugs available by then."

"You're optimistic, aren't you?"

He relaxed. She was going to stay the strong older sister.

"I am…You're not really surprised, are you?"

"I suppose not…Hey, I don't remember you being optimistic as a kid."

"I'm not a kid anymore."

"Apparently not…Well, it's a blessing you can take care of Marco. I don't know how you do it and work, too."

"Katherine, I'm not sure your life is any easier than mine."

She chuckled.

"Marco tells me the activists are on your case."

"No more than usual. But this time it's making me crazy."

"Why?"

"Because they want everyone who's infected to get AZT, before we know if it's safe, which makes me crazy because Marco should have been on AZT. But now it's too late."

He heard Katherine catch her breath.

"Sorry, I shouldn't have said that."

"No," she said shakily. "You don't need to apologize. I feel for you, Kevin. Just let me know what I can do to help."

"I will," he said in the small, fearless voice of a little boy whose older sister had begged him to find a flashlight.

Kevin brought a peanut butter and jelly sandwich, the only meal Marco could keep down, into the bedroom. Marco gave him an inquiring look. Kevin pointed to the sandwich. Marco obediently nibbled at it.

"I told her."

Marco nodded with approval. Swallowing required too much concentration for him to consider the implications. Once confident he wasn't going to vomit, he became alarmed.

"How did she take it?"

"She's scared, but she'll be fine. She's tough. You were right. It was time." Marco wasn't convinced.

"She'll be OK. You're underestimating her."

"*Sí*,' muttered Marco. Perking up, he said, "Did you talk about Douglas?"

"Not today. Next time."

"It will be so good when you do, *querido*. She's not fighting it. She's accepted he's gay. She's worried about what Ben might do when he finds out."

"She could send Douglas here."

"Sweetheart, that's exactly what she needs to hear you say. But before it comes to a crisis, you should go to Boston. Tell Douglas you're positive and what it means."

Kevin recoiled.

"*Querido*, what good will it do for you to pay his college tuition if he dies before he's thirty? You can't get him to accept the truth about himself and the precautions he has to take unless you're completely honest with him. How long are you going to wait to tell other people? Until I'm dead and there's nobody left you can confide in? Try it out. It gets easier once you've done it a few times."

Marco's sermons had always annoyed Kevin, and he tuned them out. Today he was listening.

Later, while heating a frozen dinner, Kevin overheard Marco murmuring on the telephone.

"I know. I know how hard this is. Don't worry. He's not in the least sick. And he'll come. He'll help Douglas. After I'm gone, he'll be there for you."

Kevin felt another ice pick jab into his heart. But he had cried this morning and didn't have the endurance to do it again today.

In the early evening, Marco dozed off. He dreamed he was lying on wet, lumpy life-preservers in the ribbed bottom of a weathered rowboat docked by his family's lake house. Constantly shifting his weight, moving his arms and legs, he couldn't find a comfortable position. Soreness in his back woke him. A consolation was this hadn't been the fugue state he kept slipping into, a dream in which he feverishly strove to unravel a tangled ball of string, his efforts inevitably creating more and more knots until he woke up panting and mentally depleted.

The bedroom was quiet except for the muted clacks of Kevin typing in the study. On the dresser, Marco saw an envelope Kevin had brought home yesterday, a T cell count result. They had disagreed over its significance—the same argument they had been having for two years.

After Marco returned from Mexico, he wanted Kevin to be tested, hoping against the odds that Kevin wasn't infected. Kevin had refused. Knowing wouldn't change anything, he said. There was no treatment for asymptomatic infection. And there was no risk since at this point mutual masturbation was enough to satisfy them. Kevin took the exasperating high road of stoicism, proclaiming, "There will be an answer. Let it be."

The unfairness of denying him exoneration, unlikely as it was, drove Marco to deliver the final blow. He asked Kevin if stubbornness was a family trait. Didn't his father have the same problem?

The blood test verified what for Kevin had already been a certainty. His subsequent lectures on how variable the interval between initial infection and onset of symptoms was, how it could as easily have been him who was infected first and transmitted the virus, didn't help Marco. He had made up his mind long ago that he was the one responsible. Only he had gone to bathhouses before they met.

Kevin remained optimistic, believing he would be among the lucky few who didn't get sick. He showed each result to Marco as proof his T cells were consistently above the threshold for life-threatening complications to occur. Marco focused on the downward trend of the numbers.

Downward trend, Marco repeated, which reminded him there was something he had to do before it was too late. But fatigue overcame him.

When Marco next awoke, he looked at the clock. It was midnight. He sat upright. What had he forgotten to do?

His movement woke Kevin.

"What's going on?"

Marco remembered.

"We have to talk. I've put this off too long. It's time for you to tell me, with no bullshit, what you'll do after I'm gone."

"What I'll do?"

"I need to hear you say you'll find someone."

"Marco, please. Let's not go there."

"Do this for me. It's not a betrayal."

"But…"

"I'm asking for absolution, Kevin."

Marco watched the conflict play out in Kevin's face as he was backed into a corner of submission.

"Jesus, Marco! Why did I ever believe you meant those diatribes about the church? You are such a fucking Catholic."

Kevin cradled Marco's hand over his heart. They began enumerating the plusses and minuses of every unattached man they knew.

II

HERB'S WEEKEND STARTED WITH yard work. A winter storm had passed through on Thanksgiving, clearing the oaks and maples of dead leaves. They now covered his lawn in a layer three inches deep. Martin was helping him rake and shovel the piles into garbage bags. Herb wished they could burn them, but that had been banned in the city years ago. When he was a boy, every autumn the curbs of Long Island had great mounds of smoldering leaves. The tangy scent had thrilled him, triggering bittersweet fantasies of lost fortunes and lost loves. It was one of his happiest childhood memories.

"Martin, when you were little, didn't we burn the leaves in December?"

"Yeah."

Martin stopped raking. He gazed into the distance, almost smiling.

"Remember the smell?"

"I do."

Martin returned to raking. He was thorough and efficient. He finished his half of the lawn well before his father was done and brought an empty bag over to Herb's side.

"Give me a second," said Herb. "I can't keep up with you."

"Right, the long distance runner."

"*Former* long distance runner, who has to bend and squat slowly or he'll tear something. Hey, what do you get paid for this?"

"Five bucks an hour."

"I think you should renegotiate the rate with your mother. You're worth more than that."

Martin shrugged.

After the last pile was bagged, Herb surveyed the pristine lawn.

"Looks great," he said.

Martin shrugged again, but this time Herb thought he saw satisfaction in his son's expression.

He wished he could find a way to engage Martin besides paying him to do yard work. His son wasn't interested in sports or movies. What he liked or disliked had become an enigma. He kept to his room with the door closed, and Herb had no idea what he did in there. When asked, Martin would invariably say homework or reading. He was following the precedent his older sister had set. Any conversation with his parents, beyond monosyllabic replies, was limited to school-related issues, which quickly became stale.

The leaves would be bagged soon, and Herb would have to wait another week for his next chance at bonding.

"Martin, can we talk?"

"About what?" Martin said warily.

"I'm interested in you. I want to know what you like doing."

Martin squirmed.

"I mean what you think you'd like to be doing when you're grown up, say in ten years."

The frontal attack on his privacy withdrawn, Martin relented.

"I'm not sure. Be in business or a journalist, if it's not too boring."

"There's more money in business if that's important to you."

This wasn't a direct question, and Martin didn't respond.

"Martin," he begged.

Herb couldn't continue. He knew a plea for them to be closer would only alienate his son.

At noon, Herb changed into a tuxedo. While driving downtown with Cecilia to the wedding of an in-law's daughter, he thought about the future of his marriage. In two years, Martin would be away at college. Allison's departure hadn't made much impact, but with no kids at home…

Cecilia interrupted his reverie, warning Herb to be careful about what he said to her cousin Emily.

"She's getting divorced. She's very fragile."

"What happened?"

"All I know is that Joe initiated it. Maybe it's just incompatibility. Maybe there's someone else. If so, he's not telling her."

This news was sobering. Emily was their age, and her youngest child had gone off to college in the fall. The empty-nest-divorce syndrome was epidemic, Herb realized. He knew three other couples who had split up right around the time their youngest child reached college age.

He sneaked a glance at Cecilia. She was absorbed with knitting. Had she been probing him? She had given him an opening. Should he broach the subject, explore what she'd like to do once Martin was out of the house? He considered suggesting a vacation in Europe or China. Her willingness to commit would be a clue. But Herb was feeling risk-averse today. He let the matter drop.

After the ceremony, Herb followed Cecilia and smiled at whatever people said to him. When this became boring, he went off to look for more interesting conversation. A man he hadn't seen in years waved to him. Herb knew this was a cousin of Cecilia's but couldn't remember his name. They had always referred to him as the Maoist since the toast he had made at their wedding was a quote from the Chairman's *Little Red Book*. The man joined him.

"Herb," said the Maoist with hale good-fellowship, "You still at the public hospital?"

"I am," Herb answered, taking note of the expensive suit and shoes the Maoist was wearing.

The man cocked his head.

"So what's that about?"

Herb returned the puzzled look.

"I mean, what do you get out of working there?"

Herb had never been asked this question so directly. Unable to formulate an answer on the spot, he evaded it.

"It's good. How about you? What are you up to?"

"I'm in Manhattan, working on Wall Street."

Herb was dumbfounded.

"What's that about?"

"It's about the market."

Seeing Herb confused, he said, "The market is there to be exploited. Unless you want to be oppressed by it, and that's no longer my preference."

As Herb digested this information, he noticed a Rolex peeking out from under the man's sleeve.

"So, why *are* you at City Hospital?"

Irked, Herb took the offensive.

"Not for the professional fees, bonuses, or stock options."

The Maoist wasn't insulted. He stared curiously at Herb, waiting to hear more.

Herb stumbled for the right word. Nothing came to mind. He grabbed at an innocuous adjective, one that wouldn't sound conceited.

"It's fulfilling."

As soon as he said it, Herb was embarrassed. He escaped with an excuse about having to find Cecilia.

Can't you do better than a lame cliché, he brooded.

Herb didn't see himself as an idealist. He wasn't on some utterly selfless mission to succor the poor and suffering. He aspired to be decent and caring, but he had no illusions of a higher calling.

The Maoist's question bothered him. How could he have so little insight into his own motivation? Herb was at a loss to explain why he had worked at City Hospital for fourteen years and had never even toyed with the idea of leaving. It could hardly be noblesse oblige. Though his mother believed she belonged to an elite class, Herb had grown up in the melting pot. He needed loans to pay for college and medical school. His success came from tenacity, not privilege. Thinking of his mother raised another question. Why had she never been critical of his career choice? She must know he could make more money in private practice or the pharmaceutical industry. He once gave her a tour of City Hospital, and the patients she encountered clearly stirred more revulsion than empathy. Why hadn't she ever pressed him to find a more remunerative job?

Herb walked into an empty courtyard. There was a table of gifts flanked by poster boards with photos of the bride and groom. He scrutinized the baby pictures. Each one lay in an oblong basket. Bassinets, he thought, smaller versions of cribs. They're Chinese babies in cribs. The tingling in the back of his neck made him wonder if survival guilt was the unifying diagnosis.

The combination of a wedding and several glasses of wine stimulated Herb's libido. At home, Cecilia fell asleep before he could arouse her interest. He awoke early the next morning with a mild hangover and in no mood for sex. He needed to get some exercise.

Driving across town was interminable. The traffic was being re-routed because of the San Francisco Marathon, which doubly irritated him. This was the first time in ten years he had missed the annual race. His knees could no longer take the pounding.

Halfway across the Golden Gate Bridge, the fog lifted. Sunlight filtered through the dissolving mist, and Herb's grip on the steering wheel loosened.

He parked at a Sausalito dock. The same scull he had rented the previous Sunday and had thought about buying all week was available. The bay was calm, only three inches of ripple with no hint of chop.

Herb lowered himself into the twenty-four-foot fiberglass shell. He cautiously manipulated the long oars until he was in open water. Sliding forward, he dipped the blades under water then extended his legs, pushing the seat backward on its track while pulling the oar handles to his chest and finishing the stroke. Repeating the cycle and seeing the distance he had traveled was as satisfying as running.

Twenty minutes later he was in the middle of Richardson Bay, a mile from the nearest human being. Panting from this sprint, he savored the isolation. He had left his beeper in the car. No one could make demands on him here. His freedom was limitless. The lure of being able to come here whenever he wanted was irresistible. Herb decided to buy the scull.

III

Gwen was jarred awake on Saturday morning by a loud buzz coming from the backyard. She presumed Rick was the responsible party. He had stopped running the week before in preparation for Sunday's marathon and was accumulating restless energy.

She found him on a ladder, pruning a pine tree with a chain saw.

"You nervous about the race?"

"Nah, I don't care how fast my time is. You going back to West Oakland tonight?"

"Just for a few hours."

He shook his head ever so slightly.

"This won't last long. Once Dina and I work out the routine and are sure it's safe, we'll train research assistants to recruit people."

He made no comment.

If challenged, Gwen wouldn't deny she minimized the time she spent working, nor that she had been putting in even more hours since her grant proposal was funded. Rick never complained when Gwen said she would be home at six and arrived after eight, yet she had a hunch her absence was feeding a grudge. He was far slower to burn than her ex-husband, and it troubled her that she didn't know where his flash point was.

Enough self-criticism, she thought. What I do is really important. Rick's got to accept that and find more gratification in his own life. She liked this attitude in principle but was uneasy about the possibility he might follow the advice and find gratification from another woman.

At five o'clock, there was plenty of parking on Oakland's West MacArthur Boulevard. The auto glass and tire shops had closed for the day, and the street's evening labor force were just beginning to arrive. Gwen and Dina, an African-American nurse practitioner Gwen had hired with her new grant money, parked their outreach van, a durable, dented Ford Econoline, across the street from a stucco motel in need of repainting. They grabbed umbrellas, pepper-spray canisters, bags of safe-sex kits and started searching for study participants.

The grant was a long shot, but Kevin had made a compelling case. Sooner or later, he said, the public would expect NIH to address the epidemic in women. Although far fewer women than men were infected, the CDC estimated there would be three hundred thousand women in the United States by 1991 who could potentially progress to AIDS. Even if Gwen's application wasn't approved, Kevin had argued, she could learn what the reviewers thought of her plan and use that feedback to put together a more competitive proposal when NIH finally did succumb to pressure to support such research.

Gwen had known her résumé wouldn't impress the reviewers—academic physicians and PhDs who measured an investigator's status by the number of her publications in prestigious journals. Serendipitously, the review panel met in October, one week after Surgeon General Everett Koop's report on AIDS grabbed national attention. Koop was advocating a massive federal effort to increase public awareness of human immunodeficiency virus, the new name of the retrovirus that caused AIDS. The most effective method to prevent spread of HIV infection, he contended, was for everyone to understand how HIV was transmitted. A key component of Gwen's proposal was precisely this type of outreach to an ignored, high-risk population. She received a fundable score on her first submission. Now, two months later, on the evenings she wasn't recruiting participants for her study, she drafted proposals for additional money to expand her project to more Bay Area sites.

Gwen and Dina approached four women dressed in hot pants and low cut blouses. They were huddling together against the cold. Dina invited them to warm up inside the van and learn how to avoid AIDS. None were interested, so Gwen handed each of them a safe sex kit—four condoms, a pamphlet on HIV prevention, and a square of thin latex called a dental dam. Dina gave them a thirty-second lesson in safe fellatio, demonstrating how to insert the dam in her mouth to create a barrier against semen.

In the next group, a young Latina with permed, platinum blond hair was willing to listen to them. Gwen explained that she and Dina were researchers who wanted to find out if the AIDS virus had infected girls working the streets. The woman was skeptical but agreed to enroll once told she would be paid for her time.

After an hour with no further takers, they drove to another motel. Several women shooed them away. Gwen noticed two black women in their thirties eyeing them. Both wore wigs. One was tall and lithe, the other short with large breasts spilling over her spandex top. They seemed more curious than hostile. Gwen suggested making one last attempt.

"You some kind of 'I Spy' or 'Ebony and Ivory' team?" asked the tall woman.

Gwen grinned and segued into a description of HIV infection and its consequences.

"I heard about that nasty bug," said the short woman, "but it only gets inside men who go down on each other."

"Truth is," said Dina, "if *you* have sex with a man who got the bug from using dirty needles or with an infected man who does men and women, and if that man *doesn't* use a rubber, *you* can get infected with HIV."

"Hey sister," said the tall woman, "I don't do it with no sick johns that gots sores, only healthy ones."

"I'm a doctor," said Gwen, "and I can't tell who's infected by looking at them. Lots of infected people look healthy, sometimes for years, before HIV makes them sick. But they can still give HIV to sex partners, and that can happen long before they get sick themselves. The only way you can know for sure if someone has the infection is by having the HIV blood test."

Business was slow, and when Dina mentioned the ten dollar reimbursement, the women agreed to talk in the van. They read the consent form and signed without hesitation.

"I'm happy to answer any questions you have," said Gwen.

"These 'condoms' you people is pushing," said the short woman, "I know a girl who swears she don't do nobody, never, unless they put a rubber on. She got some kind of VD anyway."

Dina jumped at this opportunity.

"If rubbers aren't put on the *right* way, they can break. Then germs can get from cum into your vagina. I'll show you the right way."

.She opened a box containing a life-size, erect silicon penis and set it on her lap. The two women hooted as she demonstrated the correct method.

"The safest thing is for *you* to put on the rubber instead of letting the john do it."

She centered the condom over the tip of the penis, pinched the pocket at the center of the latex ring, squeezing the air out, and meticulously rolled it down the shaft.

"You pretty good at that," said the tall woman laughing. "Had a lot of practice, huh?"

Dina smiled mysteriously and said, "Be sure there are no air bubbles. They can make the rubber break. If you see air bubbles, you got to roll it back up and down until they're all gone."

Dina gave each one a safe sex kit, a ten dollar bill, and an appointment slip for a study visit at City Hospital. Moments after the women left, Gwen thought of another important piece of advice.

She rolled down the window and shouted, "If you use a lubricant or jelly, make sure it's says 'water-based' on the side."

A bus had stopped in front of the van. The exiting passengers were wide-eyed as this strange white woman yelled, "Oil-based lubes make rubbers break!"

Gwen awoke alone in bed again on Sunday. Hearing Rick in the kitchen, she remembered a commitment she had made.

"What time am I supposed to be at the twenty mile marker?" she called out.

"I don't know. What did they tell you?

"Nine, I think. I wrote it down someplace. Guess I better start making lemonade now. Then I pick you up at the finish line at noon, right?"

He came into the bedroom.

"Gil's girlfriend is taking us, and all I asked you to do, Gwen, is to pick us up at noon. You didn't have to volunteer to set up a rehydration station."

"Rick, I said I would."

"I know, but I never heard you say you *wanted* to do it. Now you sound like it's a big inconvenience."

"Wait a second. Don't go into attack mode."

"Attack mode! That's overreacting."

She paused, angry and also frightened by the direction this was going.

"OK," she said. "Sorry."

Rick refused to acknowledge that she was the one who had backed down. Gwen was peeved but didn't have the stomach to continue. They had been through a similar script recently. She had challenged him, insisting he admit his resentment. His response had been, "It's not for me to tell you how much time you should spend working." Afterwards, she had pondered those words. Were they a veiled threat?

Once Rick had left, Gwen looked at the clock and realized she actually had two hours before she needed to leave. There was time to work on a textbook chapter Ray Hernandez had gently coerced her into writing. She got out of bed and hunted through her briefcase for the outline she had made.

An hour later, the noise of Eva giggling reminded Gwen of her daughter's history essay. Eva had asked for help, and it was due Monday morning. Gwen skimmed through it. While she was displeased by the many grammatical and spelling errors, she did admire the cogency of Eva's reasoning. She went through the essay again, using a red pen to circle mistakes and to praise Eva's content in the margins.

She knocked on Eva's bedroom door and entered. Eva was in her nightgown, sitting cross-legged in bed, speaking excitedly into a coral green Princess handset. Gwen pointed to the essay, then to her watch.

"Excuse me, I'm talking to Glenda. It's important!"

"I've got to go."

Eva scowled and hissed, "One more minute."

As she waited for the gossiping to end, Gwen surveyed the room. The carpet was hidden by a layer of clothes, torn notebook paper, magazines, and used tissues. Eva wasn't winding things down, so Gwen interrupted her.

"You've got some very good ideas about the Bill of Rights. All you need to do to make them clear is fix the grammar and spelling mistakes."

"Hold on," Eva said into the phone.

"I did what the teacher….."

Eva stopped as the compliment became apparent to her.

"OK," she said sullenly.

Gwen was tempted to make a snide apology for intruding but opted to accept this offer of detente. With a tight smile, she set the essay on Eva's desk, also covered by a layer of detritus.

"I'll be back this afternoon, if you have questions."

She expected no thanks and got none.

Gwen was at her assigned location in time to prepare the table, pour cups of lemonade, and spike them with a pinch of salt before the elite athletes appeared. Seeing their powerful leg muscles contract felt like an antidote to the diseased and dying bodies she examined every day. None stopped for refreshment. Each had his own personal support team, friends or relatives who sprinted alongside the runner and handed him, relay style, a plastic bottle to drink from.

She spotted Rick forty-five minutes later in a pack of recreational marathoners. Gwen grabbed two cups of juice and jogged onto the road, mimicking what she had just observed. Though most of the liquid had spilled, he gratefully gulped what remained. Watching Rick speed up, she was proud of him. He looked back and waved. She waved encouragingly in return. As the distance between them increased, he kept glancing back bemusedly at her. She kept smiling and waving.

Once he was gone from view, Gwen was sad. How long has it been since he's seen me look at him that way, she wondered. She forced herself to view their relationship objectively. They made love rarely. She rarely was curious about what he was thinking. Gwen couldn't avoid the logical next question. Was he weighing whether to leave her? He *must* be asking himself whether staying was worth it.

Dwelling on this possibility was too disturbing. She preferred dissecting the antecedents of their estrangement and recalled something Rick had said after she canceled a movie date because of an emergency meeting.

"Will any of those people come visit you when you're old and sick?"

At the time, she thought he was being selfish. He didn't appreciate how important her work was, how good she was at it. She hadn't bothered to consider his question. Now she did. The answer was obvious. Only Kevin would come.

Gwen woke up at six on Monday and typed a reference list for her chapter. She was dimly aware of Rick and Eva as they arose and left. At eight, she drove to Proctor, the middle school where Rick still taught. He had asked her to talk to his sixth grade students about AIDS.

She intentionally arrived early to watch the kids. Proctor's blurred racial boundaries delighted her. A tall, blond girl was chattering with a dark-skinned girl whose parents, Rick had told her, were black and Filipino. A boy whose mother was white and father Korean passed a note to a child whose parents were immigrants from Guatemala.

From behind her, Gwen heard a girl's voice her say, "AIDS is that kinky sex disease."

There was collective tittering. Gwen pretended to search for something in her purse.

"No, it's like the Black Plague in the Middle Ages. It's killing thousands of people."

"It's a weapon that orcs use in Dungeons and Dragons."

"Let's settle down," boomed Rick.

The room was suddenly silent, which amused Gwen. At home, Rick was laid back. At school, he was nothing but business. Three months into the fall semester, these kids had capitulated to his authority.

Gwen fantasized Rick being assertive outside of Proctor, more driven by purpose, more ambitious. She stopped herself. How could I want that? I detested it in Daniel. In fact, taking oneself too seriously was a flaw she saw in nearly all the men she knew. Rick had grown up in a small New England town near the Canadian border where he had been spared much of the indignity and damage that Jim Crow did to black men in the 1950s. Part of his initial appeal had been his open-minded, non-judgmental attitude. She felt comfortable with him, for the same reason she was comfortable with Nan. Despite occasional insecurities, neither ever behaved like they had something to prove. If this trait was appealing in Nan, why was she ambivalent about it in Rick? Did she really want him to be driven, or had she failed to root out the vestiges of sexist brainwashing she had been subjected to as a girl?

Gwen heard conspiratorial whispers.

"Quiet!" boomed Rick again.

He scanned the room, a police photographer gathering evidence for future indictments.

"We have a guest today," he announced. "Dr. Howard is going to tell you about a dangerous new disease and how you can protect yourself from getting it."

Gwen began by asking if the sixth-graders knew what caused AIDS. Their answers included blood poisoning, cancer, and street drugs. She took a piece of chalk and made a single dot on the blackboard. Next to the dot, she drew a giant, crude microscope with a disembodied eye peering into the lens. That got her a laugh.

"AIDS is caused by a virus so small it can only be seen by using the world's most powerful microscopes."

She made a circle, slightly bigger than the dot.

"Our bodies have defender cells like this one. They travel around inside us and kill invader bugs that can make us sick."

She drew an X through the circle.

"The AIDS virus is different from other viruses, like the ones that cause chickenpox or colds, because the AIDS virus can destroy these defender cells."

She paused for questions. There were none.

"OK, any idea how people might catch this virus?"

Again silence, the typical response Gwen received from middle school children. She suspected some of them did know the answer, though to say so at their age and in front of adults could entail merciless ostracism. She had given these talks at high schools and knew many teens understood how transmission occurred. A few had the self-confidence to speak up about it. Behavioral scientists had told her peer education was the best strategy to prevent AIDS from becoming a world epidemic of unprecedented mortality.

They believed sixth grade was the optimal time to encourage those with the potential to influence their peers' opinions about sex.

Gwen raised two fingers and said, "There are two ways you can catch this virus. One, have unprotected sex with someone who already has the infection. Or two, inject drugs into your body with a needle that's been used by someone who is infected. If you avoid those two activities, the virus can't get inside you. It's simple."

Stone silence.

"Now, what does 'unprotected sex' mean?" she asked rhetorically. "It's when a man who is *not* wearing a condom, also called a rubber, puts his penis into a woman's vagina...or into a woman's anus...or into a man's anus."

"Rubber" elicited smirks, but eyebrows furrowed each time Gwen said "anus."

"Or when a man puts his penis in another person's mouth, or someone puts their tongue into a woman's vagina."

"Eeeew!" shrieked the class.

"Why would anyone want to do *that*?" wailed one of the girls.

IV

KEVIN SNEAKED INTO THE clinic building through a back entrance on Monday morning. When he was safe inside his office, he phoned his personal assistant, Freddy, who brought in an armload of mail, faxes, and phone messages. Kevin noticed the door had been left open. He stood up in alarm.

"No one's out there," Freddy reassured him.

"Not yet," he said, closing the door.

Kevin had been flirting with fame since the summer of 1985 when reporters verified the rumor that Rock Hudson, icon of wholesome American masculinity and friend of President Reagan, was in Paris to get an experimental treatment for AIDS. Before the movie star was outed, the media had viewed AIDS as inconsequential, a fatal illness limited to social deviants. Afterwards, any change in the who, what, or how of the disease made national news, and Kevin had become popular as a source for expert comments.

However, once the AZT trial results made headlines, his celebrity became an affliction. The media wanted interviews in time to meet their deadlines, while the university's public relations people insisted on controlling their access to him. Activists wanted any barrier to AZT availability eliminated immediately. They were under the delusion that Kevin had the power to make this happen. Worse, he was getting twenty or more phone calls a day from desperate patients, parents, siblings, and influential friends begging for the drug, which he had no means of obtaining.

On the other hand, grants and private donations to his program had tripled in the last year, and the money wasn't likely to plateau soon. Kevin was able to recruit additional faculty. He had hired Freddy, a godsend who screened phone calls, took care of scheduling, and generally ran interference for him. Kevin also bought decent office furniture after a visiting congresswoman had looked at his scarred, institutional desk and chairs as though they were a homeless man's bedroll and shopping cart.

The intercom on his desk buzzed. Kevin punched a button.

"Are you still meeting David at nine?" Freddy responded.

"I am."

"It's nine fifteen. Shall I send him in?"

"Yes, please. Thank you, Freddy."

He heard tapping on his door. David Ross, a man in his mid-thirties with a thick black beard, wire-rim glasses, and a halo of tightly curled hair, took a tentative step into his office.

"Come on in. Making progress with the foscarnet protocol?"

Kevin had hired David directly from his fellowship at UCLA with the immunologist who in 1981 had discovered the key defect of AIDS—an absence of helper T cells. As soon as David joined the AIDS program at City Hospital, Kevin assigned him responsibility for treating the clinic's retinitis patients and urged him to develop a research plan for this complication of AIDS, a condition caused by a normally innocuous microbe, cytomegalovirus, which could infect the eyes of people whose immune systems were too weak to restrain it. The disease inevitably led to blindness, if the person survived long enough. There was only one medication that could halt the retinal destruction, and it often caused severe blood toxicity. Kevin wanted David to test a promising experimental drug, foscarnet, which had a very different side effect profile. David promptly found a pharmacologist on the Hill with the equipment to measure concentrations of foscarnet in blood samples. Together, they were designing a protocol to give the medication in escalating doses to retinitis patients.

"I was in Angela's lab," said David excitedly. "We were talking about the case reports of seizures and cardiac arrests that have occurred in transplant patients treated with foscarnet. It's going to be a major safety issue, right? Based on the drug's molecular structure, it makes total sense it would bind serum calcium, doesn't it? So that could be the mechanism by which it caused a seizure or a cardiac arrest, right?

David wasn't even giving Kevin the time to agree with him.

"So I said, 'Let's get some plasma. You can draw my blood. We'll spike it with the drug. If I'm right, the calcium will drop, won't it?' I mean, this won't win a Nobel Prize, but nobody's nailed down the toxicity mechanism. And if we know that, we can avoid killing people with the drug. Right? Right?"

David was now bouncing on the balls of his feet. Kevin instinctively shrank back, afraid David might be having a manic break. Then he grasped David's perfect logic. He patted his protégé on the shoulder.

"Good job," Kevin said. "Go for it."

David gave a clipped shout "Yes!" and bounded out the door.

V

KEEPING AN EYE ON the clock, Kevin typed furiously. It was one week past the deadline for turning in a review of the manuscript spread across his desk. Few things aggravated him more than waiting for a journal's decision on whether they would accept one of his papers. Now he was the cause of delay for another author.

The door opened slightly. He heard Gwen say, "You OK?"

"Yup," Kevin replied, continuing to type.

"Want to talk?"

"Sure."

She closed the door behind her.

"What's happening?"

"Marco's the same."

The tension that often animated Gwen, especially when she had nothing left in reserve, subsided. She crept into a chair and watched his fingers fly over the keyboard like a concert pianist. She couldn't type at half his speed.

"One minute," he said.

"No problem."

Maybe this is how he escapes, she thought. It must be nice to be fully absorbed in data—all true or false, no shades of gray, no attachment, no pain or loss.

Kevin turned off the computer screen and began complaining about the AIDS Action Committee.

"Marco won't meet the criteria for AZT. Are we whining? These people are such entitlement babies."

"Dealing with them must be so hard for you."

"It's all hard," he said, glumly.

She got up and stood behind him to massage his neck.

"You OK?" he asked.

"I'm fine," she said in a soothing murmur.

"Gwen, sit down. There's something I need to tell you."

Terrified, she obeyed. Gwen had never asked Kevin if he had been tested. No one did that here. Anything other than self-disclosure was tacitly understood to be absolutely forbidden. And if someone were to out a co-worker as HIV-infected, she imagined no one would ever speak to her again.

"I don't want to keep this a secret any more, not between us. I'm positive."

Gwen didn't move.

"But my T cells are 400, and they've been pretty much stable since I found out."

Her color turned ashen.

"I should have told you sooner."

"No, no. I understand…how difficult…When did you find out?"

"Six months ago. Marco made me get tested."

"Who else knows?"

"Marco and Katherine. That's all I want, for now."

She nodded vigorously, hoping it would keep the flood of grief from seeping into her eyes.

"I won't tell anyone."

"I know you won't. It's because I really don't want people feeling sorry for me."

She nodded sympathetically.

"See what I mean."

Gwen opened her mouth in horror and clasped her hand over it.

"It's OK. I can take sympathy from you and my sister but no one else."

"Oh, Kevin," she wept.

Gwen was appalled she couldn't stop crying. She focused on how deeply he must trust her to confide this.

I can't let him down, she thought. If I'd been infected from the needle-stick, I'd have gone to him instantly, certain he'd understand what I was going through. I owe him the same. No more selfish tears.

"I think you know that with T cells this high I may never get sick."

She tried to smile.

"And if I do, I'll start AZT. It's not the end of the world, Gwen."

"I know. I know."

Kevin sat on her lap and hugged her.

"You gonna be OK?" he asked.

Her lips trembled.

"I can't lose you," she wailed.

Two more sobs and she regained control.

Kevin hugged her again.

He's lost weight, she realized. She touched his flat belly and was dumb-struck she hadn't noticed it before.

"It feels really good to have people who care this much about me. Wish it didn't have to hurt."

"Good God, Kevin, the last thing you need to be worry about is my feelings."

"Be strong for me, OK?"

She nodded.

Arising, he said, "I'm late for a meeting. We'll talk soon."

She grasped his arm and reluctantly let go.

VI

Gwen had calmed down by the time noon conference began. Disappointed in herself, she wanted to try again at being supportive, but she couldn't talk to Kevin here. He was sitting between Herb and David. The three of them, along with all the AIDS program nurses and social workers, were looking expectantly at her.

Miranda Diaz, Gwen remembered. The case to be presented was her patient. She signaled the intern taking care of Ms. Diaz in the ICU to start.

Ms. Diaz had been diagnosed with retinitis in September and responded well to the standard anti-cytomegalovirus treatment, ganciclovir, until a recent exam showed new lesions in both eyes. David increased her drug infusions from once to twice a day. Then she became hoarse and coughed violently whenever attempting to eat or drink. David had seen a case like this at UCLA in which cytomegalovirus destroyed the laryngeal nerve of an AIDS patient, paralyzing his vocal cords. He hospitalized Ms. Diaz, ordered higher doses of ganciclovir, and asked an ear-nose-and-throat consultant to see her. The specialist confirmed her vocal cords were limp and couldn't prevent aspiration of fluids, even oral secretions, into her lungs. She soon became short of breath and febrile, signs of pneumonia. Her blood oxygen plummeted, so she was put on a ventilator. Her prognosis was grim.

Gwen already knew these details. Her mind began wandering. She wouldn't allow herself to think about Kevin. Instead, she watched David's reactions to the intern's presentation. She wondered about his priorities. Was he more concerned about Ms. Diaz or how the discussion would make him look as the hospital's new cytomegalovirus expert?

Gwen had been suspicious of David before she met him. The UCLA medical center where he had trained received far more media attention than City Hospital did as the AIDS epidemic was unfolding. Most of it was showered on David's mentor, Knowleson. It had been difficult not to be envious of the Hollywood involvement and money he was able to harness while she and Kevin were working so hard with so little at City Hospital. At first, the university ignored them. Apart from space and salaries for two nurses and a clerk, which the city's public health department provided, they had no resources until Kevin's NIH funding soared. After crossing the million-dollars-a year threshold, the university gave them modest administrative support. Donations trickled in from wealthy gays—enough money for them to expand services and hire more staff. Then came more grants, more donations, more university support, which meant they were ripe to be exploited by an ambitious junior investigator who wanted to become famous fast. Gwen had suspected Knowleson's articulate, politically correct speeches were principally aimed at getting his name in print and his face on television. Now, she couldn't help but transfer that mistrust to David.

The intern was concluding. Gwen started to listen again.

"Ms. Diaz's pneumonia and vocal cord function haven't improved despite antibiotics and pushing the ganciclovir dose higher. She's also a bit confused today. Could the CMV infection be spreading to her brain?"

Herb asked, "If this woman is developing cytomegalovirus encephalitis on supra-maximal doses of ganciclovir, what are her chances of surviving? Isn't CMV encephalitis always a terminal event?"

Everyone looked at David.

"She hasn't been on the high dose that long." David said cautiously.

Herb pressed him.

"What exactly is her prognosis?"

"It's hard to say. There are ten or so case reports of CMV encephalitis in the literature, only one of laryngeal nerve paralysis. They all died within weeks, but none were getting this aggressive ganciclovir treatment."

David looked at Gwen. She guessed he needed some backing to go out on a limb. She gave him a barely perceptible nod.

"I think it's too soon to throw in the towel," he declared. "Maybe I could get her foscarnet on a compassionate-use basis…though that would take a few days to arrange… uh, maybe longer."

"Compassionate-use," scoffed Herb. "Compassion would be considering that extending her life is prolonging her misery, given her chances of even short-term survival are so remote."

"Wait a second," Gwen interjected. "She understood the procedure and consented to being intubated. The ICU attending who explained it to her yesterday is fluent in Spanish. He offered her the option of morphine and a peaceful death. She *chose* the ventilator."

"Gwen, is this really what she wants?"

Irate, she answered, "Ms. Diaz has been my clinic patient for a year. She knows what her prognosis is, and she's told me several times her biggest priority is to see her children again before she dies."

Herb turned to Nadine, the social worker, and asked, "What's happening with that?"

"They're waiting for visas. Which could take days, weeks, months to resolve. Who knows?"

While everyone else mulled over that uncertainty, Gwen struggled to comprehend why Herb was questioning her judgment. She had made an irrefutable argument, based on the patient's wishes, something he had to respect. Was he dismissing it?

She thought of their mutual confessions two years ago. At the time, it seemed they were becoming close friends. Did he back off, or was it me? Do I have a problem trusting men at work? David, for instance? He'd be a prime example. But what about Kevin? No, that's different. Another possibility entered her mind. Her clinical judgment had rarely been challenged since her appointment to the City Hospital attending staff. Am I so used to having the last word that I can't tolerate opposition?

Kevin broke the silence.

"I'm hearing it's a very long shot that what we're doing will make a difference. On the other hand, she did opt for aggressive treatment. I think we need to determine how informed her decision is in light of what David just told us. Let's make sure she understands being on a ventilator is probably futile.

"Nadine, you're fluent in Spanish. You talked to her this morning. Is she still capable of understanding this and deciding whether she wants to quit or not?"

"She was a couple of hours ago."

"Gwen should be there. If the vent is what she wants, we should do whatever we can to keep her alive. And it doesn't have to be fixed in stone. We can revisit the decision daily."

"All right," said Herb. "But if she deteriorates to the point where she can't decide, I'm going to ask the Ethics Committee to get involved."

He asked Gwen, "Are you OK with that?"

"Of course I am! If she worsens on high-dose ganciclovir, then it's obviously hopeless. You won't need to get the Ethics Committee involved. I'll turn off the power switch myself."

Getting what she wanted didn't mollify Gwen. Herb's attitude reminded her of a sub-specialist at City Hospital who treated her as if he were a prosecutor and she a public defender representing a client charged with impersonating a critically ill patient. In fact, she was doing her job, advocating for someone under her care.

No, no, she reproached herself. Herb isn't like that. I was totally out of line. What is wrong with me?

VII

GWEN AND NADINE LEFT for the ICU when the conference ended. Kevin and Herb headed toward their monthly division chiefs meeting with Ray.

"How's Marco?" Herb asked, "And how are you holding up?"

"He's the same. I'm handling it."

"Is there anything I can do to help?"

Kevin didn't act on his impulse to decline the offer. Self-sufficiency isn't always a virtue, he thought. A veteran Shanti counselor had given him this advice after Marco's first hospitalization.

"If you're feeling guilty when friends help you out," the counselor had said, "you should think about how much pleasure they get from your graciously accepting their generosity. And the gift doesn't have to be paid back to the giver. You can pass it on to someone else later."

Kevin checked his calendar.

"You busy Wednesday evening?"

"I don't have plans. What can I do?"

"Come over to my place. We can talk."

"I'll bring dinner."

"That would be great!"

Kevin steered Herb to a different topic. He wanted feedback on Karen Packard, another junior physician he had recruited right out of training. Kevin was using one of his grants to cover her salary so she could work with Herb on Pneumocystis trials.

"She's terrific!" said Herb. "Bright, enthusiastic. Best of all, she's a very effective problem solver. I wish I could find pulmonary fellows with that kind of drive and ability. So, Kevin…How do you do it?"

"Do what?"

"Attract such great people to work with you?"

"I don't," Kevin stalled, unable to think of an answer that wouldn't sound flip or pretentious.

"Yes, you do, and I bet you know how you do it."

"It's not me, Herb. It's the work that attracts good people."

"Right, it has nothing to do with you."

"Speaking of Karen, are your studies on track?"

"Definitely. And you know those case reports from Canada and New York about Pneumocystis patients improving after being given high-dose steroids?"

Kevin nodded.

"Well, a Southern California consortium is organizing a multicenter, randomized trial. They want City Hospital to be a site. I'm having Karen represent us on the conference calls."

"Good!"

"By the way, I understand she shares an office with David. How are they getting along? They're both quite ambitious."

"It doesn't seem to be a problem. I've given them completely non-overlapping areas to explore."

"But putting them in the same office where they see each other's every success. That's a goad to keep them driven, isn't it?"

"Gosh, it might be," said Kevin feigning naiveté.

Surprised by how quickly Kevin had grown from a neophyte researcher into a wily mentor, Herb laughed.

VIII

From the division chief's meeting, Kevin went straight to a conference room above the library. He was glad to find only twenty people inside. He had faced larger hostile groups and not just AIDS activists, also those on the other side who demanded exclusion of HIV-infected children from public schools or mandatory HIV screening of anyone applying for a government job.

Kevin recognized many of the men from previous meetings. He had even established some rapport with a few of them. His temper was under control until he saw the moderator was Rebecca Wolman.

"Wonderful," he seethed through clenched teeth.

Rebecca looked at her watch and said, "Can we start, now that Dr. Bartholomew is here?"

The room hushed. All the attendees crossed their arms.

"We asked for this meeting," she said, "because it's been three months since the AZT trial was stopped—*terminated* because an independent data and safety monitoring board concluded it would be *unethical* to deprive the people on placebo from receiving a life-prolonging medication. We've read about how kind Burroughs Wellcome is being, how accommodating the FDA has suddenly become, how nicely they're working together to make AZT available to all those poor, suffering AIDS patients."

She raised her voice and lowered her pitch like an alto launching into an aria.

"But it's been three months, and nothing has happened. Ten people with AIDS are dying *every day* in this country!"

"What the fuck is going on?" she yelled at Kevin, "And what are *you* doing about it?"

Her audience pounded their fists on the table.

"AZT. Now!" they chanted. "AZT. Now!"

Unruffled, Kevin held up a hand.

"If we're going to have a dialogue, you have to let me talk too."

They kept on chanting.

"Or I'm leaving."

He took two steps toward the door. There was quiet.

How infantile, he thought.

Being as conciliatory as he could, Kevin said, "Can I give you some information about the trial that hasn't been in the press?"

Taking their cynical expressions as acquiescence, he distributed copies of his handout. He explained the study's limitations—its short duration before all those who were assigned to get placebo were switched to AZT, the restrictive entry criteria which made generalizing results to other AIDS patients problematic. He also described the severe anemia, nausea, and muscle damage that occurred much more frequently in those who had received AZT during the randomized phase of the trial.

He was tempted to mention Marco's situation as a personal example of where the harm would exceed the benefit. Then he recalled Gwen telling him that when dealing with angry people who perceive they have less power than you—whether patients, employees, or activists—it doesn't help to bring up your own personal issues. They won't be sympathetic.

"I really do get it. People with AIDS are dying," Kevin concluded, "and for some of them, AZT is likely to improve survival and quality of life in the short term. But I worry that wide release of the drug before definitive studies are done could turn out to be a terrible mistake. What if the outcome of taking the drug for longer than a few months is worse than taking nothing?"

"That's right," Rebecca retorted. "We don't know what the long term safety of AZT is, but it's clearly an immediate stay of execution for anyone who's had Pneumocystis. Burroughs Wellcome promised to make AZT available in October. It's going to be January at the earliest, if then."

"That's out of my control, Rebecca."

"You were an investigator in the trial. If you publicly put pressure on the company, if you accuse them in front of TV cameras and say delaying distribution of AZT is genocide, they'll have to respond. It will disgrace them in a way we can't."

"Rebecca, I collaborated with BW scientists in designing the trial. I am not going to make an accusation like that. Anyway, BW can't do this alone, certainly not until the FDA gives them a green light. And the FDA is greasing the wheels for AZT approval to happen at warp speed. There has never been a drug for any disease that will get out to dying people this fast and on the basis of such little evidence.

"You're also ignoring safety. The company and the FDA have to work out how to monitor the toxicity of long-term treatment with AZT. If people start dropping dead from toxicity, compassionate-use distribution will look like a greedy marketing ploy by the company and negligence by the FDA. And that would have a deadening effect on development of new drugs. Try to see the bigger picture."

"Kevin, the bigger picture is that this is a holocaust. You're a fucking stooge for a Nazi pharmaceutical company. We're done here."

As the group got up to leave, Kevin wanted to scream. My lover is dying of AIDS. What gives you the moral authority to demonize me?

Just thinking those words was enough catharsis for him to stay focused on salvaging the meeting. As the men gathered their coats and umbrellas, Kevin saw that underneath the anger, they were dispirited.

"Rebecca," he projected in his most basso voice, "Is this how you want to end things? What have you gained here?"

That caught their attention. Everyone stopped. They looked back and forth between the antagonists.

"Our mission at City Hospital is to give the best treatment to people with AIDS. Yours is to empower them. Shouldn't we be working together? Wouldn't that be the best thing for folks who have this disease?"

Kevin slowly looked around the room, systematically making eye contact with each person. Some were weighing his proposal. The others were already nodding in agreement.

Rebecca, not oblivious to the fact that she was quickly becoming a minority of one, said, "OK. We can talk about that."

Kevin offered his hand. The men clapped as she shook it.

IX

HERB RETURNED TO HIS office from the chief's meeting and paged Karen Packard. Talking to Kevin had reminded him to advise her how to stick up for their interests on the conference call with their Southern California collaborators. Karen arrived moments later. As tall as Herb, she had a taut, athletic build and straight brown hair hanging down her back.

"Don't let them railroad you," he said. "They'll want you to do all the work while they get all the credit. Make sure there's an up-front agreement about authorship. Otherwise, they may pull a fast one when their statistician drafts the manuscript."

She gave him a self-assured smile.

"I've never had a problem with people running over me."

Herb chuckled. He knew Karen had played college basketball before medical school. After she left, he reflected on how confident this young woman was. Cecilia had been confident at that age. She was even more so now, as were many middle-aged women he worked with, women like Gwen. But Karen was taking it to a new level.

Thinking of Gwen made him uneasy. Had he come across dogmatic and insensitive at the noon conference? Would she hold a grudge against him? Their connection when Laurie Hampton tested positive hadn't lasted long. Their subsequent encounters were awkward. He guessed that what she had divulged was too threatening for her to want any deeper friendship to develop. He had to admit his own confession had made him cautious too, which was unfortunate because he liked and respected her. Gwen was different from anyone else he knew well. Decidedly more unconventional, and that was appealing. It would be nice to have someone at work he could confide in besides Kevin.

Herb tapped on Gwen's half-open office door.

"Come in," she said.

She was writing on a yellow legal pad.

"What happened with Ms. Diaz?"

Gwen frowned.

"I think she understood what we were telling her, how unlikely it is she'll ever breathe on her own again. Her brother was there. She kept looking to him, but he didn't want to influence her decision. Then she shut down. Nothing was resolved."

He nodded solicitously.

"Gwen, if you choose aggressive life support for Ms. Diaz, that decides it. She's your patient."

Gwen sighed and said, "I know letting it end is the humane thing to do. But if we were to buy enough time for her kids to get here while she's still conscious…I can't discard that possibility."

"I wouldn't either. Sorry, I didn't mean to sound callous earlier."

"Herb, you're not callous. I know that."

"There's no DNR order in the chart, and there won't be until you sign one. OK?"

"Thanks."

Gwen glanced down at her yellow pad. Herb sensed she wasn't angry at him now but wanted to end the conversation. He slipped out of the office without saying goodbye.

Back in the ICU, Herb was washing his hands at the sink. He saw Laurie Hampton seated on a stool, legs crossed, making notes on a heart monitor printout.

She seems content, he thought. Has it really been two years since Gwen told me about her antibody result?

Laurie had never told him, and he had never said anything that could remotely imply he knew. He had tried a couple of open-ended questions, giving her the opportunity to talk about it. She hadn't disclosed.

She looks OK. Maybe she's one of the lucky—what Kevin calls healthy, long-term, non-progressors. And the accident was five years ago.

That was pleasant to contemplate until he began wondering how she handled the uncertainty. For him, it would be a rodent inside his belly gnawing constantly.

Laurie saw Herb looking at her.

"Got a minute?" she asked.

"Sure."

"I've been working on a quality assurance project, comparing our policies for invasive procedures to what the residents document in the chart after they've put in an arterial line or central venous catheter. I have some data."

"I've got time now."

"Great. I'll get my file."

Businesslike, Laurie described the problems she'd unearthed. Nothing too alarming, he thought, which was her assessment as well.

"We could do better," she said. "But nobody's going to find their name in the newspaper."

"That's good to hear. Thanks for the update."

He reached for her arm. His fingertips grazed her sleeve. She was closing her file and didn't notice.

An hour after Herb left the ICU, Karen Packard came in to check on a newly admitted patient.

Laurie approached her and signaled toward the break room with her eyes.

"When you've got a moment," she said.

Karen nodded.

As soon as the two women were seated, Karen asked, "Did she repeat your T cell count?"

"Yeah," Laurie replied darkly. "It was under four hundred the second time, too. They'd always been normal before."

"Does Tanya know?"

"I haven't told her yet. I'd like to have a plan for what I'm going to do first."

Karen looked puzzled.

"About the trial. This means I'll be eligible when it opens. Stanford will be a site, so I could enroll there without anyone here knowing I'm infected."

"Oh, right. God, that's a tough one. AZT or placebo, maybe for years before anyone knows if it helps."

"Yeah, tough decisionsville," Laurie muttered.

"You should talk to Herb or Kevin Bartholomew. They both have lots more clinical trials experience than me."

Laurie raised an eyebrow.

"You've got to be kidding. Besides you and Gwen Howard, nobody else here knows. And I don't want anybody else to know. I do not need people at work pitying me."

"Herb won't tell anyone. He's a good guy. You said you trusted him."

"Not that far."

"He's been doing randomized trials for longer than anyone here. He could look over the protocol, answer your questions. He'd be a terrific resource. You know he'd love to help you."

"Herb is a very nice person. I'm sure he's full of good intentions. But he's way too opaque for me to share something like this. I can't tell what he's really feeling."

Laurie looked back at her coffee. Her left leg bounced nervously.

"I'll think about it."

X

GWEN DIDN'T SEE KEVIN again that day. After a family dinner of take-out burritos, Eva did homework in her bedroom, and Rick went off to play poker with his buddies, leaving her alone. She wanted to call Kevin but resisted the urge. She chided herself on what a basket case she had been. From now on, this had to be about his needs, not hers. Marco didn't have much time left. Kevin shouldn't be wasting any of it allaying her fears. She wished she could tell Rick. She knew she could swear him to secrecy. He wouldn't break the pledge. Still, it would be a betrayal, and she'd already let Kevin down once today.

She was tempted to open her Christmas present from Nan, a fifth of good Scotch. She picked up a glass then put it away. Gwen doubted drinking would do anything other than make her depressed. For the rest of the evening, she watched stupid television sitcoms that Eva had outgrown.

Tuesday was better. She had five minutes alone with Kevin in the morning and spent it giving him a neck massage. His optimism lifted her spirits. Her mood further improved in clinic as a succession of patients told her how much they appreciated her help. Then Allen Schwartz came into her exam room.

A New Yorker in his early twenties, Mr. Schwartz had recently finessed his escape to the Castro by persuading his father to open a branch of the family jewelry business in the Bay Area. At his first appointment, he had shown Gwen a purplish growth on his leg, which she biopsied. As expected, the pathology report was Kaposi's sarcoma. The disease usually spread slowly, but she saw many new lesions at his next visit and advised him to get chemotherapy. Allen was not interested.

Today, his cheeks and eyelids were involved. He wasn't able to shut his right eye completely. Though she had taken care of dozens of patients with

Kaposi's nodules on their face, Gwen couldn't keep from imagining Allen out in public, the reactions he must get, how it would feel if everyone looked at you with revulsion.

"Have you thought any more about chemotherapy?" she asked.

"No chemotherapy," Allen said, pointing to his nose. "This isn't Kaposi's."

"It's not?" said Gwen, flabbergasted.

"Nope. I went to Dr. Williams in San Jose. He's an infection expert. He told me these tumors are caused by syphilis. Take enough penicillin, and they'll go away."

He opened his shirt, revealing a coil of plastic tubing taped to his chest, one end entering the skin under his collarbone.

"I do the infusions myself at home every six hours," he said proudly. "Dr. Williams got a nurse to bring all the supplies and change the dressing every week."

That bastard, thought Gwen. She had heard about Doug Williams and his syphilis scam. A small case series of AIDS patients who had syphilis invading their brain had appeared in a prestigious journal. It had been publicized by the lay press, even though this rare complication of syphilis had been known for a century to occur in people with normal immune systems and there was no evidence from control populations to prove it was any more common in HIV-positive individuals than HIV-negatives. A few predatory doctors had capitalized on the anxiety generated by the report. They prescribed long courses of intravenous penicillin treatment for AIDS patients who had no symptoms of syphilis and negative blood tests for the disease. In return, they received lucrative kick-backs from home infusion companies.

"My parents were ecstatic when they found out I don't have cancer. They're paying all the medical bills."

Gwen tamped down her fury enough to speak calmly.

"I don't want to rain on your parade, Mr. Schwartz, but taking IV penicillin doesn't make sense. I've checked your blood for syphilis several times, and the results were negative. The test for syphilis infection is very, very accurate. People with syphilis don't have negative results."

Allen was unfazed.

"Look in the mirror," she said, unable to restrain herself. "Those lesions aren't shrinking. They're getting bigger."

"Williams says that's just temporary. He told me the tumors might swell while the bugs are being killed and spill their guts out. See, he knows what he's talking about."

"Please, Mr. Schwartz, think it about it. Months ago we did a biopsy. If it was syphilis, the pathologist would have seen the microbes. I'm sorry, but the truth is you're being duped by a charlatan."

"You're the charlatan, Dr. Howard," Allen shouted. "All you've offered me is poison. Dr. Williams says chemotherapy will destroy what's left of my immune system and let the syphilis get into my brain. That makes sense."

Gwen backpedaled, trying to salvage some line of communication.

"Mr. Schwartz, I respect your deciding how you'll be treated. It's all right with me if we don't agree on this issue. I'm happy to keep being your doctor. Come back and see me in a month, OK?"

"I'll think about it," said Allen coolly as he buttoned up his shirt.

The next morning, Gwen took Eva to her school bus stop before driving into San Francisco. While coasting downhill in her 1966 Volvo, bleached of its original turquoise sheen, she thought of Allen Schwartz. Her rage at the South Bay physician preying on him was spent. It was the poignancy of Allen's situation that still disturbed her. He was twenty-three years old. He couldn't process his impending death. He hadn't even finished growing up. She looked protectively at Eva, who was gazing out the window.

As they passed Lake Merritt, Gwen saw geese, skeins flying in V formations, gaggles waddling across the moist green meadows. She rolled her window down to inhale the air, fresh from last night's rain. At a stoplight, Eva spoke for the first time since they had left the house.

"I don't trust any of my friends."

Gwen's initial reaction was fright. Did I just have an auditory hallucination? It's impossible that Eva would tell me something so intimate.

Gwen reined in her panic. I'm not having a psychotic break. My brain must have misinterpreted sounds coming through the window. Maybe it was the voices of joggers running around the lake.

Then she reconsidered what she had heard. The words had been spoken exactly as Eva would say them.

She rolled up her window and said, "Sorry. You said you don't what?"

"Trust any of my friends," Eva replied, as if talking about the weather.

Gwen had another extraordinary sensation, like an unexpectedly delicious bite of food. She felt a rush of joy and immediately clamped down on it. Nonchalance was the key to keeping this dialogue going. But what to say? She scrambled frantically to find the right tone.

"So, why do you think that is?"

Creases formed above Eva's silky black eyebrows.

"I don't know. I guess because they're all shallow."

Gwen quashed her amazement and maintained a pretense of mild, nonjudgmental interest.

"Yeah, I think I understand."

Eva didn't seem to be offended but said no more.

Gwen double parked in front of the bus stop.

As Eva got out of the car, Gwen said, "Hey, kiddo. It'll get better, much better. Believe me. You'll see. Your friends will become comfortable being real about who they are, and so will you."

Eva looked dubiously at the approaching bus.

"Thanks, Mom," she said with a sigh and closed the door.

At the hospital, Gwen went first to the clinic to retrieve her stethoscope, forgotten after her row with Allen Schwartz. She passed the treatment room and saw her longest surviving retinitis patient, Hubert Wilson. Once Kevin's patient, Hubert had switched to Gwen after his kidneys nearly failed during an experimental drug trial. He waved to her from a recliner chair where he was connected by intravenous tubing to a bag of ganciclovir. While the solution dripped, Hubert drew. A sketchbook lay on his lap. A tin of colored pencils was balanced on his armrest.

Hairless from chemotherapy that kept the Kaposi's sarcoma on his legs from enlarging, Hubert was the least demanding of the retinitis patients per the nurses. Although cytomegalovirus had destroyed much of his vision, he showed no signs of the profound depression that often afflicted these people.

He had no light perception in his left eye, the result of a retinal detachment. A blind spot in his right eye was large enough to eliminate half of his visual field. But he could still read. More importantly to him, he could still draw.

Ganciclovir treatment required sitting in clinic three hours a day, five days a week. Hubert used all this time to work on an illustrated book. Whenever Gwen had a few minutes to spare, she stopped by to view his progress.

Some of his drawings depicted wild gatherings in the style of Breughel—a local bath-house bacchanalia, a Castro street party, the interior of a South of Market leather bar. Others reminded her of William Blake paintings with modern stand-ins for devils, angels, and the fall from Eden. The accompanying text told the story of an art historian with AIDS trying to finish a definitive tome on the Depression-era murals inside Coit Tower on Telegraph Hill. Gwen had seen the murals, a paean to California industry and agriculture, and had read about the artist's controversial allusions to a bloody longshoremen's strike.

She sat on the unoccupied armrest and watched him color in his sketch of a priest wearing a nylon flight jacket over his clerical collar. The man was in conversation with a disheveled drug dealer whose open palms held out pills and packets of powder for passers-by to ogle. Hubert took a break and handed her a book of completed drawings. She paged through to her favorite one. In the foreground, a woman with a crew cut and huge biceps was mounting a motorcycle. Sidesaddle behind her was a transvestite wearing a slinky dress, a blond wig, red lipstick, and white pancake make-up. She had a mole on her left cheek like Marilyn Monroe. In the background marched a line of starving men, chained together at the ankles, clad only in bikini briefs. Their bodies were covered by boils and Kaposi's lesions. Above this scene, a long-bearded, elderly black man in a dashiki stood on a cumulus cloud. He held a thunderbolt over his head.

How wonderful that he has this creative outlet, Gwen mused. She wished she had one. She thought about taking an art class. Just an evening a week. I could find the time for that, couldn't I?

XI

KEVIN HAD GONE INTO work early and came home at noon. When he opened the front door, the house was quiet, too quiet. Marco always had music on during the day—jazz, rock, tango, blues.

"Hello?" he called out.

Merciless quiet enveloped him.

He found Marco in bed, eyes closed, breathing normally.

"Wake up," he shouted.

Marco didn't respond. Kevin screamed in his ear. Marco still didn't respond. He pinched the flesh between Marco's thumb and forefinger. Marco lay flaccid. He pressed his knuckles into Marco's sternum, twisting downward with more and more force until Marco moaned feebly and lifted his right arm.

Kevin curled himself into a ball on the floor and rocked in a futile attempt to repel the facts pummeling him. Marco couldn't speak. He couldn't move half his body. It was unlikely he would ever do either again. Kevin's only escape route was to think rationally. He ticked through a checklist he knew by rote. Marco must have had a stroke, or a mass was growing in the right side of his brain. There was one treatable possibility, Toxoplasma infection. If it was anything else, Marco would survive a week, two at most. Even if this opportunistic parasite was the cause, it was probably too late for any meaningful recovery.

Kevin phoned in two prescriptions to a pharmacy on Castro Street and ran to his car. On returning, he placed a pill on the back of Marco's tongue, added a teaspoon of water, massaged the sides of his throat to make him swallow, and repeated the process.

He hadn't called an ambulance. Marco had consistently been clear about not wanting extreme measures. Taking him to the hospital is pointless, he had thought at first. Now he wasn't so certain. He put the internal debate on hold. Herb would be here soon. He could decide.

Kevin went to his desk and composed a to-do list—call Mexico City, cancel everything at work for the next two weeks, find Marco's signed will. Nothing else came to mind. He gave up and sat beside Marco, who lay inert except for the rise and fall of his chest.

Herb drove to Diamond Heights after ICU sign-out rounds. He stopped on the way at a gourmet deli to buy garlic roast chicken, roasted bell peppers, a baguette, and a bottle of Sauvignon Blanc.

He had been to their apartment the previous summer. Marco had been in good spirits that evening, but his sunken frame and the anemic pallor of his lips and nails were unmistakable signs he was nearing the end of life. The idea of Kevin witnessing his lover's daily deterioration had distressed Herb, though he was uplifted by seeing how competently Kevin dealt with Marco's many needs, parsing them into smaller components, each having a practical solution—a minor medication change, setting alarms and posting reminder notes for Marco, hiring help for whenever he had to be away.

The last time he was here, the upstairs glass wall of their apartment had been ablaze, reflecting an ocher sunset. Tonight, the windows were black. He wondered if anyone was home, but within seconds of pressing the buzzer, Kevin opened the door.

"Thanks," Kevin said in a flat, numb monotone, his bloodshot eyes fixed on the bag of food Herb carried. "I should eat."

Almost as an afterthought, he said, "Marco's in a coma."

He led Herb to the only source of light, a reading lamp at the far end of the apartment. Standing by the bed, they watched Marco breathe.

"Would you examine him? I can't trust my judgment."

He gave Herb his stethoscope and rubber reflex hammer and retreated into the darkness.

Herb left the bedroom navigating blindly until his eyes adjusted. He found Kevin in the living room, staring out the window. Herb coughed politely.

"What do you think?" Kevin asked in the same monotone.

"A right hemisphere lesion," Herb said uneasily, "Could be an infection, tumor, maybe an infarct or a bleed?"

"That's what I thought."

"I'm so sorry."

Kevin's attention was directed at the waxing crescent moon setting in the western sky.

"It might be toxo," Herb suggested.

"I know. I already started him on sulfa and pyrimethamine. Not that it matters. It's better for him to stay here, isn't it?"

"Did he say he wants to die at home?"

Kevin nodded.

"Can you…?"

"It's the least I can do."

"He could be made comfortable in a hospice."

Kevin's face hardened.

"Herb, do you have any personal experience with hospice?"

"I do. Remember Sister Anna? She spent the end of her life in a hospice. I thought the staff was incredibly attentive. She had a little tape deck playing Gregorian chants. It was…serene."

"Sorry, Herb, but an impression based on a cameo appearance you made there is not a persuasive testimonial."

"Kevin, I was there a lot, daily during her last week. I was very fond of her. It was more than a doctor-patient relationship for me."

"Herb, no way! Don't tell me you had an affair with a nun."

Kevin laughed until tears blurred his vision. He arose, stumbled into the kitchen, switched on the lights, and opened two beers.

"Let's eat," he called out.

They each succeeded in swallowing a few bites of food. Kevin opened two more beers.

Halfway through the third round, Kevin asked, "Were you ever in Boy Scouts?"

"I was. Why?"

"Just curious. They have scouts in Mexico, but Marco never joined. Probably his parents thought it was beneath him. I belonged for a while.

Why were you a scout? Because your friends were, or did your parents make you do it?"

Bewildered, Herb answered, "Actually, it was my idea."

Raindrops began spattering against the kitchen windows, and Herb recalled a wet, autumn evening, standing at attention in a damp church basement. The smell of mildew was nauseating. He concentrated on the freshly laundered khaki scent of his uniform and the bright merit badges he was proud to have on his sash. The boys were clustered by patrol. His was the troop's smallest with only four members—Herb, two boys whose parents were from Latin America, and a kid who rarely spoke or looked anyone in the eye. None of them had been invited to join other patrols. Herb hadn't minded. He was grateful to be allowed to wear the uniform.

Herb saw Kevin was waiting for an explanation.

"I must have believed being a Boy Scout would make me a real American boy."

"That's great!" Kevin roared, "You wanted to be a real American boy. So did I, Herb. So did I."

Turning reflective, he added, "Boy Scouts didn't help."

Herb imagined coming of age in the early1960s, knowing you were gay. Had that fear of being discovered been worse than his own childhood nightmares of Japanese soldiers invading the United States to exterminate every Chinese who had escaped the war?

Kevin interrupted this train of thought.

"Do you remember any of the Boy Scout Law?"

"I think so."

The third beer kicked in, and Herb automatically recited, "A scout is trustworthy, loyal, helpful, friendly, courteous, kind, obedient, cheerful, thrifty, brave, clean, and reverent."

"Amazing! How did you do that? You are the *last* person I would have expected to know all twelve Scout virtues, and in the right order, too."

"I didn't realize you had such a low opinion of me."

"Touché," Kevin laughed.

He immediately became serious again.

"Did you believe in the code? You must have if you still remember it."

"I guess so. The Scout Law did embody the ethos of the times."

"Was there a hierarchy? I mean, were some of those virtues more important to you than others?"

Herb was mystified, but he could hardly begrudge Kevin.

"Let me think…trustworthy, loyal, helpful, friendly, courteous, and kind. Those all fit with what I thought Americans were supposed to stand for. I'm not sure about the rest. I do remember the oath we had to recite made me nervous. 'On my honor I will do my best to do my duty to God and my country and to obey the Scout Law.' I worried I'd be putting myself in jeopardy if I ever broke one of the rules. I even asked my mother if swearing to obey the law was OK."

"What'd she say?"

"She told me not to take it so literally. She was all for assimilation."

"Interesting," said Kevin as he gazed off into space.

Afterwards, parked in his driveway, Herb sat in the car mulling over what he had wanted to ask Kevin but of course never would. Last summer, when Marco told him how the two had met, Herb deduced they must have become lovers before anyone would have known that gay men who didn't use condoms might be transmitting a fatal disease. On hearing Marco was sick, Herb had commiserated with Gwen, but she revealed nothing. Maybe she knew no more than he did. He clutched the steering wheel in frustration. He couldn't think of any way to help Kevin.

XII

As Herb got out of his car, he saw Cecilia's silhouette pass across an upstairs window. He noticed her car wasn't in the driveway or on the street. He went inside and paused in the front hall. The only noise was the whoosh of sheets dropping down the laundry chute to the basement.

"Where's Martin?" he called out.

"Piano lesson. He took my car."

No one has to pick him up, thought Herb.

"Cecilia, if we got a car for Martin, neither of us would have to be a chauffeur again."

They hadn't discussed this since Martin got his driver's license. Cecilia had been opposed in principle then to any teenager having his own car. But now, when one of their cars was available, Martin always drove himself places and reliably returned it. Perhaps she was ready to revisit the idea.

"Cecilia?" he shouted.

Hearing no reply, Herb went upstairs. Their bedroom and bathroom were empty. In Martin's room, he found Cecilia kneeling on the floor, motionless except for her twitching hands which held a dog-eared, glossy magazine. The color had drained from her face.

"Oh, my God! Herb!" she wailed, showing him the crumpled magazine.

It had no titles or text, just photos. Nude men flexing their muscles and coupling in various positions. Close-ups of penises thrust into mouths and anuses.

Disoriented, Herb knelt next to her. It had never occurred to him that Martin might be gay. He wanted to reassure Cecilia but couldn't think of anything to say—anything that didn't include a terrifying acronym.

She looked at him, imploring wordlessly.

"I'll…I'll talk to him," he stammered.

Cecilia and Martin ate a late dinner in silence. Herb sat with them, reading the newspaper. The lack of conversation didn't seem to bother Martin. Cecilia pushed food around her plate, then said she had to call her sister and left the table.

"Martin," Herb said, "we need to talk."

"Why?"

"I'm not angry. We just need to talk. OK?"

Martin grudgingly followed his father into the living room. Herb sat on a love seat. Martin remained standing.

"Please, Martin, sit down. This will take more than a minute."

Martin sat on the edge of a stuffed chair.

"We need to have a matter-of-fact discussion about sex."

Martin rolled his eyes and whined, "Again? Dad, we've been through that before."

Herb was at a loss for how to begin.

"And I've had it in school up to here," said Martin, sticking a finger into his throat.

As Herb pondered over what to say next, Martin rose and backed away. Reluctantly, Herb pulled the magazine out of his jacket pocket.

"We need to talk about this."

Martin flushed. He stared at the carpet.

"You searched my room?"

"No! Mom found it by accident while she was changing your bed."

Martin refused to make eye contact. Herb saw shame and defiance battling across his son's face.

"Martin," Herb said, his voice cracking. "Mom and I love you. We want to protect you. It's totally fine with us if you're gay or bisexual. You know we have friends who are gay, who we respect a lot. We're scared because if you're not careful, if you got infected with the AIDS virus…so many young men have died already. Magazines are not the issue. We want to be sure you know how to be safe, that you'll be careful."

Martin looked up and saw Herb shaking.

"Jesus, Dad! Get a grip!"

"I will if you'll talk to me."

"This is humiliating. We do *not* need to have this conversation. I know about AIDS and the blood test. I'm not an idiot!"

Full of regret, Herb put a hand to his forehead.

"Look, Dad, I am being careful. All right? We're not going into details. End of discussion."

Martin stomped out of the room.

Herb didn't fall asleep until four in the morning. At seven, he was in the kitchen, half-heartedly trying to make a double cappuccino with the espresso machine Cecilia had bought him for his birthday. He couldn't stay focused long enough to follow the instructions and kept having to start over. Martin padded in barefoot. Ignoring Herb, he went to the refrigerator and took out a carton of orange juice. He stood at the sink, facing away from his father, pouring juice into a glass. Herb set down the metal pieces he hadn't been able to fit together.

"Martin, can we finish talking?"

"Dad, let it go. You need to trust me."

Herb was in check. A stalemate might be the best he could salvage.

"I want to trust you. And I meant what I said yesterday. This doesn't change how I feel about you, not by an iota."

"If that's really true, promise not to bring this up again. OK?"

Herb couldn't think of a counterargument and conceded. He shut the steam valve, abandoned his cappuccino, and went upstairs. Cecilia was dressing for work. He slumped onto the bed and told her what Martin had said.

He began to apologize. Cecilia held a finger to his lips.

"My turn," she said.

Herb followed her downstairs and stopped outside in the dining room to listen.

"Martin," she said calmly, "I'm going to trust you to be safe."

"Good, Mom."

"Will you trust me enough to give me honest answers when I have questions? That's fair, isn't it?"

"No, Mom, that's not fair. I don't ask questions about your sex life, do I? What's fair is that you respect my privacy like I respect yours."

Herb waited, but Cecilia had no reply. He trudged back upstairs. The mother's gambit, he thought, played perfectly and still a stalemate.

XIII

MORNING SUNLIGHT CREPT DOWN the bedroom wall, crossed the floor, and reached Marco's face. The heat on his left cheek woke him. He turned his head away from the light and tried to roll over. Nothing happened. On his second attempt, Marco realized his right arm and leg were missing.

"Kevin!" he tried to scream, making a barely audible sound.

He clenched and unclenched his left fist, confirming some part of his body still existed. Terrified of what he might find, Marco inched his hand across his chest. Once it passed the mid-line, that hand disappeared too, only to reappear when he pulled it back in horror.

"Kevin!" he shrieked repeatedly, making muffled whimpers.

Half asleep on the living room couch, Kevin heard gurgling noises. He ran into the bedroom. Marco's eyes were open, his mouth twisted. He was mumbling incomprehensibly. Torn between the reprieve of having Marco back and the pain of seeing his anguish, Kevin wept.

Marco had never seen Kevin cry. This final proof of love soothed him. It made everything clear. Marco accepted the missing side of his body. He was ready to leave the rest of it now and closed his eyes.

At dusk, Kevin awoke from a dreamless nap. The window shades were outlined by a chrome yellow glow. It must be five o'clock already, he thought. He sat up and suddenly felt trapped in a spinning teacup carnival ride. Afraid of falling, he didn't move. Nausea rose and crested. Kevin forced himself not to vomit. As soon as the impulse to heave subsided, he looked around the room. The floor, walls, and ceiling were fixed in space, but the swirling sensation persisted. Baffled by why he would be having an attack of vertigo, he noticed the fingertips of his right hand were tingling—the same fingers that had just brushed against Marco when he sat up. Then he understood.

Closing his eyes tightly, Kevin touched Marco. Living flesh was warm, elastic, yielding to the least pressure. Marco's skin was cool and stiff. Another wave of nausea mounted. He rushed to the bathroom in time to throw up in the toilet.

After the coroner left, Kevin remembered something Gwen had told him when her mother died, how the death of a parent removes the last blindfold keeping us from seeing our own mortality. Kevin hadn't experienced that when his father died. He did now.

At his desk, he found a pen and a clean sheet of paper. He made a list—people to call, funeral arrangements, an obituary to write. He reached into a file drawer for three folders, back-burner projects he had hoped to initiate one day.

"No more waiting," he said aloud.

Green Hills, 1988

I

GWEN HADN'T SEEN KEVIN for two months, not since he left to be a subject in a trial at NIH. Though he had sounded upbeat and energetic on the phone, confident the new medication was working, she needed to lay eyes on him to be convinced. Today would be her chance. He was flying back to San Francisco.

A year earlier, Kevin's T cells had dropped below 200. He started AZT, and his T cells rose. Despite the drug-induced anemia, which made exercise impossible, he could work. But the treatment's immune boosting effect was transient. Six months later, his T cells were below 200 again, putting him at risk for lethal complications of AIDS. He sank into bitterness then resignation as hollows formed in his temples and thighs. Simply getting dressed and driving to the hospital exhausted him. Gwen had to take over running the program. Kevin continued to come to the office, though he rarely did more than gaze across the bay at the Marin peninsula. Then a phone call had come from NIH. A newly synthesized medication with potent activity against HIV in cell culture had passed animal safety tests. It was ready to be tried in humans.

Gwen finished clinic early and drove to the airport. While waiting at the gate, she saw a middle-aged man looking in her direction. He cocked his head with an impish grin. Gwen assumed she was blocking his view of someone else and stepped aside. Then it registered. The gaunt, depressed face she had said goodbye to two months ago had filled out. He must have gained twenty pounds, she thought. Reading her mind, Kevin patted his new paunch to prove it.

Gwen embraced him. She gingerly touched his plump cheek.

"Go ahead," Kevin laughed. "Pinch and ye shall believe."

"DDI did this?"

"No," he snorted. "It was high colonic enemas. Of course it was DDI. My T cells are 300 and rising."

Pointing to his daypack, he crowed, "I've got a three month supply of pills and they'll send me refills as long as I send them back lab results."

Gwen realized Kevin's weight gain wasn't the reason she had failed to recognize him. It was his merry exuberance. How long had it been since she had seen him this happy? Life for Kevin had been constant worry about others, beginning with her needle-stick, then crisis after crisis at work, then Marco. And just as he was moving beyond that grief, his own health had deteriorated. Seven years, she counted, since she had seen him being carefree. Slipping her arm inside Kevin's, Gwen steered him toward the baggage claim area. She resolved to stop discrediting her senses. This man truly was Kevin reborn.

"Did Katherine and your mother get to visit you?"

"They took the train down to Washington last week, and they're flying out here in August."

"They OK?"

She still felt strange and was aware that all she had done so far was to interrogate him.

"They're fine. You know what's amazing? After a lifetime without affection, they're everything to me now."

Gwen pretended to pout.

"After you, I mean. So how does Eva like Boston?"

"Eva's home! On spring break."

"And?"

"She is such a pleasure to be with. Who would have guessed?"

"Not me. Remember when I told you to cut your losses, that she'd always hate you."

Gwen punched him in the shoulder.

On their way to City Hospital, Kevin asked about Rick. She shifted the topic to work, updating him on their current space shortage and who was

fighting with whom. She wasn't complaining. Kevin saw no sign the responsibility was overburdening her. Yet his concerns weren't allayed. What about
her visibility? Was that taking a toll? When Marco was sick, jealousy over the
media attention he was receiving had been the least of their problems. But
how did Rick feel seeing her picture in the newspaper and watching her on
television? Was Rick secure enough to be proud of her, not resentful of all
the evenings and weekends she was away or how distracted she must be when
she was at home? Kevin wondered if anyone he knew could be that selfless.

Wine, cheese, and fifty people were waiting for him in a hospital conference
room. Kevin didn't suspect the surprise party, even after walking through the
empty corridor to his office and being pulled away by Gwen who said there
was something on the wards she had to show him.

Kevin wasn't embarrassed when the crowd shouted his name. He knew
how much better he looked than the last time they saw him. He enjoyed their
applause.

After toasts to his return, Kevin made an announcement no one had
anticipated. The grant he submitted six months earlier had been approved.
Their program was going to be the recipient of a two million dollar award.
The room hushed. Kevin explained that while NIH had a lock for now on
testing the most promising new antiretroviral drugs, this funding would support Phase 1 trials of agents that were a longer shot for success. They clapped
when he said more research staff would be hired. They hooted "Yes!" when
told Ray Hernandez had committed to giving them additional space on the
floor above the clinic.

As the party was ending, Kevin whispered to Herb, "Let's talk."

Once they were alone, he wanted to hear about Martin.

"He seems OK, but I don't really know," said Herb glumly. "He's always
guarded with us. Cecilia and I botched this badly. He'll never trust us again."

"Herb, that can't be true. He must realize by now that your only concern
is his safety. This has got to be more about his need for privacy and having
control of his own life than coming out."

"I hope you're right. So, what was it like being a patient at NIH?"

"Those people are great. You must have loved working there."

"I did. It was the most productive time of my life."

"You think? You sure haven't been sitting on your hands here for the last twenty years."

"Well, since the boy wonder came to City Hospital, his publication rate certainly has plummeted."

"You're right,'" said Kevin, escalating the sarcasm, "You're worthless if you can't get at least six senior-authored papers a year in press."

"Touché," Herb said with a droll smile. "But the truth is you've already achieved far more than I have or ever will."

It was awkward enough to have surpassed your mentor, let alone have him be the one to point it out to you. Yet there was pride in what Herb had said, and not a whiff of envy. Kevin hugged him. Herb didn't shrink back.

II

HERB WAS UP EARLY on Saturday morning. He made coffee and began revising a manuscript at the kitchen table. He had chosen this site to intercept Martin.

His son now had a circle of friends who got together on weekends, though not at anyone's house where parents might intrude. Since going to movies and grunge rock concerts required money, Herb had been paying him to help paint the garage and build a tool shed in the back yard. A recent spell of warm weather meant Herb could stop inventing home improvement projects for a while.

"Hedges need to be pruned and the lawn moved," said Herb when Martin came downstairs.

For Martin, firing up the two-cycle gasoline engine, pushing the fierce, whirling blade through a thick tangle of grass, and molding it into a flat lawn offset the drudgery of bagging the cuttings.

"I'll mow," he volunteered.

After a half an hour of pruning Herb called, "Lemonade break!"

In the kitchen he asked, "Making the decision this week?"

Martin had been accepted by several California universities and wasn't interested in leaving the state. However, a high school counselor had talked him into applying to a few private East Coast colleges, just in case he changed his mind. The day before, an Ivy League school had offered him admission.

"It's a done deal, Dad. I'm going to Berkeley."

Herb didn't have a strong opinion about where his son should go to college, but this conversation might be an entree into understanding what motivated him.

"Because…?"

Martin, usually wary of open-ended inquiry, wasn't threatened. He knew that in five months he'd be living in a dormitory, not accountable to anyone for where he went or what he did. He could see the light at the end of the tunnel.

Martin toyed with the idea of saying he had picked Berkeley because of all the hunky boys he could fuck. But that would be a lie. There were probably as many gays at Columbia. It would be cruel, too, and Martin's conviction in his father's deep-seated homophobia was weakening.

"I've told you, Dad. There are more Asians at Berkeley than anywhere else. It'll be easier to make friends."

"That makes sense," said Herb. He doubted that friendship opportunities had been a factor in his daughter's choice of college. It hadn't been a consideration for him either. He was glad for his son.

When they finished, Martin borrowed Herb's car keys and said he'd be back late. Herb and Cecilia had nothing planned that day. They often lingered at home hoping Martin would share a meal with them. Both feared that once he went to college, they might only see him twice a year, like Allison, or even less, like Herb and his mother.

Herb went inside to tell Cecilia that Martin had left. She was talking on the phone.

"Marcia and Robbie are going for a hike in Marin," she said, "and dinner afterwards in Mill Valley. They want us to come along."

"Great!"

Herb's eagerness was genuine. They had both been grim for too long. Every time one of them brought up Martin's name, the other expected to hear the worst. How could they bear spending the rest of their life together if torment over their son's safety was at the core of their marriage?

At dinner, their friends, whose youngest child was Martin's age and also off to college in the fall, said they were thinking about a vacation in New Zealand the following February.

"We could go with them, Herb," Cecilia exclaimed. "It's after the kids' winter break. They'll be back at school."

With only one glass of wine under his belt, Herb was intoxicated by their imminent freedom.

"Absolutely we could," he agreed.

III

GWEN AWOKE ON SUNDAY luxuriating in anticipation of the day ahead. She and Eva were going to get their nails done, have lunch with Nan, and shop for clothes.

The sound of Rick's belly laugh, which Gwen rarely heard any more, came from kitchen. She went into the hallway and listened to Eva regaling him with a story about an inebriated roommate.

"A preppy who can't hold her liquor," said Eva with disdain.

Gwen wished her daughter wasn't departing for Boston soon. She wished Eva would come home for the summer instead of working as a camp counselor in the Sierras. Maybe her presence could lift them out of distrust.

"Mom," Eva shouted on seeing Gwen. "Let's go."

At the nail salon, Eva had a precise shade in mind. Gwen had always been ambivalent about fashion choices. She inevitably let a stylist or saleswoman make the decision. It delighted her to watch Eva confidently choose how to present herself to the world, even if it was only a matter of nail color. All Gwen could remember at nineteen was being desperate for validation.

At lunch, Nan asked Eva if she had a boyfriend, a subject Gwen hadn't broached, afraid it would be prying. Gwen was astounded, both by Nan's audacity and Eva's frankness in telling them about the boy she had been dating. He wasn't the love of her life, she said, but it had been fun, until he became jealous she might rekindle an old romance with a fellow counselor over the summer.

"So how does that make you feel?" Nan asked.

"Weird. I don't want commitment."

"Sounds like a downward spiral to me. Unless he can back off."

"That's what I've been thinking! How do you…?"

"How do I know? Oh, we suburban housewives have lots of time to observe and dissect relationships. It's a spectator sport in the Peninsula."

Driving home, Gwen had the courage to query Eva herself about this romance. She kept her eyes on the traffic, and Eva was as straightforward as she had been with Nan. They delved into sex, too, though the focus was more on protection than fulfillment. Then Eva asked how she and Rick were doing.

"We're fine," said Gwen. "So, what do we still need to take care of before you leave? Bank account? Housing and registration for the fall?"

"It's all good, Mom. I've got it under control."

"Good God, Eva! Are you done being a kid?"

"I guess so."

Gwen glanced from the road to her daughter. Eva was grinning.

Gwen's pride was short-lived, overtaken by melancholy. Eva's life would be elsewhere for the next three years. Gwen wanted more than these interludes, which led her to wonder whether Eva might decide to stay on the East Coast after graduation. Gwen had never considered that possibility. What if she settled down there? The prospect was disturbing enough to make Gwen think about her clinic funding proposal instead.

Eva went out with old friends from high school in the evening. Rick, ebullient during dinner, became subdued once Eva left.

"Isn't that nice," said Gwen. "Just when you want to be with her, she grows up and leaves home."

Rick concurred and opened the newspaper. Gwen estimated he spent at least eight hours a weekend walled off this way—reading the news, watching sports on television, grading tests. It could be more, but eight hours a weekend was all she could observe. That was the maximum she allowed herself not to work and be available for gardening, hiking, going to a movie, or doing anything else together.

She was sure their relationship was in trouble, though it wasn't clear to her how he perceived the situation. She had tried a direct approach. He denied being aware of any problem. When she had pressed the point, he accused her of projecting her own neuroses. Gwen didn't counter the charge. Even if it was true, she fumed afterwards, he was mean to say so. That stalemate led to simmering resentment on her part and ushered in a new period of mutual wariness. She was at a loss for how to repair the damage.

Rick turned on the television. Gwen went into Eva's bedroom to call Nan. Hearing her friend gush over Eva was only a brief balm.

"I'm worried about Rick," she blurted. "I don't know if we're going to stay together much longer."

"Whoa! I thought you guys might be drifting apart, but…"

Nan cautiously asked, "Do you still want to live with him?"

"Of course I do!"

Nan waited for specifics. Gwen refused to blame Rick, but neither was she willing to bear the responsibility.

"We're at a lull in affection."

"I gather he's not declaring his love?"

"Not really. Actually, not at all."

"Are you?"

"Umm… not like before."

"That happens as marriages age, sweetie, and by now you two might as well be married."

"This long is new for me."

"Finding out what's going to happen next can be an adventure."

"No offense, but that sounds a bit Pollyannaish."

"None taken. There's not someone else is there?"

"I don't think so. Not yet. Maybe the real issue is how much time I'm gone, and he just won't acknowledge it."

"Oh," Nan said neutrally.

There was a long pause. Nan hadn't worked outside the home in twenty years. Gwen knew saying anything more could open a mine field they had never explored. She thanked Nan for listening.

Later, during the hours it took her to fall asleep, Gwen thought about the pleasures and loneliness of being single again.

IV

OVER THE NEXT THREE months, Kevin was strong enough to bring his new trials unit up to speed as well as work out at a gym, which was where he met Barry Rose. Kevin was on a treadmill and noticed a neighbor walking at the same pace on the same incline. His curious glance was met by a shy smile. Barry's olive complexion, thick black goatee, and craggy face aroused him. Kevin was surprised he was still capable of lust. The last time he had felt it was while Marco was still healthy.

After exercising, they ran into each other at the juice bar. Kevin found out Barry was a native New Yorker who had moved to the Bay Area in the 1960s. He worked as a civil rights lawyer and had been on AZT for a year now.

It was an easy relationship to fall into. Barry made few demands. Sex was relaxed and companionable. Kevin felt none of the intense yearning that had gratified and occasionally tortured him with Marco. They kept their own apartments, sleeping together two or three nights a week.

In June, they went on a rafting trip through the Grand Canyon. Kevin drove his new car, a Japanese compact with an automatic transmission, to Arizona where they met up with old friends of Barry's at the river's edge. Their guide, a bearded, burly man in his twenties, turned wan on discovering his clients were six gay men. Though once they were rowing, his appreciation of how cooperative they were outweighed his discomfort.

"River running is about synchronicity, balance, and following instructions," the guide said at the end of the day. "And you guys have all three in spades. This is going to be a great trip!"

For Kevin it was. While floating on calm water, linear time vanished. He was only conscious of what he could sense. While rowing, he meditated on what he remembered from a pre-med physics class, imagining he could see time as a fourth dimension in the ripples his oars made.

Mid-days were windless, too hot for rowing, so they took dips in the cold water and hiked up folds in the great canyon, shaded by steep rock walls—sandstone on the first days, then older limestone, then even older schist and granite as the river cut through geologic eras. They followed streamlets studded with tufts of grass and piñon pine which they grabbed to pull themselves up and belay their descents. No one spoke, out of respect for the naked innocence of these places spared the overgrazing, logging, and mining that had ravaged surrounding lands. Twice they found ancient Pueblo pictographs. Kevin and Barry returned to camp with every muscle spent, ravenous for food and later for sex.

The river was low, the rapids little more than riffles, until the final day. Three Class V runs blocked their passage. They made it through the first two unharmed, by luck as much as skill. On the third run, turbulent water knocked them back and forth. Their oars were useless. Just as their raft's bow rose over a rock, it was slammed by a swell and upended. Sitting in front, Kevin and Barry were thrown underwater and spewed out downstream. Both were shivering violently when they reached shore. While the others made a bonfire, they stripped and held each other inside a damp sleeping bag.

In the morning, with the help of ibuprofen, they were able to hike to the canyon rim where they left their rafting partners and drove on to Mesa Verde in western Colorado. The next day, they awoke eager to explore the cliff dwellings—a honeycomb of rooms, courts, and kivas built in the same century the Black Plague was killing half the population of Europe. However, the moment Barry got out of the car and faced a cold breeze at eight thousand feet, he began coughing. They joined a tour but immediately had to turn back. Barry was too short of breath to climb the wooden ladders.

Kevin drove to Salt Lake City, the nearest town he was sure would have a hospital with ventilators, just in case. Barry's panting decreased once they dropped altitude and was holding steady when Kevin saw the city's lights in the distance. It was nine in the evening. He calculated they could easily make San Francisco in eleven hours. Though Barry was drowsy, he claimed the ride would be tolerable as long as he could lie still. He didn't feel hot to touch and wasn't bringing up the yellow phlegm typical of a bacterial pneumonia that could be rapidly fatal if antibiotics weren't given soon. Kevin was certain

Barry had Pneumocystis pneumonia, which worsened slowly. He decided waiting overnight to start treatment was less risky than trusting the doctors in Salt Lake City. They would only know a fraction of what he did about the disease, and he feared they would ignore his advice. The place wasn't exactly a haven for gay men.

He drove on. By dawn, he was climbing the eastern slope of the Sierras. Barry lay across the back seat, eyes closed. Kevin had been rousing him hourly. ICU nurses don't check vital signs more frequently than that, he thought, intent on remaining optimistic. It was time to wake Barry again. Kevin called his name. There was no reply.

They passed a sign for Donner Pass. Kevin's ears popped. Seven thousand feet, he read. In the rear view mirror, he saw Barry's lips were blue. Horrified by his stupidity, Kevin sped up to ninety on the winding mountain road.

"Hold on, baby," he kept repeating, hiding his angst. "We'll be at sea level soon."

Barry's color improved as they descended into the Central Valley, but his desperate gasping continued. On reaching the outskirts of Sacramento, Kevin followed signs to the regional medical center. Once there, he drove past a waving security guard onto the apron reserved for ambulances.

Inside the ER, Kevin observed quietly. He didn't interrupt the nurse who meticulously flicked Barry's forearm as she hunted for a vein, the respiratory technician who pressed an oxygen mask on Barry's face, or the intern who examined Barry's wrist under a bright light as he chose where to stick the radial artery. When Kevin heard anesthesia paged overhead for an emergency intubation, he left the room. Yet the fact was inescapable. He had lost Barry the instant he started climbing the Sierras. He loathed himself.

V

AFTER BARRY'S DEATH, THERE were no more boyfriends. Kevin stopped seeing clinic patients, too, and spent his days in meetings and conference calls, using the time in between to search the library for obscure articles. At home, he was a hermit monk, reading textbooks and journals instead of scripture, writing papers and grant applications instead of copying medieval manuscripts.

Kevin had a new hypothesis. He was convinced it was the most important original idea of his career. Even though the virus had been discovered four years earlier, the technical challenges in developing a method to accurately measure changes in the amount of HIV in a research subject's blood still seemed insurmountable. A promising drug's antiviral activity could be quantified in a test tube but not in an infected patient. In addition, the costly T cell assays Kevin depended upon as the primary outcome measurements in his Phase 1 trials were not precise. The effect of a drug in increasing T cells had to be huge in order for it to be detected.

Kevin delved into immunology literature, had long discussions with Rajiv Singh, and corresponded with a biochemist in Pittsburgh. Then his eureka moment came. There were assays for measuring molecules in serum that reflected the degree of immune system damage inflicted by HIV, and these assays were more precise and less expensive than T cell assays. No one had ever looked at how a proven treatment for HIV, like AZT, might affect the levels of these molecules, and he knew that Burroughs Wellcome had frozen serum samples left over from the AZT trial.

Kevin called a company senior scientist to pitch his idea. Perhaps this could be the best way yet to assess the efficacy of new drugs in patients. Forty-eight hours later, a box of specimens was delivered to Rajiv.

Assisted by two technicians borrowed from a colleague's lab, Rajiv ran assays the next day. He called Kevin at midnight with the results. Kevin spent all night entering and re-entering Rajiv's data into a statistical software program. Using the secret code indicating which individuals had been given AZT and which placebo, his analysis revealed levels of several proteins were diminished after two months of AZT treatment while remaining the same in those who received placebo. Of far greater significance, the magnitude of these changes predicted the trial participants' survival better than their T cell changes did. Kevin slept an hour, woke up, wrote a manuscript including tables, footnotes, and a reference list, and handed it to Rajiv at the end of the day.

Rajiv came to his house the next morning with his edits scribbled in the margins. They revised the paper, printed three copies, signed away their copyright privileges, and got the packet to an express mail center in time for it to reach the *Lancet*'s editorial headquarters in London before the weekend. Within a month, their article was published in what was arguably the *New England Journal*'s equal in international prestige.

The day after the *Lancet* broadcast his results in a press release, Kevin spoke by phone to reporters from the *New York Times* and *Wall Street Journal* and was interviewed by two television networks. As the last crew was packing its equipment, Ray sauntered into his office.

"This is a pleasant surprise," Kevin said. "What brings you here?"

"I have an overwhelming need to tell you how much I appreciate what you do."

Despite Ray's irony, Kevin didn't doubt his sincerity. Department chiefs were hired and fired based on the success of their faculty.

"Well, Ray," he said, savoring the moment, "You've always been most generous and kind to me. I hope this is partial repayment."

Ray cackled and rubbed his hands. He listened greedily as Kevin told him about several other papers he was working on, the journals he planned to submit them to, and a grant proposal he had in mind.

Once the conversation began to dwindle, Ray made a request.

"I'm sure you know about the annual Department dinner party, though I don't think I've ever seen you there."

"The one at Saint Francis Yacht Club?" Kevin asked, gritting his teeth.

Department of medicine faculty spread out among the various university-affiliated hospitals in San Francisco were all invited to this black tie event. Kevin had never gone, afraid it would make him feel like an impecunious relative visiting the estate of a wealthy cousin, a hillbilly in a tuxedo. Neither had Gwen. In fact, Herb was the only person he knew at City Hospital who regularly attended the affair. But Herb was amused by seeing university politics at play, how avariciously his colleagues sought power within the ivory tower and how jealously they guarded their fiefdoms. Kevin found it repugnant.

"I wish you'd come this year."

Kevin shrank back.

"Please. It would mean a lot to me if you and Gwen came."

There was no graceful way to refuse. In any case, Ray had craftily made it more bearable for Kevin by adding Gwen to his entreaty. Kevin capitulated.

At dusk on a Sunday evening, Kevin, Gwen, and Herb stood on a deck jutting over the bay. Alcatraz, a mile away, glowed red as the sun was setting behind the Golden Gate Bridge.

Herb and Gwen were on their third glass of chardonnay. Kevin was abstaining. The three huddled together in the chilly wind. Herb glanced through open double doors into the yacht club bar.

"Check out those heavy hitters," he said, pointing to a quartet of fiftyish-year-old men chatting amicably.

"Who are they?" asked Kevin.

"Milton, Reuben, Strummel, and West. Each one has a major lab on the Hill. Collectively, their grants must bring in ten million dollars a year *just in overhead* to the university. They're golden boys."

"So what does that get them?" asked Gwen.

"That and a dollar get them a cup of coffee in the cafeteria," said Kevin. "The university keeps all the overhead."

"Not true," said Herb. "They get choice space. Their needs are taken very seriously by Ray's boss and by the deans and chancellor above him. Those guys have to be kept happy. They could get recruited away to Harvard or Stanford."

"Heavy hitters," mused Kevin.

"There's another one," Herb said.

He pointed to the far side of the room where a man with a shock of white hair held forth to a fawning coterie of listeners.

"Boughton, an interventional cardiologist. Commands the highest pro fees in the entire department of medicine."

"We're heavy hitters, too," said Kevin, aggrieved now. "Between the three of us, don't our grants bring in a couple of million dollars in overhead a year?"

Herb looked doubtful.

"Two million? OK, one. That has to buy us a seat at the table."

"Maybe a step stool in the kitchen," Herb chortled.

Kevin was getting angrier. Gwen took his arm.

"Don't worry, dear," she said, mimicking a lush, aristocratic 1930s film actress. "You'll get a seat. Now please be calm. You won't make a scene will you, darling?"

Kevin finally smiled. Herb laughed so hard he stumbled dangerously near the water.

Kevin looked again at the men in tuxedos and said, "I don't want a seat at the table. I can't relate to those people."

"I think they're interesting," said Herb.

"So do I," said Gwen, staying in character. "Don't be a stick in the mud, dear."

"Myrna Loy in the *Thin Man*, right?" said Herb. "That is fantastic, Gwen."

Ray appeared, beckoning them inside.

"My, my," he said once they had shut the door. "You're better behaved here than at my house."

He patted Kevin on the back and said, "Time for you to meet some of your upper-echelon colleagues."

Herb and Gwen followed as Ray escorted him to the four heavy hitters.

"Ethan," Ray said brightly, stretching out the man's name to indicate what a rare pleasure it was to encounter him.

The tallest of the four, a pinched-faced man, responded courteously.

"Ray," he said with the slightest nod of acknowledgment and no smile.

The other three men gave Herb an infinitesimally less cordial nod of recognition. They eyed Kevin and Gwen with unconcealed arrogance.

"You've all read about Kevin Bartholomew in the newspapers, haven't you?" Ray said as he pushed Kevin into their circle. "I won't hog him to myself when he has the opportunity to meet the department's most illustrious scientists."

"You have a lab at City Hospital?" asked a short, pugnacious man.

"No," Kevin replied. "Rajiv Singh does our assay work on the Hill."

The short man tugged the sleeve of one of his companions. They were close enough to Herb and Gwen for them to hear him whisper, "In the *basement* of the Hill."

The other heavy hitters stared quizzically at Kevin.

Herb whispered to Gwen, "You're nothing in their world if you don't have your own lab."

"Rajiv and I are a couple," Kevin said with a straight face.

The heavy hitters were startled by this disclosure.

"We collaborate," he explained, "as co-principal investigators."

Ray stepped in and said, "Kevin's moving to the In-Residence series. I've just put him up for promotion to full professor, *two* years early."

They were agape now.

"Congratulations," said Ethan, circumspectly.

Ray mentioned a dean Kevin had to talk to and led him away.

"What was that about?" Gwen asked Herb.

"I'm not sure, but it's a hell of way to let someone know they're going to be the first person in university history with*out* an NIH-funded lab to be put up for In-Residence promotion *early*. And I heard Ray say '*Two* years early.' That is serious chutzpah. Ray really laid down the gauntlet. He's daring the system to make a paradigm shift and allow clinical researchers to have equal footing with basic science researchers. For Kevin's sake, I hope he can pull it off."

"Kevin won't care whether he's promoted early or not. I don't get why this is a big deal?"

"Ray's trying to change the institutional ground rules of social Darwinism here," said Herb, still astonished.

"So?"

"If he's successful, you might be next."

"Me? Hardly. I don't have a quarter of the publications Kevin has. Anyway, I could care less, even less than he does."

"Right," he said, not bothering to hide his disbelief.

VI

KATHERINE CAME TO SAN Francisco on Labor Day, and for the rest of the week, Kevin quit working at noon. They went out to lunch, then spent the afternoons wandering through the city's more affluent neighborhoods—Pacific Heights, the Upper Haight, North Beach, and the Marina—enjoying the bay views and Victorian architecture. Katherine was fascinated by the houses, especially once Kevin told her what they cost. He had been in a few of these places and helped her imagine the furniture, people, and dramas inside. It was so relaxing they put off talk of Douglas until the weekend.

They were having a late brunch on Saturday when Katherine brought up her son's conflict over coming out. He had only told his mother he was gay.

"How's Ben dealing with it?" Kevin asked.

"Denial, to the extent he can. He's unhappy, but at least he's not angry at Douglas. I'll give him that."

"Should I write to him?"

"Ben?"

"No, Douglas," Kevin giggled. "My consoling Ben because his son is queer would be pretty hilarious."

"It would be lovely if you wrote Douglas. Just be sure to address the envelope to me."

She shook her head and laughed. Seeing his sister free of worry unleashed an impulse to run his fingers through her long, thick hair. He couldn't find a trace of gray. He looked at her muscular arms and the faint creases around her eyes. He was proud of her vitality at forty-two. He wanted to say how much their shared history meant to him. He was searching for the right words when the doorbell rang. It was Gwen, stopping by on her way home from the airport after a thirty-six hour trip to the East Coast.

Gwen had never met Kevin's sister. More than their obvious resemblance, she was struck by Katherine's apparent equanimity. If she was anxious about her brother, she wasn't going to let it show.

"I would have flown back last night," Gwen said, "But I had the chance to go out to dinner with some HHS folks."

"Any money headed our direction?"

"We'll see."

As Kevin and Gwen discussed the likelihood their ideas for new clinic services would get federal funding, Katherine listened with interest.

"Is the government taking responsibility for finding a treatment?" she asked.

"There's a ton of grant money," said Kevin. "NIH, even the FDA, is giving it away to anyone with a reasonable hypothesis to test. The fuel is there. What's missing is the right tool."

"Tool?"

"We're not going to be able to cure this infection any time soon. The best we can hope for are medications that can control it, which means the effectiveness of a new drug has to be judged by how much it reduces the amount of virus in people's bodies."

"That makes sense."

"Unfortunately, we don't have an accurate method for measuring that. There's no gold standard. Labs all over the world are working on ways to quantify the virus. But so far their assays are too complicated and expensive to use in trials, and their results aren't anywhere close to reproducible."

"Hey, wasn't that what your paper in the British journal was about?"

Kevin's forehead furrowed.

"Your brother made waves by exploring whether some other markers in people's blood could be a substitute for measuring the virus," Gwen explained tactfully, "but the FDA shot down his idea. They issued a statement that any surrogate marker like the ones he reported on would have to be validated by a lot more studies before they would even consider allowing it to be the basis for new drug approval. Which basically means until we have a reliable method to measure HIV viral load in a patient's blood, we're going to have to wait for more trials to show differences between treatment arms in the number of deaths and complications of AIDS that occur."

"Which will take years," Kevin said, "With AZT on the market, it's unethical to conduct trials where people get nothing but placebo, which means new trials have to have an AZT control arm, which mean the trials have to be much larger and longer to show statistically significant differences in those kinds of outcomes. So the longer it takes for viral load assays to become reliable, the longer it will take to develop effective treatment, and the more people with AIDS will die."

Gwen wondered if Katherine shared her brother's belief the infection would eventually be mastered. Gwen was hopeful but not convinced. She glanced at Kevin, who was lost in thought, then to Katherine who turned her eyes to him then back to Gwen, smiling confidently.

Gwen was puzzled. Was Katherine naïvely optimistic or did she have a deeper source of certainty? She decided she needed to get to know Kevin's sister better.

He changed the topic by asking Katherine about the Massachusetts governor running for president. Having just returned from Washington, Gwen didn't want to talk politics. She noticed a coffee cake in a glass baking dish. She knew cooking wasn't in Kevin's repertoire of skills.

"Did you make that?" she asked.

"I did," Katherine answered. "Have some. Kevin's trying to maintain his boyish figure."

They all laughed.

That evening, Kevin and Katherine went to a restaurant in the Castro. He had no appetite and became queasy with his first bite of food. Soon a dull ache was throbbing under his left rib cage. The intensity increased rapidly. Over the past year, Kevin had cultivated a stoic approach to physical discomfort. He could ignore nausea, diarrhea, fatigue, the constant sensation of pins stuck in the soles of his feet. But pain like this was outside his range of experience.

The anguish on his face terrified Katherine.

"What should I do?" she implored him.

"Get the car. I don't know how far I can walk."

He handed her the keys. By the time she returned, the pain had subsided enough that he could stand up and avoid the humiliation of being carried out of the restaurant on a stretcher.

Katherine drove to a nearby private hospital where Kevin's doctor had admitting privileges. Art Krimsky was one of several dozen physicians in the city, unaffiliated with the university, who devoted their practice exclusively to HIV patients.

In the emergency room, Kevin had blood drawn and an intravenous catheter placed. He was transported to radiology for a sonogram of his abdomen, then to a private room where Art was waiting. After pressing gently on his belly and listening with his stethoscope, Art spoke.

"You have pancreatitis, Kevin. You're amylase is 800."

Kevin was unnerved by Art's grim demeanor. Acute pancreatitis eventually resolves, he thought. It's just pain that has to be gotten through. There's probably a gall stone blocking my pancreatic duct. Sooner or later, it'll pass through.

"I know the drill," he said. "Nothing to eat or drink. IV fluids and morphine. Surgery if it gets worse. I'll stay put here."

Art looked away.

"Why are you laying so much crepe?" Kevin demanded.

"Sorry," Art apologized.

The next morning, Art arrived more somber.

"I called NIH, Kevin. They've seen four cases of pancreatitis in patients on DDI. You're the fifth."

"OK, I'll lay off it for a while."

Now Art looked positively glum. He nodded in agreement and patted Kevin on the shoulder. Kevin turned to Katherine whose face was ashen.

"It's not the end of the world," Kevin declared.

Katherine's eyes welled with tears.

Kevin knew he was missing something. If it's so obvious to them, why don't I get it? And then he did.

"NIH won't give me any more DDI."

"I'm so sorry," said Art.

VII

AFTER A TWO DAY fast, Kevin was pain-free, though groggy from all the morphine. Herb tapped on the half-open door and saw he was dozing. One hand rested on a manuscript. The other held a ballpoint pen. His eyelids fluttered then lifted.

"Thanks for coming," Kevin croaked.

Having steeled himself to see Kevin writhing in pain or too somnolent to talk, Herb was relieved.

"I just heard," Herb began.

He stopped short, fearing whatever he said next would be clumsy.

"This isn't the end of the line," said Kevin, completely alert now. "There's a new a thymidine analogue like AZT. Dideoxy-didehydrothymidine, D4T. And it's more potent than AZT or DDI. At least in cultured cells it is."

"Can you get it?"

Herb wished he could have asked that question with enthusiasm, but it was hard for him to believe another drug like AZT wouldn't also quickly lead to resistance, and he was too poor an actor to pretend otherwise. He had recently heard Rajiv Singh lecture. The scientist's pessimism about this specific issue had been persuasive.

Failing to note Herb's subdued reaction or perhaps dismissing it, Kevin said, "A Phase 1 trial is starting soon. I already called NIH and got my name on the top of the list."

Herb did his best to give a credulous smile.

"Herb," Kevin said, suddenly downcast, "I have to get over this before I can go back to work, and by then it'll be time for me to take off for NIH. I can't keep dumping all the responsibility on Gwen. What should I do?"

Herb considered the dilemma. Glad to have an excuse to think objectively, he paced around the room until an answer came to him.

"I think you should go on sick leave. Make Gwen the temporary division chief."

"No! That'll chain her to her desk."

"I don't think so. No more than she already is. It'll give her more weight in negotiating with the hospital and the university. She'll spend less time spinning her wheels and feeling frustrated. It'll also give her the authority to appoint Karen or David as assistant director. She can offload running the clinic or supervising the administrative staff to one of them."

"Ugh," Kevin groaned. "Those two are finally playing well together. That would totally disrupt the delicate balance of power between them. I guarantee they'll each find a reason to be jealous about it."

"Not if she appoints them both as co-assistant directors."

Scowling, Kevin said, "It's still going to seem like shit flowing downstream to them. I can't risk that. Those two are the program's future. They need more of their time protected, not less."

"I don't think they'll see it as a dump. It'll be a sign that you and Gwen really trust them and think they're ready to handle more responsibility."

Kevin wrinkled his nose.

"You're right," he guffawed. "There'll be a ribbon around the turd she hands them."

Herb laughed.

"This'll have to come from me," said Kevin thoughtfully. "I'll ask them. I'll plead. If they're doing it for me, they won't resent Gwen."

"There you go," said Herb. "A perfect solution."

"Nice try," Kevin said and wagged a finger at him. "You almost made me believe I figured it out myself."

Herb looked away innocently. Then he sat down on Kevin's bed.

"So, what's the paper you're writing?"

VIII

IT TOOK TWO WEEKS for Kevin to regain the strength to go back to work, but he returned with the same tenacity and optimism. On a late September morning, he and Gwen were chatting in his office when the intercom buzzed. Freddy told him Neal Canaan from the NIH Clinical Center was on the line.

"My D4T dealer," said Kevin as he grabbed the phone.

Gwen tensed. She tried to smile. Kevin had lost more weight since leaving the hospital. She couldn't convince herself it was simply the lingering after-effects of pancreatitis. He needed to start some kind of antiretroviral therapy soon.

"Hi, Neal!" said Kevin, mustering all his buoyancy and charm.

As he listened, his face sagged. His posture drooped. Gwen felt her own heart speeding. This had to be bad news.

"Thanks," Kevin said in a monotone. "Yeah, call me when you have more data."

He hung up the phone and looked vacantly out the window. Gwen waited for him to speak until she couldn't bear it.

"What did he say?"

"They got results from an animal study. Some rats given D4T died of pancreatitis."

"But you don't have pancreatitis *now*."

"They're excluding anyone with a history of pancreatitis for safety reasons. It's a Phase 1 trial, Gwen. They have to, or the FDA won't OK it. There might be another trial I can be in, after there's data from animals given lower doses for a longer time…a lot longer time…at least a year."

He gazed at the brown hills north of Golden Gate Bridge.

"In a few months, they turn green," he murmured. "I'll see that."

Gwen sat on his lap and put her arms around him. She lay her head against his neck and heard his bounding pulse. She didn't cry.

IX

In MID-OCTOBER, KEVIN WAS hospitalized again, this time for Pneumocystis pneumonia. The work of breathing had become a marathon he hadn't trained for. He couldn't walk from his bed to the bathroom without collapsing, even with oxygen prongs strapped to his face and a nurse supporting his weight. So he wore a diaper and evacuated stool in a bedpan. His strength was totally spent by the act of sitting up. Trying to do more made consciousness flicker and wane.

He acquiesced to the facts. This was what would remain of his life. It would be brutal, and there would be nothing afterwards. But these ruminations led to questioning the truth of any certainty about "afterwards." Cycling acceptance and denial absorbed all his attention until he remembered a dying patient once telling him a story about the Susquehanna River in Pennsylvania. Kevin had never been there. Now he surely would never see it. No matter, he decided. Fantasies were better to dwell on than the void he was hurtling toward. He tried to imagine the Susquehanna as a bucolic Eden, using what he could recall from rafting the Colorado. Then memories of another, harsher river experience intruded.

In the summer of 1960, as a pre-pubescent Boy Scout of the Star rank, Kevin was expected to endure physical challenges. His first was to carry a twenty pound backpack across twenty miles of muddy, riverside trail in ninety degree, humid heat. The boys hadn't been advised to break in their boots before the ordeal. By mile five, everyone was complaining of blisters. By mile ten, pain incapacitated speech. Kevin hobbled for weeks after the hike. He considered quitting but was proud of the badge he had earned and wanted to pin a Polar Bear medal next to it on his sash.

He had to wait for the opportunity until February, when an arctic cold front drifted down from Canada. The temperature forecast was ten below zero. The boys' fathers encouraged their sons to prove their mettle by camping out on a fallow corn field near Brockton. They had volunteered to come along and supervise from inside a wood-heated farmhouse where they could play cards and sip whiskey.

The troop reached the field at sunset. While the boys scrambled to pitch pup tents, their fathers made a bonfire and served them lukewarm hot dogs with canned beans, before retiring to the warm house. Kevin shivered in his bedroll, wearing every article of clothing he had brought. Snippets of sleep came with nightmares of being alone on a frozen pond he had seen from the car that afternoon. He kept falling through the ice and couldn't climb out of the water, his numb arms and legs useless.

At first light, the boys gathered fallen pine branches for a great pyre. They rotated in front of the blaze, distributing its warmth around their bodies. They basked in the knowledge they had just come a quantum step closer to manhood. Surviving the night was proof their bodies were capable of more than they had believed. When their fathers joined them by the fire, no one spoke. Kevin looked at his scout mates and saw they shared his own cool regard for their old men. I can make it on my own, he had thought.

"And I have made it on my own, ever since," he said, not caring that he was talking to himself. "For almost thirty years. What's so tragic about not having another thirty years? What's the difference between thirty and sixty or even ninety years in the bigger scheme of things? All of those numbers are ridiculously short, and everyone lives under that condition whether they choose to think about it or not. Get over it, Kevin!"

X

Katherine and Francine flew to San Francisco on Halloween in the midst of a series of Pacific cold fronts that were battering the city with rainstorm after rainstorm. From the airport, they took a taxi to the hospital. Kevin no longer needed oxygen, but a second opportunistic infection had been diagnosed. Mycobacteria had spread throughout his body, causing persistent fevers and more weight loss.

Francine struggled for three long days at maintaining her composure before finally succumbing to grief. Witnessing her son's physical disintegration was intolerable. She returned to Boston alone.

As soon as he was in his apartment, Kevin was desperate to get outside and see the greening world. Once the rain let up, he made Katherine take him to Tilden Park, high above the Berkeley campus. She pushed him in a wheelchair to a point where they could view Mount Tamalpais to the west and Mount Diablo to the east.

"This is the place! According to Marco…"

He couldn't remember why it had been so important to come here.

"I think local Indians believed this place was… Didn't I already tell you about it?"

"You said something about Indians. I forgot the details."

Kevin looked at the jade-tinged Contra Costa hills rolling east to the horizon. He concentrated. He was sure he had been at this very spot with Marco. It wasn't an invented memory. But all he could recall now was their camping trip in the Mojave Desert.

He was buffeted by waves of anger and self-pity which vanished as quickly as they had arrived. Dust devils, he thought. He fixed his attention on Katherine.

"You're buff, Sis. That was a mile and a half uphill."

Katherine squatted down to see the panorama from his eye level.

"Guess what?" he said. "I've discovered the great irony of facing death."

"Which is?"

"Epiphanies bloom, right as time and energy are fading. It's like Dad's favorite cliché, 'youth is wasted on the young.' Well, death is wasted on the dying."

She was baffled.

"I mean there's this emotional intelligence that comes with accepting the end. Lots of people have written about it. Anyway, the irony is that it's wasted on me. The closer I get to the end and the more clearly I can see the big picture, the less I can say anything coherent about it."

"Keep trying."

"You really want to hear this?"

"Absolutely. What are your epiphanies?"

"You would ask that, wouldn't you," Kevin laughed. "All right. Here's one. Approaching death isn't about resolution for me. It's about completion."

Katherine was puzzled again.

"There goes my lucidity."

"Don't stop."

"How to explain? OK. Life's great disappointments is a good example. You'd think resolving your unmet expectations would be the key to dying peacefully, right? Not for me. I just want the kind of satisfaction a mechanic has after rebuilding an engine—knowing it all fits together—and I have it.

"And if that's too abstract, how about this? Even though I wish I'd had children, I'm not consumed by regret. Honest, Katherine, I'm not trying to rationalize my way out of self-pity. My default mode is to wallow in it. I don't know why, but I can't think about the joy I missed without also imagining having a kid who becomes a hateful skinhead or suffers from some terrible disease. So when I look back now, I don't just see the tragedy of unfulfilled fantasies. I see the pain the downside might have led to as well. So, I'm content with how things played out. It's weird."

Comprehension dawned on her face.

"Tell me more."

"Hmm… See these fir needles, the birds, the early grass. Remember the twin babies we passed. Living creatures are so tenuous, aren't they, so miraculous. It's wonderful to be certain they'll still be here after I'm gone."

Katherine shuddered.

"It's not morbid. I'll be part of it all, even if I can't influence what happens or be conscious of what's going on. At least not in the way we think of being conscious, which always relates to ourselves."

She frowned, having lost his thread.

"It's the Zen paradox at the heart of Catholicism!" he shouted.

Kevin spread his arms like a symphony conductor beginning an overture.

"I get it," she said and hugged him.

"Don't bury me in a grave," he ordered her. "The atoms that make up my body won't disappear. I want them out in the world! I want them to be building blocks for new life."

"Kind of like being here, even if it's not you?"

"Oh my God, Katherine! You're a mystic. Nobody I've talked to about this has understood but you."

XI

By Thanksgiving, Kevin was unable able to walk. The retrovirus had invaded his spinal cord and was destroying motor nerve pathways to the lower half of his body. He still had the strength to transfer between his bed and a wheelchair and could remain in his apartment with help from a home health assistant on weekdays and friends on weekends. The last Saturday of November was Gwen's turn.

After cleaning his kitchen and bathroom and doing a bit of shopping, she bundled him in a forest-green wool sweater and black watch cap and put his wheelchair in the trunk of her car. He wanted to go to St. Ignatius and the arboretum in Golden Gate Park.

Gwen had never been to St. Ignatius. She thought its two bell towers, freshly painted alabaster white and capped by bronze cupolas, quite lovely. Inside was a sanctuary with an arched ceiling. The space was illuminated by rows of stained-glass windows, each a portrait of a notable saint. An organist was playing Bach fugues. They sat quietly as contrapuntal melodies chased each other around the empty nave. Kevin hunched forward, his breathing labored from getting out of the car and into the wheelchair.

Gwen was overwhelmed by his imminent absence. She felt desolate and simultaneously grateful to have this time alone with him. She held his hand. He gripped hers tightly in return.

Kevin took a tissue from his pocket. He dabbed her cheeks.

"I hope you're not converting to Catholicism on my account," he said dryly.

"God, no," she laughed.

"That's good to hear. You know, this was always my favorite building in the city, but I'd never been inside."

"Me neither. What do you think?"

"It's like the minor basilicas of Boston. I spent too much of my childhood being miserable in places like this. Up close, it's nothing special. It's only beautiful from far away, framed by hills and the bridge."

"The music's nice."

"It's depressing in here. Let's go. I don't know why I wanted to come. What was I thinking? Churches are dismal. All the wealth and effort wasted on building a sterile vault, a monument to a non-existent afterlife, when it could have been used to help the living, the suffering."

"Hey, did you see the poster at the entrance about a service in memory of Archbishop Romero?"

"Who?"

"Oscar Romero, the archbishop assassinated in El Salvador for speaking out about government killings during their civil war."

"Romero? Didn't he try to talk the Pope into taking a stand? Not success-fully as I recall."

"Well, St. Ignatius is honoring him."

"They didn't have liberation theology in Boston when I was growing up," he brooded. "Anyway, I gave at the hospital, Gwen. I gave and gave and then gave more."

"I know you did," she said and wrapped her arms around him.

Kevin's mood improved once he was being pushed along the arboretum paths. They passed through a meadow to a stand of South African silver trees, cedars, and heathers, then stopped in a patch of California wildflow-ers—orange poppies and pink buckwheat.

"There's rosemary somewhere," he said, sniffing. "Smell it?"

"I'm not sure."

"It's spicy, pungent."

"Got it! A scent between sage and bay leaf, right? But not as sharp."

"You have wonderful descriptive powers, my dear."

Watching a pair of gulls flitting among treetops at the meadow's edge, Kevin inhaled deeply.

"I know why I wanted to come here," he said.

XII

KEVIN LOST ALL ABILITY to move his legs or control his bowels over the next week. Needing round-the-clock nursing care, he had to be placed in a hospice. A social worker at City Hospital pulled strings, and a bed became available at a derelict convent recently remodeled to house eight dying patients. The two requirements for admission were a life expectancy less than six months and a statement signed by the applicant that comfort, not prolonging survival, was his primary goal in residing there. Most of the current inhabitants had AIDS.

Herb visited a few days later. He found Kevin sitting in a wheelchair. The blanket draped across his lap failed to hide his diaper and the plastic bag full of urine attached to the footrest. Kevin's gaunt face and the pallor accentuating his freckles made him look much younger, like a wizened elf-child. Remarkably, he didn't appear depressed. Herb was astonished by how alert and tranquil he was.

"Let's go upstairs," Kevin suggested.

They took a modern elevator to the old convent chapel, renovated with carpeting and plush couches to serve as a communal living room. Its wall-high, leaded-glass windows had been left intact. Kevin pointed across the street to a small Catholic church.

"See, I can't escape," he said with half-hearted irony.

After asking if his pain, diarrhea, and nausea were made tolerable by the medications he was given around the clock, Herb had a moment of panic. What else could they talk about?

Kevin wheeled himself to a bookcase. He removed a thin hardbound volume and gave it to Herb.

"*Winesburg, Ohio.* My favorite novel in college. Would you read me a chapter?"

Happy to have something to do, Herb opened the book. Kevin picked the final chapter, *Departure*. When Herb finished, Kevin sighed.

"George Willard leaves town, his future full of possibility. Beginnings are the best part of life, aren't they?"

"I never thought about it. I guess so."

Kevin grabbed Herb's hands and pulled himself close.

Eyes shining, he said, "Thank you."

"Kevin, there's nothing to thank me for."

"Oh, yes there is. Work I could be proud of. You gave me that opportunity. It was the missing piece. Without it, I never could have felt my life made sense."

Herb tried valiantly to swallow a sob. Losing the struggle, he hugged Kevin.

"I don't know how to say this," Herb stammered. "Actually, I do know. I lack practice. It's what inertia does. No, that's a cop out, too. I'm still afraid to show feelings I can't control. But I've done it with you. And I promise, this is just the start."

Kevin wept with delight.

Certain he was on a roll, Herb said, "What a privilege it's been to watch you grow, to achieve so much. I'll remember you every day. You know that, don't you?"

"Yes, yes, yes," Kevin laughed and cried, each word diminishing in volume.

Again Herb couldn't think of anything to say, though he wasn't troubled by it now. Kevin dozed briefly, opened his eyes, and stared at Herb.

He seemed to be pleading, but Herb had the eerie intuition he wasn't asking for assistance or relief. Suddenly, Herb was convinced that Kevin had grasped some core truth of existence. He wants me to understand it, Herb thought, to share it with me.

"The void surrounding us is what makes our being in the world possible. It doesn't threaten us. It embraces us. If you can believe this, you'll be past all fear and sorrow."

Had Kevin really said that? Or was it his own imagination? He realized the answer didn't matter. Herb's mind became empty. He was only aware of Kevin's presence. For a few minutes, until mundane thoughts intruded. What was on his schedule tomorrow? What was for dinner tonight? The silence became awkward.

"Should I read another chapter?" he asked.

"Sure," Kevin said hoarsely. "The first one."

Halfway through, Kevin fell asleep. Herb sank into the couch. He endeavored to sort through his emotions with little success.

Kevin awoke. He looked out the window and pointed toward Diamond Heights.

"Your apartment?" Herb asked.

"No, the distance. How far is it to the top of that hill?"

"Half a mile?"

"That's an ideal distance, isn't it? I can see each window. Any farther and the detail would be lost. It's funny how my far vision is fine, but I can barely read."

Kevin fell asleep again. Through an open window, children's voices filtered in from the playground next door. Herb couldn't make out the words, yet he could hear the timbre of every shout and cry.

Amazing, he thought, it's a cantata.

The church tower bell interrupted this concert with four peals. The noise woke Kevin. He looked into Herb's eyes, for longer than Herb would let anyone except Cecilia.

"Go back to your life, Herb," he whispered. "It's good. It's better than you think. You deserve it."

XIII

KEVIN WANTED TO STAY in the chapel and watch the sunset. Herb was uneasy about leaving him there alone, but Kevin stubbornly insisted the hospice staff would come soon.

Once Herb had left, Kevin was fully awake, his heart racing. He hoped everyone would forget he was upstairs. There was no point in returning to his room. It was time to go. His body was useless. Without it, so was his mind, what remained of it. He soothed himself by vowing not to eat or drink. The dehydration would lead to kidney failure within days, a week at most, and at the end he'd be too delirious to feel pain.

His heart was pounding. He wasn't afraid, just surprised by the velocity of his pulse. Now he was giddy, aware of how recklessly his body was behaving. He would have giggled if he could, but he was breathing too fast.

I'm not getting enough oxygen, he thought. It must be a pulmonary embolus. He wished he could laugh. This was his last diagnosis, and he had nailed it. He was quitting at the top of his game.

Kevin had no more thoughts, only sensations—a crescendo of chest tightness, warmth ebbing from his body. His eyes couldn't focus. All he could see was rosy sunlight pouring in through the leaded glass windows. Craving the light, he reached out and toppled toward it.

Berlin, 1989

I

ON A WEDNESDAY MORNING in early November, Herb strode from his office to the parking lot. The worn leather traveling bag he had inherited from his father was hoisted on his back, stuffed with journals, a jacket and tie, and a down vest and Gore-Tex coat for long walks in a much colder climate. He looked at his watch. There was time to check in with Gwen before driving to the airport.

Gwen's door was ajar. Herb knocked. Her answer was a melodious, exasperated "Come in." She was listening on the telephone and motioned for him to sit down. She seemed relieved it was Herb, not someone from her own program with a grievance or demand. While waiting, he surveyed the room. Framed wildflowers and family photos caught his attention. It was still strange to see Gwen in Kevin's old office, her life displayed on the walls instead of his.

She hung up the phone and asked, "When are you leaving?"

"Today, at two. You?"

"Tomorrow. I'm going to spend an extra day in Berlin after the conference, then fly back on Sunday."

She looked at him with amiable curiosity. He had ambivalent impulses and immediately understood both. He wanted a deeper friendship with Gwen, like he had enjoyed with Kevin, but he was reluctant to initiate the effort. He could be rebuffed or, worse, misinterpreted as making a sexual advance. Yet here was a chance for them to be together away from work, to discover what genuine affinity they might have.

"Do you already have plans for Saturday?" he asked.

"Just sightseeing. Want to join me?"

"Sure. How about touring East Berlin?"

"Herb, that's at the top of my list! I *have* to see the Pergamon."

"Then we're on."

As soon as Herb left, Gwen reached into her briefcase for the letter Katherine had sent her. The connection she had made with Katherine on the day after Kevin's funeral when they cleaned out his apartment together, which had strengthened during their subsequent phone calls and her trip to Boston, had grown enough for Katherine to be comfortable sharing this letter. It was the last Kevin had written. Much of it was about Gwen and Herb.

Reading it had been sobering. Kevin had surmised her rift with Rick was approaching a point of no return. His warning made her choices clear. If she wanted their relationship to survive, she had to erase the slate of all resentment and start giving Rick the benefit of the doubt. She had taken the first step, and Rick had followed suit. Slowly, they were moving toward intimacy again. This letter turned out to be Kevin's last gift.

It could be a gift for Herb too, but the dilemma of having to decide whether to show to him or not was awful. She didn't know Herb well enough, nowhere near well enough, to gauge how he would react. At best, he would be embarrassed, at worst terrified. Though to withhold it, knowing Kevin's advice might help him—that wouldn't be right either.

She treasured seeing Kevin's perspective, but there was no way to be sure if Herb would feel the same. What should she do? Her stomach hurt. She slid the pages back into her briefcase.

II

SLICK FOG CLUNG TO Berlin, damping the tension of the divided city. At dawn, starlings left their roosts in outlying farmlands and marshes. They flew in lines, just above treetops and spires, aiming for bits of breakfast-on-the-run soon to be dropped in the city squares.

Herb had only slept three hours on the transatlantic flight. In the bus from Tegel airport to West Berlin's central railway station, his eyes resisted daylight despite the shielding fog and tinted windows. It was eleven at night according to his biologic clock. Yet being tired and disoriented was pleasant, taking the edge off the anxiety he had tried to suppress all week.

Traffic moved quickly in the morning rush hour. He was at his hotel by ten o'clock. A room was available, but he wasn't interested in showering or changing clothes. He pocketed a city map, headed back to the train station, and bought a subway pass.

The fog was lifting when he exited at Reichssportfeld. He walked toward an immense field where seven chiseled stone columns built for the 1936 Olympic Games stood as pagan sentries. Herb had written of these "neolithic pillars set in an earthly garden for the Valkyries' afternoon tea" in the diary he kept the summer of 1959. The night before leaving San Francisco, he reread it for the first time in decades, wincing at his naïve, misplaced romanticism.

He found the swimming stadium, climbed down its limestone tiers, and sat envisioning, as he had thirty years ago, the empty pool filled with emerald water, the cadence of glistening arms rising up and dipping down.

He saved the great track and field stadium for last. The pocked, marble plaque that enthralled him in 1959 was still there. He retraced the carved letters— "100m OWENS USA, 200m OWENS USA."

Herb spent the rest of the day wandering through West Berlin neighborhoods and visiting a museum of Art Deco furniture. He returned to the hotel, took a short nap, woke up refreshed, showered, changed, and joined the other invited speakers at a welcome dinner on the fourteenth floor.

He sat next to a German pulmonary specialist he knew from previous conferences. Peter Ramburg was polite, nonjudgmental, and colorless. Herb had yet to see him express any emotion, positive or negative. Peter was also very thin, which raised the possibility he might have AIDS, though he appeared energetic and must be capable of hard work if he was telling Herb the truth about how many bronchoscopies he did a week.

They talked shop during the salad and main courses. Herb excused himself at dessert to take in the view through the ballroom's glass-curtain walls. The fog had descended, so there was little to see—the vague outline of a television tower in East Berlin, the runway lights at Tegel. He was drifting around the perimeter, identifying other blurry landmarks, when someone shouted excitedly. The only word Herb could understand, and only because it was repeated over and over, was "Funkankündigung."

All the Germans began shouting. More remarkable to Herb, they were using their hands for emphasis, which he had never seen a German do. He asked several people what was happening, but their replies were unintelligible.

Herb saw Peter sitting alone, flushed and trembling. He didn't respond until Herb yelled, "Funkankündigung?"

Peter stirred from his catatonic state.

"Radio announcement. There has been a radio announcement. The East Germans have opened the wall. Tonight they let everyone cross to the West."

Pounding the table, Peter sobbed, "You cannot imagine what this means to us."

III

GWEN WROTE A GRANT proposal on her flight to New York, then slept through the transatlantic leg. When the pilot's voice woke her, she glanced at her watch and relaxed. They would be landing in twenty minutes. She had plenty of time to get to the conference center.

This was Gwen's fourth international trip in six months. Jet lag was becoming a manageable nuisance, like habituating herself to sleep deprivation had been during residency. She had rediscovered how to fall asleep instantly whenever the opportunity arose and use a catnap to push back fatigue a few hours.

Really, she thought, it was stupid to come to this symposium. The odds I'll learn anything of importance here are miniscule. German medical science still hasn't recovered from World War II.

But that wasn't why she had agreed to attend. The organizers were dedicating this conference to Kevin with a special opening ceremony, and Jorgen Zabel, who was chairing the meeting, was a highly regarded tuberculosis expert. Since TB was now the most serious complication of AIDS globally, he could make a huge contribution. Plus, he was trying to bring his local colleagues up to speed in treating AIDS. She needed to support him.

Then she thought of Saturday, the day after the conference. She would be alone with Herb. Gwen took Kevin's letter from her briefcase and reread it.

Katherine,

Of course I'm looking forward to seeing you, but please stop worrying. I'm not alone here. Every day a home health aide comes and lots of friends drop by. When it gets too hard, I'll move to a hospice without a fuss. I promise.

I won't lie and say this is easy, but I am making progress in accepting the inevitable. I've been reading about Buddhism and practicing how to let go—starting with material things. There's an exercise I tried, seeing my apartment as too cluttered. It works! Now I want empty space. My textbooks on virology, immunology, and infectious diseases, Marco's molecular and cell biology books, the shelves of my favorite journals, the boxes of brown manila files. They're all unnecessary. I wish somebody would cart them away. The herringbone sports coat, button down shirts and matching ties, even the dress shoes I used to love so much, are going to Goodwill. I'd be fine if everything here, including the furniture, was removed. Buddhists believe concentrating on emptiness is the key to serenity. I think they're on to something.

Enough morbid rant. I may be getting ready to depart from this life, but I'm more interested than ever in the lives of others. Weird, huh? Gwen and Herb each come by twice a week, so I know what's happening with the program, the hospital, and, most importantly, with them.

Gwen must have told you she's running the program solo, which means she's where the buck stops for every staff and faculty complaint and conflict. She's probably a better administrator than I was, but these days there are twice as many people to supervise. Anyway, that doesn't concern me as much as hearing her refer to Rick as an afterthought, a distraction. She was so in love with him. Now there's zero affection? I've asked her how they're doing. She doesn't want to talk about it. It's like she's given up on their relationship being a source of happiness. I can't believe they have nothing left or that Rick is indifferent. He'd be gone already if he didn't still care for her. But I'm afraid time may be running out. Is she telling you anything?

I'm also worried about Herb. Last week was payback time for all the doors he opened for me. He brought his son to visit. Martin is eighteen and shares Douglas and my romantic preferences. Since he came out, Herb has been terrified he's going to get infected. Sound familiar? Except he and his wife haven't handled it the way you guys have. By the way, your last letter blew me away! Please tell Ben I'm so proud of how he took the initiative and told Douglas it's OK to be gay.

It was obvious Herb wanted me to talk with Martin privately. He turned his pager off and on to make it beep, retreated to the kitchen, and pretended to be talking on the phone. Finding myself alone with his son was awkward. I had no agenda beyond being real, so I told him Herb had been my mentor. Then I asked what it was like to have him as a dad.

Martin has a lot of self-control, just like Herb. He considered his answer very carefully and said, "It's hard, actually."

I told him I was sorry to hear that because I'd had problems with my own father and never worked them out before he died. I said I was sure Herb loved him and would eventually get over the fear for his safety.

Guess what? Martin gave me this Mona Lisa smile. I've seen Herb do it a hundred times. It was wonderful. I think he's ready to forgive his dad! Wish I had been able to do that.

But a few days later, something disturbing happened. A friend took me to a restaurant in the Castro and we passed one of the only bathhouses still open. I saw a boy Martin's age leaving. In fact, it looked exactly like him. I can't be certain though. My mind plays tricks. It's part of the disease.

I was heartbroken. I couldn't stop imagining how devastated Herb would be if Martin got sick. Then I realized, OK, so what if it was Martin. Maybe he was just exploring. Why jump to the conclusion he was having unprotected sex in there? He seems to be a together young man, and of course he must be curious. Why assume the worst? It's not logical. God, I wish there was a way I could convince Herb he has to trust Martin's judgment.

So, you can see that even if my mobility is limited and my energy fading, I remain very much engaged in the world. Stop worrying about me! I do enough worrying for both of us.

Love,

Kevin

Gwen became aware of how long the pilot had been speaking. He didn't seem to be giving routine landing information. He switched to English and summarized the electrifying events of the last twelve hours. Meanwhile, passengers who had been listening raptly to the German version hugged each other and wept. Gwen was thrilled. The end of the Berlin Wall! She would be there to witness it firsthand!

IV

THE CONFERENCE WAS PONDEROUS and the presentations inconsequential, which exacerbated their burning curiosity about what was happening outside. The only useful thing Gwen and Herb learned was at lunch when Peter Ramburg explained some local slang. West Germans called the East Germans "Ossis," and the easterners called the westerners "Wessis." The terms, derived from the German words for east and west, were pejorative.

"I should be careful," he laughed. "I cannot say Ossi if anyone from the East is nearby. I like having this problem."

When the meeting concluded, Gwen and Herb declined the bus ride back to the hotel. They hurried toward upscale Kurfurstendamm Avenue where they found crowds of Ossis, all wearing muted blue synthetic fabrics. Many stood slack-jawed in front of couture and high-end furniture store display windows. Others got in and out of tiny, smoke-spewing cars apparently made of fiberglass. It's a circus stunt, thought Gwen, as seven Ossis crammed themselves into one of these toy vehicles. There were Wessis, too, stuffing Deutschmarks into Ossis' pockets. Bottles and large plastic cups of beer were circulating.

Both Ossis and Wessis looked dazed, which gave Gwen a sense of déjà vu. People were in the same mixed state of relief and trepidation she had experienced three weeks earlier after a major earthquake shook San Francisco. They had survived the cataclysm and were now unmoored in an altered world.

Across the avenue, she saw an elegantly dressed lady leaning over a second story windowsill, utterly motionless. Gwen thought it was a mannequin until she noticed the woman's fingers moving. She was pinching herself.

Dinner that night was in a museum of musical instruments. Gwen and Herb sat with Peter Ramburg again, this time surrounded by clavichords and violins from the sixteenth century. Gwen was concerned the East German government might try to stop the mass exodus. She remembered stories from the 1960s of people shot in the back as they climbed the wall to escape the totalitarian regime. What if East German soldiers invaded West Berlin, she asked. Could the situation escalate into global war?

Peter reassured her that East Germany as a political entity was swiftly disintegrating. It was too disorganized to halt the flood. His brother, a West German diplomat, had told him East German officials were resigning en masse. There were rumors the Stasi, East German secret police, were shredding documents in anticipation of the government's collapse. Peter had also heard about a spontaneous celebration underway where the wall ran alongside Brandenburg Gate, a short stroll from the museum. He urged them to accompany him there after dessert. Gwen glanced uneasily at Herb.

"Why not," Herb said cheerfully.

The sidewalks were congested with pedestrians streaming toward a wide street that ended abruptly at the nine-foot wall. Once the three reached this terminus, the crowd blocked their view. All they could see was Brandenburg Gate looming on the other side. A bronze charioteer atop the Gate's columns, a winged goddess of victory, held the reins of four horses galloping eastward, toward Moscow.

While Herb conferred with Peter on the wisdom of going any farther, Gwen stared at riflemen in Soviet army uniforms across the street. They were goose-stepping between pieces of World War II vintage artillery. Peter explained it was a memorial commemorating Russian soldiers who had died here during World War II. These Red Army troops, ferried into West Berlin from the Soviet Union, now frozen at attention, ignored the tumult. Above the ominous tableau was a statue of a caped Russian, his rifle shouldered, his hand open in a gesture of peace. She turned to ask Peter more, but he had vanished.

Herb insisted on moving forward. Frightened yet unwilling to be left alone, Gwen followed him. They inched a few feet closer, and the wall, so emblematic of impending Cold War Armageddon during her adolescence, came into sight. Instead of a battle, this was a love-in. Hundreds of denim-clad young people sat on the wall's narrow top, strumming guitars, rolling marijuana joints, chipping desultorily at the bricks and mortar with hatchets, hammers, even pocket knives. Overhead, suspended by a crane, was a prime-time television news anchor from the United States. It was astounding and silly, momentous and ludicrous. She laughed and felt tears on her face. Without a single bomb exploding, without a gunshot, the Cold War had just ended. Gwen was in the middle of a closely packed, hysterical mob, penned in by strangers, unable to move, and she wasn't afraid.

Aware that Herb was drifting away, she grabbed him. They surged in a tide of compressed flesh toward the wall and rebounded. They swayed amid the vibrating mass. Ahead, the crowd's density blocked further movement. Fortunately, the mob was not frantic at this impasse and didn't crush those in its way. Herb twisted his head around to look back at her. Gwen was shocked by his appearance, flushed and wild-eyed. She had seen him be passionate at work, but that was the focused emotion of a logician arguing about which diagnosis was correct, a detective teasing out the truth from inert data. Herb was not focused now. He shouted and gesticulated, pushed toward the wall and laughed at the slapstick of his progress impeded. He raised his fists in joy.

In the din, Gwen couldn't hear a word Herb said. It was nevertheless evident that he had surrendered far more of himself to the collective mania than she had. She used hand signals to contend they were near enough to the wall. Getting closer wasn't important. Herb conceded. They found a new current, flowing laterally, that led to a pocket of less density. They still couldn't hear each other. After an hour watching teenage high jinks on top of the wall, they agreed in pantomime it was time to leave.

At midnight, the impeccably landscaped Tiergarten was full of ecstatic Berliners crisscrossing its boulevards and radial walkways. The fog had thinned enough for moonlight to guide them. Once the ringing in their ears ceased, Gwen and Herb talked of where they had been in 1961 when the wall first divided Berlin, what they had been doing, what they had been like then. From there, they roamed to families, marriages, and children. Finally, they got to Kevin.

Herb knew nothing about Kevin's love affair after Marco died, so she told him about Barry. Herb also had something to share, but it required personal exposure at deeper level than he had risked so far. He wavered before yielding again to the impulsivity that possessed him at the wall.

"Did you know Kevin and I went to the same therapist?"

"Castlewright?"

Startled, he said, "Yes…what did Kevin tell you about him?"

"You mean what Castlewright was like," she asked coyly, "or what they talked about?"

He blushed.

"Kevin shared details. Don't be embarrassed, Herb. I've spent time in therapy, too. More than Kevin. I bet more than you and Kevin combined."

This admission put him at ease.

"Now that Kevin's gone, the only people who know I saw Castlewright are my wife and my best friend."

"Don't worry. I'll keep it a secret. Maybe we can talk about our own details one of these days."

"Let's do that," said Herb with a faint smile.

V

EARLY THE NEXT MORNING, they were heading east on an underground train. It emerged onto tracks rising two stories above street level. The fog had ascended overnight, forming a thick layer above the city. All of Berlin was exposed now beneath a dull metal sky.

Herb searched the horizon for a television tower, erected after he had lived here, which marked Alexanderplatz. He used it as a landmark to find familiar buildings—the Dom cathedral, government offices on Unter den Linden, the Bode museum. Once Herb recognized the East Berlin skyline, he was grateful the train had been so crowded that he and Gwen had to sit apart. He had expected this trip would revive painful memories but was unprepared for the distress he was feeling. He kept a vice grip on the chrome railing as neighborhoods unchanged after thirty years appeared. Looking at his white knuckles, trying to understand his reaction, he suddenly relaxed. Curiosity replaced panic.

In the summer of 1959, Herb was between his junior and senior year at Cornell. The United Nations had stationed his father with an East Berlin delegation attempting to de-escalate international tension over the large number of German Democratic Republic citizens fleeing to the west. He arranged for Herb to be hired as a temporary typist.

Herb still vividly remembered the anticipation he had felt at La Guardia and his subsequent disappointment with East Berlin—a gray, lifeless city. There was nothing to do other than work. Although he'd been tutored by a German graduate student and was semi-conversant in the language, no one would talk to him once they found out he was an American. Young East Germans assumed he was a spy from China under Stasi orders to pose as a tourist and entrap them into making subversive statements.

Herb spent his free time reading the Existentialists, especially Sartre. He stood in line at post offices and rode buses to overhear bits of conversation which he then transcribed. He planned to use his notes as dialogue in an absurdist play.

A week before Herb was to fly back to New York, his father took a rare day off so the two could visit museums. He was particularly interested in an exhibit of ancient coins that had just opened at the Bode.

It was hot and humid when they left the dingy studio apartment where Herb slept on a couch. Wanting to avoid the crowds, his father was irritated with Herb for delaying their departure by five minutes. Inside the museum, they had to climb a flight of stairs. At the top, his father grabbed Herb. Pale, sweating profusely, he said a few words in garbled Chinese and collapsed on the marble floor. Herb could recall jarring images of the events that followed but only guess at their actual sequence. His own scream for help. An ambulance's klaxon horn. His father's cold skin. Pacing the empty hallways of Charite' Hospital. The repulsive odor of disinfectants. A German doctor saying, "I am sorry. *Ist tot*. Is dead."

Herb had been a dilettante at college, toying with sciences and humanities. After that summer, he never took another course in philosophy. He never completed his play. He returned to Cornell and threw himself into the premedical curriculum.

Although the line was short, Herb and Gwen had to wait an hour to get through Checkpoint Charlie. All the GDR border guards were on the other side, inspecting passports and waving through the East German horde going west. A single unarmed functionary, unfamiliar with the crossing protocol, was gate-keeping for anyone entering East Berlin.

They walked to Unter den Linden, the central esplanade of East Berlin. Here were the same eighteenth century rococo buildings and spare, postwar communist construction Herb had seen in 1959. Only the boulevard's double rows of lindens were different, bare skeletons in winter rather than the leafy arbor of his memory.

No, he realized, something else was missing from the cityscape. None of it was imbued with menace. They were facing the Russian Embassy, a clunky, wedding-cake-shaped, marble edifice. Hammers and sickles were etched above each window. It was laughably pretentious.

He sat on a bench, trying to make sense of this disconnect between the inanity of what he was observing and the terror and alienation he remembered. He took his pulse, a calm sixty beats per minute. He saw Gwen looking worriedly at him.

"I'm all right. Just remembering. I lived here thirty years ago, before the wall went up."

Gwen didn't interrupt his account of that summer.

When he finished, she said, "I think you get to decide where we go next."

Herb studied his map, calculating directions and distances.

"First Pergamon, then Dom, then Alexanderplatz. That avoids backtracking."

"Such efficiency!" Gwen said, patting him on the arm.

"Hey, thanks for listening."

He gave her a little hug. She looked surprised. He was tempted to ask her whether she had ever seen him touch a person who wasn't a patient, but he knew the answer.

VI

CROSSING A SHORT BRIDGE led them to an island in the Spree River that housed five museums. Herb had no desire to re-visit the Bode. He followed Gwen into the Pergamon, which contained the ancient Greek altar she had wanted to see since college. Built in the second century BC, buried for millennia, then excavated by a German engineer in the late 1800s and transported to Berlin, the altar was arguably the most exquisite sculpture of the Hellenistic era.

They entered an immense room brightly illuminated by a frosted-glass ceiling. Gwen was encircled by marble panels that rippled with wrestling figures. Seven feet high, one hundred yards in length, the frieze depicted a mythic gigantomachy—a war between Greek deities and a race of giants. Gods and goddesses leapt, shoved, and stomped, defending their new order against the sons of Gaia, Earth's mother. The battle would be a victory for Zeus's clan over a matriarchal world—a victory for culture and history over chaos.

Once she had absorbed the sheer size of the frieze and assimilated the massive effort that must have gone into creating it, she looked closely at the carvings. Muscle details, precise as anatomy lessons, filled the panels. Deltoids, glutei, pronators, latissimi dorsi, many others she could no longer name. Not in a lifetime, she thought, could any individual have made more than a small part of this frieze. Who were the sculptors? What were their lives like? The bodies they had shaped, motion frozen forever in stone, were voluptuous. They made her think of Rick, of their early days together. She regretted her own ability to love passionately had been so transient.

Gwen's reverie soured. She looked for Herb and saw him sitting idly on a bench. She checked her watch. An hour had passed. She forced Rick out of her mind and walked the full length of the frieze one last time.

She was struck by something obvious. How she had missed it before? Only the front and side of each god or giant was revealed. The back of each figure was embedded in stone, unformed in amorphous, infinite space. This frieze was more than art. It was a metaphysical treatise.

Gwen was inspired. She fantasized taking up a hammer and chisel again. In college, she had broken through once, reaching the point where her muscle endurance and ability to visualize what needed to be removed from a stone block were sufficient to complete a work—a bust of Eva's head. She would readily admit it generous to call the piece folk art. Nonetheless, she was proud of it.

Gwen massaged her triceps and biceps. Why not try, she thought.

Herb was beside her.

"Meet your expectations?" he asked.

"Oh yes," she said with a mysterious smile.

VII

THE FOG HAD BURNED away by mid-afternoon. A low winter sun glared upon Alexanderplatz as they walked to the center of the square's sunken floor. Herb and Gwen were surrounded by plain, rectangular office buildings made of crumbling concrete. He was telling her about the East German secret police.

"In 1959, I heard a third of the GDR population, *including children*, were being paid by the Stasi to spy on their family and fellow citizens. I bet some of these buildings still house Stasi operatives. Or they did until yesterday."

Peering over this grim shrine to state loyalty was the television tower, a great needle with a bulbous midsection, like a snake whose swallowed prey was stuck in its throat. Gwen was repelled.

"How grotesque. The Russians had a sense of style. Why didn't they help?"

Herb began explaining how Alexanderplatz had been the artistic and bohemian center of Berlin before the Soviet occupation, but his bursts of laughter kept interrupting the story.

"I'm glad you appreciate my irony," said Gwen as she flipped through the pages of her guidebook.

I can laugh in this place, Herb marveled. Thirty years ago, it was my touchstone for existential dread. Alexanderplatz seems ridiculous now.

He was unburdened yet not quite free of guilt. Was he being disrespectful of his father? That question stopped the laughter.

My sad case of a father, he thought, all about duty, never about humor, let alone affection. Horrific as it was to watch him die, helpless and lonely as I felt, what exactly did I lose that day? Not much.

Herb had witnessed so many deaths since that first one in East Berlin. He had a thorough grasp of the physiologic changes and had seen the gamut of emotions displayed by the dying and their loved ones. But he hadn't considered his own father's death in those terms before.

What must have gone through his mind, Herb wondered, being confronted with the haphazard and pointless end of his existence. The poor man had no scaffolding, nothing other than the material present, for perspective. Death couldn't have been acceptable to him because he never could have felt his life was complete. He was entirely too linear.

Herb willingly acknowledged he would die in the finite future. He could even tolerate the idea of it happening here, right now.

Why? Because I'm connected to others in ways my father shunned, because I'll be missed, and that will be enough.

Herb laughed again.

VIII

AT MIDNIGHT, THEY WERE back in West Berlin, sipping coffee in a Kurfurstendamm café and talking about Kevin. They had to leave for the airport in a few hours and decided to postpone sleep until the plane ride home. Herb asked Gwen if she knew Kevin had been medicating himself with prednisone during his final months.

"He was taking steroids? Why?"

"For fatigue. I think it was making him manic."

"He never seemed manic to me."

"He could rein it in when he wanted to, but he let it out with me. Did he ever tell you about his virtue-knockout thought experiments?"

"What?"

"I may have been the only one he told. Well, once he got juiced on prednisone, he became convinced he had made an important discovery. He had a new method for testing ethical principles. He believed it would change the whole conduct of philosophical inquiry."

"Oh my God! He definitely didn't share that delusion with me."

"I'm not sure it was all delusional. It made sense…sort of. He said he could determine the validity of any particular virtue by performing a thought experiment."

"A thought experiment?"

"That's what he called it. He would imagine a hypothetical world in which a single virtue was missing. Then he'd think through the possible consequences. Though how he could be certain he had worked through *every* scenario was sketchy."

"Huh? You lost me."

"Kevin told you about Marco's lab experiments, right? The ones with gene-knockout mice?"

"Yes," she answered dubiously.

"He was trying to do the same thing, like eliminating a gene from a stem cell and then seeing what happens when it grows into an adult mouse. He would delete a virtue, say beauty, from his imaginary world and think through what it would be like to live in this world where nobody would care whether the things they made, their environment, even the people themselves were ugly or beautiful. And the whole point was to figure out if enough redeeming features remained to make living in such a world worthwhile. It seemed clever to me. He claimed he'd discovered there are only eight absolutely essential virtues."

"Oh, Herb, no one could possibly think of every consequence of deleting a virtue from a hypothetical world. That's textbook mania—flight of ideas, grandiosity."

"I know, but it was wonderful that he wanted to be creative and productive to the very end."

"Yeah, though it's strange because at the same time he was trying so hard to accept death."

"Right! And he was doing both with the same intensity. Isn't that amazing?"

"For sure. Hey, the philosophy stuff had to be delusional, but what about letting go? Do you think he pulled that off? Was he at peace at the end?"

"I bet he got closer than I will."

"Me too."

They cradled their china cups, each lost in their own thoughts. Gwen broke the silence.

"Herb, I'm curious. How did you and Kevin become so close? I mean there are lots of people I've enjoyed working with for years and only know the most superficial details of their lives."

"It happened right after his father died. I was always fond of Kevin, but I do tend to compartmentalize work and intimacy. Anyway, he told me about their relationship, which was as tortured and unresolved as mine with my father. So I reciprocated. Knowing we had that in common was huge. It made me comfortable sharing other private things."

"Such as?"

"Well, family issues, like the difficulty I've had connecting with my kids. Hearing his viewpoint was helpful. Incredibly helpful, actually."

Gwen's eyes widened. She cautiously slipped Kevin's letter out of her purse.

"Herb, what were Kevin's eight virtues?"

"All I remember is that he had the three core principles of bioethics—autonomy, beneficence, and justice. Hmm, I think authenticity, too."

"Did he have a hierarchy, I mean for when there were conflicts, say between beneficence and privacy?"

"Privacy?"

"No, autonomy," she said, flustered. "No, I meant authenticity."

Her lips tightened. Herb shifted uneasily in his chair.

Gwen composed herself.

"What about the conflict between beneficence and authenticity?" she asked.

"You want to know what Kevin thought?"

"No. What you think."

Herb returned her gaze.

"Authenticity has to win."

"OK, then there's something you ought to see."

She set the letter on the table. He immediately recognized Kevin's hand-writing and looked up at her. She was biting her lips. Her eyes were red.

"What's going on, Gwen?"

"I don't know what the right thing to do is. Katherine, Kevin's sister, gave me this. He sent it to her just before he died. It's about me...and you, too. Reading it was hard but so...so worthwhile."

"Don't worry," said Herb, reaching for the letter. "I'm sure you're doing the right thing."

As he read, she saw Kevin's letter reflected in his face. Wistful when Kevin let go of his books and clothes. Sympathetic when he wrote about her loss of affection for Rick. Humiliated when he described Herb bringing Martin to his apartment. Stunned at the end by the possibility his son might be reckless enough to have unprotected sex in a bathhouse.

Staring down, shoulders sagging, Herb slowly shook his head. He let Gwen hold his hands.

"Kevin was right. You know that, don't you? Believing in your son's judgment is the solution, the only solution."

Herb nodded yes.

"That would be Martin," he said with a glimmer of hope, "having to see for himself."

They finally stopped talking at dawn while huddling in a passenger line on the Tegel tarmac. It was biting cold. Orange, gelid sunlight emerged from the east. At last, a perfectly clear Berlin sky. In the flat asphalt bottomland, silver fuselages waited expectantly. They watched jets depart, one after another, ascending into ether. Sleek, free, without a net. There was nothing to protect them from falling to earth and nothing to keep them from reaching their destination, except air.

Epilogue, 1991

I

ON AN EARLY SEPTEMBER morning, Herb was orienting two new pulmonary fellows to their City Hospital rotation. As soon as he mentioned that aerosolized pentamidine would be part of their responsibilities, their smiles disappeared. They cringed when he said an average ten new AIDS patients would have to be evaluated each week for the treatment. They cringed again when he told them there were two hundred patients currently on pentamidine who would need monthly labs checked and orders rewritten. It was implicit this would be on top of the consults and bronchoscopies pulmonary fellows were always required to do.

"I'm sure you've seen the *New England Journal* article. Breathing pentamidine mist for just thirty minutes once a month significantly reduces the risk of developing Pneumocystis pneumonia," said Herb. "We're already seeing the effect. The number of new cases diagnosed every month at City Hospital is dropping. It likely improves survival as well, though we don't have the data to prove that yet."

"By how long, do you think?" asked one.

Herb thought he heard the subtext, "Why are we bothering to do this?" He was tempted to ask the fellow if he would be more enthusiastic if the procedure was handsomely reimbursed by private insurance plans.

Herb stifled the retort. He had been asked a reasonable question. It wasn't fair to assume the young man's motivation was crass materialism. His answer was upbeat.

"I don't know, but data we gather from the work you do here will answer that question."

That afternoon, Gwen had a clinic devoted exclusively to women. She peeked into the waiting room and waved to familiar faces, mostly black and Latina. Fewer of them were emaciated than a year ago when she started having these women meet to support each other in getting sober and taking medication regularly. Seeing them gain weight kept her stubbornly optimistic. She believed antiretroviral drugs with long-term efficacy would become available in time to save some of their lives.

Moments later, her sunny mood was challenged. The new patient in her exam room was a Guatemalan immigrant already consumed by the infection, her body little more than bones wrapped in skin. As Gwen entered, the woman drew her lips back in fear. Gwen gave her a well-practiced, reassuring smile.

After clinic, she met Herb in the parking lot. They drove to the large open square in front of City Hall, covered temporarily by four massive quilts. The riot of colors and textures in the usually drab, concrete plaza was jarring. They had expected something funereal. Bright reflections from rhinestones, sequins, and bits of metal made them squint.

Herb looked dismayed. Attempting to encourage him, Gwen pointed at panels made of yarn, denim, lace, leather, and taffeta. But he noticed their uniform dimensions, three by six feet.

"They're each the size of a grave," he whispered.

She lowered her head and paid attention to details. A panel at a time, she thought, will be easier to handle than this sea of death surrounding us. They began a systematic inspection. Rather than hoping to be uplifted, they simply searched for memorials to those they had known.

Gwen succeeded first. She found Hubert Wilson's name penned in large flowing letters, surrounded by Polaroid photos of his drawings. At the four corners of the panel were paperweights, the kind sold to tourists at Fisherman's Wharf, little models of Coit Tower. She guessed this was as close to publication as Hubert's work would get. His sister told Gwen at his funeral that she had talked to a number of small presses. None were interested.

Herb found Laurie Hampton next. A snapshot of her in scrubs, with a stethoscope around her neck, was set in a mosaic of popular music—original forty-five discs of *It's My Party* and *Respect*, album covers of The Beatles and Bonnie Raitt, scraps of sheet music from a fake book. She must have played the piano, he thought, which only made him sadder.

Having paid their respects, they were ready to give another try at viewing the quilts as a whole. They climbed up City Hall steps but stayed less than a minute. The sum of these panels, each capturing the quirks of someone's personality and the senselessness of his or her death, was too much.

As they were leaving, an object caught Herb's eye—a green, gabardine sash mounted on a yellow throw rug.

"Look," he called to Gwen.

Sewn on the sash were embroidered discs. Gwen knelt down to touch the threaded shapes—a moccasin, a tent, a life preserver.

"Merit badges!" they exclaimed in unison.

II

THE RINGING OF IRON chisels on Carrara marble filled a third story loft in Oakland's waterfront district. Nan's rhythm was faster, a swift down-stroke of the mallet followed by a sharp peal at two second intervals. Gwen's cycle took three seconds. Everyone wore ear plugs, including Rick, who lounged on a couch nude except for the small cloth placed decorously over his groin.

Classical music blasted from a tape deck. Nan and Gwen had discovered the sound of iron on marble could complement certain concertos and symphonies. Their choice of chisels depended on the key.

Nan was carving a Madonna, using a plaster reproduction of a sixteenth century work as her model. She needed to maintain so much focus on angles, distances, and symmetry that just to copy was daunting. Gwen, though slower at cutting stone, had a surer feel for the right depth. She had moved on to a live model.

"Anyone want tea?" Nan yelled.

"Yes, please," Gwen and Rick sang out.

On her way to the kitchenette, Nan paused at Gwen's block, cut roughly in the form of a reclining man. Separate limbs were becoming visible.

"I like the calf."

"His calf is hot! Hope I get it right."

"I'd like some tea," Rick appealed.

"Oh, you're cold," crooned Nan and Gwen.

Nan bustled to the burner, and Rick returned to his book, a history of the ancient Greek Olympic Games. Gwen stopped hammering to study his leg. He gazed at her. She met his eyes. Her lips made a kiss. The echo of her hammering continued to mark time. After three beats, Rick's attention drifted back to his book and Gwen's to chipping away grains of marble, smoothing surfaces, and turning the stone block into a statue of her lover, one that might last a thousand years.

Later in the afternoon, Herb sat with Martin and seventy thousand other spectators in a stadium nestled in the hills above the Berkeley campus. They had said little during the first half of the game. The contest, compelling initially, was boring Herb now that Cal was three touchdowns ahead of the visiting team. He realized he had never seen his son watch sports on television or read the sports section of a newspaper.

"How long have you been a football fan?" he asked.

"Since freshman year. I go to every home game."

Herb was perplexed. Why would Martin, who lost interest in soccer before high school because jostling for the ball had become too physical for him, enjoy a game in which people intentionally bashed into each other?

"Hey, Dad. There are a lot of good-looking guys out there."

Herb contemplated the linemen, their bulging thighs tensed in anticipation. Suddenly, the players were in motion. The quarterback lateraled the ball to a trailing running back while a receiver and a defensive back sprinted downfield. A perfect spiral fell inches beyond their outstretched fingers. With a stealthy glance, Martin saw his father's faint smile.

At halftime, they talked about the campus gay rights group Martin led, the work he did advocating against discrimination.

"You can tell where this is going, can't you?" said Martin. "I might have to become a lawyer like my weird sister. It's probably the only way I can make a difference."

"I suppose there are worse fates. Maybe you should consider yourself lucky."

"Actually, I do, Dad."

Herb hadn't expected this response. As it sank in, his mind was deluged with questions. He couldn't sort through them all, let alone choose which one to ask. Martin grinned and punched him affectionately. Herb draped an arm over his son's shoulders. Martin didn't pull away.

III

DE LAVEAGA DELL IN Golden Gate Park was empty at dusk on the last Sunday of September. Two hundred volunteers had been there earlier in the day, weeding, clearing dead wood, and digging out brambles. Before leaving, they planted a dozen redwood saplings and placed an engraved bronze plaque at the base of each one.

Herb reached the dell as the sun was setting. He sat down by a plaque that read, "Kevin Bartholomew Memorial Tree." Five minutes later, Gwen joined him.

"I brought tools," she said and handed him a trowel from her bag.

They dug holes at the four cardinal points surrounding the slender trunk, taking care to shape curved, perpendicular walls, a trowel-length deep. When Herb finished, he leaned back on his elbows. In the distance, he recognized Katherine. He had met her at the wake after Kevin's funeral. She was wearing a sleeveless summer dress. Her long auburn hair was lifted by a sea breeze. The pale freckles on her neck were just like Kevin's.

"There she is," he said.

Gwen jumped up and shouted, "Here we are."

The two women waved excitedly then stopped, simultaneously aware that gravitas was more appropriate at this moment. Both bit their lips to keep from laughing. They stared at each other in wonder over the identical sequence of their reactions. They had already spent hours talking since Katherine flew in from Boston. Gwen now felt she could tell her anything. The self-restraint she occasionally needed to exert with Nan and Rick, even with Kevin when he was alive, was unnecessary. Katherine had become the sister she never had.

After hugs, Katherine reached into her purse for a plastic bag. She emptied tiny portions of Kevin's ashes into each of the four holes. Gwen and Herb backfilled their excavations with loose earth and tamped it firm.

Katherine poured the remaining ashes into the trowels which Herb and Gwen held skyward. Another sea breeze arrived. They all watched as black swirls rose and disappeared into the twilight.

Afterword

*There is no testimony that does not structurally imply in itself
the possibility of fiction, simulacra, dissimulation, lie, and perjury—
that is to say, the possibility of literature.*

JACQUES DERRIDA

FICTION AND TESTIMONY

FOR THOSE INTERESTED IN learning more about how the AIDS epidemic unfolded in the 1980s, two excellent sources are *And The Band Played On* by Randy Shilts and *Virus* by Luc Montagnier.

The impetus for writing this book was the curiosity of my students and residents, as well as my children, Sarai and Mike, about the early days of the epidemic. I am deeply grateful to Ray Riegert, Leslie Henriques, and Jim Vaccaro for their steadfast encouragement and to Tom Jenks, Jennifer Walsh, Bonnie Carton, Edith Reisner-Newton, Jessica O'Dwyer, Jonas Jacobson, Susan Light, and Barbara Wright for their immensely helpful feedback. I'm indebted to the following family and friends for their suggestions and support: Ilona Frieden, Steven, Susan, Ann, and Craig Jacobson, Jesse Carton, Sarajo, Susan and Gabe Frieden, Lorraine and Anita Robinson, Hazel Becker, Felicia Liu, David Gary, Jeff Curtis, and Jim Chanin. Without the mentoring of John Mills, Merle Sande, Lowell Young, Paul Volberding, Connie Wofsy, and Donald Abrams, neither my career as an HIV clinician/researcher nor this book would have been possible. Lastly, I want to acknowledge Hopkins Stanley, Lawry Kaplan, Karena Franses, and the many other nurses, doctors, and social workers at San Francisco General Hospital who have been my role models for compassion.